Brain Game

John Donnelly

Optimus

Published by Optimus
Tideways,
Sea View Promenade, St Lawrence,
Southminster, Essex
CM0 7NE
2022

Typeset in Adobe Garamond Pro 11pt

Cover design, page design and typesetting
by John Donnelly

ISBN 978-1-3999-2770-3

For Sue

Author's Note

Brain Game is a semi-science fiction story set in the mid-twenty-first century. It follows the lives and work of two neurotechnology scientists, Lukas Hoffman and Richard Stewart who, between them, develop highly innovative products so advanced that they take the world by storm. But, while one of their creations proves to have the most mind-bogglingly positive effect on a highly-sensitive, essential element of our culture, it destroys, in equal measure, the very foundations upon which our civilisation is based.

Semi- because, at the time of writing, science has yet to match the technological achievements conquered by Lukas and Richard. But, notwithstanding this, the question their creation asks of society, as it is today, is perfectly relevant irrespective of whether real science ever achieves Lukas and Richard's level of development. In short, were we to be totally honest with ourselves, we would have to admit that we are, at the present time, living in denial of the fact that the equanimity we experience in the diverse social relationships we enjoy is not what we fool ourselves into thinking it is.

Brain Game will open your mind to the reality of life as it actually is. The science might be semi-fictional but the social implications are worryingly true.

Chapter 1

'Richard!'

'Just a moment, honey.'

. . . *always on that damn computer* . . . 'Richard!'

'Honey, I'll be one minute.'

. . . *for God's sake, go away, please. Ricky, what can I do?* . . .

'It's started again, but worse.'

. . . *Ricky, please come and help me, I can't bear this a moment longer* . . .

'Honey, I'm here, what is it?'

'It's that buzzing, that humming, oh, I don't know, but it's constant. As soon as you switch on that laptop, it's there – buzz, buzz, buzz – it's driving me insane. My head seems to have metamorphosed into some kind of digital wasps' nest.'

'Beth, honestly, I can't imagine what's happening – how could my laptop possibly cause, oh, I don't know, tinnitus? Is that what it is? It must be a coincidence. Look, I'm almost finished – I'll turn it off and you'll see it'll make no difference. Give me five minutes while I finish off this report and I'll be with you.'

With the door to Richard's study firmly closed, he removed his computer tool kit from his case, released eight small screws from the back of the device, detached the whole of the keyboard panel and duly disabled the tiny, white standby light which indicated that the machine was powered up and ready to go. He then replaced the panel, re-inserted the eight small screws, logged back on to transcription mode and got up from his seat to join Beth in the breakfast room.

'Beth, darling, I'm done. How is the buzzing?'

'It's no different, Rick, no different at all. I really can't put up with this every time you work on your laptop. I'm so sorry but would you mind switching it off?'

'It is off, honey – let me show you.'

Richard ran back into the study to fetch the computer and returned immediately to demonstrate to Beth that there was no illumination whatsoever from the standby light.

'Look here, see? The machine *is* turned off. The standby light is not illuminated. The machine has been powered off. I told you it has nothing to do with my laptop.'

Richard walked back into the study and quietly switched the machine off to conserve battery power before re-joining Beth in the breakfast room.

'Beth, why not speak to Doctor Elias, he'll explain exactly what's going on and I'm sure he'll come up with a remedy in no time at all. What do you say?'

'I'm not so sure, Rick. I don't see how he can be of help.'

. . . Doctor Elias – can't abide the man – so patronizing – and anyway, the buzzing has now subsided . . .

'Well, we've nothing to lose. Let me take you down to the surgery first thing in the morning before I start work. I'll call in to the office to explain.'

'But it's not there now, Rick. It's gone, completely gone – I can hear myself speaking, thinking. It's back to normal, really. I'm now confused. I thought it only happened when you worked on your computer but now, I just don't know what is going on.

'Oh, Rick, I'm so sorry, really. So, so sorry. I know you have to work, and I know your dedication to your work is what makes our life so easy. In so many ways. But this, oh, I don't know what it is, interference, buzz, buzz, buzz, is so awful. And it isn't anything like Julie describes her tinnitus. You know Julie, at uni, Julie Harris. She's suffered for years. Learned to live with it. And it has nothing to do with laptops, believe me!'

'But neither does this, Beth. It can't have. I'm a scientist, for chrissake. You know that. Allow me some credibility, please. Oh look, Beth, this is becoming so divisive. We need to sort it out. Let's go see the doc.'

'Doctor Elias will be powerless to help me. It isn't his area of expertise. We'd be better off calling in to see Pete in his laptop workshop above the bookmaker's – he's a whiz with computers as you well know. That's where the real problem lies.'

Richard fidgeted nervously in his seat while he surreptitiously touched the face of his watch. 'Right, right, right. Beth, listen, I've got a better idea – let's change the subject, throw on some clothes and take a walk down to the Harbour Café for breakfast. Forget all about it, eh? Eggs Benedict – with hollandaise sauce – your favourite! Will that help?'

'You always know exactly which button to press, Rick – yes, I'd love to. Let me go and change into something decent.'

Beth opened the larger of her two sizable wardrobe doors, glanced at the contents neatly arranged in front of her and, in a relaxed manner, selected what she felt might be most appropriate for the visit to the Harbour Café. What she had chosen was a clingy, black and white, elephant print wrap which, although she'd never mention it to Richard, was inclined to turn the odd male head a little more often than most of the other articles in her collection. And several compliments it had encouraged by a small but significant number of male acquaintances - voiced carefully out of earshot of Richard - suggested, somewhat flatteringly, that she might have missed a career vocation in a certain big-budget locality of Los Angeles. As she eased the wrap over her long, but not too long, auburn hair and let it drop, it accentuated her tall, but not too tall, slender figure. She felt she was ready to re-join Richard for their morning excursion.

Conversely, Richard slid his somewhat smaller wardrobe door to one side, pulled out one of his dozen, or so, pairs of designer jeans, plus whatever tee-shirt resided on top of the tee-shirt pile and, without considering the appropriateness of his choice, slung them on before stepping into a pair of trainers that happened to be within arm's length. A quick glance at himself in his full-length mirror confirmed that he had chosen wisely and, apart from a cursory scan of his slightly unruly head of sandy hair, he decided he was in good enough shape for the harbour visit. Though the thought that Beth might have gone for a flatter style of footwear to allow his nominally taller physique to register as they walked together did flash across his mind. But on balance, he felt he'd go with whatever she found more comfortable.

Regrettably, the morning's sea wall jog would have to go by the wayside on this particular day to make room for Beth's little treat and he doubted, also, that he'd have time to work out in the small gymnasium they'd recently had built as an extension to the garage. But this was TT1 trial weekend number one and there was no question that it shouldn't take precedence over whatever routines would normally take place on a Sunday morning.

Within thirty minutes the two of them were tucking into their favourite first meal of the day - one they usually reserved for special occasions. But Richard needed to keep any possible objections on Beth's part at bay without raising suspicions. This was a serious business and any chinks in the project's armour could call a halt to its development in no time. This interference blip had to be eradicated. And eradicated fast.

'How's the thesis coming along, Beth? You've not been mentioning it so much of late. Sorry, I said thesis, I should have said dissertation. My apologies – wrapped up in my own studies. Yes, how's the dissertation going?'

'I'm getting there, Rick. Over halfway through and feeling quite positive about it.'

Beth Campbell was heavily involved in studying for a master's degree in psychotherapy at Stonecroft University, an educational establishment situated some fifteen miles from where they had set up home just eighteen months previously. Both had met in their early twenties while living close-by on campus at Birmingham University with Richard Stewart and Beth working every available hour on their respective neurotechnology degrees. They'd married while still at uni but had subscribed to the popular trend of the female partner retaining her maiden name. However, while Richard went on to graduate with a first with honours, Beth had managed only a 2:2 as a result of her realising, halfway through, that, frankly, she'd chosen to pursue the wrong discipline. Whether this stemmed from a lack of thought during her post-high school planning or her quite obvious inadequacy when she compared herself to Richard, she was not quite sure. But once she had witnessed the sheer gift he had for a philosophical insight into a subject with which she was, with every best intention, never going to compete, she decided to change tack. Beth just wasn't cut out for the black and white world of binary language. Too logical. Too inhuman. Too inorganic. Beth was a people person, a feeling individual who believed she would be far better suited to furthering the understanding and improvement of the human psyche. The human experience. That was the world upon which she preferred to think she could exert a more positive effect.

For anyone who knew Beth well, her school friends, her family, her uni colleagues, the idea of her funding and studying for a major psychological qualification appeared almost a waste of time and resources. Beth showed more than a natural ability to discharge the duties of a professional therapist without the need for extra learning. The subject flowed from her personable and understanding nature. She was the friend all the girls at school would approach with their problems and it was a rare occurrence for them not to part company only a few minutes later with smiles on their faces and springs in their steps. From an early age, Beth understood precisely what it meant to be a balanced human being. She knew about expectation; how to keep it within realistic parameters. And to appreciate that others also had expectations that needed to be accommodated. In fact, the expectations of a group of friends, a school community, or even society as a whole, had to make allowance for the realisation of individuals' hopes and dreams for any one of the groups to function in an effective and stable manner. Harmony was the key to a well-adjusted society and Beth knew this more than anyone.

So, when Richard secured a position with an organisation specialising in advanced, supposedly life-changing neuro- and digital technology, she, without hesitation, agreed to move the three-hundred-odd miles south to start afresh - with her new centre of learning in close proximity to the offices of IntuTech – the company with whom Richard had impressed with his insight into an algorithmic future. A future he firmly believed would shape their lives for the better.

And while her soulmate immersed himself in his dreams of a binary utopia, she could enjoy what she felt were more realistic pursuits researching the human mind, as we know it. Working towards a more rational, care-oriented goal where everyday anxieties and tensions would, hopefully, give way to a harmonious, altruistic society free of the conflicts we have come to accept as normal made sense to Beth.

Well, that was the plan and Stonecroft presented itself as the ideal medium through which Beth felt she could achieve her objectives. Polar opposites though these objectives might appear when viewed alongside those of Richard's, Beth was of the firm opinion that their respective branches of learning would prove perfectly complementary in the long term.

There was a haze over the harbour which precluded the low morning sun from accurately defining the shapes and movements of the small number of fishermen's crafts bobbing up and down in the water. On this particular morning the boats were only mildly agitated by a light onshore breeze but they still managed to offer a calming, mesmerising even, effect to the café's clientele if stared at for too long. Beth felt this helped redirect the couple's conversation from the cold, unreality of technology to matters one could more reasonably hope to understand - expectations, loves, desires, strengths, frailties. The things that affect us all, drive us all. But, also, the very things we hold closest to our hearts and guard with our lives lest those around us, with whom we exist in constant competition, should use to reduce the value of our standing in society - sometimes without giving a moment's thought to the damage such careless abuse can do to the trust that endures between two individuals. A trust that manifests itself in a bond of friendship capable of surviving a lifetime of adversity and everything a resentful society can throw at it.

Within minutes of sitting down, the café's waiter, Freddie, was unobtrusively back at their table checking the everything was in order and to their liking – an important customer service touch.

'Rick, did you know that the most insignificant event in the life of a three-year-old can go on to shape the child's future? Without it being aware or, in some cases, even being able to recall the existence of such an episode. For good or for bad, the experience early on in life can leave an indelible mark on the psyche of the adult that can culminate in, depending on the nature of the incident, an unsuccessful marriage relationship for example. Or, in worst cases, an inability to maintain any kind of meaningful association with a person, a community or a group of work colleagues. Such is the importance of the guardianship we enjoy during our early, formative years that it can affect or dictate the whole of our future experiences.

'And the very guardians, the parents, are thrust into the role by society without the need for qualification or regulation of any kind irrespective of their ability to discharge their duties in a responsible and effective manner. It beggars belief, it truly does. I mean, could you imagine a child, at the age of four or five, being entrusted to the hands of an educational institution whose teaching personnel were as ill-trained as the parents? Most of the irreversible psychological damage could well have been inflicted before the infant first set foot in a year-one classroom.'

'Beth, this is the way of the world. This is the only way society can operate. It is not for any individual to decide who is, or who is not, capable of parenting. That's the stuff of social engineering. We've grown beyond that. Women, quite rightly, now have the vote. All members of our society are judged to be qualified to decide who, which political party, is best suited to handle our needs. Some will be more informed than others but that is democracy. There are no boundaries. No parameters beyond which any individual is considered unsuitable. We listen to everyone and achieve a kind of quantized result that is representative of the median, the average. And by this method, the electorate can rest peaceably in the knowledge that the status quo will be maintained without any possibility of an extreme opinion or dogma slipping through the political net.'

Richard was hopeful that his response to Beth's psychological awareness came over genuinely whilst bearing in mind that his current line of work was inclined to ride roughshod over her ideals as a caring member of society. This presented itself as a dilemma to him but one that demanded little time in his choosing which side of the ideological fence he should alight from. Richard and his small group of work colleagues were in no doubt as to whether their current course of action should, or should not, be pursued. So exciting was the prospect of introducing a concept of such monumental, mind-blowing proportions to an unsuspecting, and most likely, unprepared society that the team involved in the project shared a level of single-mindedness that, until now, refused to be shaken.

'I'm aware of that, Richard, but, unpopular though it may seem, reforms of one kind or another that would lift the expectations and opportunities of the most disadvantaged youngsters in our society would surely be welcomed by every fair-minded person. And ideally, these reforms should involve the very parents whose possible lack of natural ability to benefit their offspring is the root of the problems that we know, all too well, are present.'

A couple with two small children, who appeared to be on holiday, navigated their way through the tables to settle next to them adding to the general relaxed atmosphere of the venue.

'Yes, of course, Beth, and in our own ways - you with your therapy-based studies and me with my technology-driven programmes - we should work towards redressing the imbalance in society which both of us are so aware of.'

After finishing their breakfast, the couple took a short stroll along the harbour wall while the sun was doing its best to burn through the haze to reveal an unbroken expanse of aquamarine reaching to the horizon and beyond.

Beth's small autonomous hatchback was parked with geometric precision at the edge of a grass verge bordering the harbour's visitors' car park and the pair climbed in to make their way back to their modest, yet impressive, architect-designed house. They had fallen in love with the property at first sight the previous year after they spent months and months house-hunting. With its south-facing, slightly occluded glass façade offering little in the way of privacy from the odd passer-by, the house represented what they felt was a perfect balance between practicality and up-to-the-minute aesthetic appeal. Both were of the view that the property's appearance and ecological design criteria provided them with the environment of their dreams.

Once inside, Richard popped the coffee maker on to continue where they had left off at the Harbour Café and, with Beth's back turned, he carefully placed his right index finger, momentarily, on the small icon at the bottom of his wristwatch's face. A slight sense of light-headedness subsided after no more than a second or two before Beth turned around to him to suggest they take their coffees onto the front terrace. The morning sun was just beginning to make its presence known over the protruding roofline to the eastern edge of the property.

'Sit this side, Rick. You know how irritable you get when the sun shines directly onto your face. I can enjoy any amount of it but I know you say it hinders your powers of concentration. You are so funny; I can't imagine that being a problem but we are made differently. I can sometimes think of nothing better than having my powers of concentration hindered especially if it is solar radiation doing the hindering. Anyway, I want you to know that I find it so comforting when you tell me how important a truly democratic society is for the wellbeing of the individuals it serves. There are flaws in any system, as we know, but fairness and opportunity for all is paramount in a society that respects its citizens and accepts the weaknesses and strengths of each of its members. It really is so good to know we live for the same ultimate causes.'

. . . is this really true? . . . oh Rick, are you being open with me, please? . . . oh, I must stop it, I'm so full of doubt . . .

'Thank you, honey, that's why we mean so much to each other.'

. . . did I remember to send that email to Mother? . . . Oh God, I'll never hear the last of it . . . yes, I believe I did, I'm sure I did. Rick's beginning to go grey around the temples . . . won't mention it though . . .

Rick finished his coffee and excused himself to make a visit to the bathroom. *Grey round the temples? – mmm, maybe a little. But some of my colleagues are almost totally bald – a little grey can't be so bad at my age.* Richard immediately placed his finger, fleetingly, on another icon and decided to take the rest of the weekend off. Tomorrow would be Monday with study and work-place agendas awaiting both of them. He thought it best to switch off from all things project-related for the time being and to enjoy the remainder of the day with Beth. There was lunch to prepare, newspapers to read, possibly a Grand Prix to watch on the TV and, well, maybe a film later before finally turning in. Yes, the smart watch would have to satisfy itself with keeping him abreast of the time and, maybe, his step-count and heart rate until he arrived at the office at 08.00 am the following morning.

Chapter 2

'Morning, Luke.'

'Rick, how did things go?'

'Hold on, buddy, let me get my feet in the door!'

'Of course, excuse my impatience. But I need an update on the weekend's performance. This is so intriguing, Rick – my mind has been locked into you and Beth like an equity trader's eye on the world's stock markets ever since we parted company on Friday evening. Come on, come on, tell me about it.'

'I'll do a deal with you, Luke - you make the coffee and I'll give you the lowdown while we're injecting some caffeine into our systems.'

'It's a deal – go sit down – I'll be five minutes.'

Richard hung his jacket on a spare hook at the entrance to IntuTech's generous, open-plan, ground floor suite and began to wander through to a soft-seated area used for refreshments, lunch or just chilling when things got out of hand. Not that this happened often, but with a strong contrast in temperaments between the two, mega-creative techies, Lukas and Richard, there certainly were occasions when enthusiasm needed to be tempered before a democratic form of progress could be made. After all, these were two bright individuals - very bright - with highly impressive credentials driving each of them to turn the tide of technological advancement on its head in the exhilarating digital revolution known otherwise as the twenty-first century.

IntuTech was established as a commercially-focused research and development organisation funded mainly by its principal's father for the sole purpose of developing radical, computer-related concepts born of the brilliant minds of Lukas Hoffman and Richard Stewart. Lukas won scholarship after scholarship during his time at TUM (Technical University of Munich) after having grown up in the picturesque Bavarian town of Lindau. Widely recognised as the most original thinker the university had ever produced, Lukas, graduated with the world at his feet. But, without a need to concern himself with the small matter of maintaining a bank balance on account of his German, industrialist father's considerable wealth, the super-gifted Lukas set his sights on travelling the world on a fundraising mission to further whatever philanthropic causes he could turn his mind to.

He was also a fashion icon within whichever social circles he mixed. A sort of living, walking, boutique-dressed mannequin. Nobody ever saw Lukas wearing denim. Never ever. But instead, he would select his day's attire from his wardrobe of plain, lightweight two-piece suits in a colour he felt suited his particular mood. And the effect was precisely what the designer would have had in mind when creating his first, rough sketch of the concept. Lukas had the stature, the shape and the colouring that complemented most designers' mindsets.

However, by the time he reached his early thirties he fancied a change of direction where his career was concerned. A challenge. An opportunity to apply his substantial mental capacity to advancing the world of technology. To benefit not only those less fortunate than himself but to help humankind as a whole. Lukas wanted to make a difference.

Although his relationship with his parents, Max and Mia, was as close and as loving as one could hope for, he felt he needed to isolate himself from the strong influence they exerted on him as a way of creating an ethos of independence. This, he thought, would enable him to develop ideas of his own with a minimum of external stimuli. To the two senior Hoffmans, such an arrangement made perfect sense and their encouragement for their son's enterprise remained rock solid. With Lukas' fondness for the English and their quaint way of life, he spent no time in choosing to set up camp in the idyllic, southwest-coast fishing town of Falcombe. A town he found as equally picturesque as the charming Lindau in which he spent his childhood. Lukas was an aesthete as well as a technological wizard and he felt that such a setting would prove the perfect environment to attract like-minded and similarly-gifted personnel.

Richard also fell for the idea of a move from the semi-industrial midlands to the southwest-coast fishing town to continue with his vocation unencumbered by the tensions and general hubbub of a busy city. He imagined it would be like working while constantly on holiday. So, he applied for the position as soon as it appeared on his radar. And, although the posting of the vacancy in the popular technological media attracted a number of enthusiastic applicants, as far as Lukas was concerned, Richard easily presented as the front-runner. The pair, hit it off from the word go.

The small body of highly qualified technologists employed on the site were currently concerned with two major projects. Three colleagues occupying a first-floor suite were involved in the development of a substitute visual-aid device designed specifically for the blind or partially-blind. The ingenuity of the project lent itself to its dependence on CCIT (Cranial Chip Implantation Technology), the basis upon which all IntuTech developments to date were built. In short, the system employed a specially-engineered pair of what appeared to be ordinary spectacles that featured a similar kind of visual-gathering data method currently being used to collect images for 8K TV broadcasting. The technology bypassed the traditional need for the recipients to rely on their retinal optical facilities which, by definition, were likely to be in a malfunctioning condition. Instead, the devices sent data directly to the CCI which had been carefully installed by specialist German medical teams working closely with IntuTech. Once data hit the implanted chip, visual messages were instantly directed to the relevant parts of the brain to provide the immediate reception of high-resolution images independent of any external biological means. It seemed like magic but it was nothing more than nascent scientific development. This process wasn't confined only to this level of complexity as there are known to be at least ten individual brain regions that are involved with sight. However, Lukas' specialist contacts were anything but limited to his own sphere of digital influence. One of his closest friends whom he had known throughout most of his childhood and beyond was a significant neuroscientist working on the most advanced research programmes at the University of Munich. Hans Bauer, or 'Jack' as he was known to his close acquaintances, would hold conversations over the phone with Lukas for whatever length of time was necessary to be sure that the avenues being taken by IntuTech were not only correct in a scientific sense but likely to appeal to the regulating and licencing authorities. The very authorities that would judge whether the product was safe for general public usage.

But the specification of the ground-breaking optics' design protocols did not stop there. The seemingly standard-issue spectacles featured 360-degree optical sensors through both left and right temples – the arms that pass over the wearer's ears - to offer the recipient a complete, three-dimensional visual experience far superior to that of our biologically-evolved, uni-directional retinal system.

And Lukas had yet another digital trick up his optical sleeve. The team were currently involved in the development of a micro data-recording facility to allow the wearer the option to actually record incoming data for playback at a later time. In other words, the previously blind recipient could not only upload real-time, hi-definition images of whatever real-time vista to which he or she happened to be exposed, but those very images could be stored within the device to either delay the visual experience or enjoy it any number of times at a future date. If desirable, there would be nothing to stop the wearers creating their very own *Groundhog Days.*

The possibilities were endless and the healthcare benefits, immense. Furthermore, once the economies of scale kicked in with the inevitable volumes in production, in Europe alone, the cost of providing immediate solutions to those suffering loss, or partial loss, of sight would be truly negligible. IntuTech was destined to become a shining light in the world of ophthalmic medicine. Could it be that, via IntuTech, mankind had actually upgraded God's ingenious invention of biological sight to new levels of efficiency?

Whilst the development of the optical device addressed a major need for humanity in the area of restorative healthcare, the work currently being invested in Lukas and Richard's principal project concerned another equally important aspect within the culture of a civilised community; that of trustworthiness. Every successful society relies heavily on its ability to operate with highly effective controls on law and order. It goes without saying. And with unimaginably vast sums of money, principally in human resources, being poured into establishing what precisely is the truth, a means of shortcutting the process, especially one that can be shown to be ninety-nine-point-nine percent reliable, will change the game plan for authorities the world over. Lie-detectors would continue to serve a useful purpose in society but only under the watchful eyes of museum curators.

The key feature of the system concerned the implantation of an IntuTech-developed microchip into the brain of the operator through a process designed especially by Hans Bauer. All necessary surgical procedures would be undertaken by either one of the two top neurosurgeons working at the Munich Academy of Medicine with Hans having obtained all necessary permissions at government level for the practice to legitimately form part of the university's investigative programmes.

The advantages of embedding the chip within the brain of the operator rather than that of the investigatee were numerous. Firstly, after receiving the eventual approval by the regulating authorities, the thought processes being monitored would be beyond the knowledge of the individual under investigation. There were obvious human rights issues to be addressed but Lukas was satisfied that, after having taken up the matter, admittedly at a preliminary stage, with the Committee of Standards in Public Life, the end results of certain, critical legal cases would easily justify the employment of the process providing strict controls on duration of use were observed.

And secondly, beyond the world of domestic law and order, the device would prove immeasurably beneficial in a militaristic sense. It didn't need very much in the way of imagination to consider the effectiveness of its potential in determining whether a terrorist suspect was guilty or innocent. The unacceptable face of unlawful torture procedures known to be carried out surreptitiously by otherwise respectable sovereign states would be a thing of the past. IntuTech's brilliant invention would render such investigative methods to be of no use whatsoever with future suspects presenting as guilty or innocent in an environment devoid of physical and mental intrusion. How could any civilised society seriously fail to appreciate the magnitude of the humanitarian and economic benefits involved in such a technological breakthrough?

In addition to Max Hoffman's generous funding, grants had also been obtained from the British Council for Scientific Development and a small number of well-heeled, philanthropically minded individuals in North America. These were, understandably, repayable once a predetermined degree of commercial success was achieved. So, it wasn't just the residents of the small southwest-coast town who had their eyes pinned on Lukas' operation – the whole world lay in wait for the virtual miracles he performed.

'*Hier sind Sie ja*, - there you are, Rick.' said Lukas as he placed two large mugs of coffee down on the white ceramic surface.

'Just what I need.' replied Richard. 'I left home in something of a rush earlier without attending to my morning fix. Thank you, Luke.'

The two scientists sat down in adjacent comfy seats making themselves comfortable for Richard's much-anticipated report.

'Well, come on, Rick, tell me, tell me, I'm anxious to know how our little trial went.'

'Well, how can I put it? Okay, U-N-B-E-L-I-E-V-A-B-L-E!'

Richard overemphasised the word by dragging it out to maximise its semantical significance.

'No, really? Come on, Rick, tell me more.'

'Okay, get a load of this: when I logged on and activated "listen-in" mode on my smart watch, my head was, how can I put it? Well, full of my thoughts but full of Beth's thoughts as well. It was as if, as if . . . oh my God, it was A-M-A-Z-I-N-G, Luke. Like I'd gone away and come back five-hundred-years' later. Crazy, man, truly crazy. TT1 is like an omniscient deity without the attendant responsibility.

'But you know the weirdest thing of all? Get this! While I was completely aware of my own personal thoughts - just like at any other time, Beth's thoughts, kind of, appeared over the top of them. As if they were superimposed. Clear as crystal though. And you know when you hear someone else talk to you, or a number of people talking all at once in a room and you hear the chaos of the moment but still don't confuse one person's voice with another's? Well, it's just like that, really! Really, really weird. You don't ever begin to wonder who's thought patterns you're privy to. It just sounded like Beth thinking. Though, on a couple of occasions, she did refer to me as Ricky which was strange because I've never known her to call me anything but Rick. Or Richard, when I might be a little out of favour. Still, only a minor consideration, I'm sure.'

While Lukas sat hanging on every word Richard uttered he unconsciously crossed and uncrossed his legs several times unable to control his excitement at the morning's stupendous news.

'So yes, things went according to plan with, I sincerely hope, Beth not suspecting anything untoward. Real-time word reception under the control of my smart watch just went without incident with Beth's data being relayed to my cerebrum via the CCI I had installed last month by Professor Schneider. And, although I was able to determine almost precisely what Beth had in her mind, the incoming messages were different to my own thoughts insofar as they appeared to be abbreviated. I suppose the brain adopts a sort of shorthand form when compared to normal speech which, unlike one's own thoughts, needs to be clearly interpreted by the listener. But that's perfectly understandable and, for our purposes, does not prevent the receiver from understanding the transmitter's reasoning.

'There was one, I hope, small hitch, though. When I selected transcription mode on my laptop, in an adjacent room of course, difficulties began to show up. While the software showed no signs of faltering and instantly provided a clear and perfectly readable word flow on the screen, Beth reported unacceptable levels of electromagnetic interference in her head as soon as I logged on. It really upset her, and I had to fool her into thinking it had nothing to do with the computer by disabling the standby light and pretending I'd shut down. It did the trick insofar as she was still experiencing the unpleasant noise while being convinced the device was switched off. I felt awful misleading her like that – well, lying to her. I mean, I just don't do that. Ever. We have a perfectly trusting relationship - always have had - and I must say it hurt me to deceive her so blatantly. It even made me question the means by which we agreed to trial this project but, of course, there is no other way at the moment. And, in reality, it will prove beneficial for all of us in the long term, both financially and, well, as an amazing lifestyle feature. Just imagine the advances it will bring to our powers of communication. In time, intuitive, remote communication will become part and parcel of everyday exchanges of information.'

Oblivious to the pair of them, a couple from the upstairs optics team wandered into the area to enjoy a morning coffee before subsequently leaving without being noticed.

'Mmm, that is very promising, Rick, very promising indeed. And I'm really not overly bothered about the laptop interference issue. I'm sure we can overcome that by adjusting the sensitivity of the CCI providing there is sufficient headroom, to coin a phrase. Ha, ha. Sufficient headroom!'

Lukas chuckled out loudly at his own unintended homonymic witticism and continued on the alternative route along which his conversation had chosen to travel.

'Yes, with the microscopic size of these CCIs, several dozen could easily fit into the average human cranial cavity without drawing a neurosurgeon's attention during investigative surgery. But I digress, that wasn't the kind of headroom I was referring to. I simply meant we will have no difficulty in reception levels if we wind down the signal to sub-electromagnetic detection readings before logging onto transcription mode. It'll be a doddle, believe me.'

'That's what I expected, Luke. Maybe you could attend to that adjustment before next weekend's trial. Trial number two!'

'Yes, leave it to me, Rick. But can we talk about visual data images? Did you manage to secure anything worthwhile on that front?'

'Unfortunately, not. But, as I suspected – I believe I may have mentioned it to you, Luke - Beth has a strong tendency to present as a left brain-dominated thinker thereby being prone to producing worded transcripts rather than pictorial images. I can't change that, it's the way her brain functions.'

'No problem, if that's the case, we will have to find an alternative "volunteer" to help us run the visual image tests. I'll give it some thought, Rick. Unless you know someone in the meantime who you feel might score in that department?'

'Not offhand, Luke, but I will carry out a personal character assessment of all the people I know in the area to see if there might be a likely candidate.'

'But be extra careful, Rick, don't even think of approaching someone until you've discussed the situation with me. You know, I've said it a million times, if this were to find its way into the public domain before we have an opportunity to demonstrate to the authorities just how valuable an asset it poses for our society, we'll lose the opportunity to develop it. And we'll find ourselves blacklisted quicker than we could write an algorithm to pin a shortcut to a start bar.'

'Lukas, Lukas, Lukas, please! You know where I am on this.

We think as one mind and you know it. I'm as determined to see this through to its government-approving end point equally as much as you. Here, take my hand.'

Richard held out his open right hand in a gesture to grip Luke's and shake it vigorously for longer than was necessary as a symbol of their commitment to each other and they both collapsed in fits of laughter at the notion of either one of them easing their resolve.

Once their jubilation began to wane Lukas stood up and edged tentatively towards the staircase.

'Thanks, buddy – you're nothing short of a brother to me.' He added. 'Now, if you'll excuse me, I want to pop up and spend some time running through a small number of optical difficulties the boys in the upstairs studio are having. I think it's under control and on target to meet its launch date but, you know me, Rick, I can't ever risk the results of taking my eye off the ball and losing touch with the way developments are progressing. These projects belong to IntuTech, and I intend to keep it that way.'

Chapter 3

'After you.'

'No, I insist, after you, Beth.'

The head of department accompanied his response to Beth's acknowledgement of his seniority with a broad grin whilst stepping to one side and allowing her to pass first over the threshold of the automatic doors leading into the university's enormous reception hall. And before he continued on his way he checked casually as to whether her weekend had panned out as planned.

Beth visibly warmed to his usual, unreserved, courteous manner. 'Thank you, Hugh, it's kind of you to ask. Yes, Richard and I took some time out taking things easy although you know him well enough to guess how much of his "time out" was spent in front of his computer.'

'Beth, that is the Richard we both know and love and I'm sure you'd have it no other way.'

Hugh and his charming wife, Belinda, had dined out on several occasions with Beth and Richard and, in the process, the two couples had established more than a causal relationship. But Hugh was forced to maintain a constant level of intrigue at the very little he was allowed to know about IntuTech's highly guarded programmes. Beth and Belinda shared a profound interest in anything remotely associated with the human psyche and would talk for hours on the various schools of thought from Wundt to Peterson. Belinda had started her career as a therapist as soon as she and Hugh had graduated, both with BA (Hons) degrees, from King's College, Cambridge.

'You're absolutely right, Hugh, and I have no complaints. It certainly keeps me in a lifestyle to which I am pleased to have become accustomed - to coin a phrase.'

'And let's hope it stays that way, Beth. Now, if you'll excuse me, I'm running a little late for an unusually early meeting with the board of governors, must dash!'

Hugh turned and strode off resolutely revealing, indeed, an injudicious haste in his morning's preparations - an untucked shirt tail was just visible beneath the bottom, rear edge of his suit jacket.

With a wry smile on her face, Beth turned and walked in the opposite direction towards a staircase leading up to lecture room 1B on the first floor where a resident professor was due to give a talk on Questionable Ethics in the History of Psychology. The address was set to focus on a couple of programmes carried out during the early- to late-twentieth century starting with the Little Albert Experiment of 1920 in which a perfectly healthy, eight-month-old baby was allowed to be scared out of its wits in the name of science. This was to be followed by an analysis of the Stanford Prison Experiment of 1971 during which volunteers were selected to perform the roles of either inmate or prison guard. The investigation involved the would-be prisoners being stripped and humiliated, left in insanitary conditions and forced to sleep on cold concrete floors. Several of the participants went on to suffer serious emotional trauma leaving the experimenters' success confined to the demonstration of precisely how not to perform a scientific experiment. One could imagine visiting Martians choosing such investigative procedures in their attempts to penetrate the human condition but fellow human beings? The mind boggles.

These ill-judged processes, however, soon highlighted the fact that, although many consider there remains a way to go before those with more cavalier approaches fall in line with the majority of modern thinkers, adherence to a strong ethical compass is an essential component in the quest for responsible learning. This was not promising to be one of her favourite mornings on campus but she fully appreciated that a thorough knowledge of her chosen subject would prove beneficial in the long term.

By the time the hour hand had reached its Roman numeral number one on the campus' sentinel-like clock tower situated in the centre of the in-out driveway of the main university entrance, Beth was sitting comfortably at one of the melamine-topped tables in the refectory. She'd picked up some fruit, a juice and a nut bar from the well-provisioned servery that ran the length of the room and settled down to continue reading a novel she had started over the weekend. More sensibly, she should have been updating her notes on the morning's lecture but, for the moment, she felt she'd rather divert her mind from the unpleasant details of the subject matter. She preferred to think that human nature would never have led serious, scientifically-minded individuals to follow such an inappropriate and inhuman route. But there were lessons to be learnt and they certainly weren't the ones that had found their way into the minds of the twentieth-century experimenters.

As the minutes ticked by, Beth began to lose herself in her book becoming increasingly oblivious of her surroundings. With her right elbow resting on the tabletop, her corresponding hand cupping her right cheek and the paperback wedged against her mobile phone at an ideally readable angle, she could, for the moment, have been relaxing on an exotic Pacific island beach.

More commonly, she would sit with her friend Cathy who was studying the same course as her but a recent incident involving her three-year-old son at nursery school had temporarily caused her to be absent from campus. Beth was anxious for updates on the event but elected not to make contact to avoid being seen as intrusive rather than caring. The toddler had been showing distressing signs of ADHD for several months and was becoming a constant worry to Cathy. But on the positive side of things, she was beginning to feel that her chosen course at Stonecroft would help in more ways than one and prove useful beyond the plans she had for a career focusing on helping only strangers.

But halfway through her allotted sixty-minute lunch break, Beth found herself distracted. And this wasn't the first time it had happened. In fact, it was becoming something of a regular occurrence. Whether her mind was playing tricks on her in subconsciously drawing her attention to the phenomenon was open to conjecture – how would she know? And her understanding of the abilities of the human mind certainly flew in the face of the "logic" she felt she was being encouraged to accept. Some studies had shown that the sensation, known as "gaze detection" or "gaze perception", was founded on positive scientific bases with experimenters demonstrating, fairly conclusively, that their results relate to the workings of the brain's complex neural networks. But there remains little in the way of evidence to show that any such perceived notions of being stared at other than from an approximate sixty-degree forward, horizontal field of vision from one side to the other, is due to subconscious activity in one's peripheral vision beyond these limits. In other words, the concept is highly unlikely to hold water if it isn't concerned with the actual travel of straight lines of light particles from the starer's eye to the eye of the recipient. Any perception of voyeuristic activity outside of these parameters is suggestive of a preconception in the mind of the person perceiving being stared at.

That said, the reasoning behind the scientific thoughts on the subject played no part in convincing Beth that she was mistaken this time. With her mind now refocused on her immediate environment, she shifted uneasily in her seat and began to lose concentration on the novel's storyline.

On the previous three or four occasions when her suspicions were found to be true, the ensuing, impromptu rendezvous with the fellow student in question proved to be perfectly enjoyable and without any hint of untoward behaviour on his part. But was she imagining it on this occasion? Was he even present on campus today? She certainly hadn't seen him enter the refectory. Or heard him chatting with fellow students. Although, why would she have done? She had, after all, been heavily engrossed in her book and to all intents and purposes, isolated, at least mentally, from her immediate surroundings.

Without wanting to draw undue attention to herself and certainly not embarrass herself in the process, Beth decided she should continue looking down into the pages of the novel before appearing, abruptly, to become aware of the time and quickly stand up and turn in the direction of the would-be voyeur. Yes, that would relieve me of any possible suggestion of involvement, she thought and, so as not to lose the moment, she swiftly put her plan into action. But no sooner had she done so, she found, as usual, that Ricky Tremonti, with the almost shoulder-length hair, Albert Einstein-printed T-shirt and wry smile, had his eyes firmly fixed in Beth's direction. How could this be? It was not as though it had occurred at the same time each day. On one occasion it was during morning coffee break and another, late in the afternoon when she was standing at the campus' entrance waiting for Richard to pick her up while her car was in for a routine service. This was uncanny. Were the 'gaze perception' experimenters doing their job properly? Was there a rational explanation floating around out there lying in wait for a suitably inquisitive scientist to hit upon an alternative, definitive experiment? There had to be an answer to this; coincidence just didn't make any sense.

'Beth, my darling, how are you?'

Beth sprang round in her seat in no doubt whatsoever of her gazer's identity.

'I am *not* your darling, I told you that last week.' She returned with a friendly giggle. 'But, if you wish, you are welcome to join me for a quick tea or coffee before my next lecture which is in twenty-five minutes.'

'It will be my pleasure, darl . . , I'm mean, Beth. Let me get them – Earl Grey with a dash as before, is it?'

'Go on, get on with it – you choose, we don't have much time.'

Ricky, who had signed on at Stonecroft for an engineering foundation course, was too many years Beth's junior for her to take too seriously. But he was a flirt. A flirt with a manner that would have Casanova looking unprovocatively indifferent by comparison. Through and through. Beth felt that Italian men often came with the charm gene fitted as standard. And there was every reason in her mind to think Ricky came with a modded version. Tremonti – meaning three trees, carried a certain romantic flavour with it. She imagined upright cypress trees but preferred not to focus on any possible symbolism where this particular Apennine descendant was concerned. But he was thoroughly likeable and, she was sure, quite harmless.

There was little doubt in her mind that he treated every female he came into contact with in precisely the same fashion. But Beth couldn't ignore his natural congenial manner, his ease at maintaining eye contact and his ability to engage so exclusively on a one-to-one basis giving the impression of total dedication to whoever he found himself addressing. Well, she could only assume that because, in the short time she'd known him, she had been the only person she'd experienced to have been the subject of his attentions. And it didn't stop at that. Ricky emitted an aura of dependability and kindness to the point where, should the occasion ever occur, she would have no qualms in looking to him in an hour of need, perhaps. It sounded silly when she thought of him in that way, but she just couldn't visualise his character in any other light. With just a hint of reservation, Beth had no doubt at all that he'd make a wonderful partner for the right girl in due course. But there was time - he couldn't have been any more than nineteen or twenty – he had his whole life in front of him.

With the inimitable Tremonti swagger in full flow, Ricky sauntered back to Beth's table with two plastic beakers of her favourite Earl Grey blend – hers with a dash and his without.

'So, the weekend, tell me, what did you get up to with that inattentive other half of yours?' Ricky enquired.

'Now, now, he's my husband *not* my other half and he's anything but inattentive, I've told you that before.'

'I'm sorry. Really, I am. But you've told me more than once that he spends more time on his computer than he does with you. Your words, not mine!'

'You make me laugh, Ricky, I should be offended by your directness, your impudence even, but I can't somehow take you seriously. And I know you mean no harm. Look, why don't you tell me what *you've* been up to? I'm sure it'll be immeasurably more interesting than an account of my boring existence. Come on, tell me what you have been doing?'

Beth folded her arms in a manner suggestive of her unpreparedness to engage further with her acquaintance until such time as he provided her with a chapter and verse update on his life since the last time they sat down together some four or five days before.

'Why have you folded your arms, Beth? Come on, you're the psychotherapist - you should know all about body language. Or is it that you didn't think I'd pick up on it?' Ricky said, cheekily.

'Right, in case you were off sick when that particular lecture was given, I'll explain. Folded arms can indicate anxiety, resistance, insecurity, tension, or fear. There, now you know. No need to ask the professor for a one-to-one on the missed module!'

'You really have the cheek of the devil. You really do. You, the engineer student, and now the expert on kinesics. Are there any limits to your talents, Ricky Tremonti?'

Beth unfolded her arms awkwardly and slowly placed her hands on the table in front of her.

'Is that better?'

'It certainly suggests a more comfortable level of confidence. And friendliness, even.' Ricky replied while slowly sliding his hands across the table and gently placing them on top of hers.

Beth felt herself flush while momentarily keeping her hands in place. She was enjoying the physical contact and experienced a sort of mental paralysis as if she no longer had control of her body. But, as the feeling passed, she unhurriedly slid her hands out from beneath Ricky's and, with just a hint of regret, placed them on her lap under the table.

'Ricky, you're being very naughty. I asked you to tell me about your weekend and before I know where I am, we're sitting here hand in hand like two lovers. Now tell me, what did you get up to?'

Ricky raised his eyes towards the ceiling as a means of aiding his concentration while considering which events might prove most entertaining.

'Oooooookaaaaaay, now let me see. I took the beautiful Alice to the cinema on Saturday afternoon then went back to the cinema with the absolutely stunning Sofia in the evening. Watched the same movie twice, would you believe? That American teenage fantasy pic that's doing the rounds, you know the one? Quite entertaining, actually. In fact, both visits were equally enjoyable with the girls cuddling up close to me, in the back row, during the scary moments. They needed some masculine protection!'

Ricky subconsciously accompanied his report with an "embracing" mime that would have impressed even Marcel Marceau.

'Hold on, hold on.' Beth interrupted with a chuckle. 'Never mind "entertaining" and "cuddling up", how can you justify galivanting around with two different girls on the same day? And having the audacity to take them on the same outing at that? It's preposterous! Go on, tell me they both know what you're up to and have no problem with sharing you between them.'

'You always see the worst in me, Beth. And you a psychotherapy student with plans to help and understand people's problems and anxieties. You surprise me.'

'I surprise *you*!' Beth replied with a sarcastic grin on her face. 'What about the poor unsuspecting young ladies? Wouldn't they be surprised too?'

'No, no, not in the slightest. As soon as I took my younger sister, Alice, home after the matinée performance, Sofia, her elder sibling who'd just arrived back from a shopping trip with Mum, started playing up and refused to leave me alone until I agreed to treat her to the same outing. You need to think these things through before jumping to the wrong conclusions, Beth.' Ricky replied smugly.

'Ha, ha, ha, don't sit there with that "butter wouldn't melt" look on your face. You purposely misled me into believing you had the choice of the town's females in the palms of your hands: the beautiful Alice, the absolutely stunning Sofia, how was I to know they were your sisters? But, if you're telling me the truth, then all power to you, Ricky, for being such a lovely big brother.'

'I'll take that as a compliment then, Beth, because there wasn't an element of untruthfulness in my account of what I got up to on Saturday. But, on reflection, okay, I can see why you might have got the wrong end of the stick. But only just.'

The two of them sat laughing at a conversation that pleasantly passed the few remaining minutes before they each needed to move on to their respective afternoon lectures.

Chapter 4

'Rick, we've been working on this project for eighteen months now and we've yet to give it a name. A title. Something as a reference. *We* know what it is, but it won't be too long before a number of other people are going to be involved in it. There'll be medical trials, demos, seminars, launches, you name it. At the very least, we should apply some sort of identifying term. Until now, it's been just you and me but quite soon it's going to be out there. Out everywhere most likely. So, I thought, Teletuit - what do you think? As you can see, it's an amalgam of telepathy and intuition – Teletuit. Sort of speaks for itself, don't you think?'

Richard stared into the middle distance momentarily while he contemplated Lukas' suggestion.

'Yes, sounds good to me. Let me write it down. Mmm, the word looks good in an aesthetic sense – important, in my mind, how it will come over in promotional blurb. And in lights above us when we're introducing it to the respective authorities on the world's stages. Yeah, I like it. But how about, TT1 when we're referring to it between ourselves, you know, during the working day, on the phone? A code name, if you like – a working title.'

'I'll go along with that, Rick, no problem. TT1 – Teletuit version 1.00. TT1. Okay, that's settled - now let's get on with it. With TT1 - yes, I like it.'

The two scientists felt they'd moved on just by naming their invention. It felt as though it had grown into a kind of established item ready to be recognized within the world of technological advancement. After all, there would be papers published in the coming months, BMA reports, Medical and Legal publications analysing its value as an instrument of the twenty-first century and beyond. TT1 was going to make a big splash in a big technological pond, and it needed to be easily identified, easily called to mind, easily poised to trip off the tongue.

A code name for the optical project being developed upstairs had been established some time before as work had begun some eighteen months earlier than TT1. The designated title was OptTech to, kind of, keep it in line with the general nomenclature being employed by the company. Due to the device's current state of play, having endured two significant developmental revisions, OptTech had become known internally as OT3 - OptTech version 3.00.

Jennie popped in briefly to hand a wodge of envelopes to Lukas that she'd found in the mailbox several minutes earlier.

'Thanks, Jennie – I'm sorry but would you mind closing the door behind you? Thank you.

'But, Rick, for now, there is the small question of trialling,' said Lukas. 'So far, we've only run a preliminary test over the course of one weekend at your house with Beth, bless her, as the unsuspecting laboratory rat, as it were. If you'll excuse my referring to your lovely wife as a rodent. No, don't answer that, I don't deserve to be excused, my apologies!'

Lukas had attended to the small matter of interference and Richard had tested the results on Beth as soon as he returned home on Monday evening. The process took no more than a few minutes on his laptop which he chose to boot up in full view of Beth hoping she would immediately dismiss any ideas she might have had about computer-related noises in her head. And it worked like a dream. Richard used the excuse that he needed to log on to quickly find a telephone number and neither of them mentioned a word about the previous morning's problems.

When Richard had first secured the position at IntuTech, Lukas had taken great care to have his legal team produce watertight confidentiality agreements specifically applying to himself and Richard. And they included a special clause precluding Lukas from having the TT1 chip implanted into his own cranial cavity without prior, written agreement being given by Richard. This enabled Richard to rest easy in the knowledge that he was not, at any time, being monitored by his superior leaving him to proceed with confidence during the course of the project's technological progress.

Lukas removed a wad of papers from his briefcase and shuffled them into some kind of obscure order.

'So,' he continued, 'we need to move on as quickly as possible with the trialling exercises. Beth's unsuspecting involvement was immensely helpful, and we both felt she'd genuinely have granted us permission had we asked. But the anonymity aspect of the exercise was of great value to us and, of course, in the fullness of time we shall have to own up to her. However, we now need guinea pig number two and that isn't going to be so simple. We can't possibly expect our next candidate not to know what we're up to. Not that the process calls upon any actual physical intrusion – just a matter of, well, listening-in. Like phone tapping, I suppose. Or the act of overhearing a conversation on public transport, say. I mean, how intrusive is that? People do it all the time.'

'Of course they do, Luke, but we both know we have to play this by the book. There are laws against this kind of behaviour and IntuTech can't afford to get off on the wrong foot as far as the authorities are concerned.'

'Yes, I know, Rick, I was just, sort of, thinking aloud. So, we must fully brief the next contender and have everything thoroughly documented with signatures provided by both parties on all relevant aspects of the procedures involved. That's all we need to do if we find a suitable participant.'

'I agree, but it would be particularly good if we could identify a right brain-dominant person who is likely to think in pictures rather than words. Somebody with an inclination towards architecture, say, or engineering. That would be interesting. It is thought that those types of mindsets are most likely to result in picture thinking. While Beth's word-thoughts came over ideally, in a telepathic sense, and provided perfectly legible texts in transcript mode, it'd be amazing to see what a laptop would churn out with a picture thinker.'

'Yes, I can't imagine what a computer screen will decide to do with incoming, mind-generated graphics data – infinitely more exciting than any mega-budget, multi-screen blockbuster I've ever queued up to see. Mmm, if only we knew such an individual sufficiently well to make an approach. While you're thinking about that, Rick, I'll move into my office to get started on the permit documentation which we'll be needing as soon as we find somebody. And I'll have to run it past the legal bods before we can expect to start applying signatures. Catch up later, Rick.'

Lukas hurried out of the room with his briefcase in one hand and the wad of papers in the other.

While Lukas got on with the necessary paperwork, Richard stayed put and racked his brains for a suitable candidate. Over the course of an hour, or so, he made several phone calls to friends and acquaintances to furtively sound them out before discussing the subject further with Lukas. But nobody appealed to him in an intuitive sense and he was, naturally, reluctant to involve anybody known closely to him as there could easily prove to be complications following exercises of such an intrusive nature. This was proving to be more difficult than he had first thought.

But just when he was beginning to get a little bogged down with the matter, Lukas emerged from his office with a big smile on his face as if he'd had some kind of brainwave.

'Rick, listen, I think I've got the ideal guy. You know, someone likely to see images in their mind rather than all those boring words. Only likely, mind you, because I've yet to approach him. But from what I know, I'd put money on him really wanting to get involved.'

'Who is it, Luke? Do I know him?'

'I've no reason to think you do, Rick, but I believe the two of you would get on great. He's a really likeable guy – only young - about nineteen or twenty. Still lives with his parents - in the next turning to me, actually. Lovely Italian family -

Mum, Dad, two young daughters and him. His name's Ricky, Ricky Tremonti.'

'No, can't say I do know the guy – no reason why I should, I suppose. So, how are you imagining we should go about approaching him? And what is it that makes you think he'll be up for it?'

'A kind of intuition, Rick. Like something my mind has made sense of before letting me in on the secret. I've chatted with him in the local food store and he's a nice fellow – easy-going personality. Comes over sort of trustworthy, you know, seems the kind of guy who'd speak our language.'

'Any idea what he's involved in at present?'

'Hmm, I believe he's doing a foundation course at some uni not too far away but I really can't be too specific. Engineering, possibly.'

'Be great if it is because, as I say, there'll be a better-than-evens chance his thought processes will appear as graphics. The mind boggles at how Adobe will handle this. I really can't wait – this has to be one of the most exciting aspects of the project so far.'

'I hear what you say, Rick, but, when you think about it, it's not very much different to the way our software deals with word transcription. Remember, when we transcribe word-oriented thought patterns they start out as graphical images before being converted to text. Not a lot different to the speech recognition software we've known and loved for years. Ours is, naturally, more advanced but that's the way computing goes. It's just one long process of digital evolution with each stage presenting itself as the pinnacle beyond which other developers will struggle to outdo. But it never is the pinnacle – given time, somebody, somewhere will always better it.'

'Yep, with you, Luke. So, how do we approach the guy? Be nice to think we could both chat to him before carrying out a suitability post-mortem once he's left.'

'Yes, sounds perfect - let's give it a go. Let's see how he feels about it. We could invite him down to show him around the lab and fill him in on what we're up to.'

Lukas' facial expression clearly suggested he wasn't quite so certain.

'Not so sure that's the best idea, Rick. After all, we don't have clearance on this yet. We've not even applied for permission to carry out trials – something I'm thinking of dealing with as soon as I can get my head around the best way to describe what we're actually involved with. OT3 was easy. Nothing untoward about our objectives there. Sure, it's a complex bit of kit but its purpose in society is pretty straightforward: provides folk who've lost their sight, through retinal means, a whole new way of getting it back. And they get a choice of any number of cool pairs of shades to wear in the process. What's not to like or not to trust about that?

'But TT1 is a whole different ball game. Licencing is going to have to be super strict in case it gets into the wrong hands. I mean, it's law enforcement authorities and military bodies, possibly, who are going to be using it and that's about it, period. And those guys aren't going to want any Tom, Dick or Harry getting himself implanted just for the fun of it. I mean, imagine the bad guys laying their hands on TT1 before the cops do! No one is going to thank us for where that ended up. No, we have to show that we're squeaky clean in every department before anyone other than you and I breathe a word.'

'I get that, Rick, but think about it, when the medical team in Munich dealt with your recent TT1 implant we used precisely the same documentation as we did for the OT3 surgery. We're fully licenced for OT3 and the surgeon wouldn't know the difference between one IntuTech microchip and another. The products look identical – it's only the programming that differs. We can't possibly risk anyone other than you and me knowing what TT1 is about until we have the full documentation suitably drawn up and signed off like OT3. And, as you know, I haven't even finalised the first draft yet. Look, our reasons for being so careful with the TT1 registration are solely to ensure the ultimate product that reaches the respective authorities, post launch date, is protected up to the hilt and ready for use without any chance of alternative versions existing on the wrong side of the fence. The IP involved in TT1 cannot, I repeat, cannot get leaked into the wrong hands. So, what are we worrying about? When Ricky comes on board as a paid volunteer, we sit him down with you to engage in a chat about the general business of developing highly-advanced computer hardware and software applications and let him go after an hour or two without him, or anyone else for that matter, having the slightest idea of what it is we're trialling. And all the time he's with us, you will have the perfect opportunity to monitor his every thought, which will hopefully be in picture form, while I'm sitting in an adjacent room logged on to transcription mode downloading his entire thought process which will never see the outside of this building. Tell me where that can possibly go wrong.'

But the idea just didn't sit comfortably with Richard.

'Mmm, it could go wrong. I mean, why would he think we'd be interested in talking to him in the first place? On what pretext would he feel he's been asked to sit down and talk to us? Look, the guy's a student and probably wouldn't say no to some pocket money. Why don't we offer him a part-time job doing, let me see, what could we do with here? How about a position that would require him to handle all of our backup files? There's no way he could log in to anything sensitive. I mean, come on, the guys at Area 51 would be amped with our levels of confidentially. It'd be no more than a file management exercise. You know, someone who could tidy up things on a peripheral basis which is actually something we could do with. You and I spend so much of our time with the more important aspects of TT1 that there are certain areas that could genuinely do with some attention. And, after all, we don't really care what it is we talk to him about as long as we're able to check out the efficacy of the software we've produced. In fact, what is the difference between what we're proposing and what any serious commercial organisation would be doing when they inform a job applicant on the phone that an ensuing conversation may be recorded for, how do they put it? Yes, *recorded for training purposes.* Come on, what's the difference?'

'You've got a point there, Rick. That's brilliant! No one ever mentions the means by which the *training purpose* recordings will be recorded. If we switch our objective to simply offering the guy a part-time job and conduct the interview in accordance with industry-standard protocols, i.e., by recording it after advising him first about the training purposes, we're doing nothing different than anyone else. The fact that our recording will be taken care of by TT1 technology instead of the more usual audio-to-digital interface, is a mere technicality. Wow, that's it – we have a cast-iron case if anything untoward were ever to be suspected. Right, leave this with me - I'll see if I can orchestrate a chance meeting with Mr. Tremonti ASAP.'

Chapter 5

On the first floor of the IntuTech building, the team in control of OT3 were labouring for more hours than could reasonably be squeezed into a working day in an effort to meet their end-of-the-month deadline when the grand launch of their product was due to take place. In all fairness, they only had a few loose ends to tie up but there was an understandable degree of anxiety floating around because of the importance of the event.

However, amongst all the panic and stress, any visitor wandering around the building's general communal areas during working hours could be forgiven for thinking the property had been vacated as the proverbial pin would be heard to drop anytime day or night. But this is par for the course with computer technicians who, the world over, are inclined to work in an environment of total silence. It has been said that, if you listen very carefully, you might just hear the odd sound of a neural transmitter's axon tip connecting to a receiver (a synapse). But this is probably more down to binary folklore than reality. However, unlike some other commercial premises that may house the same number of, say, bank dealing room traders or telesales staff, computer technology organisations do little to promote hearing loss and deafness amongst their workforces.

To date, no one outside of IntuTech had an inkling of what they were up to. The world beyond remained, for the moment, blissful in its ignorance of what would likely, at some time, prove its residents' redeemer. And to say the product they were about to unveil to the world was radical would be a gross understatement. OT3 was about to turn the world of ophthalmology on its head and, in the process, earn Lukas' IntuTech company unimaginable sums of money.

Ralph Henriksen, originally an ophthalmology student from the University of South-Eastern Norway, headed up the OT3 team and, in the time he had worked with Lukas, he had convinced his superior that he was suitably possessed of a devotion to IntuTech's highly innovative programmes. His enthusiasm for his work at the company's Falcombe headquarters knew no bounds. Arriving well before his contracted start time each morning, Ralph would have his head down until well after going-home time while, sometimes, not even stopping for refreshments.

The two lab technicians under his command were James Richardson, a PhD/MPhil neuroscience graduate of Manchester University and Meghan Annabel Byatt, an MSc graduate in digital biology also from Manchester. James had graduated two years previously and had joined IntuTech as a junior research technician while Meghan, whose parents had either an uncanny sense of humour or an inexplicably prophetic insight into the ultimate career choice of their progeny, had been on board since the organisation's inception some years' earlier. Whatever the reality of her appellation, Meghan was more than happy to sign her name, Meg A Byatt despite having endured all the jokes, and the rest, throughout the course of her computer technology education and eventual career. Meghan perfectly refuted Ms. Capulet's contention concerning the semantic insignificance of a title.

Such was the attraction to Lukas' particular brand of world-shattering creativity, each of the three academics discharged the duties of their respective disciplines with unparalleled loyalty in the knowledge that they were, unquestionably, heading towards a goal of unprecedented achievement in the world of scientific development.

The stage was set, so to say, for the product's launch to take place in the George Bartisch Hall at the International Ophthalmic Council headquarters in Brussels, such was the anticipated significance of IntuTech's product release. Invitations had been sent to all known ophthalmic bodies throughout the world in addition to members of a wide variety of medical organisations and specialist publications following an introductory, yet carefully guarded, article published in the World Medical Journal three months' before. The event was limited to one hundred and twenty-five places with a ticket price of £200 per applicant with all proceeds going to a range of ophthalmology charities. Details of how and when bookings could be made were contained on both the invitations and in the journal's article. Within two hours of the sales desk going live on IntuTech's website, all seats had been reserved and monies transferred. This was going to be an event to remember.

Lukas had engaged the services of a leading PR company with a suitable level of experience to ensure that all marketing issues, including brand awareness, product visibility and each aspect of a successful event promotion, were covered and geared towards portraying OT3 in a light commensurate with the predicted impact it would have on the future of worldwide optical healthcare.

Final preparations were going well with no hitches expected with regard to OT3 meeting its launch-date deadlines. Ample samples of what were perceived, in all probability, to be the most popular designs were assembled from components commissioned and manufactured at a far-eastern optical fabrications specialist and large overhead projection screens were in place to facilitate a running visual record of the evening's agenda as it unfolded. The event was shaping up to be the ophthalmic equivalent of the king of all rock 'n' roll extravaganzas.

But, most critically, a volunteer suffering with total visual impairment had been flown out on an all-expenses-paid trip to the Munich Academy of Medicine to undergo the implantation procedure. The individual would be key to the success of the evening by demonstrating the efficacy of OT3 in front of some of the world's most prominent authorities on ophthalmology. The candidate had been carefully selected and was well known within the sphere of ophthalmic healthcare insofar as his treatment had featured as a particularly noteworthy case study. For those involved, even remotely, in the subject of innovative optical procedures, it would be highly unlikely for them not to have been aware of the challenges this individual brought to the profession, so comprehensively was his journey documented. And it was only in recent times that his medical team had finally called a halt to further remedial procedures having reluctantly accepted that medicine had nothing more to offer him other than palliative care where the question of his sight was concerned. Bill was a typhlotic wild animal ensnared by science's inability to release him from the chains of his retinal inadequacy. The applicant had experienced retinal failure in mid-life following a virus contracted during an otherwise routine operation unconnected with his eyes.

When approached by Lukas for the purpose of becoming involved in OT3 he expressed little in the way of hesitation in taking part. The risks concerned with the experiment were deemed to be minimal as the OT3 microchip implant had passed every known medical test and diagnostic procedure for both pathological and non-pathological conditions in the human body. The general anesthetics and standard non-intrusive cranial surgical techniques posed certain risks, although nowhere near as hazardous as those of the intrusive kind prevalent during the early part of the century.

Ralph, James and Meghan had also undergone implantation for the purposes of trialling OT3 and, apart from a small number of minor issues, everything had gone swimmingly. Although none of them was visually impaired, tests could still be carried out with the simple fitting of blackout lenses to the OT3 frames. This exercise negated any possibility of the three candidates' biological visual processes operating in their normal fashion thereby confining all relevant incoming data to that generated by the OT3 technology.

Tests had been carried out on the candidate at IntuTech but these were confined to their psychological rather than biological suitability for which Lukas was totally comfortable.

He was concerned that the grand launch event should not expose the candidate to any undue trauma once the OT3 demonstrations were executed in the presence of the esteemed members of the audience. And the applicant was well aware of the implications of what he was due to face acknowledging that he would be generously compensated for his cooperation. There was also the not inconsiderable matter of having his sight restored, albeit by an alternative means to that with which he had evolved as a member of the human race. This was going to be ground-breaking stuff.

Seated on the low stage at the George Bartisch Hall were Lukas, Richard, Ralph, James and Meghan: *The Lukas Hoffman Five?* Decent name for a cool, jazz quintet, maybe. But none of the five scientists on duty tonight was intending any kind of improvisation. Not at all - each stage of the OT3 launch had been planned to the nth degree leaving absolutely nothing to chance. Not one note would be played out of time. The team occupied five of seven easy chairs, upholstered stylishly in a green, faux leathercloth and carefully positioned to form a gentle arc able to afford every one of the eminent guests a full view of their hosts for the evening. At the front edge of the platform were two multi-directional, microphones connected, wirelessly, to a personal in-ear PA system designed to carry every nuance of the ensuing address directly to the ears of each member of the audience. No one would miss a syllable.

In the sixth chair was Sir David Jensen MBBS BSc PhD FRCOphth, a world-renowned authority on all matters ophthalmological and present on the evening to take the chair to preside over the general run of events. The agenda was relatively simple involving an anticipated twenty-minute introduction by Lukas followed by three fifteen-minute résumés by Ralph, James and Meghan on their respective areas of expertise in the development of OT3 before a certain Bill Evans, seated in chair number seven, was to be brought forward and fitted with the first pair of IntuTech OT3 DigiSpecs ever to be seen in public. And more importantly, the first pair ever to be used to demonstrate the miraculous application of the invention. Bill would be shown to experience a completely new visual facility for the first time since contracting the virus that had led to the destruction of his eyesight some three years' earlier.

Richard would take a back-seat during these items on the agenda but make himself available to take part in a later Q & A session which was likely to include brief references to the ensuing launch of IntuTech's TT1 sensation due to surface some months' later.

But Sir David was very much involved and was the first scheduled speaker to take up his position at the microphone. Bang on the dot, he stood up, straightened his tie, brushed his hair back with his hand and, with consummate self-assurance, cast his eyes over the sea of guests.

'Good evening, everyone. And thank you all for making your way to this delightful conference hall to witness what may prove to be one of the most outstanding evenings of your life. Many of you have travelled a number of miles to be here and, I can assure you, you will not leave disappointed. Indeed, you will recount what you are about to learn to your children, your grandchildren and, if you are fortunate enough, to their children too, such is the magnitude of the revelation soon to be unveiled before your eyes.

'For those of you who are, maybe, unfamiliar with me or

have yet to cast your eyes on this event's programme, my name is David Jensen. I have devoted my life to exploring every possible means of furthering the cause of those members of our society unfortunate enough not to enjoy perfect eyesight like, in all probability, some of us assembled here tonight. It is easy to regard the miracle that is vision, as a birthright and not give the subject the consideration it so richly deserves. However, at the last count, some 2.5 billion individuals, world-wide, were known to suffer from one kind of vision impairment or another and if it weren't for the continual hard work that many of those amongst us this evening put into their lives as a matter of course, this figure would be many times greater, I'm sure.

'But progress knows no bounds. Progress continues along its interminable journey through time without ever pausing to take note of who is at the helm. Progress refuses to recognise a helmsman even exists. Progress has its own agenda for which it, single-mindedly, pursues its goal oblivious of those responsible for providing solutions en route; the oarsmen tasked with delivering the power with which the helmsman achieves his momentum.

'But enough from me. Seated with me on this platform this evening are the very oarsmen in control of the world's latest advancement in technological achievement, the unparalleled team working for the UK's incredible IntuTech organisation. I give you the company's chief executive officer, the incomparable Lukas Hoffman.'

The audience received Sir David's opening address with warm enthusiasm and rapturous applause providing both he and Lukas with a fitting welcome to the evening's affairs.

The star of the show rose from his seat and to the occasion. With arms outstretched in a gesture to quell the sheer volume of the welcome, for just one night and maybe one night only, Lukas Hoffman was the Freddie Mercury of the neurotechnology world.

'Ladies and gentlemen and most distinguished guests . . . it is my greatest honour and privilege to stand here in front of you tonight. I will be forever indebted to your presence on this auspicious occasion but, before I start my demonstration, I would like to tell you something about the development of my organisation. It is called IntuTech, which is short for Intuitive Technology and our philosophy is to look for new ground to break in areas where we feel the enhancement graph's Y-axis has flattened to the extent that further advancements in its particular field have become extremely unlikely. Once identified, we step in with, if you like, some outside-the-box thinking. Okay, I know that's somewhat clichéd but it's what we do. We look to develop the next stage in the growth of whatever technological field we're working in and set a progress path that will run in a completely new direction. A direction that will accommodate fresh ideas, fresh reasoning and enable its further development the power to expand into areas for which it had previously been forbidden access.'

The audience remained deathly silent, hanging on Lukas' every word.

'Ever since Italy's Salvino D'Armati brought us the first eyeglasses sometime during the thirteenth-century, mankind has profited immeasurably in combatting the results of any number of causes of vision impairment and, irrespective of what is unveiled on this stage tonight, we must not lose sight of the inestimable benefits this great man afforded us over the intervening centuries. But his work didn't provide answers to every challenge presented to those working within the ophthalmic industry and I would like to think the solutions we are about to reveal, although in many ways revolutionary, owe much of their value to Signore D'Armati.'

Lukas ran through various aspects of the development of the OT3 hardware without giving anything away regarding the actual means by which it bypassed the need for a subject's retinal facilities to play a part in his or her ability to enjoy full eyesight functionality. And for the moment, left his audience's understanding of what was to come on a knife's edge.

No illusionist or magician in the history of deception and wizardry had held an audience more rapt than had Lukas Hoffman on this momentous occasion.

Ralph Henriksen followed on by giving a brief resumé of his role in the progress of OT3 before James and Meghan did the same for their respective areas of expertise. By the time the IntuTech team had collectively briefed the one-hundred-and-twenty-five guests, one could sense a palpable air of tension throughout the auditorium. History was about to be made.

As Meghan returned to her seat, Lukas rose from his to take his position again at the front of the stage.

'Without wishing to leave you in suspense for a moment longer, I should like to introduce you to a gentleman I have only recently had the pleasure of meeting. His name is Bill Evans and I had the good fortune to be introduced to him through an ophthalmologist acquaintance of mine. Three years' ago, Bill suffered a minor injury at his place of work that required him to undergo some routine surgery to get him back on his feet. The injury concerned the crushing of the index finger on his right hand, an exercise totally unrelated to his eyes. However, on being admitted to hospital as an out-patient, by one means or another, Bill came in contact with a virus wholly unrelated to the injury for which he was being treated. And within no time, it found its way into his ocular system and quickly went on to destroy his eyesight. Bill's cornea and retina were damaged beyond repair and had sent their last messages along the optic nerve to his brain.'

Lukas paused for a whole minute-and-a-half to allow the full weight of this last sentence to fully sink in.

'But that is exactly where OT3 intends to take over and, tonight, you are about to witness the very first nominee to be equipped with our creation. A creation that places no demands on the body's damaged optical organs. Instead, the OT3 device, when linked to the specially-designed IntuTech chip that Bill has had implanted into his cranial cavity, will send all necessary visual data to those parts of the brain responsible for interpreting the images to which the device will be exposed and, in turn, enable Bill to enjoy the results in Ultra High Definition. A resolution equal to that which he previously experienced before his fateful hospital admission.

'But not only that. Bill's newly-acquired OT3 device is fitted with image-gathering sensors along all sections of its design, including the temples – what some people call the arms - and their rear sections to provide 360-degree vision. Bill will be equipped to see where he's going, where he could have been going and where he's already been. Bill will enjoy vision like no other human being.'

There was an audible gasp almost in perfect unison from each member of the otherwise silent audience. They were about to receive more than the full value of their £200 admission fee.

Chapter 6

'Come on, Ricky, you're kidding me.'

'No, no, no, I promise you I'm not, Harry. I am not kidding you, really. This lady at uni, I promise you, has got me completely hooked. Seriously.'

Ricky felt an inexorable need to share his emotional disposition with someone close. Someone he trusted, someone likely to be non-judgmental. And, in this instance, he chose to burden his good mate, Harry Stevens with the discreet specifics of the story so far.

'But she's several years' older than you and, by all accounts, happily married.'

'I know that. And I'm not looking to upset anybody else's cosy little nest but there's something about this lady that I just can't get out of my head. She's attractive but not the most stunning female I've ever set my eyes on. She's sort of curvy but, well, not a catwalk model. And she's taller than me. Yes, I have to, kind of, look up to her if we're walking together. So, on paper, she's not ticking all the boxes. But there's a box somewhere in my head that has a whopping great tick in it and, for two months now, my mind has been fixated on it.

'It sounds ridiculous but it's the way she insists on rejecting me that I find so irresistible. Honestly. She looks at me, straight into my eyes, and says things like, "Ricky, I'm not available, not in a million years. I'm happily married to a guy I'm desperately in love with and who's going places in his career. And I'm too old for you".

'And when she says, 'Ricky' she sort of trips over the second syllable and does a little glance to the side at the same time and it does me in. No one else I know does that. They all say, 'R-i-c-k-y – straight and simple – like you and I would. But Beth says, 'R-i-c-k-e-r-y. No, that's not it. Oh, I can't do it the way she does it and that's probably why she comes over so magical. She's just different, Harry, and when I wake up every morning she's just pinned to my "start menu". We both boot up together. She's there, sitting on my taskbar all day long. I've tried everything: re-booting, deleting, uninstalling, you name it, but Beth just hangs on in there twenty-four-seven and I'm lovin' it.'

Since first setting eyes on her, Beth had taken up permanent residence in Ricky's consciousness. And he had no plans to terminate her tenancy. Beth was free to enjoy gratuitous occupancy for as long as she wished providing he was allowed unrestricted access.

'Wow, you're not kidding me then. You've got this Beth lady real bad, mate.'

Ricky and Harry had been good friends since junior school and regularly hung out together. Nobody knew either of the guys better than they did themselves and, if Harry was convinced of Ricky's passion for Beth, then it was clearly more than a mere whim.

On this particular evening, they were relaxing with a couple of pints outside one of the town's busy bars with little on their agendas until bedtime.

'So, what are you going to do about it, Ricky?'

A herring gull landed on the path no farther than a metre from when the two were sitting but it singularly failed to interrupt Ricky's train of thought.

'Do about it? Hmm, I'm going to buy her a birthday present – nothing too grand – just a small gesture.'

'Isn't that a bit premature Ricky?'

'Premature? No, not at all, Harry – we're good friends, me and Beth.'

'But how do you even know when her birthday is?'

'I don't, but I can only be six months out at the most!'

'A birthday present when you don't even know her birth date – you're crazy, Ricky, completely crazy.'

They were sitting on a wooden bench running along an outside wall, adjacent to the bar's restaurant area, with their legs stretched out in front of them casually observing the comings and goings of the local's diverse clientele. But while, in normal times for Ricky, this would have been confined to those of the female gender between the ages of sixteen and twenty-five, tonight he was noticeably oblivious of that particular demographic. And Harry was more than aware of the fact.

'Ricky, what are you thinking? Man, I've never seen you like this. Erica from the doctors' surgery just ambled past - no more than two metres away - and you remained motionless, just staring into the middle distance. What's come over you, mate?'

'Chocs or flowers, Harry?'

'Chocs or flowers! I just asked you a question about Erica Brinkley for chrissake, and you come back with, "chocs or flowers". What are you talking about?'

Ricky's mind was on a different planet.

'Sorry, Harry, do you think Beth would appreciate a box of chocolates or a bunch of flowers, you know, for her birthday?'

'Ha, ha, ha, there is only one Ricky Tremonti, that's for sure. Okay, a bunch of flowers, I say. They always go down well even if this time they'll be all stinky and droopy by the time the birthday arrives. You are priceless, Ricky, truly priceless!'

Ricky was actually quite serious about buying a birthday gift for Beth – it was in his nature to charm his way through life and presenting Beth with an early, or late pressie didn't faze him in the slightest. A bunch of red roses it would be.

Beth had mentioned various random aspects relating to her home several times to Ricky during their casual conversations and it wasn't difficult for him to work out precisely which property belonged to her and Richard. The town wasn't large and most of the residential developments had been, understandably, concentrated around the coastal areas. Both Ricky's parents' house and Richard and Beth's property were east of the town centre and within no more than a mile of each other – an easy walk with no need to announce his arrival by driving up and parking outside. Ricky planned to approach the front door by walking diagonally across the lawn from the left-hand, stone-cladded side of the house. By doing this, it would avoid a direct line of sight from the living room to the pathway that led from the pavement. And it would maximise the surprise element by taking Beth off-guard when she opened the door. He was confident it would be Beth opening the door because she had mentioned Richard's Brussels trip to him earlier in the week. What could possibly go wrong?

It was a warm summer evening with only an-hour, or so, to go before the sun was due to disappear and Ricky pondered over the attire in which Beth might have, unintentionally, chosen to greet her secret guest. A pair of tight shorts and a loose-fitting shirt undone and tied at the waist would have been his choice for her but, hey, he had made no announcement so he'd have to accept whatever she appeared in. But in truth, Beth could have presented herself in a trench-coat and gumboots for all the difference it'd make to Ricky.

At 08.30 pm, Ricky rang the doorbell and stood poised for a likely flustered reaction from his unsuspecting host. Her little autonomous runabout was parked in the drive to the right-hand side of the property so he had no reason to think she wouldn't be in. But after a minute, or so, there was no answer. Perhaps she was upstairs with the TV on and failed to hear the bell. Or in the bath, maybe. He rang again . . . one minute . . . two minutes . . . nothing. It was beginning to appear that, instead, *he* was to become the surprised party and he felt anything but comfortable returning home with the bunch of roses intended for Beth.

But thinking on his feet and improvising was never something Ricky had trouble with and a furtive sneak around the side lawn leading to the rear garden seemed a decent plan 'B'. He was totally prepared to be the one caught out of position but, no problem, he'd made it this far and wasn't going to fall at the first hurdle.

He crept stealthily along by the cladded wall to the left of the door, turned sharply to his right and followed the property's side-elevation which led him to the rear garden. And there, before him, was a large, decked area housing an elaborate hot tub bubbling away vigorously to the accompaniment of a slinky smooth jazz track of unknown provenance. And there in the tub, with her back to the unannounced visitor, was a bikini-clad Beth swaying to the rhythm of the music with a glass of something in her hand.

While Ricky had fantasized about shorts and a loose-fitting shirt he hadn't dreamt of a skimpy, two-piece swimsuit. From behind, she looked nothing short of stunning and Ricky was beginning to think he couldn't have planned things better.

Pull yourself together, Ricky, control yourself.

Without hesitating further, he sneaked up towards the tub and quietly extended his right hand over Beth's right shoulder to reveal the dozen red roses he'd brought as a gift. And before she had a chance to respond, he whispered '*Happy Birthday*' in her ear without giving a thought to how she might react to his most outrageous conduct.

Beth immediately grabbed a towel, covered herself and leapt out of the bubbling water.

'Ricky Tremonti, how dare you! When did I give you permission to enter my property? And it is NOT my birthday anyway. And how did you know where I lived? And on a night when my husband is away on business. The audacity of it. Who do you think you are?'

'I'm sorry, I really am, Beth. I thought it might be a nice surprise for you. And, being a gambler, I took a long shot on it possibly being your birthday.'

'Well, it isn't and it was wicked of you to spend money on

flowers expecting me to receive them with good grace. You can remove them and yourself from my property at once.'

Beth stood there, dripping from beneath the towel and found herself completely lost for anything further to say. She was infuriated. And Ricky cut a miserable dash standing just a few feet away holding the unwelcome gift. With the speaker system now playing a more upbeat Bossa Nova track and the woeful pair utterly stumped for any possible contribution to a meaningful conversation, they looked across at each other and simultaneously burst into fits of laughter.

Although she would never admit as much, Beth was invigorated by the situation, sensually enlivened. And in an aberrant way, she was enjoying a moment of exhibitionism without fear of accusation.

'Mr. Tremonti, why do I always let you get away with this audacious behaviour?'

'I guess it's the way you're made and the way I'm made. I thought a bunch of beautiful flowers on an evening when you were likely to be feeling lonely would be a nice gesture. But we think differently. I now realise that and I promise I will never behave this way again.'

'Here, give me the roses and come inside before the neighbours start talking.' dictated Beth as they passed through the property's rear sliding glass doors into a spacious, open-plan living area.

'Sit down there while I go upstairs and get dressed. And don't move an inch!'

Beth walked hurriedly across the living room and began to climb the winding, oak-treaded staircase while Ricky, not daring to move a muscle, watched, furtively, from below. She was an attractive lady, he thought, and worth every minute of the dressing-down he had provoked on his arrival. *Yes, every minute.*

While he sat motionless on his allocated seat by the window, he mused over the elegant way the room had been decorated. The mix of colours was unusual yet stimulating in a kind of unapproachable way. Bold greens were sitting uncomfortably alongside pastel blues and salmon pinks as if to suggest a disagreement had occurred between two separate, yet equally dominant interior designer minds. But it worked. It worked in a sense that unashamedly drew attention to the fact that two strong-minded individuals were in occupation of this dual-fulfilling setting. Why should anyone expect it to be otherwise?

Beth re-entered the room dressed casually in jeans and a loose-fitting shirt.

'Ricky, now you're here you might just as well stay and join me for a glass of something. Gin? White wine? Bubbly? What will it be? No, on second thoughts, I'll choose. As it's my birthday next month, it'll be bubbly – okay with you?'

For the opportunity of joining Beth for a, possibly romantic, evening drink, Ricky would, unquestionably, have settled for a glass of dirty rainwater.

'Well, I wasn't far out, was I? Happy birthday for next month, Beth. Yes, a glass, or two, of bubbly will be most welcome.'

'I said a glass, Ricky. A glass is one glass.'

'One glass will be perfect.'

The two fellow students settled down by sitting next, but suitably distanced, to each other on one of the room's extravagant, white leather sofas and held their glasses aloft in celebration of Beth's, almost, timely birthday. But one glass soon led to two. And then three. And then another bottle until only a drain remained.

'Yours or mine?' Beth enquired with a slight hint of a tremor in her voice.

'Oh, yours, Beth. I'm here on false pretenses, after all – I couldn't possibly finish off the last two swigs of your excellent champers. No, you go for it.'

'I couldn't possibly. Tell you what, we'll share it.'

'But there's no more than a dribble. How can we share it?'

'Come over here, Ricky, closer, no, not like that, right next to me and lean your head back. That's it. Now, put your lips next to mine – yes, like that - and I'll pour what's left vevy, vevy, carefully so that it drips into both of our mouths at the same time.'

The alcohol had empowered Beth to enter a world where there were no rules. No responsibilities. No concept of conscience. Where forbidden fruits were temporarily suspended. Where her basic senses were granted the freedom to delight in life's pleasures without fear of repercussion. A world where Ricky Tremonti was already a fully paid-up member.

Beth's egalitarian method of fairly distributing the remaining liquid between the two of them was wholly unsuccessful. Most of the fluid trickled down her shirt front while the remainder found its way onto Ricky's necktie. But neither appeared to notice anyway, instead, returning to their previous state of uncontrollable laughter.

Beth awoke at first light with a start. Then she remembered that Richard was away and wasn't due to return until just after lunch. He promised he'd be back to prepare a special post-

OT3-launch meal for her that evening and it wouldn't be in Richard's nature to let her down. Then Ricky stirred next to her. She glanced uneasily to her left. *Oh my God, oh my God, no! What have I done? I'm sharing my bed with Ricky Tremonti. Oh God, somebody tell me this is not happening. Please! Please! Please!*

Beth had abruptly re-entered the world of reality. The world of rules. The world of responsibilities. And she had absolutely no idea how she would avoid its inevitable consequences.

'Ricky, for God's sake wake up! NOW! Ricky! Wake up now! Ricky Tremonti, you've got exactly two minutes to remove yourself from my bed . . . and leave my house . . . and not let the neighbours see you . . . and don't ever come back . . . and don't ever talk to me again at uni . . . and I don't ever want to see you again. Just go! Just go now! Go, go, go! Now!'

Ricky opened his eyes to see Beth in a state of sheer panic. Completely out of control. This was not how he liked to see her. This was not the Beth he'd seen while being dragged upstairs just five hours earlier after spending the evening knocking back Champagne and dancing arm-in-arm to her collection of slow love songs. This was a Beth he'd never seen before. A Beth he'd never contemplated seeing before. A Beth he didn't wish ever to see again.

'Of course, of course, Beth, I'm going. Just give me a minute and I'll be away from you. I understand what you're saying – please, please, just one minute.'

Beth was weeping hysterically while she sat up in the bed with her head flopped forward and her hands clutching her unruly hair. Her whole body was shaking.

'Oh, Ricky, how did this happen? How did we end up in

this awful, compromising situation? This is just not me. I just don't do things like this. I've never, ever, ever, ever, done anything like this before. I'm in love with my husband. He'll be distressed beyond all comprehension when he finds out. Oh, Ricky, oh, Ricky.'

'Beth, Beth, Beth, please, it's not your fault. Neither of us intended the evening to end up like this. We were drinking, remember? We drank far too much and we lost control of our senses. And Richard doesn't have to know anything about it. I'm going to slip away now without anyone seeing me and we just don't ever have to refer to it again. We can just pretend it didn't happen. It's not a problem, really. Look, I'm dressed now and I'm going home. Lie down again and go back to sleep. Things will be better when you wake up in a couple of hours.'

But Beth was already out of bed and halfway through dressing herself.

'I know, I know, But just go, Ricky, just go and let me clear up whatever mess we left downstairs before this . . . this degrading situation developed.'

The crying had subsided and Beth was beginning to come across a little more intelligible. No longer shaking, she started to regain control and, though frantically trying to run a brush trough her dishevelled hair, she was beginning to look more like the Beth Ricky had seen before the two of them had been drawn into this unintended affair.

But she found herself slipping back, uncontrollably, into the no rules, no responsibilities world.

Beth ambled over to him, hairbrush still in hand and planted a kiss on his left cheek.

'I'm so sorry, Ricky, it's all my fault but I'd like your assurance that you will never, ever breathe a word of this to anyone. Ever, ever, ever. Will you promise me that? Now, please leave and I will straighten things out and attempt to get my head back into some kind of rational shape. Goodbye, Ricky, goodbye.'

Ricky made his exit via a side door taking care not to be seen leaving the house by avoiding direct lines of sight with windowed elevations of the adjacent properties.

Chapter 7

Lukas waited the several minutes that were necessary for the audience's gasp to subside and then paused a few more minutes for various inaudible remarks between guests occupying adjacent seats to abate before continuing.

'Now, my learned guests, if you are ready, I would like to invite Mr. Bill Evans to join me to say a few words to you before we introduce him to OT3, his new technological companion who, I believe, is likely to remain by his side throughout the rest of his life. Bill, if you're ready, perhaps you could please come over.'

Lukas bore the facial expression of a man about to learn the magnitude of a single-ticketholder lottery win, so confident was he of the ensuing event's potential to become a world-shattering news story.

Bill was sitting in the farthest comfy chair to Lukas' left and immediately rose to walk the few steps to the microphone where Lukas was addressing the audience. As he left his seat, he intuitively grabbed his smart stick as a matter of habit rather than necessity. Many brands of computerised, visually-impaired persons' canes were available on the market these days but Bill had chosen the popular SatLab product which featured every imaginable technological trick in the book from simple satellite navigation to obstacle detection and beyond. The creative people at SatLab had clearly paid due deference to the time-honoured work carried out by, amongst other canine breeds, labrador retrievers whose presence, for many years, had become synonymous with those suffering from blindness.

Bill made his way over to where Lukas was standing with the help of Meghan who had positioned herself next to his chair in readiness for the moment he was due to be introduced. As he reached Lukas, Meghan gently guided him to face the guests and he, instinctively, set his would-be gaze straight ahead, effectively, above the heads of the audience. Although it was doubtful that Bill appreciated the appropriateness of this pose, it was, in fact, perfectly in line with the method taught to budding stage actors. Apparently, training your eyes on a point at the back of the auditorium, above the heads of the audience, gives the impression that you are focusing on everyone at once.

'Ladies and gentlemen, a round of applause please, for our very special guest, Mr. Bill Evans.'

Bill managed a nervous smile but was noticeably uncomfortable at being the centre of attention. Though he was unable to visually witness the level of interest present in the one-hundred-and-twenty-five-strong audience, the general level of audible activity was obvious to anyone - sighted or otherwise. And, of course, he had been visually challenged for just three years so his powers of perception were well-tuned to deliver such information via his remaining senses to his primary visual cortex regardless of his retinal capability.

'Good evening, Bill, we are delighted to have you here with us this evening and I wonder if you would mind telling me just a little about the history leading up to your visual impairment. I'm sure our audience will have more than just a sympathetic interest in your journey.'

'Good evening to you, too, Mr. Hoffman. And all of you out there as well. It's good of you to ask me to come. Really good.'

Lukas interjected, 'Bill, I am sure I can speak on behalf of everybody here tonight in saying that the pleasure is, without question, all ours.'

Lukas' response to Bill's opening words was met with enthusiastic applause from the audience.

'So, perhaps you could cast your mind back to the incident that led to your unfortunate disability, Bill.'

'Well, where shall I start? Right, it was roughly three years' ago when I suffered a minor injury at work. It was all my fault, not my employer's. I disregarded an important safety measure to meet a delivery deadline and ended up paying the price. I crushed the index finger on my right hand in a piece of machinery and was rushed to the local hospital to have it stitched up. But what should have been a routine exercise for the medics turned out to be a nightmare for me. I had to have eighteen stitches sewn into the top segment of the finger. Though, because a particular doctor had checked out prematurely, due to a stomach upset or something, and the fact that the hospital, unusually, had a couple of spare beds, the sister suggested I stay overnight while the local anesthetic wore off. And, that way, I'd be able to see the morning-shift doctor when he turned up.

'But I soon learnt that hospitals aren't always the safest places to be and I ended up catching a virus that went on to destroy my sight. I had no idea I'd got it until a week later when my vision started to become blurred and, to cut a long story short, within eight weeks I couldn't see a bloody thing in front of me. I apologise, I'm sorry - please excuse my language. But I imagine all of you have heard these stories a million times over so I shouldn't feel too sorry for myself in your company.

'Anyway, I won't bore you any longer. Thank you all for coming along tonight – really appreciated. Erm . . .'

Bill glanced round to where he sensed Lukas was standing.

'Mr. Hoffman, that's all I've got to say, really, was that okay or do you want me to say something else?'

Lukas put his arms around Bill and gave him a big man-hug.

'No, what you've told our friends here tonight is absolutely perfect. You did a great job, Bill.'

In actuality, since Bill had begun to endure life without vision, he had failed to perceive himself as a disabled person. That was for others. Others whose physical challenges had been evident to him throughout his life. People who parked in special, parking lot locations. People who used designated toilet cubicles. People who others awkwardly forfeited their train seat for. No, he was a perfectly healthy individual who'd simply suffered the misfortune of losing his sight. Bill didn't belong to their club – he'd never enrolled - and he constantly felt he needed to explain this ambiguity to those who doubted his true status. After all, he knew perfectly well what it was like to interpret incoming visual data – he'd spent a lifetime doing it. His imagination, he was certain, adequately compensated for the deficiency others mistakenly identified in him. And Bill was about to be miraculously returned to where he felt he rightfully belonged.

Meghan duly returned to escort Bill back to his seat while Lukas prepared himself to run through the various technical points of the device before asking Bill to revisit the microphone position for his *pièce de resistance:* the fitting and commissioning of his OT3 device.

At this point, an oversized OT3 image appeared on a huge overhead digital display screen while Lukas used a long pointing stick to draw the guests' attention to its various features. The image slowly turned on its axes to reveal its key attributes during which time the audience remained deathly silent. One could be forgiven for thinking each and every guest had serious reservations regarding what OT3 purportedly had in store for them. But, on the other hand, it would be likely they doubted IntuTech would have gone to all the time and expense involved in staging the event were the innovation to eventually come to nothing.

While the OT3 device gently revolved, the image of an accompanying smart watch appeared on the left-hand side of the screen showing elements of the control software essential for the wearer to manipulate the almost infinite number of functions available. These included the elevation of the visual image, its panoramic value, real-time definition, real-time or delayed playback programming, recording, transfer to external hard-drive, even print-out options. All resources were able to be regulated from the watch face via either a normal eye-to-wrist viewing angle or, in busy environments, with the watch face's image superimposed onto one or other corner of the principal lenses. Nothing, it would seem, had been overlooked by Ralph Henriksen and his team.

When Lukas felt he had given as comprehensive a presentation as possible he prepared to move on to the evening's main attraction.

'I hope my little demonstration was sufficiently clear for you to get an overall picture of what IntuTech's latest piece of hi-tech equipment is all about but, to put this extraordinary device into its proper perspective, I am now going to make history by commissioning the very first pair of OT3 digital spectacles the world has ever seen. And our chosen recipient will be our good friend who is with us tonight, Mr. Bill Evans.'

Lukas' initial demonstration served well to whet the appetite of the audience but his impending revelation was surely poised to challenge the significance of John's New Testament apocalypse.

The hall, once again, broke out into loud, rapturous applause as Meghan led Bill back to the microphone. Lukas shook his hand warmly and asked him if he was sure he wished to proceed.

'Mr. Hoffman, how could I refuse? You have placed your trust in me by fitting me out with the world's very first working IntuTech OT3 chip and are now about to reinstate my sight without it costing me a penny. It is me who is indebted to you and I shall be forever grateful. Thank you, Mr. Hoffman.'

'If you could bear with me, ladies and gentlemen - James, would you be good enough to bring me the pair of OT3 spectacles and the corresponding smart watch you have been closely guarding in the case by the side of your chair? Thank you.'

James removed the contents of the case and walked

purposely over to where Lukas and Bill were standing and placed the items on a small table next to them.

'One pair of OT3 spectacles and one pre-programmed IntuTech smart watch, Mr. Hoffman.'

'Thank you, James. Now, if you wouldn't mind, please stay here with me and Bill while we continue.'

James moved two paces to the right-hand side of Lukas and while doing so, placed a reassuring hand on Bill's right shoulder as if to say, *'everything will be just fine'*. Bill immediately turned and nodded in acknowledgement.

'Now, Bill,' Lukas began, 'I first want you to feel comfortable with the watch on your wrist. Which will suit you best, left or right?'

The hall became deathly silent. More than deathly silent in fact. The audience was so uncannily quiet in anticipation of the incredible event they were about to witness that a sound level meter would unquestionably have returned a negative decibel reading. But their minds were working overtime. Each member was abundantly aware of the very special place the evening's revelations would occupy in the annals of history.

'I usually wear a watch on my left wrist so, I suppose, left, please.'

'James, would you please place the smart watch on Bill's left wrist? Ladies and gentlemen, James will now be placing the watch's Kevlar strap over Bill's hand and up to a suitable position on his wrist and, as soon as the movement stops for two seconds, sensors around the strap's perimeter will automatically adjust its size to optimize comfort for the wearer. Is that done, James?'

'All present and correct, sir.'

'No need to be quite so formal, James.' Lukas returned with

a chuckle.

'Okay, now Bill, I want you to simply place the index finger of your right hand on the face of the watch for five seconds while it registers you as the wearer and then we'll be ready to go.'

Bill did exactly as he was told and, to recognise the registration, the OT3 specs began to emit a soft, yet perfectly audible beep to both inform the wearer that they had been linked to the watch and to enable the visually-impaired user to locate them.

'Bill, would you please locate the position of the glasses by the beeping sound you can hear, pick them up carefully and place them on as you would any normal pair of spectacles.'

Once again, Bill obeyed Lukas' instructions and cautiously put them in position.

'How do I look?' Bill replied jokingly into the microphone.

'Well, let us ask our audience, Bill. Humble guests, how do you think the OT3 specs suit Bill?'

This time Lukas' address to the crowd provoked a loud cacophony of replies amongst which, most audibly, was the cry *"very cool"*, which Bill acknowledged with a somewhat embarrassed grin.

His humorous response to Lukas' light-hearted plea to the audience went some way to breaking the ice with an almost tangible easing of tension perceivable amongst all of those present.

'I agree, Bill, you look a million dollars. But, before we get carried away with your new image, striking though it may be, I want you to reserve any judgement you may have, concerning our invention, for the next stage on this evening's agenda which is the actual commissioning of the device. However, ladies and gentlemen, we are now going to break for twenty minutes, or so, for refreshments. If you would all like to rise and find your way to the large dining hall adjacent to the reception you passed through when first entering the building, you will find a variety of light bites and drinks to prepare you for the next leg of our journey. Thank you.'

While most of the guests rose from their seats and made their way to the dining hall, several groups remained seated, leaning in towards each other busy in conversation. One could only guess at the diversity of opinions that might have been floating around the auditorium, and indeed, the dining hall just a few metres away, but any prevailing reservations were soon very likely to be quashed once the guests reassembled after the interval.

Lukas and his team took advantage of the refreshment break to double, treble and quadruple their checks on the equipment to ensure the next stage of the evening's presentation would go without a hitch. *So far, so good*, he thought.

Within minutes, small groups could be seen returning to their seats whilst still engaged in enthusiastic conversation. Lukas wished he could have been a fly on the wall. But the idea stopped him in his tracks immediately triggering a thought process that led him directly to the exciting times that lay ahead of them all when TT1 was ready for its own launch – probably just a matter of months hence, he imagined.

The guests promptly returned to their allocated seats like miniature avatars in a computer game. And after a little more than twenty-minutes had elapsed since Lukas announced the refreshment break, the auditorium was, once again, fully occupied and ready for the final stage of the evening's revelation. And the team occupying the stage were looking suitably confident that they could successfully deliver precisely what they had travelled to Brussels for. The next half-an-hour, or so, would surely tell.

'Distinguished guests, ladies and gentlemen, I hope you are suitably refreshed and prepared for what you are about to witness. Bill's smart watch and his cool OT3 spectacles have been introduced to each other and are anxious to get to work in offering him a remedy to his hitherto impaired vision. Are you ready, Bill?'

'I'm ready, Mr. Hoffman, but I have to say I'm feeling a little apprehensive now.' Bill replied with a touch of nervousness in his voice. 'You see, in all the time that has passed since the incident, I have seen nothing of those who are dear to me: my children, my grandchildren and, most of all, my lovely wife, Sarah.'

Bill paused for a second finding it difficult to form his words properly with the mixture of emotions swirling around in his head.

So bewildered was he by the immensity of the occasion, Bill started to question the credibility of his impending jackpot payout.

'Oh, I'm sorry, everybody, you must think I'm stupid but I've spent all of that time conditioning myself to accept that I will never set eyes on them again and here I am on the precipice of having all of that hopelessness . . . that impossibility . . . that bleakness, if you like, turned completely on its head. And I'm thinking, what if I don't like what I see, what if it works a dream and then, excuse me saying this, Mr. Hoffman, what if it packs up one day and the IntuTech team don't know how to get it up and running again? All these things are haunting me and I'm finding it difficult to hold myself together.'

'Bill, Bill, we all understand your apprehension, of course we do, but I promise you, you'll have no regrets. We have tested OT3 so thoroughly that I cannot conceive of a situation that could possibly arise where the clock, in a manner of speaking, would be turned back again. So, let's waste no more time mulling over these quite understandable thoughts and get on with the business in hand. Right, Bill, will you please lightly touch the frames of your new OT3 companion with the same finger you placed on your new smart watch and tell us what happens?'

'What, just touch them? Not switch them on? Or enter a password into the watch? Surely anybody could inadvertently brush past me and touch them.'

'Don't worry, Bill, nobody else has your finger.'

There was an audible chuckle from the audience at Lukas' suggestion.

'Okay, Mr. Hoffman, here I go.'

Bill tentatively raised his right arm, pointed the required digit in the direction of the frames and, gingerly, made contact. But instead of him turning round to Lukas and the team in elation, he instantly dropped to the floor with both hands clutching the temples of the device.

In one instant Bill had, involuntarily, carried out a valuation of his missing sense. A facility he had never really appreciated during their previous relationship.

The auditorium became silent. Nobody moved a muscle. Except Meghan who rushed to Bill's side and bent down delicately.

'Bill, are you all right? It's Meghan.'

Lukas had stepped back a couple of paces and seeing

Meghan's swift response, the remainder of the IntuTech team, together with Sir David continued to sit anxiously awaiting a response from Bill.

'Can you hear me, Bill?' continued Meghan nervously.

Her mind had virtually blotted out her surroundings though she was vaguely aware of movement, mild panic and a general sense of disturbance.

'Oh, my dear good God. Jeeeeeeeesus Christ. Could somebody please help me up?'

Bill was returned to his feet by Meghan and Lukas only to display an emotional response that alternated between the heights of ecstasy to the depths of despair. Tears of joy flowed into tears of happiness; the man had clearly lost all control of his emotions. But there were no signs of anything physically or mentally untoward – he could have been an over-excited football fan witnessing his team's first cup win of a lifetime. Or an anxious mum and dad at the birth of their first child after an against-all-the-odds pregnancy. On balance, Bill was celebrating as if it were his birthday, Christmas, the country's first ever World Cup victory and a record lottery win all rolled into one. You could say he was a happy man.

'Bill, no rush, really, but when you feel you've collected yourself, we'd rather like you to describe, in just a few words, what it is you are experiencing,' offered a relieved Lukas.

By this time half of the audience were on their feet applauding having realised that Bill's physical and mental health were not in question.

'Mr. Hoffman,' whispered a sobbing Bill Evans 'I am truly lost for words. No, that's not right, these are words. No, I mean the right words. Words that are able to describe my feelings at this moment.'

Bill stood looking down into the audience rather than over their heads. But he wasn't staring. He was slowly turning his head as if to be memorizing every single guest's appearance. Every single guest's facial expression. Every single guest's everything. And then the IntuTech team seated around him. He calmly turned away from the audience to examine the faces of those who had spent months, years dedicated to undertaking every subtle modification to a process that led nowhere but here in the George Bartisch Hall in the International Ophthalmic Council headquarters in Brussels. Tonight, in front of some of the world's most distinguished ophthalmological minds, William Geraint Evans' eyesight had been restored after he had irresponsibly failed to follow a simple set of guidelines just to meet a stupid deadline. How could he begin to repay these wonderful individuals?

And unbeknown to Bill, he would be able to relive the moment at any future time as Lukas had, sympathetically, set the device to RECORD mode.

But Bill didn't need to repay anybody. Lukas Hoffman's IntuTech organisation had just demonstrated that it was not only able to return Bill Evans' sight to a state of normality but to turn eighteen months of hard work into more cash than the likes of an unfortunate factory worker from a humble valley in south Wales could ever imagine in a million lifetimes. Lukas' wealthy industrialist father need never ever put his hand into his pocket on behalf of his proud son again.

Chapter 8

'So sorry I'm late, Luke. That little autonomous hatch of Beth's is playing up again.'

'Not a problem, Rick – Beth called me earlier to let me know you wouldn't be in first thing.'

'Oh, good. Yeah, come to think of it, she did mention you two had spoken. It's so frustrating that those auto-tech guys at the garage can't seem to find a simple fault. You know, we left the house at 07.30 am dead, dialed in the uni's postcode then sat back chatting while the little demon gave us a tour of Falcombe's seafront three times before navigating itself back home again. I mean, that is not what you want to be doing when there is work here waiting for you.'

Richard was noticeably frustrated at having been forced to surrender control for over an hour to what was ostensibly a piece of machinery. The psychological implications didn't sit comfortably with him.

'Rick, calm down, it really isn't important. Go make yourself a coffee and come back here – I've got something you're going to be really interested in. Go on, get yourself a coffee.'

Richard marched over to the kitchen where he found the coffee pot burbling away with a fresh-brew Lukas had set up while he was admiring the views from the seafront.

'Okay, I'm back. What is it that's going to make my Monday morning? Sorry, Luke, did you want a cup?'

'No, I'm okay. Listen, sitting over there in meeting room L1, waiting for you to arrive, is a certain Mr. Ricky Tremonti. Remember that name? The guy who lives round the corner from me. The one who's studying to be an engineer. The one I suggested might be interested in some part-time employment at IntuTech, remember?'

Richard was still seething from having wasted his time on a non-guided tour of the seafront and was thinking maybe these driverless car makers should supply them complete with tour guides if they can't sort out the navigational software problems.

'Oh yeah, right. Yeah, of course I remember. We thought he could be good for some picture thinking TT1 trials. Yeah, I'm with you, Luke. How did you manage to reel him in?'

Lukas brushed a speck of fluff from the sleeve of his jacket.

'Easy-peasy. I used to see him almost as a matter of habit popping into the mini-market to pick up a lottery ticket or something like that. It might have been scratch-cards, I wasn't concentrating enough to know exactly what he was buying. But it did suggest to me that some extra cash was pretty much at the front of his mind so I thought I'd join him in the queue one morning to buy myself one as a means of striking up a conversation. Like we were both sharing the same kind of interest. And I found him quite chatty. Nice guy, actually. And when I steered our little exchange around to the subject of our needing a reasonably bright young person to do some tidying up of our file management systems, he immediately showed some interest. I didn't make any promises, Rick, but suggested he might call in to chat things over with you sometime, and here he is.'

'That's great, let me go and meet him.'

'Hold on, hold on, before you rush in, let's agree on what it is precisely we want to ask him. He seems to be quite conversant on operating systems so I thought, maybe, we should just talk around the subject to get an idea of what he could offer us.'

'No problem, Luke, leave it to me. I'll set up the laptop while I'm introducing myself to him, make sure it's logged on to transcription mode and activate it via my smart watch without him realising what I'm up to.'

'Sounds good to me, Rick. I've got an OT3 meeting with the guys upstairs so you get going with Ricky and we'll catch up later.'

Richard swung the meeting room's door open to reveal a cool-looking dude sitting, quite comfortably, at the far end of the twelve-seater, polished bamboo, boardroom table as if in readiness to chair the meeting himself. At first glance, he didn't look to be short on confidence and immediately stood up to greet his host.

Tremonti was slightly shorter than Richard with an athletic physique and was markedly comfortable holding eye contact.

'Hi, I'm Ricky Tremonti, Mr. Hoffman warned me that you were running a little late this morning.'

'Yes, I'm sorry about that – I'm Richard, Richard Stewart -

may I call you Ricky?'

'Of course.'

Richard explained that he needed to log on to a system on his laptop to check a couple of items before they started their chat and sat there tapping away while Ricky casually contemplated his surroundings. When finished, he duly tapped the face of his watch as if to check the time.

'Right, that's done. Oh yes, we don't pay too much attention to formalities here at IntuTech. You can call me Richard. Richard and Ricky – I presume you're a Richard too?'

'Yes, but my family coined the shortform early on and it stuck. So, yes, I'm Ricky and I'm pleased to meet you . . . er, Richard.'

'Pleased to meet you, too. Oh, I'm sorry, Ricky, I've walked in with a mug of coffee for myself without thinking of offering you one.'

'That's fine, I've already had a little too much caffeine for one morning so, not a problem.'

'Great. But before we start, here at IntuTech we record all meetings as a matter of course. It just serves as a record for future reference and might, possibly, be used during training programmes we run from time to time. Are you okay with that?'

'Absolutely, Richard, record away.'

Richard imagined Ricky Tremonti rather fancied the idea of his voice being recorded.

'Excellent. So, tell me something about yourself. Like, what is it you're up to these days?'

'So, I'm in my first year at uni studying for a BSc in mechanical engineering. Not too sure where it's going to take me but I love the subject and people tell me it won't be too hard to secure a decent position almost anywhere in the world once I graduate.'

'I'm sure they're right.'

'Mmm, hope so. It just seemed the thing to do with the way my mind is wired. You know, I just love anything that involves logic. Anything that needs to be thought through and kinda proven. Creative, but, well, not in a sort of airy-fairy way. I like to be able to account for every detail of what I'm thinking before making a proposal. Oh, that sounds a bit vague but I'm sure you understand what I'm getting at, Mr. Stewart, sorry, Richard.'

'I'm sure I do. You like things to be precise, accountable for themselves, provable.'

'Yes, that's the word, provable. I like that a lot. You're spot-on there, Richard. I don't like to open my mouth unless what I'm about to say holds water. That's me. I have to be able to visualize perfectly what it is I'm thinking before I attempt to articulate it. Apprehension, Judgement, Reasoning – the three basic acts of intellect. You have to do things in this order if you want them to make any sense. Like, no one's going to understand what you're talking about if you haven't really thought it through yourself.'

Ricky sat back in his chair with a satisfied look on his face as if he'd provided his would-be employer with an unequivocal description of himself. He sure was a confident guy and seemed to know precisely where he was at, leaving Richard feeling more as though he was looking to engage the services of a new CEO.

'Ricky, I'm with you all the way and that's an interesting way of putting it. But look, the part-time position here hardly requires a high level of intellectual application though it does call for an appreciable degree of thoroughness. You know, insofar as the organisation of our operation's computer file management has to conform to a strict sense of logic in order for any of us to follow the reasoning behind its design. Particularly when you might not be available, say.

'Here, take a look at these pages on my laptop – they'll give you an idea of how we go about things. I have to tell you that our work here is extremely confidential so, nothing personal, but you won't get access to any of the actual files – just their positioning, their updating and, of course, the multi backup procedures we observe with zero tolerance efficiency.'

Ricky returned to his seat at the head of the table, dragged it back a few inches and sat with his legs crossed.

'If you fancy the position, we'll start you on a short trial period to be sure that everything works for you and for us. But I have to say, your little resumé describing to me how your mind . . . how did you put it? Oh yes, how your mind is wired, intrigued me. You seemed to be suggesting that you automatically employ a method of considering things that has a kind of infallibility about it. Like it almost guarantees the listener that your account of whatever it is you're discussing can be relied upon to such a degree that it is the listener's responsibility to interpret you correctly. Is that how you meant to come across?'

Ricky uncrossed his legs and sat forward on his chair as if in contemplation of how he should respond. And he paused before replying.

'Well, put like that, it makes me sound sort of, well, egotistical, I suppose. Like I always think I'm right. But, in a sense, rather than it being a statement of how I am, I'd prefer to regard it as a statement of how I hope I come across. It's really a question of how accurately I picture a concept or an image in my mind before I attempt to convey it as an argument or an instruction. Or a piece of advice, even.

'Let me give you an example: imagine you're about to embark on a journey - say, a car journey. And you're about to have your vehicle navigate you and your passengers along a relatively complicated route with which you are fairly familiar. And one of your party enquires which route it is you've chosen to accept from those offered to you by the vehicle's navigation system.

'Now, you don't have a map or an on-screen image to refer to so you have to supply the information direct from your mind's eye. How do you do it?'

Richard looked interested but realised it was he who was on the spot now, not his interviewee.

'Wow, let me think. Mmm, I'd look at the road ahead of me. Then I'd look straight into the distance to, say, the first turning – maybe a T-junction – and then imagine the distance along that road to the next turning, advise my enquirer of an approximate number of miles before we turn off again, for instance, then, well, then keep on going until my report reaches our destination. How does that sound?'

Ricky's facial expression did little to inspire confidence in Richard's response.

'Well, if you don't mind me saying, not too good. I doubt you'd manage to get every detail of the route correct when you're using a method that requires you to visualize the journey which your mind is only capable of recalling in stages. Stages that you're having to piece together as you go along. Don't get me wrong, Richard, I believe it's how most minds work. But mine doesn't. And it's no credit to me, it's just the way my mind operates. Upon being asked the question, I immediately see a two-dimensional map in my mind, as if I'm viewing the journey from an aerial position, and it allows me to just, sort of, read off the various stages of the route whilst, also, being fairly confident of the directions in relation to a compass. Every road registers with me as either a north-south road or an east-west road. Or, of course, other relative compass degrees within those parameters. That's how I see things.'

Richard felt he was receiving a lecture on the subject of mental perspectives – something he really wasn't expecting when he sat down with Ricky half-an-hour earlier. But he was enjoying it and found the part-time job applicant an absolutely fascinating individual. But, more importantly, he felt sure he'd identified an ideal candidate to test TT1's efficacy at reproducing digitalized images from a picture thinker. If Ricky wasn't a picture thinker, no one was.

'Ricky, that's an amazing way of looking at things and I have to say I've thoroughly enjoyed our conversation here this morning. We must do this again. But for now, I'd like to terminate our little rendezvous and let you get on with your day. I will discuss the matter of you joining us – that's if it appeals to you – with Lukas Hoffman and will ping you over an email in the next couple of days. How does that sound to you?'

'It sounds fine to me and I will look forward to hearing from you.'

'Great. If you could just jot down your email address on that pad in front of you, I'll see it gets entered on the HR database. Thank you so much for calling in today.'

'The pleasure was all mine, Richard, really.'

Ricky waited for his host to stand up first before casually

following him and accepting his offer to shake hands as a sort of end-of-meeting gesture.

The two of them left the room and Richard showed his guest to the exit door leading to the small car park at the side of the property.

He then returned to the meeting room, buzzed up to Lukas, who was still with the OT3 team on the first floor, and suggested he come down as soon as he was finished so that they could run the transcription programme together in the hope that TT1 was, in fact, able to reproduce identifiable graphics following his conversation with Ricky Tremonti.

'I'm going to be five minutes, Rick. But don't run the software until I'm down – I want us to see this together. Can't wait, mate!'

Richard sat at one of the chairs that ran along the side of the meeting room table staring at the machine in front of him desperate to know what sort of job it had done with Ricky's mental pictures. He just couldn't imagine how they would appear on the screen. Lukas seemed to be taking a little longer with his OT3 meeting than his five-minute ETA had suggested so Richard took the opportunity to set up a wireless link to a large, high-definition display screen installed in the room for the purpose of addressing larger groups of guests when they held small conferences and seminars. If Mr. Tremonti's thoughts were going to be worth watching, they might as well be seen in true movie fashion. This was history in the making.

'Sorry, Rick, I couldn't get away as sharp as I had hoped. Tell me you haven't started without me.'

Richard chuckled. 'Just sit down, Luke. I'm as nervous as you are on this one. Hold on, I'm going to lock the door – I don't want us to be disturbed during this . . . this world premiere. And I don't want any uninvited guests bursting in halfway through the showing. I know, I know, I'm paranoid, but I'm taking no chances – I want to enjoy this in peace. Shall we go?'

'Let's go, Rick!'

Chapter 9

Richard had used his not inconsiderable programming skills to adapt an off-the-shelf video editing package to run in conjunction with the TT1 software and was reasonably confident that it could reproduce Ricky's thought patterns graphically and facilitate his manipulating them into some sort of useful document. Where, in reality, neither he nor Lukas had any idea what was likely to arrive on the screen, Richard's unerring optimistic nature had unconsciously banked on a scenario where perfectly-formed graphic representations would manifest themselves automatically when confronting the digital domain. Such was his expectation that he never once considered an alternative outcome where approximations of a visual depiction needed to be interpreted by the observer.

He duly opened the file he had used to record Ricky's responses to the conversation that had taken place just minutes earlier. Then he selected transcription mode, left-clicked on the graphics icon, set the counter to zero and sat back in his chair opposite the big screen ready for the verdict. Although the recent exercise to transcribe Beth's "word" thoughts had met with unmitigated success, the possibility of recording "picture" thoughts was judged by the two digital wizards to be many steps up the technological ladder. This was, in many ways, the make-or-break moment.

'Are you prepared for this, Luke? Come on buddy, we've dedicated our lives to this moment for longer than I care to recall and, let's make no bones about it, the next few minutes are going to define our future in more ways than one.'

'I know that, Rick. Well put. But hold on, let me buzz Jennie to ask her to fetch us some fresh water – we might need something to help us cool down.'

'I've a better idea, get Jennie to bring in the bottle of bubbly that was over from the little OT3 celebration we arranged last week when we returned from Brussels.'

'Excellent suggestion, Luke – we should approach this event with the confidence we'll have something to celebrate.'

Jennie had joined IntuTech some twelve months' earlier and handled anything from tidying up the offices, keeping the place clean, booking taxis, welcoming guests – you name it. And she had the perfect personality for the position – forever bright and cheerful, polite and eloquent when contacting business acquaintances and totally reliable.

Richard unlocked the door while Lukas buzzed Jennie over the intercom with the request that she should bring in the bottle and two glasses. And, within minutes, the two of them were sitting uneasily in their seats with the meeting room door suitably secured and the unopened bottle in ceremonial standby mode on the table in front of them.

'Go, Rick.' said Luke. 'Press the PLAY button!'

Richard did as he was told and, without hesitation, the screen came to life. The audio track of Richard and Ricky's conversation began with the screen remaining blank apart from some very minor signs of static.

'Hi, I'm Ricky Tremonti, Mr. Hoffman warned me that you were running a little late this morning.'

'Yes, I'm sorry about that – I'm Richard, Richard Stewart - may I call you Ricky?'

The audio track perfectly reproduced the introductory part of their conversation but was initially devoid of any visual accompaniment.

'Press PAUSE for a moment, Rick. This is what I expected.' said Lukas.

'When the mind is wholly focused on a pattern of speech – under a degree of stress, for example – I wouldn't anticipate there'd be sufficient mental capacity available for it to form visual images – pictures. But, hopefully, as the two of you become more acquainted, I'm imagining Ricky will relax a little and allow his mind to concentrate also on, well, in the very least, his surroundings. Sorry, press PLAY again.'

The audio – the conversation – got underway again beginning with Richard's confirmation that Ricky was welcome to refer to him by his Christian name. And then an image appeared. A shape. In colour - vaguely.

'Wow!' yelled Lukas.

But it was difficult to discern. Definitely an image but neither of them could begin to identify it. A fictional image. An otherworldly image. An image with its own agenda. An agenda one could imagine deriving from an uncharted region of the subject's visual cortex. Of anyone's visual cortex. This was new territory.

'Press PAUSE again Rick. What was in this guy's mind, for chrissake?'

'Luke, it's not so much what was in his mind as to what else was occupying it. Listen, he's fully absorbed in what I was talking to him about. And his responses to me – all of that was in word-form which we can hardly expect to be translated into pictures. That must be the way a picture-thinker sees things. If he's occupied with a conversation, especially one with a new acquaintance – an acquaintance who's possibly going to offer him a job – he's only going to think of words – the words in the conversation. What possible purpose would be served with the mind spending time converting those words to pictures? It might happen but probably only when the subject is so relaxed. Only then will he see regular, familiar words as visual patterns. Like, let me think, what would be a good example? Yes, the word DOG. Or the word, TREE. Everyday words like these conjure up a typical, generic image as soon as you see them. Or speak them. But why should we think examples of these will be filtered out of yours and Ricky's discussion earlier?'

'I see your point, Luke.'

While TT1 represented the absolute peak of technological innovation, it was by no means beyond further development. For a start, word- and picture-thinking patterns had shown they could be interpreted, imported, transcribed and output to analogue media with no inherent problems. But the patterns required the subject to be within certain parameters of a predetermined range – usually between zero and 5 metres – though the technology could not yet operate across more than one person. As soon as a second DNA brain configuration was detected, the software was programmed to switch off to save cross-platform thought contamination. But, of course, at this stage, not being able to download more than one individual's thoughts at one time appeared totally insignificant. The sheer act of successful thought transfer between two persons was so mind-bogglingly magical that any further enhancements couldn't be properly appreciated.

'Shall we carry on?'

'Yeah, go for it, Rick.'

Richard immediately left-clicked the triangular transport icon to restart the video and the images continued to appear in their previous vague and abstract manner. But when the audio moved on to the part of the conversation when Ricky was suggesting that one has to have a clear understanding of a concept in one's head before being able to hope to articulate it – the bit about Apprehension, Judgement, Reasoning – the video images began to sharpen up. As if they felt an innate need to communicate with their human conspirators. As if in sympathy with the experimenters' objectives. As if playing ball and getting in on the act of breaking new scientific ground somehow appealed to them.

Ricky was clearly beginning to feel more comfortable. And, unsurprisingly, an almost perfect representation of Richard appeared on the screen in front of them. And why not? Ricky was wholly focused on his host and it was understandable that his host's image should be dominating his thoughts. And that was precisely what the video graphics' programme had no option but to reproduce.

'Wow, wow, wow, wow, wow!' Lukas shouted at the top of his voice. 'Press PAUSE, press PAUSE, Rick, we need to celebrate!'

Both men were up on their feet doing some kind of

embarrassing "dad" dance but neither appeared to care what he looked like even if an audience had have been allowed to watch.

'We've done it, Rick! We've successfully converted analogue thought patterns into the digital domain and made them wirelessly transferable to any bog-standard video screen of the sort that virtually every household in the country possesses. Okay, it was mind-blowing that you could import Beth's thoughts a couple of weeks' ago into your own head as if they were your own but this . . . this is several mega-technological strides further than that. Forget moon landings, this was a successful touchdown in another universe - a small step for engineering students, maybe, but a giant leap for IntuTech. We're now *seeing* what Ricky Tremonti was thinking – not just thinking it. This is utterly amazing. Come on, pop that bottle – we may never ever make a breakthrough again on anything approaching this scale. Look, nobody else can be party to this innovation just yet but we are, you and me, Rick, and we definitely deserve at least one glass each of France's finest.'

After sinking their first glasses of the exhilarating fluid while prancing, clockwise, around the long, oval boardroom table more in the style of a couple of excited pre-school toddlers, the two grown men began to regain their composure and, again, take on a demeanor more fitting of their unequivocally significant standing in life.

'Wow, Luke, this is truly amazing. Just think, with this brainchild of ours in the hands of the country's CID, suspects will not only provide investigating officers with undeniable thought patterns, they will, unwittingly, serve the police with actual images of their guilty accomplices. The cops will be able to transcribe the suspect's thought patterns to furnish them, directly, with lists of implicated individuals, and they will also have a ready supply of photographs graphically transcribed from the picture-thinking suspect. Game, set and catch! We are making history, Luke.'

'Yes, there is no question about it. But it goes further than that. Just imagine TT1 in real-time graphic transcript mode say, in an interview room. You'll have the CID officers interrogating the suspects whilst simultaneously watching picture-thought patterns accompanying the actual lies they are having to listen to. But, unbeknown to those being interrogated, a real-time movie is running the unlawful event in the background not with character actors but with the actual perpetrators themselves. And a simultaneous word-mode transcript is coughing up an admission to the crime. There'll be no need for film producers to spend millions making "based-on-true-story" movies when the CID can boost their funding by selling the actual footage! Okay, I'm getting carried away now but, wow, the possibilities are endless.'

'No doubt about that, Luke, but there is going to be the question of legality. You know, whether society will accept the data as evidence. This is so new it's going to have to be properly vetted in Parliament – both houses – before we'll get a green light. Even to this day, positive polygraph tests are not admissible as evidence.'

Luke sat back and considered the ceiling for a minute or two. He viewed ceilings as useful blank canvasses eminently skilled at filtering out intrusive or unwanted thought processes when a fresh perspective needed to be comprehended and IntuTech's meeting room's uppermost horizontal surface served this purpose admirably.

'No, I understand that, Rick. But our evidence is far

stronger. We will have actual videos of the culprits admitting, on film, that they participated in the crime. And the efficacy of the evidence will easily secure the approval of any police department or government specialist scientist asked to vouch for the technology involved. We will, of course, have to apply for licencing and undergo all sorts of verification procedures but it's going to be impossible for any expert of any persuasion to seriously put forward an argument that will counter the veracity of TT1. Surely, it's foolproof.'

The two elated working colleagues sat back in their seats silently contemplating where their invention might lead. Neither was particularly money-driven but it was difficult for them not to be aware of the inevitable financial rewards that would be coming their way. There were loans to be repaid, of course - most notably where Lukas' father was concerned - and it was true that, being the operation's principal, Lukas would attract the lion's share of future earnings. But this division between the two was a mere technicality when it came to the likely scale of the windfall ahead of them. The repayment of Richard and Beth's mortgage was not going to present them with a problem.

'I'm sure it is, Luke, but let's take control of ourselves, settle down and get on with watching this little movie we've made. This little world premiere of ours.'

There was no red carpet and there were no flashing paparazzi cameras. No glamourous models draping their bodies over drooling film directors. But in our two scientists' eyes the significance of this particular first night dwarfed any epic movie production ever to find its way onto celluloid.

Richard activated the PLAY icon and the pair of them relaxed again in their seats to enjoy the rest of the video.

Richard's image figured largely on the screen for the next few minutes, presumably while Ricky was summing him up and concentrating on little else. But then the graphics started to become significantly more defined and, suddenly, a computer screen appeared, as it were, within the main screen showing an array of file directory icons. Hundreds of them. With a hand passing over the screen pointing to various details. It was, quite clearly, a replay of Richard's file management demonstration. Ricky was, doubtless, quite relaxed by this time and had crystal clear images in his mind whilst staring at the laptop. It was no different to watching a home movie. And it continued this way for several minutes with perfectly predictable images appearing one after another. And then, sometimes the flow of the images would go back again as the thoughts followed a random course, chronologically, in his mind. There was a coffee cup, an image of the outside of the building – possibly his initial view as he walked round from the car park. Then the image of a middle-aged lady of quite noticeable Italian ethnicity – might have been his mother who was likely to have prepared his breakfast an hour, or so, earlier. This was pure magic. A real live story in pictures. No pinholes, no black cloths, no shutters, no telephotos, no dark rooms, no developing fluids, no digi-cams, no lighting, no CGI, no saying "cheese" - these pictures were straight from the source. No means of reproducing visual images could ever be as unadulterated as TT1.

Though, it didn't stop there. These were images of actual events that Ricky Tremonti had experienced prior to his meeting with Richard. Images that could previously have been captured with a traditional camera. But TT1 technology was able to reproduce fictional images. Moving images. Moving images resulting directly from a person's imagination. Moving images in no need of a film set. No need of a film director. No need for actors. The potential was mind-boggling. In time, whole films could be developed from the mind of one creative, highly-imaginative individual.

The Italian lady was followed, curiously, by three little elephants grouped together for a couple of seconds before they slowly disappeared. Then a Ferrari. Or it could have a Maserati - neither Lukas nor Richard could be described as car enthusiasts. But it was certainly sleek and, to most people, they felt sure, highly desirable. And, of course, Italian. This was becoming extremely interesting. While Ricky appeared to gain more confidence as the meeting moved on, his thoughts became less focused and began to move onto random recollections that could have emanated from almost anywhere. Richard certainly had a coffee cup in his hand when they first met and, if it was his mother, then, that was fairly understandable too. The supercar could well have featured on a breakfast-time TV advert and it wouldn't be too difficult to conjecture that Ricky harboured aspirations in that direction. How many young men didn't? But the elephants? One facing left, one facing forward and one facing right - in a carefully assembled arrangement. They weren't quite sure where they'd evolved from but how could they be privy to everything to which their interviewee had been exposed?

As the visual transcript neared its end – maybe with about five minutes to go – Richard's moving image continued to dominate the footage while other, quite plausible, apparitions came and went as, no doubt, his mind wandered. There was a scene that could have represented a classroom, or a lecture hall, with a tutor standing on a platform waving a pointer stick at what looked like a white board. And another where a group of friends were gathered at some kind of social occasion each with drinks in their hand. Totally normal thoughts occupying the mind of a typical young man. And the funny thing was, in each portrayal, Ricky, unsurprisingly, failed to feature. And why should he? One's own image would never be included in real-time observations. How could it?

No, as the 'movie' approached the end of the encounter, both Lukas and Richard felt satisfied that the visual transcripts were perfectly comprehensive representations of what was running through Ricky Tremonti's mind during the course of the meeting.

The clock above the digital screen was close to indicating the afternoon was about to begin. It was 11.57 am and Lukas and Richard felt they'd already done a day's work such was the intensity of the past hour, or so, analysing the visual transcript of the earlier meeting. They remained in a state of heightened euphoria having had their dreams come true before their very eyes after so many months of anxiety and apprehension and were finding it difficult turning their minds to the more mundane tasks facing them for the rest of the day.

'Hey, Rick, how about we both take the rest of the day off? I don't know about you but I can't imagine I'll be able to concentrate on anything while this morning's revelations are still swimming around in my head. What do you think?'

'Well, you're the governor, Luke, it's totally up to you. But I have to say I'm precisely of the same mind. Why don't we each return to our respective homes, take a shower and lie back on a garden lounger contemplating how we plan to deal with the next phase of this crazy enterprise we've got ourselves involved in?'

Taking the afternoon off meant nothing more than the two

scientists choosing to be somewhere other than in the IntuTech building. The prospect of either of them switching off and chilling for the rest of the day was about as likely as encountering a snowstorm in the middle of July in the centre of Birmingham. Lukas' and Richard's minds were in permanent alert mode – only the venues were likely to change.

'Sounds good to me – do you need a lift? Beth's taken your car to uni, remember?'

'That'd be great, thanks, Luke.'

Chapter 10

Reality returned at 08.30 am the following morning when Lukas and Richard entered the building almost simultaneously. Both felt their feet had begun to reconcile their individual differences with anything vaguely resembling terra firma and they were as ready to continue with their work as they would ever be.

While Richard got down to the business of digitally documenting all of the previous day's proceedings, Lukas set about formulating a plan to award international licences that would establish commercial relationships for OT3. It was thought that, initially, one licencee per country would be prudent with contractual limitations imposed to disallow cross-border marketing. This would assist in maintaining a desirable level of exclusivity to enable the successful licencee to enjoy adequate rewards while the product was in the process of gaining ground in its particular domain. Whether, in reality, this would be necessary was open to conjecture given the clear head-start it had over its already-established competition but, to Lukas, the model appeared sensibly cautious and easily amendable providing suitable time clauses were written into the respective contracts.

He had set up meetings at various times during the week. First, was his City of London, Eton-educated, international solicitor, Edwin Crowther-Brown, whose long, familial line of lawyers had been known to Lukas' maternal family for some three generations – *sein Schutzengel* – his guardian angel. Then there was an international licencing agency specialising in identifying and negotiating foreign commercial contacts around the globe. And, finally, an intercontinental, internet-based, marketing agency boasting adequate credentials to ensure that the OT3 message would be relayed world-wide in a manner that would appeal to whatever mix of cultures it found itself confronted with. Lukas thought that should be enough to get the ball rolling. Enough for one week, at least.

Richard's tasks were less intellectually demanding though far more arduous and repetitive than those facing his superior. But they were just as important in their own way and he gained a certain satisfaction in seeing that everything concerning the meeting with Ricky was saved in an orderly fashion with back-up, analogue printouts filed away for easy access should anything untoward happen to their electronic counterparts. The system was as failsafe as he and Lukas could imagine. Nothing was being left to chance.

Lukas' solicitor arrived in the usual, inimitable Crowther-Brown style by parking his immaculate 1976 Bristol 411 haphazardly in the car park at the side of the IntuTech building. Edwin's lack of interest in parking his car was no doubt borne of an expectation that a uniformed chaperone might best be present to deal with the menial task of positioning the vehicle and generally caring for it until he returned. Though impeccably eccentric, the 6.5-litre, scrupulously British, gentleman's sports tourer didn't begin to compare with its owner's dedicated lack of convention. ECB, as his close friends were accustomed to referring to him, burst in through the electronically-sensored, main entrance doors wearing a classic, pale-chestnut, Henry Herbert bespoke Harris Tweed three-piece suit. In his right hand was a Berluti E'mio leather briefcase and on his feet, a pair of size 14, Church's Burwood brogues. Crowther-Brown cut a pretty impressive dash if anyone did.

But his value as an interpreter and advisor on British and international law far outstripped that of his chosen attire for the day and Lukas' family had long trusted the legal experts the Crowther-Brown lineage had, over the years, managed to produce.

'Lukas, I'm here.' announced Edwin in his usual loud, extravagant RP accent as he ventured into the premises' reception area. 'Where are you?'

IntuTech's infrequent number of visitors didn't warrant the services of a full-time receptionist so those dropping in from time to time were inclined to feel they were being left to their own devices where the subject of being welcomed was concerned. But that wasn't the case. The main entrance doors were fitted with a face recognition device that, when primed, allowed the visitor to enter. And as soon as the image was identified by the sensor, each employee's smart watch received a notification to alert them to the visit. And the first one to tap on the icon cancelled all other displays thereby signalling that he or she would be receiving the visitor.

Within seconds, Lukas had acknowledged the small face recognition icon and was making his way down the stairs to greet Edwin. As soon as their eyes met, Edwin yelled, 'Lukey' at the top of his voice. While Edwin would now have been in his late sixties, at the youngest – a different generation to Lukas – the two went back many years to when 'Lukey' would sit on the solicitor's knee during meetings with his mother. The maternal branch of Lukas' family were businesspeople and there always seemed to be something to meet about. So, Lukas and Edwin went back a long way and enjoyed a relationship way beyond that of client and lawyer. Edwin flung his arms around his younger acquaintance almost completely enveloping him in the process. ECB was a giant; at six-and-a-half-feet tall he towered above most people he came into contact with. One could quite imagine Charles Atlas wilting under the welcome Edwin chose to hand out to Lukas.

'That'll do, Edwin, I'll be left with a cracked rib if this goes on any longer.'

'Sorry, my boy, I never did know my own strength. How are you? And what is the purpose for my visit?'

'Let's not stand here talking, we have a meeting room just over there where we can sit down comfortably and catch up properly. Would you like something to drink? A coffee, tea or iced water, perhaps? We have a non-alcohol policy in the workplace which I'm sure you'll appreciate.'

Edwin elected to sample a cup of IntuTech coffee and Lukas buzzed through to Jennie to place his order.

'Looking as dapper as ever, Edwin.' Lukas observed.

'Clothes maketh man, Lukey. You must have heard me say

that many times over.'

'Yes, I can't say it doesn't ring a bell. But you will forgive our more casual way of dressing here in Falcombe, Edwin. Much as I have to say you look by far the suavest gentleman I can recall setting my eyes on since moving to this lovely seaside town, I just couldn't imagine spending a ten-hour day working in that regalia.'

'Oh, come on, Lukey, you know full well that when I'm in the office I'm likely to be slopping around in a casual pair of plus fours, silk shirt and cashmere pullover. Oh, and a cravat, of course.'

'Precisely my point, Edwin.' Lukas replied, with a chuckle.

The pair shared a moment of light amusement while Jennie was preparing their drinks.

'Come through to the meeting room and relax, Edwin, you've had a long drive this morning. Here, take any seat you like and put your case up on the table.'

Jennie walked in with the coffees while Lukas grabbed some coasters to preserve the furniture's finely polished bamboo finish.

'So, tell me why I've been summoned here this morning, my dear man.'

Lukas gave his long-time friend a detailed summary of where the development of their OT3 project stood and described the likely route he expected it should take before arriving at its final destination as a universal solution for those members of society unfortunate enough to suffer from vision impairment. He filled him in on the meeting he had arranged with the licencing and marketing agencies and asked for his advice regarding any particular issues he should be placing on the respective agendas. Edwin took everything on board as if it were something he dealt with before breakfast each morning and furnished Lukas with notes relating to each of the forthcoming consultations.

One area he showed interest in was that concerning the speed with which IntuTech should roll out the programme. Were they to attempt to licence and market the product to too wide a territorial range, he felt unforeseeable teething troubles could compromise the success of the exercise.

'Why not start with, say, just the UK where it will be relatively simple to keep an eye on things, if you'll excuse the pun! I can't see you being knocked back at all during the preliminary stages and would expect the device to go to market within three months of your awarding the first licence. That way, you'll be at hand to monitor its progress every step along the way. You'll even be readily available to meet the inevitable national media demands post launch without needing to travel too far afield. You're going to be a busy man for a few months, Lukey. But do remember to run everything you receive from the licencing and marketing agencies past me before committing to signing. I might just spot something important that your legally-untrained eye might miss.'

The two longtime friends spent a couple of hours going over every possible legal aspect of OT3's impending launch before Edwin announced that he felt all areas had been covered. And to mark the moment, there was a gentle knock on the door.

'Come in.' responded Lukas.

'Oh, my apologies, Luke, I didn't realise you were in conference.' offered Richard.

'Not at all. Please, Richard, do come in and join us.' replied Lukas.

The three of them were now standing in preparation for the appropriate introductions.

'Richard, this is my dear legal advisor friend, Edwin. Edwin Crowther-Brown. He is here to offer some guidance prior to the meetings I have arranged with the licencing and marketing people. Edwin, my colleague, Richard Stewart.'

Richard and Edwin immediately clasped hands and shook vigorously.

'Good morning, Mr. Stewart, I am truly honoured to meet you.'

'Likewise, Mr. Crowther-Brown, I have heard a lot about you. All positive, I should add.'

The three men enjoyed a light, jovial moment for a few seconds before Lukas suggested they sit down and get to know each other a little better. It was quite likely that Richard would have some involvement with Edwin during the immediate and subsequent stages of OT3's progress. But getting to know ECB better wasn't as straightforward as it might have sounded. Edwin was not only from a different generation to Richard but from a different generation to himself. Quite why he chose to present as a late nineteenth-century lord of the manor was anyone's guess. His English upper-class education certainly lent a degree of credibility to his image though he was still several generations adrift. But that was Edwin's choice and there was no doubt whatsoever that it suited him. Designer labels, distressed denims and air trainers would have seriously compromised his authority and probably cost him dearly.

'Richard, Edwin is my long-time solicitor friend but is also a virtual uncle insofar as he used to sit me on his lap when my mother met with him at his office to sort out various legal matters concerning her family's business. And here he is with us in Falcombe, providing the very same, reliable service for IntuTech.'

'That's a fascinating story, gentlemen. A valued friend, indeed.' replied Richard.

'But gentlemen,' interrupted Lukas, 'I need to pop upstairs for just a few minutes to run through an algorithm with Meghan. I know she's waiting for a little bit of input from me before being able to move on with a project she's involved with. So, will you excuse me, please?'

Luke left the room leaving the two men to their own devices until he could rejoin them a short time later. And, as Richard began chatting away with his newly found colleague, he casually glanced down at his smart watch to check the time and, in doing so, brushed several bits of fluff from the face that must have gathered there when he retrieved it from his briefcase a short time earlier.

Before five minutes had passed, Lukas was back in the room continuing their conversation before he'd even reached his seat. Never one to take his eye off the ball, Lukas had clearly engaged PAUSE as he left the room and then RESUME immediately upon re-entering. However, within another quarter of an hour, Edwin announced that he really needed to get going in the hope that he would miss the rush hour traffic around the London orbital on the final leg of his return journey.

The three partook of the customary handshakes with Lukas and Edwin adding an affectionate man-hug to the proceedings before the three of them stepped out into the car park to furnish their guest with a more demonstrable, hand-waving sending off. Edwin's Harris Tweeds, exquisite accessories and 6.5-litre Bristol automobile certainly warranted it.

As the image of the somewhat eccentric supercar of

yesteryear slowly disappeared into the distance, Lukas and Richard remained standing on the slightly raised composite-decked surround to the car park discussing the remarkable relationship that had endured for so many years between Luke and Edwin.

'He certainly is a character, Luke.'

'Yes, a dear old boy, our Edwin. I can't somehow imagine trusting my legal trials and tribulations to anyone else. He's, sort of, always been there for us. For our family. Come on, let's get back inside – I need to prepare for the licencing meeting.'

The two men stepped back inside and went their separate ways: Lukas upstairs to his first-floor office and Richard back into the meeting room.

Once inside the room he glanced at his smart watch. He had felt a gentle vibration a couple of times suggesting there might be one or two notifications advising him of updates and, true enough, there was an icon indicative of some impending TT1 recordings. But he had no recollection of activating the device. He pressed the menu symbol and found two separate, unread word-thinking recordings represented by tiny green flashing LEDs. Mmm, how very strange, he thought - why on earth would he have done that? He could only think that he had, somehow, inadvertently initiated a recording during the brief meeting he'd had with Lukas and Edwin Crowther-Brown – when he brushed the fluff from the watch face, possibly?

Richard sat for a while considering the responsibility he had towards his partner, Lukas, and was minded of the unwritten agreement they shared regarding the logging and recording of trial data. They both felt it was right and proper for any word- or picture-thinking activities to be made known to both of them whether, or not, the exercise had been planned. Mistakes were bound to happen but Richard knew it would play on his mind until he made Lukas aware of this particular accidental recording. In being the only one with the implanted TT1 chip, the occurrence of such an incident would, by definition, only take place with his intervention – wittingly or otherwise. And he was aware that, while all generated data automatically entered itself on the relevant directories, he could, if he wished, erase any such record as he enjoyed computer access at all levels of confidentiality. This privileged position was something he determined he should never take advantage of.

But there was no reason why he should feel he had done anything underhand here. He would simply buzz through to Lukas, advise him of the error and suggest they evaluate the files together. He immediately contacted his superior and requested a short get-together in the meeting room.

'Hi Luke. I have absolutely no recollection of having activated this exercise, none at all. But I believe it must have occurred while I unconsciously accessed the relevant menu item on my smart watch. But don't worry, I will see that the protocols governing any such future event are re-coded to avoid it happening again.

'However, let's see what the data reveals.'

Richard set the machine running and an indicator alerted him to the fact that the data they were about to observe was from a recording in word-thinking rather than picture-thinking mode. Had it been set to "real time" instead of "record", he would have experienced the imported thought patterns at the moment they occurred. However, the time of recording suggested it was triggered during the time he and Edwin chatted while Lukas had popped up to see Meghan. He selected AUDIO and raised the volume to an appropriate level.

Chapter 11

The playback began with several predictable word-thoughts reflecting the initial pleasantries exchanged between Richard and Edwin and the two listeners were encouraged by the clarity of the audio. Even though this was an unpremeditated recording, it was proving to show the technology in a very favourable light.

But the thoughts of ECB soon moved on into areas unconcerned with the conversation. Presumably, involuntary ideas floating around in his head while Richard was, maybe, talking. The interesting bits, one would suppose. The bits that would lead to TT1 having a real application – primarily, the couple thought, in the field of criminal investigation. The audio track continued:

Nice little set up Lukas has here. From what I've been allowed to see, this could turn into an immensely successful enterprise. Never did like the precocious little upstart from the word "go" but

I have to hand it to him – he's done an excellent job here.

'Can you run that again, Rick?' Lukas asked, with a disconcerted look on his face.

'Mmm, of course, Luke.'

Richard left-clicked on the REWIND symbol and then again on PLAY once the clock had returned to its original position. The pair of them listened a second time.

'My word,' said Lukas as he slumped forward in his seat. 'This is not what I expected to hear. Oh wow, my old friend . . . my family's old friend, for chrissake, harbouring thoughts like that over so many years. I'm shocked, Rick, truly shocked. God, we just don't know how we're viewed. Even by seemingly close friends. I really don't know I want to hear any more of this, mate. I need to go and sit down in a darkened room. Apologies, Rick, but would you excuse me for a while?'

Lukas got up from his seat and strolled wearily to the door to make his exit while Richard sat dumbfounded. But his thoughts were more orientated towards the fact that this was precisely what they had signed up for. This was the very essence of TT1. What use would it be if it were confined to reproducing only spoken words. That could be done in the early part of the twentieth century with a simple reel-to-reel tape recorder. No, what was wrong here was that the sheer magnificence of the invention had merely back-fired on its inventors. Unfortunate though that may be, in reality, it did justice to all the arduous work the guys had put in over the many months they'd been working on it. TT1 was up and running - and running superbly.

He stood up feeling somewhat disorientated. Though nothing in the way of emotional commitment existed between him and ECB, he sympathized deeply for his colleague and genuinely wished he'd not witnessed the disappointing and embarrassing incident Lukas had encountered. TT1 could prove to be an absolute monster completely devoid of any form of discretion whenever it wished but that was the nature of its functionality. As he mused over its shortcomings he had no choice but to accept that the prospect of a "tact" gene modification was simply one technological dream too far.

He sat down again wondering what to do next but couldn't somehow justify not playing the recording through to the end. Lukas was clearly in no mood to join him so he leant forward and clicked on PLAY. The audio took up from where it'd left off and Richard listened to the conversation as it evolved while the three of them advanced towards to main exit doors and round to the car park to wave Edwin off. Nothing more untoward about what he heard until, just before the end, when Edwin's car was disappearing into the distance, another unwelcome word-thought, this time from Lukas, came through loud and clear:

Well, hopefully, that's the last of the silly old sod I'll be seeing for the foreseeable future.

Richard couldn't help but see the funny side of this second revelation and sat back in his seat quietly chuckling to himself. Luke has got to hear this, he thought. He has to see the out-and-out irony of this. It totally cancels out the thoughts in Edwin's head towards him. Neither party was aware of the sentiments being concealed towards their otherwise close, highly valued acquaintances. Lukas just had to hear this to mitigate his disappointment.

He buzzed Lukas on the intercom to suggest that he should return to the meeting room as soon as he gets an opportunity. But instead of making his way back, he pressed the CHAT button to communicate with his colleague over the system.

'Hi Rick, what is it?'

'Luke, if you're not too tied up, you need to join me back in L1. Just for a few minutes if you could.'

'Sure, buddy – I'm just running through some legal forms concerning OT3's government approval process. And feeling sorry for myself at the same time.'

'Well, I think I have a perfect antidote and it's not a glass of your favourite thirty-year-old single malt.'

'Okay, sounds intriguing – I'll be right down.'

Richard quickly clicked on REWIND, set the clock to the appropriate position and waited for his superior to arrive.

Lukas re-entered the room a little sheepishly, no doubt as a result of a degree of emotional discomfort, and unhurriedly pulled out a chair adjacent to where Richard was sitting. As he sat down in a somewhat measured fashion he placed a computer tablet he'd been carrying on the table in front of him before spending an undue amount of time positioning it with metrical precision parallel to the edge of the polished bamboo surface. He was clearly in a thoughtful mood.

'Okay, I'm here – what have you got for me?'

'Make yourself comfortable, mate. I'm going to play you the only other non-verbalised word-thought patterns in the Edwin conversation that occur towards the end of the recording while we were both enthusiastically waving him goodbye. Are you ready?'

'Of course, but please don't play anything that might upset me – I found that last playback really quite depressing.'

'I don't think it will cause you any real concern, in fact, I think you'll see the funny side actually.'

'Right, let's hear it, Rick.'

Richard clicked on PLAY and the two men sat back and listened intently. When the passage had run its length, Richard clicked on PAUSE and turned, apprehensively, to Lukas.

'What do you think, Luke?'

His colleague had a stern, perplexed look on his face but, within seconds, he burst out into fits of uncontrollable laughter. Lukas could hardly contain himself.

'Ha, ha, ha, I got the old bastard back. I got him back good and proper. And he won't ever know I have – the old bugger. A moral victory for me, I say. After all, he started it. Rick, that is the funniest thing I have heard for years. But you don't have to like your lawyer to get good legal advice from him so I'm quite happy to leave everything business-related exactly as it is. Thanks for inviting me back in, Rick. I can now get on with my day unhindered by that dear old creep, Edwin Crowther-Brown's negative thoughts.'

Without another word, Lukas got up and left the room.

Richard had some pressing file management issues to deal with and decided to get down to reorganising several directories. And he thought he should, maybe, start a whole new section dedicated to logging details of the word- and picture-thought audio and transcription files before they got out of hand.

But as he was delving through the records, naming this and re-naming that, his mind began to think ahead with regard to the forward journey of TT1. Leaning back in his chair while gently massaging his eyes with the heels of his hands his mind involuntarily switched to meditative mode. *Where was this behemoth taking them? Which party was actually in the driving seat.* It looked more and more as though TT1 was beginning to take control.

Their initial thoughts on the subject concerned its suitability in the world of criminal investigation and he had no reason to change his mind on that. But he was more than a little concerned that, should it fall into the wrong hands, all hell could be let loose. IntuTech would need to impose very tight restrictions on its licencing structure. In a similar way to those concerned with the application of polygraphs where usage is largely confined to the USA's federal, state and local law enforcement agencies. Apart from the military, he found it difficult to imagine an alternative environment where it would serve any kind of useful purpose.

The file management updating exercise was something that needed constant attention and, with the way that developments with OT3 and TT1 were occupying so much of his and Lukas' time, his thoughts turned to the subject of Ricky Tremonti's job application thinking how much of a bonus it would be were Ricky to be attending to the tasks he, himself, was spending so much time on. He vowed to email him later to request that he attend a second interview prior to IntuTech offering him the position. Richard duly triggered the company's omnipresent speech facility requesting a direct-to-implant thought reminder at an appropriate time. This particular resource was, at the present time, available only to him due to the exclusive application of the imbedded TT1 unit he was enjoying. But within time there was no reason why the feature couldn't be marketed as a standalone amenity – a valuable offshoot of the technology's original functionality.

Lukas had finished running over several items with Ralph's team on governmental approval issues and decided it was time to contact his good friend Mark Broderick, a detective chief inspector in the CID with the Metropolitan Police. Lukas and Mark had first met a number of years ago whilst on holiday in Marbella. Both were staying at the same hotel with their then girlfriends and had struck up a relationship almost immediately. The girls also got on but they both tended to take a back seat once Lukas and Mark got chatting in the cocktail lounge. The one-week holiday turned out to be a great success in an unexpected way insofar as the two men formed a friendship that, if anything, had strengthened as the years passed.

However, with the intensity of work over the past year, or so, the two buddies hadn't spoken a great deal. A change-of-address email arrived in Lukas' inbox some six months' previously with the announcement that Mark and his wife, Stephanie, had relocated to west London. Lukas had sent the customary welcome-to-your-new-home eCard and that was the last time, he believed, they had communicated. But with the TT1 project in its present stage of development, Lukas felt the time was right for an "off the record" discussion. Mark knew nothing of its existence and Luke was sure it would be met with interest. He was aware that only a small number of the UK's police forces used polygraphs in their lines of duty and had always suspected their usage would be more widespread were the device able to offer a greater degree of reliability. But in his mind, any further advances in polygraph technology would prove of little consequence once TT1 was introduced to the market. He couldn't wait to have an opportunity to sit down with Mark to run the logistics of his and Richard's invention past him.

Lukas reached for his mobile phone and keyed in the number. And as he did so his body language spontaneously transformed to reflect the relationship he and Mark had established all those years' ago. Although ignorant of the change, a broad grin appeared on his face and a certain restlessness became evident in his composure.

'Mark, my old mate, it's Luke. Lukas, remember me?'

'Remember you, of course I do. So good to hear from you. How're things?'

'Things are absolutely fine here, Mark. In fact, they're better than fine. Richard and I have been hard at work developing, amongst other ideas, two major projects that we feel sure will take their respective markets by storm. How is life with you?'

'Wow, I've always had confidence in you. And with what I know of your colleague, Richard, it is no surprise to me that things are happening.

'Life with me, you ask, busy, busy, busy, mate. It's a criminals' market – too many of them and too few of us. What we need is either more officers on the ground or better detection facilities to nail them earlier. With current regulations as they are, bringing the little horrors to justice is just too longwinded, too tiring and too draining on our hopelessly limited human resources. But that's not what you want to hear when you call me up for an overdue chat, Luke.'

'Well, it's strange you should say that, Mark, but it's exactly what I want to hear. I'd be happy for you to go on all afternoon if you like.

'Listen, one of our projects is just reaching its final testing stage and I'm wondering if you would be prepared for me to pop up to the capital sometime soon to meet up and run it past you. It very much addresses the reservations you have with your current workload and I would appreciate an opportunity for you to give it the once over. What do you think?'

'Luke, you know you are more than welcome to visit me anytime you like. Or, if it suits you better, I'd be delighted to motor down to you and catch up in your neck of the woods rather than mine. Come on, what's not to like about calling in on an old mate in the idyllic southwest-coast fishing town of Falcombe. With a little latitude, Luke, you just go ahead and name the day - odds are I'll be able to make it.'

At 10.30 am on the following Monday morning, Lukas and Mark were seated on the front terrace of the Harbour Café carefully shading themselves from the morning sun under one of the café's generous cream-coloured parasols. Life could be worse. Both had partaken of early breakfasts before leaving their respective homes - very early in Mark's case - so an Americano and a skinny latte were more than adequate for their mid-morning refreshments.

While they had all the time in the world to enjoy their meet-up and relive old times, they were perched forward on their seats each anxious to get the next word in. There was lots to tell and, contrary to their usual more sophisticated, more mature rules of conversational engagement, on this occasion, telling trumped listening by a considerable margin.

'Luke, you've cracked it. I presume this is where you hold your business meetings each day. Nice work if you can get it.'

'Ha, ha, Mark, no, life is not exactly like that. In fact, we can have pretty harsh winters down here when we huddle up on our way to the office with temperatures well below zero. So, you really are seeing the working day at IntuTech in its best possible light.

'But this is half business and half pleasure. Business because

I'd like to run our latest project past your not inconsiderable, criminal investigation department-tuned ears and pleasure because we've not caught up properly for some time'

Mark was fully aware that something of significance was in store for him due to Lukas having lured him all the way from the Metropolis. And it was abundantly clear that he had more than a modicum of curiosity - anxiety even - with regard to its nature. The latte duly disappeared at a similar speed with which his mind was working leaving Lukas in no doubt as to the captivation level of his audience.

'Well, that's all good for me because I've taken the day off work to spend as much time with you as you wish. But, Luke, put me out of my misery, what on earth have you got in store for me that has taken you and your team all these months to develop? You're digital wizards not coppers – what is it you've got yourselves involved in?'

Lukas sat up straight, placed the palms of his hands face-down on the small table in front of him and looked Mark in the eye.

'Okay, sit still, concentrate and try not to doubt what it is I'm about to say to you. This is not some sort of yarn. I promise you. Are you ready?'

Lukas spent the best part of the following hour running through both the technological and applicational aspects of TT1 while they downed two more coffees each in the process. Mark was trained to be a good listener so as not to miss the smallest nugget of information during questioning procedures so Lukas could rest-assured that he had understood the philosophy behind the enterprise. And he was having trouble imagining a situation in his own line of work where the product wouldn't prove unimaginably beneficial to every police force in the country.

'Are you sure this works, Luke? You've not got yourself involved in sniffing naughty substances since I last saw you, have you?'

Lukas politely ignored Mark's humour, rose from the table and walked calmly around its perimeter before replying.

'We have run tests, Mark – only preliminary tests – but they have worked impeccably. With word-thinkers we get pages and pages of perfectly legible textual transcripts and with picture-thinkers it's page after page of flawlessly distinguishable graphic images. In colour!

'And what I want from you is an idea of how well you think it might be received by the Met. We've obviously got to go through the necessary governmental approval procedures and get the product licenced for manufacturing purposes but do you think it would be taken up, Mark?'

'Taken up, what are you thinking, my good buddy? The Met will bite your arm off. Both arms! There is nothing I could imagine that the Met's procurement department would put before signing up for this technology. Nothing! Get on with it – it's a clear winner. And you are going to be a wealthy man, Luke. Very wealthy indeed.'

'That's great to hear. Especially from you, Mark - thanks a million. Really. You've switched the lights from amber to green.'

'That's one way of putting it. But let me assure you, they ain't ever gonna turn back to red. Get on with it, Luke, there's no going back now.'

Chapter 12

Mark spent the remainder of the day with Lukas enjoying a light lunch at the Harbour Café, a short tour of the IntuTech headquarters in the afternoon and an early evening meal that Richard had set up at his home with he and Beth providing the necessary culinary skills. Quite appropriately, the conversation didn't venture towards the IntuTech projects but that didn't stop the proceedings from going off with a bang. Mark was quite a character and it didn't take long for him to feel a rerun of his Marbella karaoke rendition of Charles Penrose's 1926 recording of The Laughing Policeman would be worth dragging out of the closet. The three onlookers were in hysterics. The sight of a detective chief inspector from the CID cavorting around in Richard and Beth's open-plan living area attempting to sing what was ostensibly a comic children's song from the early part of the twentieth century was one to behold. After all, this was their first introduction to the man from the

Met – an introduction they would have difficulty forgetting.

Mark was no lightweight and soon finished his party piece just a few Celsius degrees hotter than when he started. But, other than one shirt tail hanging out and some nominal adjustment required to the height of his waistband, little was sustained in the way of serious dishevelment. With his handkerchief mopping a somewhat sweaty forehead he, quite unashamedly, sat himself back down and suggested the two male onlookers should reveal their lighter sides. This wasn't the kind of activity either of them generally participated in but, after several refusals to accept their declines, Lukas and Richard decided a rerun of their earlier dad dance might satisfy their guest's enthusiasm.

By 09.00 pm Mark felt he should hit the road if he was ever going to be fit enough to face his New Scotland Yard desk just twelve hours later. The three hosts duly thanked him for a thoroughly entertaining evening and bade him farewell.

'Well, that was a little different for a Monday evening.' suggested Beth.

'Mmm.' added Lukas, 'It's been a while since Mark and I have met and I must have put his overtly extrovert character to the back of my mind. But I promise you, what you saw was DCI Mark Broderick in all his glory and, I can assure you, he never changes. And Beth, I have to say the success of our evening was in no small part due to yours and Richard's magnificent hosting and culinary skills – thank you so much.'

By this time, Richard had donned his comic man-apron and was attending to the clearing of the table, the loading of the dishwasher and, in general, the returning of the place to its pre-Mark Broderick state. Not that he had any objection to the impromptu fun and games, but tidiness was an essential lifestyle prerequisite for him and he wouldn't be settling down for the night without, first, ensuring that the following morning showed no hint of the previous evening's recreational proceedings.

Lukas gave Beth a peck on each cheek before creeping up on Richard at the dishwasher and giving him the customary man-hug. He then bade his two good friends farewell and let himself out to make his way home.

'A fun evening,' remarked Beth.

'No doubt about that.' returned Richard. 'Mark certainly knows a thing or two about entertaining. Come on, let's turn in – I'd like to get an early start in the morning.'

Inspired, no doubt by his guest's unadulterated capacity for self-expression, Richard placed one hand around Beth's waist, the other in her right hand and uncharacteristically launched into a Gene Kelly-style routine around the kitchen. An apt finale to a most unforgettable evening.

By the time Friday arrived, the licencing and marketing meetings had come and gone without incident and arrangements had been put in place for applications to be made to the relevant authorities. These concerned who would be allowed to sign up for commissioning and trial periods were built into the agreements to protect both party's interests once TT1 went live. Governmental approval was a tricky one but most of those concerned with the applications felt permission would be granted on a provisional basis as long as the extraordinarily strict monitoring measures, proposed by IntuTech, could be seen to be viable.

The marketing agency would be employed to develop a

brand image commensurate with the intended target clientele which, in this case, would be, in the first instance, confined to the Metropolitan and City of London police forces. No time was expected to be spent on sales strategies as it was anticipated the two selected forces would be automatically signing up for the system without the need for persuasion. Off the record, Mark Broderick had already vouched for its unquestionable fitness-for-purpose so all involved agreed that appropriate branding was all that would be required. However, while all associated marketing plans would be put in place straightaway, there was no urgency to finalise matters until the relevant government departments had consented to its use. Both Lukas and Richard felt the week had gone exceptionally well and locked the premises up for the weekend with an air of optimism and fulfilment. All in all, a decent week's work.

Richard and Beth's radio alarm clock gently swung into action at 07.30 am on Saturday morning with the usual news channel updating them on what it deemed was necessary for them to consider themselves suitably informed. And it served as Richard's signal to throw on his dressing gown and amble down to the kitchen to prepare the couple's first cup of tea for the day – an essential component of their waking process.

He cut a somewhat listless figure as he meandered around the room in a semi-sentient state - a stark contrast to his mid-week, post dinner-party frolic.

As he wandered around the room waiting for the kettle to come to a boil he shifted a basket of freshly-washed clothes Beth had left on the floor by the breakfast bar and took them into the utility room where they would stay until the local, mobile ironing service van came to collect them. But as he placed the basket on the room's granite worktop and returned to the kitchen, something struck him as odd. He turned around and walked back into the utility room. One left, one forward, one right. Strange, he thought. Three elephants. Where, he pondered, had he seen those before? It was very recent. It was at work. In the meeting room. It was when he and Lukas were watching the final stages of Ricky Tremonti's picture-thinking graphics. He looked again. One pointing left, one pointing forward and one pointing right. Three little elephants arranged in the same group. He was astounded by the coincidence. But, hey, he thought, maybe Ricky'd passed by the same fashion retailer that Beth had purchased the wrap from. Not much of a coincidence at all. They both lived in the same town.

But something still didn't feel quite right. He stopped what he was doing, paused for a few seconds and, leaning against the breakfast bar, ran the event over and over in his mind. *Could it have been a coincidence? They both studied at the same establishment, after all. Am I being unduly gullible? They say you're always the last to know. But this guy's young enough to be . . . well, young enough to be a lot younger than Beth. God, how can I reconcile this?* Richard felt decidedly uneasy.

He made the tea and took it back to the bedroom where Beth was still wanting to talk about the fun evening they'd had with Mark and Richard.

'You've talked to me about Lukas' friend, Mark, over recent years, Rick, but I didn't realise what an amusing character he was.'

'Well, to be frank, I didn't expect to be dancing around the house myself. Lukas and Mark first met in a holiday environment where everyone is, kind of, exercising their extrovert tendencies but I hadn't really thought he'd still be in Marbella mode. Yes, it was an evening to remember.'

Richard arrived at work on Monday morning, poured himself a coffee and sat down to go through various bits of mail that Jennie had placed tidily on his desk. He opened the first envelope to find a letter from a young student enquiring after part-time work and duly ran off an email to her suggesting he'd keep her details in the event that something might crop up. The request immediately triggered a return to the thoughts he'd been having over the weekend about Ricky Tremonti and the three elephants. The connection with Beth's wrap was bugging him and he needed to resolve the issue to get it out of his head. As it had been only a few days since Richard had promised he'd be in touch and thought reminders were registering on his implant periodically, he thought it might be opportune to call him up and invite him back for a second short chat before offering him the position. He punched in the contact number.

'Hi, is that Ricky?'

'Yep, Ricky Tremonti here.'

'It's Richard Stewart from IntuTech, is it a good time to chat?'

'Of course, no problem, Richard. I'm just between lectures. What's on your mind.' Ricky replied with his usual air of confidence.

'I was wondering whether you would fancy popping down again to discuss some final details concerning the part-time position you were interested in. Assuming it still appeals to you, of course.'

'That'd be great Richard, it's a defo from me – you name

the time and I'll see if I can arrange things.'

'Right, let me think - would later this afternoon suit you – when you've finished lectures? I presume you're at uni all day, is that right?'

Ricky paused for a second or two while his eyes locked onto a group of young female students walking away from him arm-in-arm along the corridor and momentarily wondered whether an approach to the one on the far left might be a better way to spend the afternoon.

'Erm, let me see, erm, yeah okay, I can make that, Richard. My last lecture is over at 14.30 hours so I can be with you around three o'clock if that suits.'

'That will be perfect – I'll look out for you.'

'Okay, thanks – see you then.'

Richard touched the call-over icon on his cell phone and sat back in contemplation. He would have to be upfront with Lukas regarding his wish to transcribe the conversation's thought-graphics and didn't see a problem with this. There was certainly no need for him to clear the line of questioning he had planned with his superior as it would largely be concerned with Ricky's suitability for the post. He sat back in his seat contemplating the way in which he should plan the discussion to be sure the three elephants issue, and any implications associated with it, was put to bed once and for all.

The remaining items of mail were of little significance and, after acknowledging several inconsequential communications, he switched on his phone's voice recorder to make a few notes in preparation for the ensuing meeting.

'Ricky, good to see you again – come in and sit down.

Coffee?'

'That'd be great, Mr. Stewart, sorry, Richard. Yes, black without, please.'

'I'll be two minutes.'

Richard strolled over to the kitchen feeling a little apprehensive but kept telling himself he was letting his imagination run wild. But as he reached for the coffee cups he uncharacteristically knocked his hand on the corner of the half-open wall unit door immediately causing him to drop one onto the hard-tiled floor. To his immense irritation the cup smashed into a thousand pieces and he silently reprimanded himself for being so careless. But he was all too aware that it was Ricky Tremonti's presence that was the real cause. Without wishing to draw undue attention to his stupidity, he quickly scooped up the shards, deposited them in the waste bin and took a replacement cup from the cupboard.

'There you go, one black coffee – without.'

Richard, surreptitiously, touched his right index finger on the face of his smart watch and sat down opposite his guest.

'I know we covered most things during our last conversation but there are a couple of details I didn't check with you, Ricky. For a start, your availability. While I'm happy for you to choose your own working times, I'd like to think you could manage around seven or eight hours a week. How does that sound?'

'I don't think I'll have any trouble with that. As long as you don't mind me, say, coming in for one hour here and three hours there.'

'That's fine with me. In fact, it might be best for you to monitor the backing-up and directory rearranging tasks to suit

IntuTech's working programmes rather than the other way around. I mean, sometimes when Lukas Hoffman and I have been out for several consecutive days you'll find there will be very little to do. But when that is the case, we will, naturally, understand if you need time to catch up after we've returned and logged all manner of new items on the system.'

'All good with me, Richard. I'm sure we'll work well together.'

'Well, I don't think there's very much else except for you to fill in the two-page questionnaire in front of you. It's just personal details like your address, other contact details and a little bit of your education history etc.'

'I'll do it now, if that's all right.'

While Richard sat there in silence watching Ricky fill out the form, he planned to engage with him, casually, once he handed it over. But he couldn't help noticing his guest's large, bold, confident handwriting. Everything about this young man yelled out extrovert, outgoing, self-control and he wasn't sure he could compete if that's what lay ahead of him.

'There it is, Richard, I think I've completed all of the necessary items.'

'Thank you, Ricky. How was your weekend, by the way?'

'Oh, my weekend was great. Hung out with some friends on Saturday afternoon after helping Mum with some of her household chores. I'm close to my mother and enjoy the chats we have while I'm doing a few bits and pieces for her. And I've got two absolutely gorgeous younger sisters who are always demanding this, that, and the other from me. They're great fun. Then . . . mmm . . . now let me see, oh yes, me and a mate went to see a film in the evening. And Sunday, I didn't do much except write up some lecture notes ready for the next part of the module I'm working on at Stonecroft.'

'Oh, you're at Stonecroft – how's it going, if you don't mind me asking?'

'Oh, it's great, Richard. I just love the course I'm taking – suits my mindset. As I've already told you, I'm not too sure what I'll do with the qualification but, if I achieve a worthwhile grade, it should stand me in good stead for a whole bunch of opportunities. And the people, the tutors, the students, they're all amazing – I'm having a ball, really.

'Mind you, if you don't mind me sharing this with you, there is a student who's causing me a bit of distraction at the moment. Oh God, why am I telling you this? Sorry, Richard, but I'm a little preoccupied with a lady I keep bumping into on campus. A married lady. Honestly, I have no intention of upsetting her marriage but, well, I just can't get her out of my mind. I don't know about you Richard – but I find it difficult to control my emotions sometimes. You know, the chemistry that kicks in when you chance upon someone you just seem to click with - involuntarily. Are you with me on this?'

Alarm bells rang out loud in Richard's mind. *Preoccupied with a lady . . . a married lady . . . upsetting her marriage . . . chemistry . . . seem to click with.* This was not what he wanted to hear. Definitely not what he wanted to hear from the young, cool, fit, Italian Lothario sitting in front of him.

'You know, there was an app I heard about that was going around some years' back, Richard, where you logged all of your details into an enormous, world-wide database to find the one person – just one – who figured more accurately than anyone else as your most ideal partner. Lots of people shied away from it on the grounds that the database would have examined not only millions of possible matches – people, that is - you'd never set eyes on but that it would definitely have included your present partner, or spouse. And, of course, the chances of her coming out top were less than those deciding whether you'd won the lottery four weeks on the trot. So, those of a possessive tendency were inclined to give it a miss but those a little more sure of themselves were up for a bit of fun.'

'Sounds crazy, Ricky. But, if I'm to be absolutely honest, and I'm not proud to say this, I think I would have fallen into the former group – the group where they didn't really want to know if they weren't the ultimate partner. An inadequacy, I'm sure, but I don't think it would have sat comfortably with me knowing my wife would have been more suited were she to have met another guy. I mean, there would be nothing to stop him being your next-door neighbour. Or your brother, dammit!'

The two men sat back in their seats and had a chuckle at Richard's somewhat remote suggestion.

'Well, I think we've covered everything now, Mr. Tremonti, er, I'm sorry, Ricky. I'll update our records and get an email off to you later in the week advising you of our acceptance of your application. Thanks so much for calling in at such short notice.'

'The pleasure is all mine, Richard. I shall look forward to seeing you on the allotted start day.'

With that, Richard escorted Ricky to reception and bade him farewell as he passed through the exit door to the car park.

Chapter 13

Richard immediately returned to the meeting room and booted up his laptop. His conversation with Ricky had been recorded and he braced himself for watching a run-through of the graphics transcript that would be ready to load from his smart watch for instantaneous viewing. As he manipulated the controls he ran his fingers through his hair, once or twice, crossed and uncrossed his legs several times and unnecessarily wiped his handkerchief across his forehead. He was nervous. Nervous that his worst fears were about to reveal themselves as entirely warranted. This type of situation had occurred before. Many times, in fact. There was an incident when a beautiful, unmarked bouquet of flowers had arrived at the house from an unknown sender only for it to materialise, later, that it was a gift from a far-flung cousin of Beth's who'd learnt, several months' late, of the death of a favourite aunt of hers. It took a day, or two, before either of them managed to marry up the two events.

Then there was a case of mistaken identity when two, or three, incoming calls on Beth's cell phone looked uncannily suspicious with the caller insisting that Beth should recognise his voice and recall times they'd spent together several years' previously. The guy turned out to be a well-known scammer who preyed on elderly ladies but who'd got hold of some inaccurate data concerning Beth's age. So, poor Richard was vulnerable to anything looking remotely questionable and couldn't rest until each such incident was able to be resolved. And at the back of his mind, he felt sure this would go the way of the other events once he'd combed through the latest Ricky Tremonti footage.

However, the possibility of discovering something shocking whilst sitting there in the IntuTech meeting room filled him with horror. He could hardly justify locking the door without a plausible explanation should Lukas happen to wander down. Or anyone else, for that matter.

No, he would be far more comfortable sneaking out for a short period to put the episode safely to bed without the chance of anybody else being involved. He duly mentioned to Jennie that he would be uncontactable for the next hour, or so, and to let Lukas know should their paths cross in the meantime.

The Harbour Café seemed a peaceful enough venue to partake of a drink before making his way back to the office to get on with his busy work agenda. So, with a cup of his preferred Earl Grey blend in front of him (though a glass of Napoleon brandy might have been more appropriate) and the laptop ready to run, Richard activated the PLAY icon to access Ricky's visual thought patterns that had been recorded just half-an-hour earlier.

The "movie" began to run with the expected images of

Richard shaking his hand, a coffee cup with a small biscuit on the saucer, some computer directory icons, a questionnaire form being filled out – all the usual picture thoughts as they came into his head real-time. These were followed by the lady Richard had previously, in the last recording, identified as Ricky's mother, two young girls with big smiles on their faces then a multi-screen cinema reception area he was, presumably, visiting with his pal in the evening. All in line with what had passed between them in the meeting room.

But then, probably at the point when Richard had enquired about his weekend, an image appeared on the screen, in perfect high-resolution, of Beth. He left-clicked on PAUSE and sat staring at the image - stunned. Thinking the worst. And reluctant to continue. He spontaneously stood up - traumatized. And acutely embarrassed – the café was busy and he imagined every customer in sight had somehow gained access to his predicament. Then he made things worse by pretending to brush away an imaginary wasp. Quite erroneously, he felt he was drawing attention to himself. The Harbour Café was not proving to be the best choice of venue. Then, after furtively glancing around him, he casually took to his chair and began to reconcile his thoughts with the idea that Ricky could easily have chanced upon his wife while walking the university's corridors being aware that both of them attended the same learning establishment. He mentally rebuked himself for being such an idiot and began to relax before restarting the machine. The "movie" carried on running and, unsurprisingly, a number of shots of the campus flashed past as if Ricky was recalling his route from lecture hall to reception and beyond to the main student car park. Then the images seemed to slow down - as if his recollections were running in slow motion. And Richard began to recognise the area outside his own property. The wall at the left-hand side of the house. And round to the back garden, to the hot tub. The hot tub with his wife, Beth, merrily partaking of an evening drink and being handed a bunch of flowers. Roses. Then nothing except confusion. Flashes of images that made no sense as if the thinker's mind was in turmoil. Unable to think straight. Unable to gather his thoughts sufficiently to render a decipherable picture.

Richard didn't want to watch any more. He'd seen enough to confirm his worst thoughts and was in a state of total shock. Without thinking, he advanced the footage through to the end intending to log off and return the laptop to its case. But before the final images were due to cease, the whole screen suddenly came alive, left-to-right, top-to-bottom, with the image of Beth lying naked in bed – his bed - and, in the foreground, the occasional man's leg or arm appearing whilst, seemingly, engaged in the process of getting dressed. There was nothing left for Richard to assume – he'd seen more than enough to incriminate the pair of them. He sat there a broken man. His world was crumbling around him. When could it have happened? After all, he's always at home with Beth in the evening. He couldn't remember a time in the recent past when they'd been apart. Perhaps it was fiction – all in Ricky's imagination. Yes, that could be a distinct possibility. But how would Ricky Tremonti know how to visualize the house, the hot tub, the bedroom, for chrissake? No, he was going to have to get used to this – Beth and Ricky were a lot more than mere students passing each other periodically in corridors. They'd shared Richard and Beth's bed at least once. God, how many other times could this have happened?

He nervously looked around – imagining all eyes were focused on him. He could have been trapped down a hole, a pot hole, a sink hole, with dozens of eyes peering down in sympathy but unable to help. And his predicament, his emotions, his inadequacy, scrolling on a screen before them like some kind of dystopian, Edvard Munch-inspired horror movie.

He traipsed back to the car, set navigation to reverse-last-route mode and sat there with his eyes closed. He felt he had little left to live for. Too bad if his autonomous vehicle had a software blip during the short journey and failed to avoid something terrible in the absence of any human intervention. Too bad.

One hour later he was back in the car heading for home having tidied his desk and said his goodbyes to his work colleagues. He couldn't contemplate not returning home for his usual meal with Beth and an evening either outside in the hot tub, inside watching TV or crashing out early and doing a crossword together before turning out the lights. But he wanted to be smart about what was going on. Didn't want to show his hand, as it were, before envisaging exactly how he planned to deal with the matter. It was his turn to be calculating, scheming, to be sure he ended up turning the tables on the two lovebirds. He fully intended to come out on top irrespective of how bad his position appeared to be at that moment. No, he would walk in, greet Beth in the usual manner and proceed to give the appearance of enjoying every minute of the evening as it unfolded.

Richard carried out his plan without giving Beth the slightest reason to think she'd been found out. In a way, he felt sorry for her – felt desperately sad for what he knew she would be forced to confront in the coming weeks – or days, even.

But he held no such sympathies for the cheating son-of-a-bitch, Ricky Tremonti. If he were allowed, he'd have him hung, drawn and quartered without blinking an eye. Richard's mind was wholly preoccupied with nailing the little creep. Part-time job with IntuTech? – he should be so lucky.

At ten-thirty, they switched off the TV and made their way upstairs. Beth went straight to the bathroom while Richard walked over to the bed to turn back the duvet – a silly habit he followed religiously every night before he climbed into bed. But this evening was different. He stared down at the sheet and couldn't erase the image of Ricky taking his place next to Beth. Undressing and settling down for the night felt positively repugnant to him. But he was determined to play things cool and get to the bottom of the situation. He needed more evidence than he'd already collected if he were to choose the divorce route. And he decided that the court's response to him declaring he'd read Ricky Tremonti's mind and printed the results out in picture form weren't likely to cut it. No, he had to play his cards right to deal with this mess in an orderly fashion.

He could hear Beth attending to her final lady procedures for the day through the half open door to the en suite and, for the first time in his life, began to wish they'd opted for separate rooms.

Richard used the bathroom after Beth and duly put himself to bed making every attempt to behave normally the following morning at breakfast. Unsurprisingly, he had a restless night's sleep.

The following morning he made light conversation and cleared away after they'd finished. Beth loaded the dishwasher and Richard wiped around the sink and worktops. Nothing would have seemed untoward to Beth as he planted the usual peck on each cheek and made his way through to the garage to set off for the office.

'Good morning, Rick.' said Lukas as they almost collided in reception. Richard was entering via the car park doorway while Lukas was, simultaneously, about to nip out to retrieve some items he'd inadvertently left in his car.

'It may be for you, Luke, but things aren't looking so good from my perspective.'

'Oh, that's not like you, Rick. Mind me enquiring as to what's unsettled you?'

'No, you're very welcome and I'll be pleased to explain things if you could give me until, say, ten o' clock. I've a few bits and pieces I'd like to attend to first thing but, yeah, how about a coffee in L1 at ten?'

'Sounds good to me, mate – but keep your chin up, Rick, it's not good seeing you like this. Leave it to me to organize some coffees with Jennie.'

'Thanks, buddy – see you at ten.'

The two colleagues went their separate ways with Richard running the past few hours' events round and round in his head trying to decide the best way to unload his troubles to Lukas in a little over an hour's time. This wasn't going to be easy.

How did he know who to trust anymore? Was Luke really the confidante he'd always taken him to be. Jennie? The guys up on the first floor? After all, TT1 had him believe no one got anywhere near a pass mark in the trustworthy stakes. He trudged around in a self-induced stupor finding it difficult to focus on anything work-related. His tasks for the day seemed trivial when set against the backdrop to his personal life.

'Come in, Rick – I came down a little early to clear away some papers that were left lying around after a short meeting I hosted last night – after hours.'

'Not a problem, Luke, but thanks.'

Richard stood for a moment or two just inside the doorway and kind of lingered there as if in anticipation of being granted permission to take a seat.

'Sit down, mate, come on, what are you waiting for? You're not exactly yourself this morning. Where do you want to start? Is it something concerning me? Or IntuTech generally? Or something at home? Do feel free to talk to me in strict confidence, Rick, you know it won't go anywhere else. Or, if you'd rather not, then fine, I'll perfectly understand.'

'Oh, God, this is tricky. It's about home and it's also about work. I've got myself in a right mess and at this stage, I don't have a clue how to get out of it.'

'Is it money, mate? You know you can talk to me if you've got any financial demands at home. Really, Rick, with OT3 now well underway, we are going to be literally swamped with the stuff within a couple of weeks. Opticians the length and breadth of the country are placing advanced orders on an unprecedented scale – all subject to the final approval certificates arriving from the Department of Health and Social Care, of course, but I'm expecting these to turn up by Thursday at the latest.'

'Luke, stop, stop, stop, it has nothing to do with money, really. My salary easily covers my expenditure with a comfortable sum left over each month. No, it's to do with Beth and me.'

'Oh, Rick, I'm so sorry, what's happened?'

'And it's to do with IntuTech as well. TT1 to be specific.'

'I don't follow. Surely, Beth knows nothing about TT1. We agreed to keep it under wraps until all planned trialling was complete. Have you reneged on our agreement?'

'Luke, you know me better than that. Of course not. When I carried out that first test at home recently, I assure you she knew nothing about it. The interference issue was quickly sorted out as you know and Beth didn't suspect a thing. I mean, how could she, it isn't exactly something you'd conjure up in your mind on a whim.

'No, Beth isn't party to TT1 and neither is anybody else. But it isn't as simple as that. We now have the potential of knowing precisely what's going on in people's minds – once we agree to activate listening-in mode, of course – and before this little experiment of ours has got out of the traps, we've already run into trouble. Well, I certainly have. Big trouble. Life changing trouble.'

'What on earth has happened, Rick? I can't begin to imagine what TT1 has been getting up to.'

'Well, listen to this, Luke. It isn't going to be easy for me to get this off my chest but bear with me, please. And promise you won't tell a soul until the whole ghastly affair comes out in the open.'

'You have my word, Rick – in your own time, buddy. By the way, do you need a top-up before you carry on?'

Richard sat with his hands on his knees and his head lowered as if to isolate himself from the world. He spoke slowly and barely audibly.

'No, I'm fine. Listen. You'll remember the two short meetings I've had with that Tremonti fellow. Well, I don't know precisely how much you understand about the guy but I'll run through the relevant bits to put you in the picture. Stop me if I'm spending too much time telling you what you already know. Okay, here goes. Ricky Tremonti attends the same university as Beth. Different faculties but the same establishment. This is something I doubt either you or I knew prior to his visit here.'

'Sure, I had no idea.'

'Well, neither did I until he listed his current education details on his post-interview questionnaire. But that was okay, nothing untoward. No reason to think they'd even set eyes on each other. In fact, I'd already ignored references to someone called 'Ricky', that I'd transcribed from Beth's very first word-thinking exercise at home, thinking it referred to me. I knew she usually called me, Rick, but thought nothing of it – put it down to the idea that people might have personal ways of thinking that differ somewhat from the ways they verbalise concepts. I just didn't think another thing about it.

'But when the little bastard, I'm sorry, when our Mr. Tremonti came in for his second interview, I decided to approach him in a slightly different way. Oh look, Luke, there was a small incident at home the previous day when I was moving some of Beth's laundry about. I noticed a dress of hers that she'd carefully folded and placed on top of the laundry basket. Okay, I do tend to have something of a suspicious mind but this dress, or wrap, call it what you like, featured a printed elephant design in which three of the beasts were arranged in a formation where there was one facing left, one facing forward, and one facing right. Do you remember seeing something like that before?'

'Of course, Rick, it was at the end of the graphics transcript that we recorded during Ricky's first interview.'

Richard raised his head focusing his attention on the ceiling and paused for a few seconds before turning to face Lukas eye to eye.

'Precisely. And it wasn't until I noticed the same image on the garment in the laundry basket that I started to smell a rat.

'Anyway, to cut to the chase, when I carried out the second interview, I started to question the guy on some personal aspects of his life – nothing too intrusive, just about what he got up to over the weekend, you know, things like that. And all was fine until we terminated the interview several minutes later. We shook hands, said our goodbyes and he duly made his way to the car park.

'But when I returned to L1 and replayed the footage of the conversation, things went horribly wrong.'

Richard's voice began to break up. He was clearly having trouble getting his words out.

'Oh, I'm sorry, Luke, this is so difficult. Look, I ran the graphics through to the end and, when it got to his responses to my questions about his social life, an image appeared on the screen of . . . oh, I really don't know how to say this . . . it was a full screen image of Tremonti and Beth naked together in my bedroom.'

Richard broke down in front of Lukas sobbing uncontrollably while his superior did his best to console him.

Eventually after managing to regain some sort of control he continued.

'I can only think it was while we were away in Brussels for the OT3 launch, Luke. I just can't believe this is happening to me.'

Chapter 14

'I don't know what to say, Rick. I'm truly lost for words.'

'You don't have to say anything, Luke – we've been good friends long enough for me to know this will be hurting you too. But it's so ironic. I mean, the ingeniousness of TT1 is precisely in inverse proportion to its ability to destroy lives. And in our case, we are already counting the cost. If TT1 hadn't been invented, my marriage to Beth would still be sound. Okay, I accept the flaws that have now been uncovered wouldn't have failed to be present were TT1 not to have been developed but, who knows, if I never found out, the affair could have run its course without me ever knowing. And things between me and Beth might never have come into question. But now – now I can't unknow what I've already discovered. If I choose to forgive her, it will always be at the back of my mind ready to surface at any time were she to put another foot wrong. Oh, I know there are guys who'd just wave the Ricky

Tremonti episode away and get on with things but that just isn't my character. And if I didn't have my character – fastidiousness, demanding, meticulous, you know what I'm like, Luke – I probably wouldn't have been able to assist in the development of the project in the first place. It's a vicious circle. And I really can't imagine our relationship surviving this.'

Lukas shifted uncomfortably in his seat trying to find an angle that might relieve his partner's misery but could find little in the way of consolation.

'Rick, you know full well that I've never crossed over the threshold into the merry world of wedlock and, frankly, this experience of yours does rather reinforce my nervousness. I'm like you in many ways insofar as I'd be totally unforgiving. I couldn't live with myself if I had to endure the knowledge that I'd been double-crossed. No way, mate. But I feel I should be taking a different angle with your situation. A more conciliatory stance in the hope that you and Beth could get things back on track.'

'Thanks, Luke, but it would make no difference. I know my own mind and I will have to think long and hard before I decide which way to go on this.

'But there will be difficulties if I can't orchestrate a situation where I can offer the pair of them irrefutable proof that they're up to something. Think about it, Luke, all I've got is an argument based on my having gatecrashed this Tremonti fellow's primary visual cortex to produce an A4 print of him in bed with my wife. What's he going to say about that? What's *Beth* going to say about that? You and I know full well it's bloody illegal. You can't go around inventing devices able to, uninvitedly, infiltrate people's minds and then expect the evidence to stand up in a court of law. Can you imagine: "Excuse me, my Lord, but I've got this printout of my wife and her lover engaged in a sexual encounter. I downloaded the image directly from the culprit's cerebrum so there's no question to answer regarding its authenticity. Can I have a divorce, please?"

'Well come on, Luke, this just isn't going to work, is it?'

'Of course not, Rick. Without any form of permissible evidence, you've got to confront Beth, or Tremonti, for that matter, to get a confession.'

'Yeah, that's what I've got to do. But I can't allow this matter to get between me and my work. You and I are in the middle of some especially important issues concerning TT1 and OT3 and I can't be spending the whole of my working day contemplating my relationship with Beth. As far as you're concerned, Luke, it's a separate topic and, while I'm here, IntuTech projects must come first.'

'Okay, I get that, to a degree but I'm pretty much involved, mate. I mean, were it not for IntuTech, you'd know nothing about Beth and Tremonti.'

Richard stared into the middle-distance taking time to consider Lukas' angle.

'Mmm, you're not wrong. But the weakness in my marriage is not IntuTech's fault. It is the very essence of IntuTech's success that is responsible for my downfall. IntuTech is not the flawed party – my marriage is. To put it more graphically, if you'll excuse the pun, it is the sheer brilliance of TT1 that has caused the problems. We should be celebrating its effectiveness.'

'Okay, I agree, but, with your marriage at stake, let's hold back on running the flags up and hanging out the bunting.

Yeah?'

'You've got a deal.'

Richard and Lukas understood the situation perfectly and knew where their individual priorities lay. Richard needed to sort out his personal problems, in his own time, and Lukas had no option other than to concentrate on the IntuTech projects.

Richard managed to force something resembling a smile and began to feel there might just be some positives as well as negatives in store.

'Okay, let's move on, Rick. So far, we've tested TT1 on two or three accounts and it's come up trumps each time. In a sense, we've nailed three victims and have shown the product to be faultless. Let's recap - our success record to date is as follows: 1. We've established that Edwin Crowther-Brown isn't my number one fan. 2. We've ascertained that I'm not Edwin Crowther-Brown's number one fan. And 3. We've shown that Tremonti has compromised your marriage.

'All of these "successes" have been proven by TT1. Were they to have been the subject of criminal investigations, each would have provided irrefutable evidence for justice to have been served in a court of law. Once we have permission from the relevant authorities to proceed, the world of criminal justice will have advanced beyond all recognition.'

'Yes, Luke, this is what we should be celebrating, no question about it. But it has to be restricted to use within the legal system and our applications for approval must be clearly defined. Just imagine a product like TT1 getting into the wrong hands - the consequences could be catastrophic.'

'So, Rick, for the time being we'll leave things as they were. I will proceed with monitoring the product's approval status and you get on with the matter of procurement. We have to be sure we will have a reliable, cost-effective source for the manufacture of the chips and the smart watches by the time TT1 is ready to drop. Oh, and what shall we do about Tremonti?'

Both appeared stumped by Lukas' question. The engineering student was taking up too much of their time and none of it in a productive fashion. He'd become the proverbial thorn in their sides but neither of them could figure out a way to remove the disruptive barb. Richard finally broke the silence.

'We'll go ahead and offer him the position. If we decline, he's likely to smell a rat. And it'll be better for me to have him around and earn his trust if I'm to accumulate any sort of legal system-friendly evidence. I'll drop the SOB an email right away'

'Okay, Rick – we'll catch up later.'

It was the beginning of the following week and Lukas and Richard were on a solar express train heading for the capital. They'd caught the 07.10 am from Camchester to be sure their planned arrival at their London, Victoria Embankment destination would materialise without having to rush around. A coffee before they went in for their appointment was likely to fit into their agenda. A train journey always held a certain fascination for the guys. And probably for most people. A kind of excitement built around the idea of a huge piece of machinery travelling at speed through a rural landscape inaccessible to the more common transport mode, the autonomous car. While the current generation of rolling stock hardly competed, romantically, with the steam-powered locomotives of yesteryear, there remained a small-child mindset in most individuals where anything railroad-related was concerned. The landscape rushing past at close to one-hundred miles an hour never ceases to give the traveller an exaggerated impression of the distance being covered whilst still satisfying the aspiring explorer's appetite for a perceived abundance of flora and fauna they could take an avid interest in. The truth, however, was quite different in that the fleeting vista from the carriage's window offered no more than the minutest opportunity to examine the richness of the rural wildlife and its environment. A more detailed manifestation of all things natural was readily available in one's own back yard.

But the warm, bright, cloudless spring day made for a very pleasant trip that would ultimately afford them time to take in a glass, or two, of wine when they met up with Mark Broderick early evening at a west London restaurant of his choice. Mark had arranged for Lukas and Richard to visit a New Scotland Yard colleague of his, Peter Williams, who was the Met's top polygraph trainer. Mark had, somewhat evasively, suggested that two friends of his, who had a particular interest in lie-detectors, were in town for the day and would appreciate a few moments of his time if he could find a slot. Being the amicable guy he was, Peter agreed to forgo his lunch hour to accommodate the two friends and insisted that Mark should think no more of it.

'We need to be prepared for what could come up in this meeting, Rick.' Lukas said cautiously but with an edge of humour. 'Well think about it, this guy Williams heads up the Yard's lie detector facility and here are we calling in for a demo almost completely on false pretenses. I mean, what if he wants to run a test on one of us?'

'Yes, that could be highly amusing. And embarrassing at the

same time. Mmm, I hadn't considered the possibility, Luke. But, hold on, there are many aspects of the polygraph that we're genuinely interested in so it shouldn't be too tricky to focus on the bits we actually want to find out about and have one over on the machine. I'll do a deal with you: if such a situation crops up, I'll take the test as long as you foot the wine bill when we eat later.'

'You should have been a salesman with tricks up your sleeve like that, Rick. Okay, go on, let's shake on it.'

In actual fact the two IntuTech delegates were, principally, interested to learn a little of the polygraph's efficiency in establishing the veracity of would-be villains' statements and the degree to which TT1 would prove to be superior. They were aware that their own innovation was as close to one-hundred-percent failsafe as could be imagined but they were anxious to know how close the traditional lie-detector might come.

So, shortly after a pleasant interlude in a coffee shop not far from the Met's Victoria Embankment headquarters, Lukas and Richard were making their way up in a lift car leading to Peter's office on the seventh floor.

'Come in, guys, it's a pleasure to meet you – Mark has filled me in on your more-than-casual interest in my role here at the Met. My name is Peter, Peter Williams, by the way, and I believe you are Lukas and Richard. Which one is which?' Peter added with and accompanying chuckle.

'Great to meet you, too,' said Lukas, 'I'm Lukas and this is my good friend Richard.'

The three men turned and ambled into Peter's surprisingly compact office, took off their jackets and sat down on two comfy chairs in front of their host's impeccably tidy desk.

'Wow, some view, Peter, how do you get any work done with a panorama like that?'

'Yes, it is difficult at times but one tends to take even the most outstanding aspects of one's life totally for granted given enough exposure. I find myself walking past the Palace of Westminster each morning and each evening on my way to and from the office without giving it a moment's thought. And all the while I'm ignoring its breathtaking architecture, there are dozens of tourists from all corners of the globe eagerly snapping away on their digital SLRs. But, of course, when I'm holidaying somewhere in the region of, say, Paris, I find myself behaving in the very same fashion while sauntering around the Palace of Versailles, maybe. We're all so predictable.

Peter Williams averted his gaze from the spectacular view of the capital and politely turned the conversation back to the purpose of the meeting.

'But my friends, we have approximately an hour to cover a fair bit of ground concerning the wonderful invention that is the polygraph.

'Now, where to start? Right, briefly, the first polygraph was invented in 1921 in California as a joint effort between four individuals, two of whom worked for the police department, one as a psychologist and another as a cardiologist.

'Present day machines differ greatly from their more basic early twentieth-century counterparts and accuracy has, understandably, improved over the years. However, even today, we can only expect a "truth" rating in the order of between 80% and 90% which is rarely sufficient to convince a court of law of a person's guilt or otherwise. But the information gleaned from those being tested invariably provides the examining officers with invaluable material that will contribute to the overall evidence and go on to ensure that a conviction or an acquittal are deemed to be safe - in the eyes of the law, of course. Incidentally, it is worth noting that an average person's ability to detect lies correctly is thought to be roughly 55% accurate.

'Right, the means by which a polygraph gathers its data, or, rather, the polygraph operator gathers the data, concerns the examinee's heart rate, blood pressure, respiration and skin conductivity.'

Peter was an outright professional at imparting knowledge in the most lucid of fashions, a skill that made his demonstrations both comprehensible and enjoyable. He continued along these lines delivering as much information he found possible during the period he would normally have spent consuming his packed lunch. But Lukas and Richard sat there for the duration transfixed. Unbeknown to Peter, these two individuals were so far ahead of his game that they began to feel a little disingenuous in, unconsciously, registering, his actual subservience to their almost infinitely advanced technological minds. However, it was not in their nature to advertise this point in his company and both prepared to bid Peter farewell following his most enthusiastic and comprehensive guidance on the subject.

'But before we go, Peter, I'd like to ask you what is probably an obvious question.' begged Lukas. 'Why do you think we are still placing our trust in a machine that is unable to provide one-hundred percent accuracy after being in commission for nearly a century-and-a-half?'

'That's an excellent question, Lukas, and one I am certainly not qualified to answer with confidence. Or, more to the point, officially. However, I will give you my opinion for what it is worth and suggest that the technology required to provide absolute truth on every occasion is positively beyond the capability of the most intellectually-gifted human beings. One would need to be an equal to God to achieve such an outcome.'

Lukas and Richard wished Peter a pleasant afternoon, thanked him prodigiously for his time and made their way back to the lift lobby. Once inside the lift car, with the doors closed, they burst into fits of laughter at Peter's intimation that they were God's equals. Without wishing to assume a patronising view of their more-than-generous lunchtime tutor, neither could resist a chuckle at his expense when reconsidering his closing remark. God's equals – they weren't likely to forget that for some time.

Once out of the building, they had the whole of the afternoon to kill before they were due to meet up with Mark Broderick for an early evening meal so the pair decided to take a stroll along the embankment, take in a few sights and while away the time relaxing.

Relaxing wasn't something either Richard or Lukas was terribly expert at. But environment plays a significant part in accessing the necessary state of mind. And the Thames embankment proved to be a quite different setting to the IntuTech premises in Falcombe where escaping from the all-pervasive neurotechnological ambience was simply not an option.

After an hour or two, they found themselves sitting in a teashop overlooking the Thames with their conversation, inevitably, leading back to their pride and joy, TT1. In an unusually jovial mood for that time in the afternoon, Lukas' thoughts turned to naughty-schoolboy mode. They were seated at a small outdoor table on the café's grassed terrace area several metres away from the nearest guests as he leant forward to address his colleague - as if to ensure nobody could overhear their conversation.

'Here, Richard, as we're miles and miles away from base and never likely to set eyes on anyone remotely close to this establishment again, what do you say to us activating your TT1 chip and recording the short chat with whoever emerges from the rear of the building to take our order?'

'Are you sure, Luke? I mean, you're the boss. I'm up for it if you are.'

'Yeah, set your smart watch to record mode, trigger auto-word/picture detection and we'll take a look at the results on our return train journey later.'

'All good with me.'

Richard did what Lukas suggested but while doing so, found himself glancing around furtively as if to check for lurking figures of authority poised ready to expose his misdemeanors. He secretly smiled to himself in acknowledgement of the absurdity of the impulse. Within a few minutes, a pleasant-looking gentleman, possibly the proprietor, made a beeline for their table.

'Good afternoon, gentlemen, my name is Manuel and I'm your waiter for this afternoon. I trust you've taken a look at the menu? Is there something I can I tempt you with today?'

'Good afternoon, Manuel' replied Richard. 'Yes, now let me see, we'll have a pot of English breakfast tea – for the two of us. And I'll go for the blueberry cheesecake while my friend here will have – what'll it be, Luke?'

'Oh, yes, I'll have a toasted teacake with unsalted butter, if I may.'

'You certainly may. But, sir,' Manuel said turning to Richard. 'can I suggest you go for the salted caramel cheesecake instead of the blueberry? It's so much more popular with our clientele.'

Richard feigned an expression of deep contemplation while musing over the matter of which item of confection he should go for. But then broke into a conciliatory smile suggesting he'd, of course, be happy with either option. Manuel responded with a friendly, mock attempt to perform a headlock on Richard. The little moment of light relief went down well with all three guys.

'I've no objection to that – I'm happy to go with your recommendation if customers are inclined to prefer it. Yes, salted caramel, please, Manuel.'

'Excellent, I will be back to you in a short while. Thank you, gentlemen.'

As their host turned and walked back to the premises, Lukas and Richard, sitting there like the well-behaved young men they certainly weren't, shared a chuckle

'It's hardly going to be groundbreaking stuff, Rick, but it could prove amusing.'

'Here you go, gentlemen – a pot of English breakfast for two, one slice of homemade salted caramel cheesecake and one toasted teacake with two pats of unsalted butter. Enjoy your meal.'

The two pranksters set about their refreshments with gusto given that their last meal was from the buffet car on the morning's London-bound express. When finished, they wiped their lips with the paper napkins provided, rose from their chairs and dealt with the necessary monetary transfer that more than covered the cost of the meal. When they reached the pavement, Richard turned to Lukas and gave him a thumbs-up as they headed off in the direction of the Met building to meet up with Mark Broderick.

Chapter 15

By the time the two techies arrived back at the police headquarters, Mark was waiting for them in the large reception hall on the ground floor. He maintained an almost dummy-like posture according him the kind of presence that might lend one to imagine he owned the building. Upright, commanding, consummately able to remain still without sporadically shuffling from one foot to the other and eminently capable of holding eye contact with whomever he confronted. Mark Broderick was a guy who was in control.

'Hi guys, great to catch up again. I hope you've both had a pleasant day.'

'Good afternoon, Mark.' the two replied in unison before Lukas continued. 'Yes, we've had an interesting trip, thank you. Due, in no small measure, to Peter Williams, your excellent polygraph trainer. What he crammed into sixty minutes was nothing short of a miracle – one of the most coherent, eloquent instructors I believe I've ever come across. Strangely, our first impressions, on entering his office, were that he was possibly under utilised at the Met - going by the total absence of papers on his desk. But it soon became clear that he was so impeccably organised that everything he was working on had been carefully tidied away prior to our arrival. And a nice guy too, Mark – thanks again for arranging the meeting – much appreciated.'

'Did it offer anything interesting concerning your project development?'

'It certainly did,' replied Richard. 'It confirmed what we suspected all along. And that was that, even though improvements have been made over the years to the polygraph, the tolerance for error remained a worry. Additionally, while the device scores highly on identifying liars, it doesn't perform at all well at detecting truthtellers. But, all-in-all, it has served authorities around the world well over the years.'

Richard spoke with a certain confidence borne, no doubt, out of the somewhat negative light in which the polygraph had revealed itself.

'Excellent, guys. Right, enough talking shop, how about we make out way round to Antonello's – I've booked a table for four. Oh, I forgot to tell you that I've invited Peter along – I was sure you wouldn't mind.'

'That's great, Mark.' said Lukas, 'He'll be most welcome.'

'Here's Peter now.' said Mark, 'Come on, Pete, we haven't got all evening.' Mark joked as the polygraph wizard quickened his pace to join the party.

'Hi everybody, this is really kind of you. Where are we off to?'

'Antonello's, Pete – I thought you'd approve.'

'Excellent choice, Mark.'

The four of them trundled off in the direction of the Italian eating house mindful that Lukas and Richard's train would be leaving Paddington station at 20.30 pm. They had a couple of hours to relax over their meal.

By the time 20.00 pm arrived, they'd finished eating, got to know each other a little better and vowed to keep in touch more regularly. The short taxi ride to Paddington took no more than fifteen minutes and as the terminus clock's minute hand pointed down to its roman numeral six, the train pulled away from platform nine en route for Camchester.

As they sunk back into their sumptuous first-class seats with the small carriage to themselves, they both agreed it had been a tiring day. And almost simultaneously, they stretched their legs out in front of them, their arms towards the ceiling and both inhaled deeply as a means of releasing whatever pent-up energy they'd taken on board during the preceding hours in the capital.

Then, for a little light relief, Lukas urged Richard to boot his laptop up and run the transcription of poor, unsuspecting Manuel's unverbalized contribution to their earlier conversation. If nothing else, it should raise a laugh or two. Within seconds, the screen had begun to scroll with perfectly legible text. Their waiter had clearly been a word-thinker.

'Here we go, Luke.' Richard suggested, as the storyline started to reach the part when the cakes were being ordered. 'Let's concentrate from here.'

Although the words Manuel had spoken appeared as a simple account of the conversation, there were additional bits of narrative that represented his thoughts – thoughts he'd generated in between the actual dialogue and Richard set the software to show only the thoughts and not the spoken parts of the exchange. They expected nothing incriminating but felt the plot would prove amusing nonetheless. The transcript began as the waiter approached the table.

Please, please, no Fawlty Towers jokes, guys – I hear them a million times a day . . . mmm, blueberry cheesecake . . . let me try to steer him towards salted caramel – he can have that piece left over on a previous customer's plate . . . comes to £19.65 – they won't notice if I add another fiver to their bill . . . so, £24.65 . . . tourists never do . . . no doubt about that . . . there, he didn't have the slightest clue I'd already sold the cheesecake earlier . . . oh, they've left the table . . . quite fancied the one with the German accent . . . wish I'd plucked up the courage to ask for his phone number . . . dammit.

'Not the first time I've been identified as gay, Rick. But who cares? – we're all human beings, for God's sake! I've even got some good friends who swing both ways.'

'Yes, me too, Luke. But I've no idea how Manuel came to that conclusion. Mind you, how could we possibility know what it's like to see the world through another person's eyes? After all, that's the preserve of TT1. That's why we invented it.'

The impromptu exercise was certainly proving amusing but there was something niggling Lukas. Something that didn't quite sit right with him. Something about the way TT1 was developing.

'But Rick, consider what we've got here. The conversation lasted no more than a few minutes – five at the most – and we've collected at least half-a-dozen negative or discreet, filtered-out thoughts without even trying. Okay, we only have a small sample of transcriptions to date but this is looking crazy. I'm beginning to wonder who on earth any of us can actually rely on. The social system we've all come to know and love is proving to be fraudulent. The very people we spend every minute of our lives engaging with, depending on, trusting, are suddenly being exposed as . . . well, not exactly enemies but something coming close. If TT1 isn't restricted to the law enforcement industry I can't imagine what will happen.'

Richard was sitting staring at the screen while he scrolled through numerous lines of predictable narrative with the feeling their intended insight into Manuel's mind was over. He began to recount periods of his childhood when difficulties with his parents' relationship created a general aura of unrest within the family. The finer details of the cause of whatever particular rift he was having to deal with were, understandably, never imparted to him as a child leaving his auto-suggestive powers to work their magic and, probably, arrive at the wrong conclusion. But looking back now, it appeared quite likely that, were TT1 to have been available, the degree of monitoring accessible to them could well have averted any forbidden fruit that may have found its way onto their table. A deterrent? A warning? A guiding light? A wake-up call? Who knows? But he felt sure that society could only have benefited from such an insightful facility. A facility that encouraged honestly and discouraged deception. What were the gods thinking when they wired our minds with the duplicity gene? What possible purpose could it serve other than to nurture deceit?

'You're not wrong, Luke, looks like we might have invented our own monster. We must take care to see that it remains tethered within its cage. But when you think about it,' Richard continued as he turned towards his partner, 'most inventions have a negative side to them.'

But it was too late, Luke had nodded off and was slouched back in his seat with his head to one side breathing heavily. It had been a long, tiring day and Richard thought he might just join him for the rest of the passage. The train was scheduled to terminate its journey, in approximately one hour, at Camchester so there was no danger of them missing their stop.

But as he went to log off on the laptop, he noticed a fresh dialogue appear on the screen with a narrative far removed from Manuel's earlier, inopportune meanderings. In the excitement of the day's events, he'd not taken care to deactivate record mode on his smart watch and had, inadvertently, proceeded to transcribe another person's thoughts – in word-thinking format. But they were still being recorded in real-time. In the train carriage. It had to be Luke. Luke's thoughts were appearing on the screen as they materialised in his mind. Luke must be dreaming or possibly running through things in his head while dozing on and off. He was certainly tired but not that tired. No way. Would it be wise to delve into the thoughts of his, hopefully, trustful partner when the odds would overwhelmingly suggest that negativity of one form or another would feature in the playback?. Was he ready for this?

Richard left-clicked on the PLAY icon and immediately started to read the narrative.

. . . I thought OT3 was a winner . . . a money spinner beyond my wildest dreams . . . but this TT1 is on another level . . . infinitely more sophisticated . . . no need for the subject to be aware of any intervention . . . the transcriber is the only one involved . . . the only one needing any kind of surgery . . .not the subject as is the case with OT3 . . . this project is going to earn millions,

billions, even . . . if I can establish a market beyond the realms of the legal industry . . . if I can sell this on to the right organisation, I'll never have to do another day's work in my life . . . I'll be rich enough to choose whatever lifestyle I'll like . . . but now the bulk of the technological development has been completed, why do I need to continue filling Richard Stewart's pockets? . . . he's been invaluable in contributing to parts of the software that I wasn't adequately versed in but that's now water under the bridge . . . in a week or so's time I'll be getting approval from the authorities to get this thing up-and-running and Stewart's role will be virtually non-existent . . . I'll sort him out some redundancy money but I should be able to get away with a figure that will hardly make a dent in IntuTech's present funds . . . with his current marriage troubles he could, psychologically, be a spent force by now anyway . . . his problem, not mine. . . . I'll leave things for the time-being . . . never know if there'll be some odd ends to tie up . . .

Richard had read enough. He was truly stunned. His marriage was in pieces and now his career was all but over. A career he had imagined would provide him with employment throughout his life. Not just employment but camaraderie with a certain Lukas Hoffman who, until today, he had considered as one of his closest allies. He'd even had thoughts of the possibility of being offered a directorship in recognition of the substantial contribution he'd made to OT3 and TT1. This was soul-destroying – no other way of putting it. Richard was devastated.

He had entered a world of ultimate isolation where every other member of society appeared alien to him. Disinterested in him. Oblivious of him. Uncaring. Ready to dispense with him without contrition if it suited them. Surely this couldn't be the work of the maker. It felt more as though the universe was the brainchild of the Devil.

He finally logged off, placed the laptop in its carry-case and sat back in contemplation. This wasn't going to leave his mind for some time to come. If ever. It would be doubtful that, along with the marriage situation, he'd avoid suffering serious psychological after-effects. Yes, this was going to be a life-changer. But soon, Lukas was going to wake up and Richard had to be sure how he was going to handle things. However, in true Richard Stewart style, he decided to act as if nothing had happened. Far better, he thought, to stay in control and not let the enemy read your next move. A next move that would need plenty of thinking time so a "hedging-one's-bets" strategy appeared the most sensible option to him.

Before long the 20.30 pm solar express from London Paddington began to slow for its approach to the Camchester terminus and, sensing this, Lukas started to stir. He'd been in a deep slumber for fifty-minutes, or so, and was finding it difficult to snap out of his drowsy state.

'Where are we, Rick?'

'Just approaching Camchester, Luke. On time as usual.'

'Oh, excellent. Though I apologise, it was impolite of me to nod off like that.

'But what a brilliant day we've had. Tiring, I know, but fascinating, nonetheless. Did you enjoy it?'

'One of the best days of my life!' replied Richard with a generous helping of undetected irony.

'Yes, me too. That meeting with Peter Williams confirmed everything we had hoped for with the latest polygraph machines. The guy's going to have to look for another job once TT1 breaks. Polygraphs will be a thing of the past – confined to the museums.'

'Don't get too enthusiastic, Luke, we've yet to receive approval from the relevant authorities. Without it, we have no product and nothing to get excited about.'

'Stop being so pessimistic, Rick, I can feel it in my bones. TT1 is heading for the top and we're going all the way with it. Come on, mate, you've got to be positive - if this doesn't prove to be jackpot material, we might as well shut up shop and go home.'

'Yes, okay, Luke – I'm sorry, it's been a long day.'

The two weary travellers stepped off the train and made their way to the taxi rank adjacent to the main station entrance.

'Well, I'll see you at the office in the morning, Rick. Goodnight and sleep well.'

'Yes, you too, Luke.'

The two taxis pulled out together, one carrying a guy with not a care in the world, the other, a broken man.

Richard's cab was the first to reach its destination and he stepped, slowly out of the vehicle with his laptop and an equally heavy heart. All signs of zeal, commitment, enthusiasm, had deserted him. Evaporated into the ether. His head was low and his whole demeanor despondent as he ventured towards the house. He now had to confront the woman he'd lost all faith in while maintaining an air of resolute enthusiasm for the hours he had spent in the capital.

'Hi honey.' Beth called out as he ambled in through the front door. 'How did it go?'

'Oh, really well, Beth, really well.'

'Let me make you a nightcap and you can sit up in bed and tell me all about it.'

'Thank you, my usual, please.'

Beth prepared a frothy, decaffeinated coffee for Richard

and some kind of aromatic infusion for herself.

'Here you are, Rick. It's late, throw your things on the floor and we'll tidy them up in the morning. Tell me about the meeting you had at New Scotland Yard.'

Richard eased himself into the couple's oversized double-bed, scrunched his pillows up behind him and laboured to give Beth a comprehensive account of Peter Williams' tutorial.

She had little idea of the relevance of Richard and Lukas' interest in polygraphs but accepted it had something to do with one project or another the pair were working on at IntuTech. The train journey, the meeting, the stroll along the embankment and the meal with Mark Broderick appeared to be no more than a jolly to her but that was fine – everyone needed a little variety in their working lives and a day out of the office did no one any harm.

The couple finished their beverages, turned the bedside lights off and snuggled down into the comfort of their sumptuous feather mattress. But while Beth dropped off into a sound sleep within minutes, Richard lay awake, on his back, with his hands behind his head for a good hour. He had more than enough to remove from his mind before he could switch off and join Beth.

As he lay there he contemplated the sorry state of his marriage, the forthcoming presence of Tremonti in the workplace and the impending confrontation with Lukas Hoffman once his governor had decided how to dispense with his services. And the predicament he'd inevitably find himself in once he had no job to go to. No money coming in to support a home and a wife. A wife he'd begun to have little interest in supporting anyway. He couldn't imagine how things could actually get any worse. And while all of this was materializing, he had the very real prospect of entertaining the idea that no one in society appeared to have anything remotely resembling an altruistic bone in their body.

But, of course, the ultimate irony was that he was the very creator of the technology that was destroying him. The architect of his own demise.

Chapter 16

Lukas arrived at the office several minutes before Richard and, by the time the two met, head-to-head in reception, Lukas was in a heightened state of animation. A positive contrast to Richard's disposition.

'You okay, mate? You don't look yourself this morning.'

'Excuse me a second, Luke – I need to visit the bathroom.'

Richard entered the gent's, headed for the mirror and was confronted by a poorly shaven individual with a shock of bed-hair, a shirt buttoned up out of sync and, on glancing down, one shoelace undone. He immediately ran a brush through his hair, splashed some water on his face, removed a couple of areas of missed stubble with a cheap throwaway razor he found in the cupboard, refixed his shirtfront and attended to his errant shoelace. Not perfect but more appropriate for a meeting with the boss. He returned to reception and made a half-hearted apology to Luke.

'Not a problem, mate! Here, look what I've got. In my hand.'

Lukas was holding an unopened, buff A4 envelope which appeared to be generating an undue level of interest in him.

'What is it, Luke?'

'Take a look at the franking mark. Look, there, at the sender's logo.'

Richard focused his eyes on the small, rectangular strip bearing the postal levy alongside the logo of the sender. It bore the words, Medicines and Healthcare Products Regulatory Agency. This was the government body responsible for approving and licencing all things medical – medicines, medical devices etc., - the main governmental body as far as IntuTech was concerned.

'It's arrived way, way early, Rick, which, to me, indicates that granting approval was such a no-brainer that they simply signed our application off without the need for a prolonged process of consideration. Come on, let's sit down in L1 and read their letter together. I'll go grab some coffees.'

Ten minutes later, the two creators of TT1 sat together staring into the middle distance with downcast expressions on their faces. Their application had been rejected.

'Well, I was not expecting this, Rick. Not expecting it at all. The agents handling the application gave us no reason to doubt its suitability for use in controlled environments within the Criminal Justice System. We even offered our own, extensive caveats concerning the usage restrictions we were comfortable with. I can't believe this.'

Lukas' disposition had quickly plunged pretty much all the way down to Richard Stewart levels. The two colleagues were now in the same beleaguered state mentally.

'What do they offer as a reason, Luke?'

'Let me see, Reasons for Declination of Application – turn to page three. Right, page two, page three, here we go.'

At the bottom of the page there was a large, rectangular box in which the regulatory agency's description of their reasons for disapproval were entered. The box looked big enough to accommodate well in the order of a hundred-odd words but, in this case, they needed to enter just six: UNACCEPTABLE BODILY INTRUSION NECESSARY FOR EXAMINER. Nothing more, nothing less.

Lukas stood up kicking the chair from beneath him so forcefully that it toppled over and came to a halt against the meeting room wall some two metres from the table. He was mad, livid, enraged.

'But that's absurd.' He roared, 'They had no hesitation in granting us approval for OT3. And OT3 requires a cranial chip implant in precisely the same way as TT1. It doesn't make any sense.'

'Well, there is a difference,' suggested, Richard, 'The implanted chip in OT3 is concerned directly with the patient - the person receiving the treatment. In TT1's case, the process requires a perfectly healthy individual to be involved in a medical process for the purpose of examining another person's condition. In a sense, the implantee is acting as a surrogate. That is the difference, Luke, and I would imagine that is the thinking behind the ruling.'

'Well, it rules us out of the picture. It invalidates everything we've worked on for the past eighteen months and it renders the whole TT1 project untenable. And I have to ask the question, are we able to justify our existence on the strength of OT3 alone? I mean, OT3 is done and dusted, out there in the marketplace earning its keep. As a research and development facility, we no longer have anything to research and develop. We might as well lock up shop, go home and live on the proceeds of OT3.'

Whilst of a similar emotional view, Richard was uneasy about exhibiting the same kind of demonstrable response. Though he felt compelled to state his case which, as an employee, was many times weaker than that of his superior.

'Well, that might be something you can do but I'm a mere employee, Luke, and I don't share your luxury of being able to enjoy the legacy of a previously developed, highly successful project. Where does this leave me?'

Lukas retrieved his chair and sat with his head in his hands appearing to ignore Richard's rhetorical response before grabbing his phone and calling the licencing and approval agency who were handling the application. But the person dealing with the case had called in sick and nobody else had been briefed on the matter so Lukas had no one to vent his feelings on. But, of course, when it came to influencing the regulatory agency's decision, the application agency was as impotent as was IntuTech. His frustration was simply causing him to abandon all reason and hit out at anyone or anybody appearing on his radar. He needed time to think and, in his current frame of mind, Richard was hardly the ideal candidate to offer assistance.

'You'll have to excuse me, Richard, I need some space, some time to think this through.' And with that, he seized his briefcase, left the room, and made his way to the car park before speeding off into the distance.

Just when he felt things couldn't get any worse, Richard's situation started to rapidly deteriorate even further. A week in technology can be a long time, he thought.

Without the mental energy to apply himself to the simplest of tasks, he buzzed through to Jennie and asked her, politely, if she would be so good as to leave what she was doing and bring him a strong, black coffee.

If Lukas thought he had problems, how would he describe Richard's predicament? OT3 was a mega money spinner for life. TT1 was no more than a rich boy's toy. With the volume of cash IntuTech's ingenious, retina-replacing technology would be bringing in, Lukas had zero need for any additional income. But in a very short time, Richard could imagine he'd have no income at all.

His position was intractable. He felt impotent to exert any kind of control over the situation. Sat at the meeting room table, he glanced towards the window only to witness a darkened sky, a raging squall and heavy spots of rain pounding against the glass. His world had become a picture of gloom from whichever angle he viewed it.

With Jennie's coffee in front of him on the meeting room table, Richard sat back with his legs stretched out in front of him and his head thrown back contemplating his future. IntuTech had, so far, cost him his marriage and his career all because the development of one particular product had been so successful. He found this difficult to reconcile in his mind – how could two negatives still create a positive? If he hadn't found out about Beth and Ricky and had witnessed only positive sentiments when he transcribed Lukas' train journey thoughts, TT1 wouldn't be seen to have the potential of being an outright success in the world of criminal investigations. It seemed crazy but that's just how things had turned out.

So, what was he to do? IntuTech had been knocked back

with their first application for acceptance of TT1 and, by Lukas' immediate response, it would seem he acknowledged the decision as being final. No way back. Wow, this was hard to stomach. A real gut-wrencher.

But as he mulled over the minute details of the technological steps they took in the early stages of its development, it occurred to him that certain areas of their progress were dealt with by just one technician rather than two simultaneously. This would, typically, occur when either Lukas or Richard might have majored in a particular skill and realised the benefits of their attending to separate tasks. Such decisions were taken regularly and the two of them got used to standing back from time to time in deference to the other's superior expertise in a specific technique. After all, what they were handling here was not only advanced computer technology but cutting-edge cognitive neuroscience philosophy. They had complementary rather than shared skills. Both brilliant in their individual ways but not carbon copies of each other. While the storm continued to beat against the property, Richard's mood began to brighten.

His thoughts started to meander towards the time they perfected the method of linking the software that was downloaded into their smart watches with the central nervous system of the subject – the thinker. This was a particularly tricky part of TT1's development and, if his memory served him correctly, it involved weeks and weeks of intricate, detailed refining before the eventual, mind-blowing wireless connection between a human-derived artefact and the human brain could be established. And, being the neurotechnology graduate, Richard was the one responsible for this element of the development. Although there were moments of despair -

many of them - along the way, it didn't deter him from finally reaching his goal. But it was a goal that was reached as a result of the brilliant philosophical and neurotechnological mind of one Richard Stewart.

So, he thought, why would it not be possible to develop both ends of the signal chain to behave in the same fashion. Not precisely the same but one designed to perform in reverse of the other. It would certainly take hours and hours of deliberating but, on the spur of the moment, he couldn't think of any logical reason why it shouldn't be worthy of investigation. It might take six months of painstaking, hair-pulling, unremitting hard work but, wow, just imagine if it paid off. The Medicines and Healthcare Products Regulatory Agency would sign it off without a moment's thought. The complex process of cerebrum-to-smart-watch-to-cerebrum communication would totally comply with their philosophy of precluding any form of invasive surgery on the part of the transcriber. Brilliant or what, he thought? But he had to be resolute in keeping his thoughts to himself – so, it was fortunate he was the only one to have received the implant.

The prospect of finding a way out of the technological maze the two scientists had found themselves in was inclining Richard towards feeling he might have discovered the correct path after all.

But there was a hitch. Lukas Hoffman was head of the lease on the premises and he was also the principal of the organisation. And he owned all of the laboratory equipment necessary for Richard to develop his perceived enhancement of TT1. Everything belonged to Lukas and the idea of branching out on his own just wouldn't be possible without the help of his superior. Or at least a significant win on the Lottery to set himself up with a premises and a suitable level of professional equipment. And with Lukas' involuntary admission that dispensing with Richard's services looked to be a favourable commercial move in the not-too-distant future, Richard was beginning to think that a change of career to, maybe, that of a construction site labourer or highway hygienist might be his only choice.

It was now nearing lunchtime and there had been no sign of Hoffman since he stormed out several hours' earlier. A confrontation wasn't even on the cards. And a long shift in the afternoon working on some, now, irrelevant administrative tasks was the last thing he imagined he could muster up enthusiasm for.

Though the storm outside had begun to ease, the once pounding rain seemed to have transferred its energy to Richard who felt a headache coming on – not something unusual for him and certainly something he could relate to when under stress.

He reached for the intercom. 'Jennie, you don't, by any chance, happen to have any headache pills in the first aid cabinet, do you?'

'Hi Richard, I believe I do. Is it for you?'

'Yes, things have been a little stressful this morning and I am, sort of, prone to migraines when my brain becomes overloaded. Oh, I'm sure that's not an accurate medical diagnosis but all I know is that it's hindering my concentration.'

'Are you in the meeting room?'

'Yes I am.'

'Well, stay where you are – I'll bring them down to you with a glass of cold water.'

'You're a saint, Jennie, thank you.'

Richard swallowed 400mg of a popular, over-the-counter analgesic, relaxed in his seat and closed his eyes for a couple of minutes. But the pill was having an uphill struggle competing with the predicament swirling around in his mind. After half-an-hour he decided to call it a day and make off for home oblivious to whether his domestic predicament coupled with IntuTech's problems might even cause his tension to intensify instead of offering some sort of refuge. But he gambled on the fact that a change in environment would be likely to absorb some of the pressure he was under whilst remaining in a work setting.

'Jennie, it's me again, Richard. I really can't shift this pain and I've decided to take the afternoon off. Lukas is out of the office and may not be returning today so if anything important crops up - anything you can't deal with - buzz through to Ralph for guidance. And explain what's happened down here, would you?'

'Of course, of course, Richard. You get off home and try to relax. Hopefully see you in the morning.'

'Yes, I'm sure I'll be back to normal after a good night's sleep. Thanks again, Jennie.'

Richard decided to throw caution to the wind on the journey home by closing his eyes and trusting his autonomous vehicle to deliver him safely to his driveway. The short drive turned out to be uneventful and, within twenty minutes, he was undressed and tucked up in bed. Beth had a full day at uni so he could rest in the knowledge that the next three-to-four hours would be sufficiently calm so as not to interrupt his sleep.

Half-an-hour before Beth aimed her remote sensor at the

front door, Richard was out of bed and dressed again in the clothes he'd worn earlier. He remade the bed and chose not to recount the events of the day at the office as he was now seeing Beth as an adversary rather than an ally. With his aching head considerably eased they exchanged the usual welcomes and engaged in a short embrace before Beth climbed the stairs to change into something more informal for the evening. Richard called up to her suggesting he should start to prepare something for their evening meal.

'That's great - you choose, Rick, I'm easy.' came the reply.

To the casual onlooker, everything in the household appeared to be a picture of domestic harmony. And that was exactly what Richard had intended. To his surprise, his ability to continue the masquerade of appearing perfectly at one with the marital side of his life was becoming particularly effective with Beth seemingly ignorant of any shifts in their relationship.

When he entered the IntuTech reception at 08.00 am the following morning he was taken aback a little to see Tremonti and Hoffman engaged in conversation just outside the meeting room door. Tremonti's start date had momentarily escaped his mind due, no doubt, to the state of confusion he was having to live with. But before he had a chance to join them, Ricky Tremonti could be seen shaking Lukas' hand before promptly disappearing through the car park doorway without glancing in Richard's direction.

Lukas strolled over and apologised for handling the new recruit by himself explaining that he'd decided to renege on his decision to take him on in light of certain changes he was now planning to introduce. When he had time to bring Richard up to date, all would become clear regarding his cancelling of the computer file management post.

'I'm sorry, good morning, Rick.'

'Yes, good morning, Luke – things seem to be moving apace.'

'You could say that. How are you fixed to meet with me in L1 before we get on with the day?'

'I'm fine with that, Luke, what straightaway?'

'Why not – I'll buzz Jennie and get her to organise some coffees.'

'Thanks, Luke.'

'No problem, let's get started.'

Chapter 17

Lukas and Richard entered the meeting room, sat down in their usual positions and turned to each other rather awkwardly. Richard had half prepared himself for an uncomfortable confrontation with Lukas in light of the somewhat calculating thoughts he had revealed during his dozing off periods on the Camchester express. He could quite reasonably be excused for imagining that Lukas held little sway in the value of loyalty.

Before either had a chance to say a word, Jennie arrived with the drinks and left the room hastily.

'First of all, Rick, I must apologise for my behaviour yesterday morning when the news arrived from the Regulatory Agency. I think you'll understand why I was so disappointed.

'However, I have thought things through – long and hard – and have decided to make some radical changes in my life. I've taken stock and have realised the full potential, financially, of OT3. No one in the world has anything comparable as a remedy for impaired or total loss of vision. I have begun issuing licences to all European countries and can't imagine the magnitude of the rewards that will start to accumulate.

'So, I have asked myself a question, "What is the function of my striving to produce a second, world-beating product?" More money? I wouldn't know what to do with it. Come on, I'm going to be rich beyond my wildest dreams on the back of OT3. Fame? Status? Admiration? Power? Not for me, mate. Not important in the slightest. No, I will be happy setting up my own foundation in an effort to satisfy my philanthropic goals to do some actual good in the world. Look at OT3 alone and imagine its application in third world countries where the people have no access to even a pair of second-hand National Health specs. I will be able to hive off millions from my wealth to provide them with my new digital solution. I will be in a position to see that the developed world subsidises those less advantaged. It will be within my power – that's the kind of power I'm interested in. Richard, believe me, I will not be needing additional funding from a new project that we've yet to come up with. TT1 looked promising but it's now dead in the water, as they say.

'Right, I've not finished yet. There is, naturally, the question of your position here. I can't fail to recognise the invaluable contributions you have made, not only to TT1 but to OT3 - the OT3 that will be providing me with the wherewithal to move on to the next chapter in my life. So, I have wrestled with the subject of a redundancy payment which I am committed to compensate you with by law, but something about it just didn't seem enough. So, I have devised a plan that I hope will be more attractive to you. As you know, I am the owner of the lease on this property which has five years to run. What would you say to my settling the remaining rent commitment and the local authority business rates etc., for the same period and leaving you in place to, hopefully, develop the next IntuTech project?

'The deal will include my passing ownership of every piece of equipment over to you to provide you with a ready-to-go setup. And, in addition, there will be a generous cash payment to tide you over. What would you say to that?'

Richard's reservations about Lukas' commitment to him as a valued member of the organisation who deserved to be dealt a decent hand had, unexpectedly, made a U-turn. Which occurred to him as rather strange. Thought transcriptions, generally, to date, had proved, without exception, to weigh heavily towards negativity when it came to the matter of faithfulness to one's colleagues. But now, it seemed Lukas' altruistic gene was fully functioning and ready to dish him out something in the order of a royal flush. He found this thought provoking. *Could it be that there was a margin of tolerance in the degree of accuracy within individuals' minds' evaluations when it came to judging the true value of others? Was TT1 really recording a subject's sentiments accurately?* Richard was beginning to feel that this could be a factor that needed consideration when interpreting transcriptions but was comforted by the thought that this possibility would have zero impact on the efficacy of factual assessments.

'Oh wow, that gives me something to think about. On the face of it, it sounds unduly generous of you but, notwithstanding that, I'm still going to need some thinking time. I'm going to have to "talk to the wall" – did you ever see reruns of that old, early twenty-first century, entrepreneur-funding TV programme? – oh, never mind. But yes, can you give me twenty-four hours, Luke?'

'Of course, Rick, you can have longer if you wish.'

'No, that's all I'll need. How about we agree to meet back here at the same time tomorrow morning?'

'Fine with me, Rick. I don't expect you to beaver away here for the rest of the day with this on your mind so, by all means, take the rest of the day off.'

'Thank you – I will do that. See you in the morning, Lukas.'

With that, Richard got up and made his way to the car park. Once seated in his autonomous SUV, he sat motionless trying to make some sense of the situation.

So, my marriage is about to fail with the likelihood of an expensive divorce settlement around the corner and I'm now being offered an opportunity of a lifetime from a guy who, a little over twenty-four hours' ago, was considering turning me out onto the street when he envisaged TT1 hitting the jackpot. And now that has turned out, in his eyes, to be dead and buried, he decides to gift me the whole bloody caboosh. What is it with people's psychology? With the small sample of tests we've carried out with TT1 it would appear that everybody, without exception, is quite happy behaving in an altruistic manner when they expose their intentions to others through the usual channels of communication but when they feel they are safe in the knowledge that no one will be privy to their thoughts, they throw altruism out of the window. I'm no psychologist but this seems crazy. And not only that, it appears the very foundations of our social system hang on the fact that access to a person's private thought processes is not accessible to us. Maybe my thoughts on the matter of a possible tolerance margin when it comes to TT1's accuracy really do hold water. And now, even Luke believes that access remains impossible. If I am correct, I'm the only person in the world who, conceivably, holds the key to this access.

I don't have anything to think about - my response to Luke's offer is a no-brainer. But if I cut short my thinking time and go back this very moment to accept, he could well become suspicious. No, I'll give it the twenty-four hours we agreed. Jeez, now I'm doing it. I'm orchestrating a response to Luke that will optimise his inability to gain admission to my motivations. God, we're all at it!

Blimey, is there any such thing as altruism? It seems to be nothing more than a façade – a means of presenting ourselves in our best light while, all the time, not giving a shit for anyone. And society's been happy to go along with the process, ad infinitum, in the mistaken belief that we are a caring people. Okay, Lukas' current plans would appear highly altruistic on first consideration but how much of his actual wealth does he plan to give away? All save enough to keep his new-fangled foundation going? I don't think so. He's more likely to be managing his affairs from the luxury of the promenade deck of his super yacht moored somewhere along the Côte d'Azur. Here I go again!

Richard selected HOME on the navigator screen before immediately cancelling it to key in the address of the Harbour Café – he needed some time on his own and wasn't quite sure what Beth's movements were that day.

When he reached the café he selected a table situated in a less occupied area of the terrace in the hope that he could enjoy a little peace and quiet to get on with some serious thinking.

'Good morning, Freddie, how are things down here at the harbour?'

'Same as ever, Mr. Stewart – I have a menial job waiting on tables overlooking the marina but wouldn't change it for the world. What would you like me to bring you?'

'Oh, just a double espresso, please - if you wouldn't mind.'

Freddie strolled off and Richard mused over the likelihood

that the young waiter would probably give his right arm to anyone offering him double his salary. Richard's mind was beginning to reinterpret everything he was told in accordance with his newly discovered insights into the human psyche. And it was Beth who was supposed to be studying the ways of the mind. He seriously wondered whether the current teaching on human psychology needed a complete shake-up in the same way that the Met's polygraph programme was about to get in the not-too-distant future.

'Thank you, Freddie, what do I owe you?'

'Oh, I'll bring you a chitty in a short while – I'm sure I can trust you, Mr. Stewart.'

'Of course you can.'

Of course you bloody well can't, mate. He feared with a wry smile on his face.

Richard sat staring into the middle distance in deep contemplation over what was in store for him career-wise. He'd never been wholly responsible for running an organisation and found the prospect extremely daunting. But it looked likely he'd have little in the way of money worries with the deal Lukas had proposed and felt sure this fact alone would make for a smooth transition from the current arrangement.

After several minutes of being oblivious of all around him, he heard a small voice addressing him. A child's voice. He looked down and there before him was a young Afro-Caribbean-looking boy of no more than seven, or eight, years of age.

'I'm so sorry, I was miles away, little man. What was that you said?'

'I said, are you all right, mister? And I said it because my momma said you looked lonely and might need some company.'

'Well, that is so very thoughtful of you and your momma, little man. Do you mind if I ask you your name?'

'I'm Jerome but everybody calls me Jerry. I like that better because I think it's more friendly.'

'Yes, I agree with that – Jerry is a lovely, friendly boy's name. My name is Richard.'

Out of his peripheral vision, Richard could see a lady with a young daughter, maybe a touch older than Jerry, sitting a few tables away and could sense her approval of her son's natural sociability.

'Well, Jerry, I'm pleased to tell you that I'm absolutely fine but rather deep in thought about some aspects of my life that have come as a surprise to me. When you grow up lots more things happen in your life and they sometimes need some very careful thought. But you don't have to worry about that yet. You can concentrate your mind on being happy, having lots of fun and being kind to people. And let me tell you; when you show kindness to others they will always show kindness to you. That is one of life's first and most important rules.'

'Thank you, Richard. I didn't know about that kindness rule but I will always try my best to remember it. And I'm pleased that you're okay. Byeeee.'

With that, Jerry made a quick exit and re-joined his mother and sister while Richard looked over and offered a wave in acknowledgement of Jerry's very welcome friendly nature.

Being heavily involved in their respective careers, he and Beth had rarely broached the subject of children but this heart-warming encounter with little Jerry certainly diverted his mind away from matters neurotechnological. One day perhaps.

With his coffee finished and his thoughts on the future beginning to take on some kind of workable shape, Richard got up from his seat, offered his payment card up to the electronic chitty left by Freddie and decided to take a stroll along the seafront.

Falcombe offered walkers a good mile-long, well-maintained boardwalk to take in the views and, if that wasn't enough, a pebble path continued along the top of the sea wall to deliver them, eventually, to Foxbridge, the next seaside town along the coast. The walk, in total, was in the region of five miles. But Richard had little to attend to that day and the Foxbridge route would allow him more than enough valuable contemplation time than any alternative option he could think of. So, it would be lunch in the Four Season's restaurant at the eastern end of Foxbridge's boulevard, which the local council liked it to be known by, before a slow meander back to where his SUV was parked in Falcombe.

By the time he was back in his vehicle, he was on target to arrive home at the usual hour when he could begin his preparations for the evening with Beth. But when he walked in, he found she'd beat him to it and was busy arranging the rear terrace table for their evening meal. He felt he had a dilemma: on the one hand, he lived with a partner who was an absolute pleasure to get along with and perfectly versed to involve herself in the machinations associated with the upheaval he was confronting. But on the other hand, she had shown herself to be untrustworthy which, by definition, precluded her from acting as his advisor and confidante. Society's rules of engagement, he surmised, had been thrown into question by TT1. Although the turmoil it had generated was, largely, restricted to his own cognizance, its potential to play havoc with a community of individuals was nothing short of alarming. He needed to get a perspective on how the technology should be handled given that he would be successful in developing it to operate without the need for cranial implantation.

He had no option other than to continue exercising patience where his relationship with Beth was concerned and to bide his time until he felt it was appropriate to make a move.

The couple partook of their usual home recreational evening agenda which consisted of the meal, the clearing away, an extra glass of wine while they summed up their individual day's events and then either a quiet read on the sofa or a TV programme of one sort or another upstairs.

This evening while they sat chatting away after the meal, Richard found it a little difficult to play his part in developing a flowing conversation. They certainly knew each other well enough to endure a silence without feeling socially inept but, Richard was beginning to wonder how meaningful a casual chat really was when the underlying conflict he was now more than aware of was unable to be erased from his thoughts. Things between him and Beth would never be quite the same.

But with plans to accept Lukas' offer firm in his mind, he felt it would be unacceptable for him not to break the news to her.

'Beth, if you're okay to sit here for a while, there is something I need to bring you up to date on.'

'Of course, Rick, I'm going nowhere, fire away.'

During the course of the following hour-and-a-half, or so, he gave Beth a detailed account of the changes that were underway but left out the subject of TT1 and its rejection by the regulating board. So far, he had managed to keep her in the dark regarding the project he was working on ever since its first trial, for which, she was the involuntary guinea pig. And it wasn't difficult to gloss over the details of his present assignment any more than it would have been for her to avoid going into the specifics of whatever psychotherapy module she was currently engaged in.

'Well, that's a turnaround for the books, Rick. I had no idea anything like this would happen but I can entirely see the sense of it. No, you go for it – it's probably precisely what you need at this moment in your life. Where could you ever expect to be handed an opportunity like this again? Bite his hand off, Rick.'

'So, I have your approval, Beth. That's very encouraging. I will confirm my acceptance with Lukas first thing in the morning.'

With that the pair retired to their upstairs snug room and relaxed with their noses in books for the duration of the evening before it was time to retire. But Richard had mixed feelings about the situation. Beth's blessing was one thing but how sure could he be that she was going to figure in the arrangement? As his wife, it would be quite normal, and economically viable no doubt, for her to take on half of the shareholding and he felt certain that his accountant would advise him as such. But for all he knew at this juncture, she could be swanning around with Tremonti someplace else as soon as the legal formalities needed attending to. Not the best basis for future planning.

'Good morning, Rick, how are things shaping up?'

'Let's sit down in the meeting room and I'll give you a detailed account.'

'Okay, let's go.'

Once inside the room, the two colleagues took up their usual positions in readiness for a meaningful exchange.

'Well, Luke, it hasn't taken me long to make my mind up. We are clearly at a crossroads here at IntuTech with the demise of TT1 and I think your offer is very generous. Yes, very generous. And I fully appreciate that, in financial terms, it far exceeds the minimum legal requirement for a straightforward redundancy settlement. So, thank you. And yes, I'm pleased to accept your terms unreservedly. I'm going to start off with nothing of any substance in the pipeline though I've got a few ideas that just might warrant development. But that isn't your concern, of course – all you need to know is that I'm definitely up for what's on the table, as the saying goes.'

Richard felt there was no need to confuse the matter at this stage with the mention of Beth. Though Lukas was aware of the situation any complications would be unlikely to appear as urgent to him. Besides, his colleagues' domestic affairs really weren't his concern.

'That's marvellous, Rick. I will get in touch with that twit, sorry, my best friend, Edwin Crowther-Brown to instruct him to draw up an agreement for both of us to sign. As we agreed, I will be extricating myself from everything under development at the point of signing with the exception of OT3 so whatever you wish to proceed with will be entirely up to you. I don't imagine it'll take ECB more than a week, or two.

'I'm really thrilled, Rick, and I have no doubts that, with your level of technological expertise, you'll make an excellent go of it.'

Lukas pressed a button on the intercom. 'Jennie, I know it's not the ideal time of day but could you bring me down a bottle of Champagne from the fridge, please? I'm in the meeting room. Oh, and two flutes as well.'

'Right away, Mr. Hoffman. I'll be two minutes.'

'This warrants a celebration, Rick. I think the plan will work out best for both of us. Did you discuss it with Beth, by the way?'

'Well, yes, actually. I know things are all up in the air what with recent events, but, for the time being, I'm letting things carry on as if nothing had happened.'

'I think that's very sensible if you can handle it, Rick. I mean, come on, with the way everything seems to be changing on a daily basis, it wouldn't seem prudent to rush into something you might well regret later. No, good for you, you certainly do think things through thoroughly.

'Ah, Jennie, put them down just there, thank you. That was kind of you to stop what you were doing.'

Jennie left the room without giving any hint that she was confused at the idea of an 08.30 am bubbly celebration but put it out of her mind the moment she returned to her room.

'There you are, one glass of France's finest – bottoms up!'

The two one-time buddies turned business associates emptied their flutes in one go before recharging them and coming to terms with their newfound relationship. Maybe the future wasn't looking quite so bleak after all, Richard reflected.

Chapter 18

With the celebrations over, Lukas and Richard went in separate directions each eager to get on with their respective strategies now they, effectively, worked independently of each other. Lukas had promised he'd arrange a meeting with Ralph's team during which he intended to offer them positions in the new foundation. This made perfect sense as the three of them were heavily involved in the ongoing development of OT3. Although it had already been launched with great success, he had no plans to stop there. A mark two version would certainly be announced in good time.

In addition, he would make allowance for Ralph, Meghan and James to be available to Richard, on an advisory basis, in view of their wider experience and knowledge on neuroscience-related matters. It was inevitable he'd need access to their expertise at some time or other. And furthermore, Lukas' long-time neuroscientist confidante, Hans Bauer, would always be available at the other end of the phone to discuss anything concerning the biological aspects of whatever project he might find himself involved in.

Before returning to his office, Richard made a visit to the men's room for a pee. As he turned around to wash his hands he felt the formality, on this occasion, had a dual, symbolic function. He stood up and stared straight ahead into the mirror as if to address the image looking back at him. *Come on, mate, this is a chance of a lifetime. You can do it. You can make it work. You're still a young guy. A young guy who's, arguably, operating way ahead in his chosen field. Look behind you, the runners up aren't even in view. Your legal advisers will deal with the Beth issue without giving it a second thought. Stand up straight mate and give it your best shot.*

His alter ego had somehow lifted his spirits - introduced a spring into his step - and seemed to have given him the mental energy to promptly start work on the zero-intrusion TT1 development. The process involved, in the first instance, thinking time rather than hands-on procedures. The software handled by his dedicated smart watch was critical to the revisions he was hoping to achieve and a laptop screen image of the neural network system he had devised for the original scheme was set up in front of him to aid his visualisation process. He ran over and over the networking infrastructures he'd mapped out concentrating on every aspect of the design to envision the prospects of reversing one half of the overall method that he'd devised many months before. It wasn't going to be easy but he failed to understand why such a revision couldn't be possible. He was convinced that he could be held back only by his own personal powers of intellectual perception. A major factor by any account but Richard wasn't short on self-confidence and he firmly believed that, with time, he could crack it.

After sitting there for two hours solid he was getting nowhere. Every time he contemplated altering the routing or switching frequencies he hit a brick wall. The system he'd devised when he and Lukas first set out to develop TT1 seemed more and more perfect the more he considered it. While lowering the frequency slowed down the data transmission unacceptably, leaving it in place restricted the signal range. Whichever way he turned, he seemed to compromise the effectiveness of the original circuits. It just wasn't working. There was only one thing for it, he needed to scrap everything and start again from scratch. So, without wishing to burn his bridges, he carefully backed up every single file concerned with TT1 data, several times over, locked the sealed hard drives away in the company's safe and copied the master directory to IntuTech's cloud-based account. He now had no need to worry about the possibility that he might, at some later date, need to revert to the original model. It would now be easily accessible at any time. And, for the foreseeable future, he would make no plans to reverse the implantation procedure he had undergone just in case there was a need to revert to the original model at some time or other.

Richard became positively animated in his work. His alter ego's little pep talk seemed to have instilled an enthusiasm into his objectives and eliminated any notions of doubt he may have been harbouring prior to their consultation.

He decided the time was right to apply a new name to the revised design – a name he would rightfully recognise as an identification of his own creation. After deliberating for longer than he cared to admit, he came up with Brain Game for which BG would serve as its short form, its working title. So, Richard was now ready to start with his first version of a whole new technological development, Brain Game version 1.0, or BG1 for short. Mmm, sounded good. And it had the effect of ridding his mind of the, now, old technology enabling him to begin with a blank canvas as it were.

By this time he was ready to break for lunch and to clear his mind further, he thought he'd take a stroll down to his favourite haunt, the Harbour Café, where the vista over the marina and beyond might assist in accelerating his first BG1 conceptualizations. A more inspiring outlook than the office's four walls.

Richard felt more in control of his life. Well, certainly on the career side. No longer did he have to consider being accountable to Lukas. Not that Lukas ever placed unacceptable restrictions of any kind on his working programmes. But to be at the helm and to have the freedom to steer a course wholly of his own making, made an enormous difference. And additionally, having what should prove to be a highly lucrative project hidden in the galley, shone a very bright light on his immediate future prospects. Things were definitely looking up.

'Good afternoon, Freddie, how's your day going?'

'It's going too quickly, Mr. Stewart. You know how much I enjoy spending my days in this beautiful spot by the water. But don't ever tell my boss, he might expect me to work for nothing.'

'You're a lucky young man, Freddie. You never appear to have a care in the world.'

'Well, I don't know about that but I might do if the boss sees me chatting here for too long and not serving the other customers.'

'Of course. Right, I'd like a cold lager from the fridge and one of those hot pasties I had last time I was here – if you can remember.'

'Not a problem, Mr. Stewart. I'll be back in a few minutes with your order.'

Richard found the location particularly conducive to coming up with new ideas which was precisely what he needed - in truck loads.

He sat there applying his mind to the task in hand so preoccupied with the technicalities involved that he hardly remembered Freddie serving him with his lunch or, indeed, his consuming it. But after an hour, or so, he had a brainwave. Rather than reproduce the TT1 model with some new-fangled routing ideas, he would design the BG1 system to link directly to the subject's DNA. This would allow him to develop a programme that would enable multi-subject transcriptions able to operate when more than one individual was being questioned. The scheme he had in mind would facilitate switching from multi- to solo-mode by applying a DNA code to each individual within range and producing a link to separate the eventual transcriptions. In theory, the TT1 software could well have proved adequate in that the listener's incoming data signals' circuits could have been removed entirely leaving the system to rely solely on screen transcriptions. However, while this would certainly bring forward the launch date, it would compromise the investigating officers' ability to develop a case more effectively with the would-be offender in real-time. It would cut out possible delays in having to call the questionees back in after reading the printout. No, a completely revised system with multi-identity coding would be far superior.

Richard had never considered himself much of an athlete

but were BG1 to have qualified as an Olympic event, he felt pretty sure he'd soon be occupying the centre tri-podium spot with a gold medal hanging around his neck.

As the weeks went by Richard made good progress with the new technology and found the occasional consultation with Ralph's team and Hans Bauer invaluable. The setup was absolutely ideal in that he could call upon their technical assistance at any time without feeling he was putting upon his old boss.

The necessary paperwork forming the agreement with Lukas was duly signed and countersigned to put the business side of things in order and life at home was jogging along as if nothing had happened. Lukas soon vacated the premises along with Ralph, James and Meghan but Richard decided to keep Jennie on for the purpose of monitoring phone calls, handling unannounced visitors and dealing with the general administrative duties. Everything appeared to be satisfactory and by the end of the third month, he had got a trial version of BG1 up and running. But he needed to test it, ideally, with the subject unaware that anything was going on. Without wanting to make things worse between him and Beth by discovering yet more unwelcome revelations concerning their marriage, he thought Jennie might be a more sensible guinea pig.

It was essential that he fully trialled the new system before completing and sending the application to the regulating agency. With one IntuTech rejection already on their records, he didn't want to think he might be starting a trend.

'Hi Jennie, if you're not too tied up, any chance you could get me a coffee?'

'Of course, Richard, it's time I stopped for one myself.'

'Then why don't you join me in the meeting room where we can both take a break?'

'Sounds perfect. I'll be down in five minutes.'

Richard programmed his smart watch to handle the real-time audio transcription and waited for Jennie to arrive.'

Surely Jennie isn't going to continue with the negative thought processes. Jennie never has a bad word to say about anyone. This must be the exception that proves the rule. I can't believe her brain is wired to harbour derogatory feelings about anything or anybody. Brace yourself, Rick, there might be more surprises in store.

'Here you are, one black coffee without. She placed his on the table in front of him and moved around to the other side of the table to sit opposite. This suited Richard perfectly because there would be no chance of her seeing him touch the watch in the event of him needing to make any kind of adjustment. He tapped the START icon and sat back as if to relax.

'So, how's life with you, Jennie?'

'Oh, you know, up and down. But more ups than downs, I'm pleased to report.'

Jennie was a young mother living with her husband, Harry, in a small fisherman's cottage not very far from the IntuTech building. Her mother lived close-by and, luckily for Jennie, enjoyed looking after her three-year-old daughter, Rosie, while she worked to supplement the family income. Harry was a hard worker but struggled to keep the wolves from the door. Jennie's contribution was invaluable and helped them enjoy some of the luxuries that Harry would have been hard-pressed to fund.

'Well at least that's the right way round. How is the proud father these days?'

'Oh, he's a darling, my Harry. He works all the hours God gives him to keep us in the black.'

'That's great - sounds like you make a good team. And how are you adapting to the changes we've seen in the past few months?'

'Oh,' Jennie had a habit of starting almost every sentence with the exclamation. But it added a sort of endearing charm to her conversation. 'I can't say it's made much difference to me – I still seem to be doing the same jobs I used to. How about you, Richard?'

'I'm quite enjoying myself, actually. And I'm so heavily tied up with a new project I'm working on that I don't really notice the difference.'

The two work colleagues finished their drinks and Richard suggested he should be returning to his work - he was having some difficulty keeping up with deadlines. Jennie picked up the cups and made her way back to her office.

During the short conversation, Richard had checked that real-time thought transfer mode was working before switching to record mode so that he could transcribe Jennie's thoughts on the laptop once she'd left the room. The subject matter couldn't have been more innocuous but he was still keen to see that everything functioned as it should. He turned to the computer screen and pressed PLAY.

. . . black without . . . meeting room . . . mmm, it'll be nice to sit and chat for a few minutes . . . I wish there were more ups than downs . . . the proud father? . . . I really don't have a clue . . . haven't seen him since that night in Ibiza . . . good team? . . . be nice if Harry put the vacuum cleaner around once in a while . . . it'd be great to have more variety at work . . . it does get a bit boring sometimes with only the tedious Richard Stewart to

communicate with . . .

Richard tapped on the PAUSE icon and sat back with a disconcerted look on his face. He didn't find it easy to take on board this newly-found truth he'd discovered about what appeared to be every single member of society. It didn't seem to matter whose thought patterns he transcribed, without exception, they all had negative things to say about someone or other. And they invariably included unwelcome thoughts about the transcriber.

His mind began to work overtime. He kicked his chair back, hoisted his feet onto the tabletop, clasped both hands together and tried to make sense of things. *Okay, so Jennie has vindictive thoughts too. Well perhaps not so vindictive – maybe realistic. Maybe Harry is a bit of a slob. And maybe her own moral compass isn't quite as well calibrated as one would have imagined. Why should it be? And it would stand to reason that my personal inclinations are no different to anyone else's. That seems to be how society works. After all, when do we ever witness positive reports from media agencies? They have blank canvases on which to paint whatever topical picture they wish to exhibit to the public. But virtually all of their reports are negative. They're feeding a public with an appetite for negativity. But, of course, factual thoughts remain factual.*

As well as for himself, Richard was now feeling sorry for poor Harry who, it would appear, had no idea that he wasn't the paternal father to dear little Rosie. And what about Rosie, he pondered, is she ever going to know who her real dad is? We're living in a world we simply don't recognise, he thought. But, as if that wasn't enough, he now had to stomach the fact that Richard Stewart was tedious! No one had ever said that to him. But, of course, they wouldn't have done, would they?

Jennie would never have said it and he doubted she ever would. He realised that people just don't say what they think, rather, they assume a sort of altruistic façade, a sort of persona that only they are privy to. He was becoming more and more depressed about the state of today's society until he pulled himself up quick – the system was working. Working perfectly as it should. Damn, society, he thought. The realisation that the hours and hours he'd put in on BG1 had paid off was more than enough to cheer him. He was now in control of a totally new version of TT1 that not only functioned flawlessly but stood an excellent chance of being approved by the regulatory authority. He leapt out of his seat, punched the air and performed his dad-dancing routine without giving a thought to whether Jennie might walk back in. Richard Stewart tedious, he thought to himself? He certainly didn't think so. Well, definitely not today anyway.

Now that BG1 posed no problems in use, it was time for Richard to reapply for regulatory approval. This needed to be carried out via the licensing and regulation agency he and Lukas had used previously so he duly contacted them, tendered the required information and requested they submit the application as soon as they were able. Being aware of the implications of the system getting into the wrong hands, he took great care to ensure that suitable caveats were attached to restrict usage to only the criminal investigation divisions of the country's police forces. This would cover him for introducing the product to the forces up and down the country but he fully intended to confine his representations to the Metropolitan and City of London police in the first instance. Although there appeared to be no hitches in the product's functioning in its latest guise, a full trial in the real world of legal interrogation would reveal any possible teething troubles were they to exist.

Richard felt satisfied that all was heading in the right direction but he was missing the camaraderie he enjoyed when he and Lukas worked alongside each other. Beavering away on his own just wasn't the same. But he acknowledged that it really was the company he could do with rather than the technological expertise. And after his short chat with Jennie, he began to wonder if he might be able to make use of any latent skills she possessed by promoting her to the position of his personal assistant. He felt it might also offer her the opportunity to discover he was far from tedious.

He reached for the intercom. 'Jennie, have you got a minute?'

'Oh, of course, Richard, where are you?'

'Still in the meeting room – it shouldn't take more than fifteen minutes, or so.'

'Oh, no problem, I'll be right down.'

'Excellent.'

Without thinking, Richard wiped off several marks his shoes had left on the polished bamboo surface, drew his chair back to its usual position and tidied up some papers he'd scattered over the tabletop to ensure everything was neat and tidy for Jennie's arrival – all part of his fastidious nature rather than a thought out, purposeful exercise. OCD? Who knows? Maybe just the way his brain had been wired. But certainly a personal characteristic that played an important role in the development of BG1.

'Ah, Jennie, sit down. I've been thinking about the changes we've undergone here at IntuTech and am wondering whether you might like to be more involved in the day-to-day workings of the projects I'm responsible for. It won't involve anything too pressing but it will give you a better insight into what we're actually up to and also provide me with an assistant I badly need. You will still have time to attend to some of your present tasks but I thought we could employ, say, a part-time administrative member of staff to fill in the necessary gaps. And there will, naturally, be a pay rise commensurate with your extra responsibilities. What do you think? Or, rather, would you like to think it over and come back to me when you've arrived at a decision?'

'Oh, Mr. Stewart, sorry, I mean, Richard, I would absolutely love to take you up on your offer. I really don't need any thinking time, really. No, please make the necessary arrangements straightaway.'

'That's great news, Jennie. Let's start now. For your first assignment, could you please place an advert with a local recruitment agency for the part-time employee? I think you and I will get along well.'

Chapter 19

Just over two weeks after the application to the Medicines and Healthcare Products Regulatory Agency was submitted, Richard was sitting at his desk when Jennie walked in with the morning's post. Seeing an ominous, large buff envelope amongst several items of otherwise unidentifiable mail, he nervously took the wodge from her and beckoned her to stay with him. The opening of the reply was, hopefully, going to be met with a wholly different response to that when the TT1 answer arrived several months' earlier.

Since offering Jennie promotion and receiving her immediate, unequivocal, on-the-spot acceptance, Richard had, quite sensibly, found time to bring her up-to-date on the scientific and commercial objectives concerning the BG1 programme.

'Jennie, I believe this is the reply from the Regulations Agency following our recent BG1 application - the one I've been boring you with these past few weeks.'

'Oh, you've not been boring me, Richard. Since you've talked me through the workings of the project, I think I'm as anxious as you are to know whether they have approved it this time.'

'I'm sure you are, Jennie. Right, shall we open it?'

'Here, let me do it, you'll be fumbling with it all day.'

'Go ahead, it probably does call for a woman's steady hand. It's the contents of a rectangular box on page three that we're most concerned about.'

Jennie tore the flap off the envelope with one swift motion and removed the leaves of A4 paper from within.

'Okay, let me see, now, page one, page two, here it is, on page three - the rectangular box at the foot of the page. Well, they certainly haven't gone into much detail, it just says, APPROVED. I think that's what we want, isn't it?'

'Did you say, approved?'

'Yes, Richard.'

'Well, we've done it! We've done what the previous administration failed to do – we've succeeded in creating a properly marketable technological device that has an actual function in today's society.

'What else does it say?'

'Well, let me see . . . erm, it states here, in a separate rectangular box, that it can be used, at the present time, in connection with the United Kingdom's Police Forces but no other body either public or private.'

'Let me take a look, Jennie.'

Richard silently chuckled as Jennie handled the papers as though they were made from some kind of priceless, antique, priceless parchment - an automatic but wholly unnecessary response probably borne from an unconscious preoccupation with the value they represented.

She passed the whole package over to Richard who flicked through the various pages before stopping at the usage section's rectangular box.

'Right, well, that is precisely what we applied for. We've been granted unequivocal approval for use within the auspices of the UK's police forces. Which means, from now on, and I'm trying not to get too excited about this, Jennie, from now on, the lie-detector, officially known as the polygraph – invented in 1921, will be obsolete. Yes, outmoded. Passé. Outdated. You name it, it'll be it. As from this day, IntuTech's Brain Game version 1.0, or BG1 as we know it, will become *de rigueur* within the law enforcement agencies of the United Kingdom. Mandatory. Obligatory. Wow!

'Well, I am jumping the gun here a bit but I can see no reason why we won't have total control over the means by which the British police forces will test subjects for their honesty during criminal investigation procedures. All we've got to do is tell them we've got the solution. And, when I manage to regain my composure, I'm going to contact the head of polygraph training at Scotland Yard to see if I can get the ball rolling.

'Without overreacting unnecessarily, Jennie, how about we celebrate with a cup of coffee each?'

'Oh, that sounds an excellent idea, Richard. Leave it to me.'

Jennie went to take care of the coffees while Richard checked to see whether he had a number for Peter Williams.

After they celebrated their achievement for another quarter-of-an-hour, or so, Richard announced that it was time for the two of them to come down to earth and get back to work and he asked Jennie to let Kate know that he'd rather not be disturbed for the rest of the morning. Kate had recently been taken on for the part-time post they had discussed that would facilitate Jennie's promotion. Jennie took the coffee cups away and left him to his own devices.

He cleared his desk and picked up the papers from the agency to read through them carefully in case he'd missed anything important. It wouldn't do to begin proceedings with the Met only to find that an item of unread small print was likely to compromise the whole operation.

So, he sat back in his chair and read the agency's accompanying letter thoroughly before scrutinizing every possible detail contained within the attached pages. And, after almost an hour of painstaking examination, he was delighted to find that there was absolutely nothing he could see that should stop him from making an initial approach to Peter Williams.

From what he could see in front of him nothing had been left to chance. The BG1 trials had functioned impeccably, the agency had approved their use unequivocally, all necessary software was ready for uploading and dedicated smartwatches ware available at the press of a button – what could possibly go wrong? Richard picked up his handset and dialled in the Met man's number.

'Hi, is that Peter?'

'Yes, who am I talking to, please?'

'It's Richard Stewart from IntuTech – I don't know if you will remember me but I visited you with my colleague, Lukas Hoffman, some weeks back to learn a little bit about the polygraph and you were kind enough to give us a free demonstration.'

'Of course I remember you, Richard, it was a most enjoyable meeting. What can I do for you?'

'Well, if it's no trouble, I'd like to come along again to discuss a new technological device we have developed down here in Falcombe. I want you to know that I strongly believe it will prove extraordinarily successful if adopted by the Metropolitan Police and that, at this moment in time, I doubt you'll believe that the facilities it offers could be possible. An hour of your time will be all that is required.'

'Mmm, I must say that, had we not met recently and this was, instead, a cold call from some computer software outfit, I'd probably ask you to write in first and attach some literature. But, from what I remember of you, I will be perfectly happy to arrange a meeting. But just one proviso, if you don't mind, Richard, could we meet during my lunch hour as before?'

'Of course, Peter, that is no problem at all. I am indebted to you for being so accommodating.'

'Perfect, how about next Tuesday?'

'Tuesday will be ideal. So, same time as before, Peter.'

'I shall look forward to it. Goodbye for now, Richard.'

'Yes, me too, goodbye, Peter.'

Richard came off the phone, got up from his chair and walked around the room several times contemplating his future. And in the process, gave himself a little pep talk. *This is it, mate . . . the big one . . . the one all those years of studying were about . . . a rare chance to leap from non- to premier-league in one go . . . don't foul it up . . . it's been clean sheets all the way so far with just the one regulating body red card to spoil things . . . give it your best shot.*

He then buzzed through to Kate.

'Hi Kate, I trust your day has started well.'

'Yes, Mr. Stewart, nothing to complain about.'

'Would you be good enough to book me a first class seat on the 08.10 am solar express from Camchester to London Paddington for next Tuesday?'

'Of course I will. I'll do it online and pay via the company debit card if that's okay?'

'Thank you, Kate. Just message me when you've done it so that I will know everything's in order.'

'Shall I email you, Mr. Stewart, with the confirmation details and attach the ticket for you to print out?'

'That's even better, Kate – thank you.'

Kate was following well in Jennie's footsteps - a pleasure to work with. Richard was beginning to get used the idea of employing people and found himself enjoying the whole exercise. While his initial qualification for the IntuTech position only concerned his scientific capabilities, he was now beginning to feel the art of running and delegating to a small team might also figure on his list of talents.

He duly boarded the 08.10 am London bound train and settled into his comfy seat ready to go through things one final time to be sure he was fully prepared for the meeting. He had allowed himself enough time to disembark at Paddington and grab a coffee before making his way round to the Met building by taxi. He'd always preferred to be early rather than late to avoid any last minute panics especially before an important meeting.

The train journey proved uneventful but was of sufficient length to grant Richard more than adequate time to run through his intended pitch. He had two smart watches with him plus his laptop so that he could conduct a demonstration if time permitted. The software programmes were primed and ready to go and he'd set the watches to multi-transcription mode as he couldn't be sure whether Peter Williams would prove to be a word- or picture-thinker although he suspected the former.

The train pulled into Paddington at 10.50 am and, within a couple of minutes, he was enjoying a double-espresso in one of the station's coffee shop franchises. He felt the strong blend would keep him as alert as he would need to be to stay on top of things with the limited time Peter had allocated.

Once the coffee was finished, he got up, nodded a sign of approval to the friendly barista and headed for the taxi rank situated at the side of the terminus. It was very rare not to find a cabbie ready and waiting to whisk you off to your destination without a delay. And, within what seemed like only minutes, he was making his payment and alighting onto the pavement outside the New Scotland Yard police headquarters.

With several minutes to spare, Richard stood for a moment contemplating his surroundings. And whichever way he turned he found innumerable people going about their busy days. High numbers were pedalling along the Embankment's busy cycle lanes carefully demarcated alongside those designated for autonomous vehicles. And the thought struck him that, fundamentally, the bicycle had changed so very little over the course of its close-on two-hundred year existence. How remarkable, he thought – a true testament to the perceptive powers of the inventor. BG1? Two-hundred years? A sobering thought.

On entering the building he found the commissionaire had been advised of his visit and, after making a brief check of his credentials, waved him through the somewhat imposing stainless steel and glass revolving doors. Once inside, he was met by a security officer who duly deactivated the electronic barrier leading through to the main reception area and suggested he should walk over to the left to check in with the receptionist who was ready to greet him with a welcoming smile.

'Good afternoon, Mr. Stewart. I will let Mr. Williams know you are here and I expect his PA will be down shortly to accompany you up to his office. Do take a seat while you're waiting. By the way, the wash-room is through the revolving doors and round to the right and there is a water dispenser just next to the seating area.'

'Thank you, I'll wait here until I am called for.'

A few minutes later, a smart-looking, middle-aged lady emerged from the left-hand revolving door and walked, confidently, up to where he was sitting.

'I presume you are Mr. Stewart. I'm Geraldine, Mr. Williams' personal assistant. Pleased to meet you.' she said without pausing for breath and with something of a stern expression on her face.

'Yes, that is right. I'm pleased to meet you too, Geraldine.'

Geraldine didn't appear pleased to meet *him*. In fact, Geraldine didn't appear she'd be pleased to meet anyone. *Mustn't judge - maybe she's having a bad day.*

'Would you please follow me, then, and I will take you up to his office on the seventh floor?'

'Thank you.'

During the several minutes it took to walk over to the scenic lift, travel up to the seventh floor and negotiate the long corridor leading to their destination, Geraldine remained silent giving Richard the distinct impression she was in no mood for exchanging pleasantries.

'Mr. Williams, Richard Stewart.' she announced as Peter opened the door with an amiable air about him in contrast to that of Geraldine.

'Richard, it's so good to see you again. Please come in and make yourself comfortable. I did warn you that I can only afford an hour of my time so I hope that offers you an adequate opportunity to show me what it is you have travelled all this way for.'

'Good to see you too, Peter and, yes, I'm sure you'll get the gist of the product I am about to show you well within that time.'

'In that case, let's start right away.'

Richard had his smart watch set ready to activate and removed his laptop from its case. He thought a transcribe-only session to start with would be favourite so that he could catch Peter's attention by allowing him to be privy to the subsequent scroll down of his thought patterns. He planned, afterwards, to run a real-time exercise in which he could simultaneously comment on what he was picking up directly from Peter's thought processes. But before launching into the first session, he needed to advise him what it was he was about to demonstrate. Reading a potential client's mind without warning might not be the most judicious of decisions he'd make that day. But a mere verbal explanation of the product's capabilities wouldn't scratch the surface of a real, live presentation and Richard suspected, anyway, that Peter would probably go ahead without fully appreciating what he was letting himself in for.

'Peter, before I begin with the demonstration, I feel I owe it to you to give you a short briefing on how the system functions. And I must warn you that it may take you by surprise. When Lukas Hoffman and I met with you some months' ago, our interest in the polygraph was linked to this creation insofar as we wanted to see how it compared with what we had produced - check out the competition, so to speak. Anyway, when we left you, we had the distinct impression that we were sitting on something that would prove immeasurably valuable to your organisation. And in the months that have passed, we have, not only completed and signed off all necessary trialling procedures but have been granted carte blanche approval by the Medicines and Healthcare Products Regulatory Agency to go right ahead and offer it to a potential end-user. However, I should add that the use of the device is unequivocally restricted to its intended application for operation within the auspices of the criminal investigation divisions of the UK's police forces.

'So, to cut to the chase, I have to tell you that our product, BG1 – that's a working title, by the way - is a highly advanced neurotechnological device that allows the operator to read the mind of a subject which, in practice, will mean the mind of a suspected criminal. Investigative procedures within your profession will never again be left to chance with lie-detection results needing to be interpreted and judged on their truth-percentage rating. BG1 will reveal exactly what is in the would-be culprit's mind to appraise whether he, or she, is guilty or otherwise.

Richard braced himself before asking the inevitable question.

'Now, to provide you with a demonstration, I will need the services of a volunteer to play the role of the suspect. How do you feel about this, Peter? We're on our own here and I will be quite happy to proceed with you taking that role but it would be presumptuous of me to expect you to do so. Are you happy to continue on that basis or would you prefer to locate a volunteer rather than be involved yourself?'

Peter looked Richard straight in the eye then glanced at his wall calendar. It appeared his mind was beginning to spin out of control. He felt more like a magician's foil after being dragged from the front row of an audience. How could this end up with him looking anything but stupid?

'Just checking it's not April the first, Richard.' he proffered with an uneasy grin on his face. 'Is this some kind of prank? I mean, you appear to be a professional in your field but, Richard, we get all sorts of strange individuals pass through these doors and, I have to say, this is the most ridiculous suggestion I have ever come across in my life. Is this for real? You know how busy I am – I really haven't got time to play games with you.'

'If my new system didn't come across as unbelievable as it does, it wouldn't have the potential to replace the, in my opinion, outmoded lie-detectors you guys are using and depending on every day. This conversation can't go any further without me being allowed an opportunity to demonstrate BG1's capabilities to you. But I'd understand if you'd prefer not to participate yourself. That always remains your prerogative.'

'No, I have no problem taking part in the demo and, if there is any truth in what you say, I would rather keep things between you and me at this stage. But Richard, we have been talking for well over twenty-minutes and I must stress that you will need to vacate my office before the hour is up because I have other, extremely important meetings scheduled that simply cannot be missed.'

'I understand, of course I do. Can we, in that case, get on with the first demonstration? I was hoping to move on to a second presentation but, from what you say, we might have to arrange that for another time.

'Right, what I'd like you to do, Peter, is nothing more than simply answer my questions. They won't be difficult and they won't need to be connected in any way to the subject of criminal investigations. I just need you to provide me with answers. And they don't even need to be truthful – it's entirely up to you. Are you okay with that?'

'Perfectly okay, Richard but I have to say it feels a bit like a game we might play at home while we're digesting our Christmas lunch.'

'Ha, ha, ha, I understand. But I think you'll have a different perspective once we've finished.'

Chapter 20

Richard checked that his smart watch was set correctly before turning to Peter to begin the questioning.

'Peter, what would you have had for lunch today if I hadn't travelled up to London to hijack your lunch hour?'

'Probably two crispbreads, a tomato, a chunk of mature cheddar and a piece of wedding cake – there was a family wedding at the weekend, by the way – my wife doesn't have a habit of buying me slices of wedding cake for my packed lunches, you'll be pleased to know.'

'My sort of lunch, Peter.'

Richard was noting Peter's verbal responses while being aware that additional non-verbal responses were present also in his mind. These responses were very likely not to have been quite so evident to the participant until revealed in the ensuing transcript. The demonstration continued.

'I noticed some graffiti on a wall just around the corner

from the Met building's entrance, is that something you and your mates did?'

'Ha, ha, ha, Richard. I saw it too – it's been there a couple of months and isn't especially complimentary to this police force. However, the answer is no, not guilty, officer.'

Peter was clearly pleased to join in with the humour Richard was injecting into the demonstration.

'Excellent, I was hoping it wasn't you, Peter. One last question, how do you get along with your boss here at the Yard?'

'Well, that's a moot point, really. No, I'm joking, honest, M'lud. Sir David Meakin is a pleasure to work under. A hard task master, for sure, but he is a top man and somebody no one has a problem deferring to.'

The exercise was complete but Peter was still not taking the matter quite so seriously as one would imagine the forthcoming revelation should demand.

'That's it, Peter – I told you there was nothing difficult about it. Now, if you'll give me a minute or two, I will move onto the second phase of the demonstration.'

Richard reached for his laptop, booted it up and set it to multi-transcription mode to facilitate the programme being able to detect either a word- or picture-thinking subject to ensure it displayed the appropriate scrolling images.

'Okay, if you'd like to come around to this side of the desk, Peter, and sit next to me so that we can both view the screen together, it might make things easier.'

'I can do better than that - use my Wi-Fi link to send the image to the large screen on the wall then we can both sit in comfort and watch whatever it is you have planned.'

'Perfect, what's your password?'

Peter read out the key and within seconds the curser flashed on the top left-hand corner of the wall screen indicating that it was ready to display Peter's thoughts.

'Ready, Peter?'

'As ready as I'll ever be.'

'Okay, here we go. Oh, I'm sorry, before we start, you will see that your verbal contributions are automatically filtered out and the reason for this will soon become apparent. Right, keep your eyes on the screen.'

Richard applied the relevant keystroke to activate the transcript and the screen suddenly came alive. It was soon apparent that Peter was a word-thinker.

. . . crispbreads be damned . . . a real man would be tucking into a chunk of crusty bread . . . be pleased when this diet has run its course . . . thank God for the wedding cake . . . makes having to endure the tedium of that ghastly affair on Saturday just a bit more bearable . . . if I could lay my hands on those little bastards it wouldn't be probation I'd be giving them, it'd be half-a-dozen lashes . . . Sir David Meakin, the stuck up son-of-a-bitch . . . whose bloody idea was it to put him in charge? . . . effing politics! . . .

Peter Williams' jaw dropped as he sat there motionless staring at the screen. Then, with a deadpan look on his face, he got up slowly, snatched a data card from the desk and remotely locked the door to his office. He then turned to Richard and looked him in the face while he tapped the PA icon on his glass communication pad.

As Richard had suspected, Peter reached the position where he couldn't fail to properly judge the efficacy of the product.

'Geraldine, Peter here, would you please cancel all of my afternoon's meetings and advise everybody that I must not be disturbed. And that goes for you too. Rearrange everything for another day and I will talk to you later. Thank you.'

Still holding Richard's gaze, he placed a finger on the icon again but this time until it disappeared.

'How the holy fuck did you do that? This is outrageous. Who else knows about this? I'm sorry, this is not the sort of response people get after demonstrating new equipment to Mr. Peter Williams BSc, Head of Polygraph Interrogation Procedures for The London Metropolitan Police Force. I just don't react like this.

'Richard, forgive me and please give me a few minutes to properly digest what I have just witnessed.'

Peter walked over to the window where he had a panoramic view over pretty much the whole of east London and beyond. To his left was Charing Cross station and straight ahead, in the middle distance, Canary Wharf and London City Airport. Then, way beyond that, and barely visible, the Thames estuary – a view he enjoyed on a daily basis. And all of it looked completely logical. Were one to refer to a map of the areas over which he sometimes felt he had dominion, each of the landmarks in his line of sight would coincide precisely with their charted positions on a cartographer's two-dimensional representation. And why not? Why should it not follow that one image would appear as a prefect replica of the other? That's what logic dictates. Simple reasoning. Everyone knows that.

But what Richard Stewart from IntuTech had just demonstrated, defied every possible interpretation of the semantics surrounding the word "reason". What Peter had just seen was simply impossible.

He was almost lost for words.

'I'm assuming you didn't spike my drink, Richard.'

'No, Peter, I did nothing of the sort. Look, if you need a

little time before I move on to the next demonstration, I perfectly understand.'

'No, I think I'm okay, really. It's just, it's just. Well, it's just that you've taken me completely by surprise. You've turned my whole understanding of science, as I've known it all my life, completely on its head.'

'It's not magic, it's a new invention, Peter. And sometimes it takes a little time to grasp something so new that it appears to defy logic. But it doesn't defy logic. If I were to run through all of the neurotechnological procedures that have led me to produce this . . . this, well, let's call it a device, you would recognise that it strictly complies with the laws of science in every respect. You just need time to adapt.'

Peter's mind ran through a whole host of ridiculously ungraspable concepts such as a Neanderthal being confronted with smart phone, Napoléon being presented with a Challenger 5 tank or Archimedes taking a tour of the Large Hadron Collider at the European Centre for Nuclear Research near Geneva. He'd had no idea how out-of-date his understanding of modern science had become.

'Of course, Richard, I know you're right. No, please, let's move on to the second demonstration. I promise to behave myself this time.'

Richard reset his smart watch to word-thinking, real-time mode and turned to a still noticeably-stunned Peter Williams.

'Okay, Peter, I'm now going to change the device's mode to show you its real-time capability which, I think you will agree, is where it will come into its own when used for interrogation purposes. Now, my demonstration is going to be extremely simple so that the function takes precedence over any complexities it is able to deal with. In other words, I'm opting for the easiest way to enable you to understand what is happening leaving any further, particularly valuable applications, for you to figure out yourself. And I promise you, you will not find that difficult.

'Right, we're going to swap hats, as it were, insofar as you will be registering, in real-time, what is going on in my head rather than mine in yours. So, I want you to ask three simple questions about me that you will be pretty certain you don't know the answers to. Anything you like as long as you are sure you'll be unfamiliar with my responses. And, to make things even more interesting, I am not going to verbalise the answers. Here we go.'

Peter felt a bit like Shakespeare's blundering Dogberry character being confronted by the Bard himself.

Richard touched the watch in two separate locations to start the process rolling.

'When you're ready, Peter.'

'Okay, Richard. What time did your solar express leave the station this morning? Oh my God! . . . Which was the last educational establishment you attended? . . . Jesus Christ. . . What colour car do you drive? What the holy fuck? Richard, this is crazy, bloody, crazy.'

'I know, I know, but we haven't quite completed the exercise. Right, I'm now going to ask you the same three simple questions. Here goes: What time did my solar express leave the station this morning? Which was the last educational establishment I attended? What colour car do I drive?'

'This is crazy. Okay, 08.10 am, Birmingham University, Burnt Copper.'

Both Peter and Richard were now in fits of laughter. Gone was Peter's initial, incredulous reaction, his, *someone's-having-*

me-on response, his gobsmacked facial expression, now he was seeing a funny side to Richard's presentation which he had, very quickly, come to take on board. He was finally believing what he was seeing. He doubted he'd ever understand how it worked but, hey, he thought, how does a five-year-old reconcile itself to the technicalities of a holographic TV broadcast when sat in front of a real-time hologram in his nursery?

Peter was starting to enter grovelling mode by pleading to Richard to let him in on the secret. But without the vast scientific training necessary to understand the concepts there was little his visitor could do to explain the technological aspects of what he had witnessed. Besides, what benefit would it be to divulge the mysteries behind BG1 were it even to be possible?

'Come on, Richard, come on, tell me how you've achieved this.'

'All right, all right, I give in. You ask Arabella Rosa White for the recipe for her favourite Christmas dish, and, in exchange, I'll let you have the neurotechnological algorithms for BG1. Deal?'

The pair fell into more fits of laughter before collecting themselves, sitting up straight and wondering what to say next to each other. Peter broke the silence.

'Okay, Richard, game, set and match to you. Well bloody done, my friend. So where to from here?'

'Well, I have carte blanche approval to proceed with signing up agreements with any of the UK's police forces and have started the process with this afternoon's demonstration. Consider yourself lucky to have been granted one of only two available seats for the world premiere of BG1. Peter, I can assure you that nobody, but nobody, has witnessed what you have experienced this afternoon. Not even Lukas Hoffman who you met when I last visited you. Lukas and I came to a commercial decision to go our separate ways some weeks' back – totally amicably, I must add – with him pursuing a project of his and me pursuing BG1.

Richard's confidence in the product eliminated any ideas he might otherwise have had regarding closing the deal there and then. He imagined Peter would still manage to track him down to place an order were he to disguise himself as a nun and leave the country under a false passport.

'So, my intention now is to leave the matter with you to mull over for a couple of days before we touch base again in a week, or so, to see what suggestions you might have. There will be the question of cost, hardware availability, the number of modules you will require if you plan to take the technology on and, probably most important of all, support programmes. Remember, this is as new to me as it is to you.'

'That sounds fair enough, Richard. But I really can't see it taking me more than a couple of minutes to decide whether or not I am interested.'

Peter looked up to the ceiling pensively.

'Although, on reflection, maybe I'll come up with some fresh questions if we wait a little while. So, yes please, let's talk in a couple of days.'

'Excellent. I will pack away my equipment and leave you to catch up on your busy afternoon, Peter.'

'Just a minute, Richard. Before you go, I have to say how grateful I am that you chose me to confide in instead of any number of other parties that would have bitten your hand off to acquire the rights to this exceptional creation of yours.'

'Well, that's nice of you to say but remember, I only have approval from the regulating body to market this within the auspices of the country's police forces so, with you being at the top of the most famous force in the UK, it was logical to start here at the Met. And I have to say, so far, the pleasure has been all mine.'

Richard picked up his belongings, bade his host farewell and, on meeting Geraldine at the door, made his way to the lift car to begin his journey back to Falcombe.

Once the office door had closed behind them, Peter sauntered over to the window again and stared out into the distance. Without focusing on anything in particular, his mind began to wander in sheer amazement at what he had just witnessed. He'd worked in criminal investigation for over two decades and had become a master at interpreting the results of hundreds of polygraph tests without ever considering their fallibility. He was, of course, well aware that their findings were not foolproof and that many other procedures needed to take place before a case could be considered sufficiently viable to put before a court of law, but he could now see a whole new future emerging where the business of establishing the truth would become a mere technicality. The whole legal process, from charging an individual to his eventual committal, need take no more than a few minutes in some cases.

And the changes wouldn't be likely to stop there. Once the new system had become known by virtue of the media, he imagined a new deterrent materialising where potential culprits would think far more seriously before committing crimes. With police forces holding the ultimate trump card, there would be little chance of acquittal were guilty parties to find themselves up against the bench. BG1 could not only turn the legal system on its head but, also, that of the world of criminals. Richard could almost imagine BG1 turning the nation's moral compass on its head.

But before anything further could be done in the way of trialling the system, there was one very important question that needed to be answered: would the law courts accept BG1's revelations as permissible evidence? And what were his thoughts on establishing this. There would certainly be a lengthy process ahead of them if it were to go through the necessary authorisation channels but, he just wondered whether there would actually be any need to worry insofar as guilty pleas were likely to become the order of the day once culprits realised they had been irrefutably found out.

As Peter had full control over his own budget, he would have no trouble justifying the purchase of the IntuTech BG1 system. Richard had run through the costs involved which required an initial sum for the primary software licence and additional amounts for each extra user-licence. All prices included a specially-adapted smart watch to control the programme and an ongoing customer support package payable on an annual basis.

Peter felt he needed zero thinking time and planned to make contact with Richard the very next morning to begin the registration process.

To say Richard had a spring in his step as he strolled along the Embankment looking to hail a cab would be understating his disposition at that moment. The positive response he'd received from Peter seemed to add significantly to his standing.

Chapter 21

Almost as soon as Richard arrived at the office the following morning, he had a call show up on his phone from Peter Williams.

'Richard, it's me, Peter'

'Oh, hi, Peter – good morning to you - it seems only a matter of hours since we parted company. I hope you haven't decided to give the project a miss.'

'I presume you are joking – have I not allowed you sufficient time to write up your notes? Look, I was actually tempted to call you yesterday afternoon scarcely before you'd left the building.

'Listen, I want it, Richard. I want it now. There isn't anything for me to consider – the system is nothing short of ingenious and you know that. What is more, your price is entirely reasonable so, yes please, can we get the registration procedure underway for one unit? Just one for now. I believe

I'll be back to you within a couple of weeks to sign up for several additional user licences, but I want to trial the item first and I have a very good idea which way I am going to approach the means by which we'll use it.'

'Well, that's fantastic, Peter – thank you. As you know, you are my first customer and, as such, this calls for a celebration. I will toast your good health, as well as your good sense, with a fresh cup of coffee once this conversation is over.

'But I'm intrigued, what is the approach you wish to make and what is the thinking behind it, if you don't mind me asking?'

Peter explained, in detail, the idea he'd had regarding bypassing the need to undergo painstaking authorisation procedures with the courts being likely to deal with the process in a long-winded manner. And he filled Richard in on his suspicion that BG1's usage would lead, very quickly, to guilty pleas and their accompanying bargaining opportunities. The first the courts would know of individual cases would be the serving of a guilty pleas. Their function thereon after would be for the judiciary to apply its expertise to the matter of sentencing.

'I see your point, Peter. That's an educated insight into the way BG1 may well come to be used in interrogation processes. I have to say, that possibility hadn't crossed my mind and I shall be fascinated to hear how this unfolds once you get the system up and running.'

'I promise you, Richard, you'll be one of the first to know. Anyway, I will email you an official order later this morning and look forward to receiving your confirmation that everything is ready to be downloaded.'

'Thank you. I will get onto it immediately. A single-user

licence, convertible to multi-user at a future date, will be issued and a dedicated IntuTech smart watch despatched under our controlled delivery programme. This will ensure it will arrive safely at your office this time tomorrow. Peter, it has been a pleasure to do business with you. I am sure we will talk again very soon.'

Richard terminated the call, breathed an especially long sigh of relief then buzzed through to Jennie to invite her to join him for the celebratory cup of coffee he had promised himself.

'Oh, and Jennie, ask Kate to pop in too if she's not too tied up.'

While the ladies were organising things, Richard mused over the position he now found himself in. For the time being his attention would be focused on sales and marketing rather than scientific development. He had little choice in the matter. Until such time as there needed to be a version 2 his job description would change drastically. Not a problem he thought, all of the serious legwork had been done leaving the product to establish its own reputation and pass through whichever end user doors happened to invite it in.

Within five minutes, the three IntuTech employees were gathered together in Richard's office to toast the good health and good sense of one Peter Williams of New Scotland Yard.

'Ladies, I am pleased to announce that we have, today, received our very first order for BG1 from no less a customer than the London Metropolitan Police Force. Which, in the absence of anything more appropriate, warrants a special celebratory cup of IntuTech coffee. Please lift your cups to toast our one and only client, Mr. Peter Williams, head of polygraph testing at New Scotland Yard.'

The coffee cups were, summarily, held aloft while the three

colleagues cheered their hearts out. IntuTech had steadied itself on the first rung of the neurotechnological ladder and were determined climb farther up in the months to come.

'And not to put too fine a point on it, ladies, this auspicious event will generate the first item of serious revenue since Lukas Hoffman and I decided to move in separate directions several months' ago. It will enable me to embark on an investment programme that will not only secure our futures for some time to come but establish BG1 - Brain Game version one - as *the* major player in the field of criminal investigation interrogation techniques. I see no reason why this shouldn't herald the passing of the polygraph, otherwise known, affectionally, as the lie-detector.'

Within the hour the festivities had run their course and Richard suggested Jennie and Kate should return to their respective offices to re-establish a sense of proportion. The point had been well made and all agreed it was time to park the morning's success to one side and get the IntuTech show back on the road. Richard dealt with sending the necessary digital files to Peter Williams while Kate organised the safe despatch of the dedicated smart watch via the company's controlled delivery programme. Meanwhile, Jennie raised the relevant digital documentation to ensure the Met's finance department would have everything they needed to set up the agreed interbank GBP transfers. Things were beginning to move in the right direction.

Richard was existing in a sort of trance-like state not knowing when he was next likely to return to terra firma. Though it would appear probable that this would occur somewhere around the time Peter Williams applied BG1 to an actual, real, live case. Although he felt the possibility of the system failing virtually non-existent, he couldn't help but endure a sense of anxiety until he received a conclusive, positive report from his client.

Forty-eight hours later, Peter Williams had completed all of the essential tasks relating to the BG1 registration process and everything appeared to be ready to go. All he needed now was an appropriate investigation case upon which he could test the new miracle software. And for its inaugural run out, he decided that it would be he who sat in the driving seat rather than Richard Stewart. He turned to his computer and duly logged on to Current Investigations which brought up a long list of unresolved cases complete with details of when suspects were questioned. In the first column was the date when the investigation was first initiated and in the far right column, the date of the most recent interrogation. In random positions as Peter scrolled down, certain entries were shown in flashing red text. These were examinations that were being carried out at that very moment. Details of the investigating officer, suspect and suspect's solicitor were also shown and, when he right-clicked, anywhere on the relevant row, a summary of the crime popped up in a separate window.

He scrolled down viewing only the live investigations and read through their respective synopses to decide which might be an appropriate questioning to interrupt. Peter's seniority at the Met was such that it was likely the investigating officer was of a lower grade to him so he felt interposing and politely pulling rank wouldn't be a problem. Several cases appeared unsuitable for a variety of reasons but when he came across a drugs case that involved a south London man, George Cooper, who'd been questioned a number of times already, he decided his intervention might be appropriate.

The investigating officer was a certain Detective Inspector David O'Connor who appeared to be experiencing great difficulty in persuading the suspect to name his supplier. So, Peter immediately sent a note down to the room requesting a brief word with O'Connor who duly advised the suspect and his legal representative, Edward Jenner, there would be a ten-minute intermission. The audio recorder was, accordingly, set to PAUSE and the officer left the interview to meet with Peter in an ante-room.

Peter did his best to curb his excitement at having a chance to put BG1 to the test. He was so confident the product would perform brilliantly and couldn't wait to see the face of his colleague once the exercise was complete.

'Good morning, David – my apologies but I have something I would like to introduce to this investigation if you don't mind.'

'Peter, you are most welcome. I am getting absolutely nowhere with this. For the past twenty-minutes, the suspect has repeatedly answered 'No comment' to every question I've thrown at him What is it you want to introduce?'

'It's a new item of technology that I will run through with you in some detail later. But, for the moment, I would appreciate you taking me with you into the room and allowing me to briefly address the suspect.'

'By all means – let's go.'

Peter set the smart watch to DNA separation mode in order to focus on only the suspect's thought patterns and selected auto-detect word/picture-thinking as it was not known which particular thought patterns the interviewee would present with. He then tapped the RECORD icon before following his colleague into the room. David looked at the suspect and his solicitor in turn and advised them that Chief Inspector Williams would be joining them for a short while.

'Mr. Jenner, I would like to ask your client a couple of questions. Do you mind if I call you George, Mr. Cooper?'

'No comment.'

'Very well, I will decide for myself. George, who was your supplier for the cache of cocaine found in your possession by my colleague, DI O'Connor, last Wednesday morning? And where will we be able to find this individual?'

'No comment.'

'That's fine, David – thank you. I shan't be wanting to ask anything further at this juncture and I would suggest you bring this interview to a close. Thank you, gentlemen.'

With a somewhat perplexed look on his face, David averted his gaze from his superior, turned to the solicitor and his client and announced that they were free to go for the time being. Peter duly left the room.

All three of them, O'Connor, Jenner and Cooper, looked flummoxed. What was happening? None of them; an experienced police investigating officer, a veteran solicitor and a serial small-time criminal had witnessed anything of the kind in a Scotland Yard interrogation room.

'Gentlemen, will you please remember to report to the duty officer for this department before leaving the building. Thank you.'

With that, David walked swiftly out of the room and chased along the corridor to catch up with Peter.

'Excuse me for questioning your motives, Peter, but what on earth was that about? You asked two questions that stood no chance of eliciting a response other than 'No comment' then simply got up and left. Did your new item of technology suddenly give up the ghost?'

Peter chuckled. 'No, I don't believe so. But give me a few minutes and I'll get back to you on this, David. Will you be available during the course of the next hour, or so?'

'Definitely – I'm intrigued.'

'All will be revealed, I promise you.'

Peter returned to his office on the seventh floor and logged onto his laptop. David O'Connor might be intrigued, he thought to himself, but not half as much as he was. Unlike Richard Stewart, who had trialled the system many times, this was Peter's first foray into physically entering the mind of another person and he found the prospect of what he was about to uncover nothing short of staggering.

The IntuTech software booted up within seconds and he immediately ran through the uploading process in accordance with the online manual that Richard had made sure formed part of the package. He selected word-thought transcript mode, clicked on the "recent data" icon and sat back in his seat. Nothing. The screen flickered slightly but nothing in the way of text appeared. He tried again – clicked on the "back" arrow twice, selected word-thought transcript mode, re-clicked on "recent data" then waited. Same again. Nothing. He could feel a tension building inside him as if he were a rookie member of a bomb squad in the process of defusing his first device.

Peter reprimanded himself. He knew it wasn't the product that was failing. He slapped his forehead in a symbolic gesture to suggest his mind needed a shake-up. *Calm down, mate, you're too excited. It's not the software, it's you – you're not thinking straight.*

No point in trying a third time, he thought. He must be

doing something wrong. Or worse, the programme was unreliable or flawed in some way. He sat back again to collect his thoughts. No, he was too anxious to achieve a result – re-reading the instructions again had to be the next port of call. He scrolled up to the contents page: Remote Recording/DNA Separation/Auto-Detect Word-/Picture-Thinking/RECORD . . . hold on, Auto-Detect Word/Picture-Thinking? He hadn't considered that. What if George Cooper thought in pictures rather than words? Why not? He'd taken for granted that transcript mode would simply spew out the suspect's responses like some sort of ticker-tape message and never dreamt he might be thinking graphically. It was certainly worth a try. Okay, here we go, transcript mode, picture-thinking, recent data - WOW! This was amazing. Mind-blowing. Totally and utterly mind-blowing.

He couldn't believe what he was seeing. He stood up. Looked around the room. Sat down again. Stood up again. Walked around the room. Twice. He was playing a part, a significant role, in making history. This very moment would be documented and studied by law students, history students, for years to come.

Peter was staring at a near high-resolution picture of an individual he'd never ever set eyes on and, on scrolling down, a front entrance door of, what looked like, a high-rise apartment with the number 42 displayed to the right-hand side of a standard-looking letterbox. He scrolled up again to take a longer look at the figure whose image was confined to the upper part of his chest, his neck and his face. He appeared to be wearing a smart, expensive-looking, tan-coloured, leather zip-up jacket with, possibly, a white, silk shirt beneath. Around his neck was a chunky, gold necklace with some kind of large, inscribed coin hanging down towards the front. And facially, he could have been of eastern European origin, maybe, but that wasn't so easy to determine. Age? Probably mid- to late-thirties.

As he scrolled back to the entrance door, he noted that he was viewing it from just the central letterbox area up to the white-painted horizontal frame at the top. The door itself was plain, without any architectural features - as if constructed from a kind of sheet material – plywood or fibreboard, maybe – and painted in a dark shade of maroon. The letterbox appeared to be made from a cheap alloy of some kind – silver-coloured - with the adjacent, black numerals fabricated from a sort of textured, black plastic. All pretty much run-of-the-mill stuff.

But what it did reveal was that the two images seemed to appear precisely as the observer - the picture-thinker - would have viewed them in real life. And, from the parts of the images that the screen was able to display, both had been quite clearly observed by a tall, rather than a short individual. And George Cooper was significantly tall in stature.

Wow, wow, wow! Peter could not believe his eyes. What he was witnessing was precisely what David O'Connor's suspect was visualising during the course of Peter's questioning. The results of this new IntuTech BG1 software were nothing short of miraculous. The world of criminal investigation would never be the same again.

Chapter 22

Peter immediately touched David O'Connor's icon on the glass communication pad at the side of his desk to suggest he might want to join him. Two minutes later he was tapping on the door.

'Come in, David. Sit yourself down – I have something I think you'll be extremely interested in.'

Peter couldn't suppress a half-smile as he addressed his colleague.

'I'm sure you do, Peter. If the new technology has given us anything to go on after your two-minute stint in Interview Room 12, then you've got something quite remarkable.'

'But look, before I show you the results, I'd like to run through the basic philosophy of the device with you. First of all, I believe it will totally preclude the need for us ever to use the polygraph again. And not before time. The lie-detector, as it has become commonly known, has been with us, in one guise or another, since the early part of the twentieth century which, for me, suggests it is well past its sell-by date.

'The company that has developed the new system is IntuTech, a small, but highly professional, neurotechnological enterprise on the southwest-coast. Their speciality is innovative work on linking the human neurological system, which you will know transmits and processes information received through our senses, to manmade neuro-network software designed to mimic the human model. In a crude sense, it is similar to the way computer technology engineers produced analogue to digital convertors many years' ago to enable them to function on digital platforms. And back again, of course.

'So, without getting into too much technological digi-speak, what our IntuTech friends have created is a digital conversion programme that will read human cortex-generated signals and transform them into a digital format. Which, in simple terms, means we can read other people's minds. Either in real-time or by recording data and transcribing it later.'

David sat motionless with a quizzical look on his face.

'Now, when I posed those two questions to George Cooper with the BG1 device – sorry, that's its technical name – it stands for Brain Game version one – suitably set to record his mental responses, I simply recorded his thoughts via software built into the dedicated smart watch I was wearing. Then I returned to my office to transcribe them.

'But, one more thing you need to know before I continue. You might already be aware of this but people, generally, think in either words or pictures – some will see in a mixture of the two but they are comparatively rare – so the BG1 software has to be primed to know which thinking format it needs to transcribe. Now, with our Mr. Cooper, it's all pictures so, rather than seeing a list of textual transcriptions on the computer screen, we get actual graphic images – like photographs.

'So, what you are about to see, and I'll reproduce the images onto my large wall screen over there, will be precisely what George was visualizing when he refused to verbally respond. Right, are you ready?'

'Wow, I don't know that I am, Peter – this sounds quite incredible. It's not April 1st' is it?' David added jokingly.

'Ha, ha, that's precisely what I said when it was first demonstrated to me. No, I kid you not, David, I am as gob-smacked as you are. However, shall we move on?'

'Yes, please, I'm sitting comfortably.'

'Well brace yourself, buddy, what you're about to see will play havoc with your powers of reasoning. Your logic circuits will start to update and remap themselves.'

Peter tapped a couple of times on the face of his watch and the "slide show" began to play. He had left the audio running so that David could relate to the timing of the suspect's visual responses and, as soon as Peter's first question regarding Cooper's supplier was heard, the image of the eastern European-looking individual immediately appeared on the screen. Peter clicked on PAUSE and looked round at David.

'That's Vladja Sekelsky. We've known about this operator for months but just can't track him down. From what little intel we have on him, it seems he's linked to some major eastern European players - could be a big catch if we manage to nail him. But, wow, what an image. This is truly amazing.'

'Well hold on, there's more – watch.'

Peter ran the transcription on and almost immediately heard himself asking, 'where will we be able to find this individual?'

And, without interruption, the dark maroon entrance door came to life on the screen.

'Number 42! That's magical.' said David. 'Not that I recognise the property but, at least it eliminates all other door numbers from our investigation. Peter, let me tell you, there is nothing, bar nothing, you could more wisely be spending your budget on. I am lost for words.'

'You and me, both, David. Anyway, that is it and I'm sure you now have more to go on than you did before my intervention. So, good luck with your ongoing investigations and do let me know if you come up with anything.'

'I sure will. Any chance of pinging these images over to me?'

'They'll be on your terminal before you arrive back at your office.'

'Thanks, Peter – big time. I'm sure we'll speak again soon.'

With that, David O'Conner left the room to make his way back with more than a positive spring in his step.

Peter stepped over to his favourite east-facing, panoramic window in search of further inspiration. What he had acquired from Richard Stewart was not even the tip of the iceberg when it came to BG1's further purchasing potential throughout the fifty-odd UK police forces. And he simply couldn't perceive of one single force choosing not to sign up. In fact, he wondered whether a Parliamentary law shouldn't be passed to deem it compulsory for all British law enforcement agencies to adopt the system. He was enjoying this immensely but what would he not give to swap shoes with Richard Stewart.

However, he appreciated that IntuTech's sales development programme wasn't of a direct concern to him – what he needed to concentrate his mind on, for the immediate future, was the number of additional user licences he should be applying for from Mr. Stewart. A question he found difficult to answer at this stage. It clearly called for a decision at the highest level and a full presentation to all senior officers at the soonest opportunity. He decided to have a word with the man himself.

'Richard, it's Peter Williams here – is it a good moment?'

'Of course, Peter – always good to hear from you. How is the new software going?'

'How is it going? I can tell you it's manna from heaven, the stuff of my dreams, a gift from on high and a godsend – all rolled into one. You can't begin to imagine how well this has gone down here.

'However, what I'm calling you for is to put you on notice that we will be requiring several more user licences in the very near future. I'm planning to hold a seminar here at the Yard to brief all interested parties on the functioning of BG1 and to establish precisely how many licences will be appropriate. This will be as soon as I can arrange it and I was wondering whether you would be available to come along and give a talk on the system's background – you know, and some instruction on its usage, maybe. As far as you're concerned, there're bound to be a number of orders placed immediately after - not to mention the interest that will be generated once the word gets out. In fact, I will be inviting several colleagues from neighbouring forces so, from a business point of view, the sky will be the limit. What do you say?'

Things were clearly moving apace for the IntuTech boss and the invitation was impossible to pass on.

'I'll be delighted to attend, Peter, thank you for the invitation. Just let me know when you plan to book the event and I'll drop everything to be with you.

'You, no doubt, have your own programme in mind for the evening but may I suggest we treat the audience to some actual real-time demonstrations. If you have one of those large TV monitors suitably positioned, it could prove to be an unforgettable event. So, it's a definite "yes"– just notify me of the date once you have it.'

Peter promptly set up a meeting with his immediate superior and put the question to him. He briefed him on the BG1 events to date and after the excitement died down it was suggested a more high-level, broad-reaching event should be held to enlighten forces far and wide.

Though the growth of the BG1 application throughout the country would hold only limited benefits for the Met, the two senior operators felt they had an almost moral duty to promote its usage.

Both agreed this was an excellent idea and duly booked the soonest available evening for the main auditorium at the King William V conference hall on the South Bank. Capacity was a little over two-and-a-half-thousand which the two officers felt could easily be achieved providing sufficient notices were posted ASAP. Once the details of BG1 were bandied around, they imagined the event could even be oversubscribed.

During the weeks leading up to the South Bank evening, Peter wasted no time in expanding his user licence to accommodate five more interrogators though he doubted that would prove sufficient in the long term. However, considering the speed with which interviews were now being conducted, it quickly became apparent that economies on a considerable scale were being made. No longer were investigators having to labour away, interview after interview, building up necessary levels of evidence to justify a suspect being brought before a court of law. One or, possibly, two short sessions were all that were needed. And, invariably, with so much indisputable proof either way in relation to whether, or not, the correct arrests had been made, solicitors were almost falling over themselves to persuade clients that a guilty plea was really their only option.

Also, with the accompanying increase in efficiencies predicted, once cases were set to reach the courts, the total funding structure of the legal industry in Britain was expected to be turned on its head.

If BG1 didn't lead to Richard Steward being awarded special recognition for services to science, services to industry and services to the British economy there would need to be a serious shake up in the whole UK honours system.

Invitations for the grand BG1 exposé were duly sent out to the heads of police forces throughout the length and breadth of the country as well as significant dignitaries closely associated with the British legal system: the Secretary of State for Justice, the Home Secretary and the Minister of State for Crime and Policing were just a few of the names on a guest list that would result in the BG1 message reaching everybody who was anybody. In addition, members of PA Media (once upon a time, the Press Association) and significant journalists from leading online news providers were offered a limited number of seats to assist in spreading the message to all relevant sections of the general public.

By the time the big day had arrived, Richard Stewart had acquired intellectual property rights for all related aspects of the BG1 design. The level of protection he had secured ensured his invention would be safe throughout significant parts of the developed world to provide him with the peace of mind necessary to continue with its development.

The King William V Conference Centre was buzzing with activity a good hour before the presentation was due to start and the anticipation evident on the faces of everyone in the vicinity was almost palpable.

It was a beautiful warm, still, autumn evening and the river Thames, glistening in the sun, appeared intent on lifting the collective air of optimism that pervaded the numerous guests standing around admiring its spectacle. Several hundred others were assembled in the vast reception area where drinks were being served and tickets being checked. The general aura surrounding the majestic assembly hall was more suggestive of a grand evening of entertainment rather than that of a pronouncement concerning an item of police equipment. But for Richard Stewart and Peter Williams, who stood chatting just along from the main entrance doors, the prospect of the event quickly turning into something more akin to the world premiere of a long-awaited, star-studded comedy movie looked more likely to be on the cards.

Although Peter's position at the Met had brought him ample experience when it came to the matter of public speaking, the subject was something Richard had little involvement in. But whatever he lacked in familiarity was outweighed many times over by his confidence in the product and a personal ego at having masterminded its development.

When the ten-minute signal echoed through the building's extensive public address system, tens of hundreds of guests simultaneously began to scramble for access to their seating locations. And in time-honoured tradition, almost every seat in the auditorium appeared, proudly, to accommodate its occupant for the evening with ample minutes to go before the curtains were due to be opened.

First to address the gathering was Sir Keith Wilkenshaw, the current Minister for Crime and Policing.

'Good evening my Lords, Ladies, Gentlemen and esteemed guests. I am privileged to have been invited here tonight to introduce you to a British invention that can only be described as *the* most innovative, advanced, revolutionary piece of equipment I have ever had the pleasure of setting my eyes, or, rather, my mind on. The product, which is the brainchild of a certain Mr. Richard Stewart, who will be introduced to you later, has been borne of such extraordinary ingeniousness that I doubt most of you will believe what you are about to witness. This is not a show exploiting the cunning expertise of the one-time, world famous escapologist, Harry Houdini, or a demonstration in possible mind-blowing trickery by the likes of history's more recent Uri Geller, but the serious development of a miraculous scientific device, totally free of deception, by a man, not possessive of strait-jacket circumvention powers or spoon-bending illusions, who is steeped in the highest levels of intellectual resourcefulness enabling him to deliver, to the country's law enforcement agencies, an instrument that will alter the world of criminal investigation forever. But before I ask Mr. Stewart to come to the microphone to explain the workings of his brilliant invention, I would like you to welcome the Home Secretary, Dr. Susan Reynolds, to say a few words.'

Sir Keith turned to face Dr. Reynolds and gave a discreet nod to indicate that the stage now belonged to her for the next few minutes.

The audience broke into loud applause at his introductory speech but one couldn't help feeling a large part of it was directed towards the yet-to-be-announced neurotechnological guest.

'Good evening all. I am also here tonight to observe the wonder of Mr. Richard Stewart's invention which, I have to say, I am yet to see demonstrated, but I would like to take the opportunity to celebrate his creation's predecessor, the polygraph, which has helped investigators solve crimes the world over since its American creators developed it in the early part of last century. It would be difficult to recall a device with a success record that compares with that which we have all grown to refer to as the lie-detector. But I fully understand and appreciate that its retirement party is well overdue and that it will, hopefully, show due magnanimity in allowing IntuTech's BG1 device to step up to the mark as a worthy successor. So, I will say no more now other than to ask you to put your hands together to welcome, on stage, Mr. Richard Stewart.'

Chapter 23

The full two-and-a-half-thousand-strong audience broke into rapturous applause as Richard calmly walked up to the microphone.

'You are so kind, really. This is not the sort of activity I am used to but I would like you all to know how much I appreciate you making the effort to be here with me tonight. My comfort zone, like most computer techies, extends little further than a one metre radius around my office workstation so you will understand that I am now having to perform in an environment that is something like the polar opposite of what I am accustomed to.

Richard was feeling somewhat ambivalent about facing an audience comprising of so many highly esteemed individuals. While he had acknowledged that he himself was amid unfamiliar surroundings he was also aware that each of his twenty-five hundred onlookers appeared, quite justifiably, in awe of him.

'Anyway, before I begin, I want to assure you that I am no magician. Although this stage and, indeed, you, the audience, appear more suited to welcoming, maybe, valued members of the Magic Circle, what I am actually here for is to brief you on a new creation that I am confident will prove to play a very positive and very functional role in fighting crime. And not only that, it will lead to unprecedented economies for our law enforcement agencies which, in turn, will result in savings for us all.

'However, enough of my rambling, I would now like to carry out a few demonstrations.'

Richard went on to invite members of the audience to take part in a number of live presentations in which both word- and picture-thoughts were shown to be gleaned from unverbalized thoughts. And transcriptions of both formats were streamed to a variety of large format screens positioned at various points around the auditorium. At every new revelation a loud, collective gasp could be heard from the audience presumably in sheer disbelief of what they were witnessing. So revolutionary was the IntuTech invention that, planned or not, the evening provided the esteemed audience with both education and entertainment in equal measure.

It would be easy to believe that there was little doubt in every audience member's mind that the Magic Circle would have had a difficult job competing with Richard's BG1 demonstrations for sheer entertainment value alone. But with the knowledge that there was no sleight of hand involved, the evening provided a truly remarkable spectacle.

At the end of the programme, every one of the two-and-a-half-thousand guests rose to their feet to give Richard a standing ovation. There were the customary calls for "more" but instead of returning to appease the crowd with further demonstrations, Richard simply walked to the microphone and suggested that any number of encores would be seen to be performed in the coming months in law enforcement establishments throughout the country. The audience responded with more applause.

As the hall eventually began to empty and the four uniformed stage technicians started work on breaking down the various pieces of equipment, an atmosphere of heightened enthusiasm amongst everyone within earshot seemed to remain. And, as one particular stagehand, who was carrying a huge, reeled cable, walked past Richard, he couldn't resist setting the item down and stopping to shake the inventor's hand vigorously. Everyone, it would seem, was in total awe of the IntuTech executive.

There was no doubt that he had gained a huge following in just a couple of hours and had to admit to himself that he couldn't wait to see what the media made of the demonstrations in the following morning's news feeds. He felt like a celebrity for sure.

Then, as the technician continued on his way, Richard turned at random to one of the remaining guests to remark on the strength of the stagehand's grip suggesting it was, no doubt, the result of his excitement following the evening's events. Even the hired staff had thoroughly enjoyed the occasion.

Half-an-hour later, Richard was installed in his taxi and heading for his hotel. The evening had been every bit the success he had hoped for and he felt it doubtful that he'd be coming back down to earth any time soon. But before he could think about moving on to the next chapter, he needed a good night's sleep.

The hotel was everything one comes to expect from a central London overnight facility: compact, traditional, meticulously clean and hellishly expensive. But the latter feature hardly needed to bother the inventor who, by the most modest of estimations, was heading, confidently, towards the realms of society's financial elite. Whether he'd planned it or not, Richard was looking forward to a future of fiscal security.

He checked in at the ground floor reception desk which was being manned by a cheerful-looking, young Scandinavian lady and collected his door fob before making his way over to the lift car. On entering his room on the second floor, he dropped his bags, kicked off his shoes and collapsed on the king-size bed. But, shattered though he was, it wasn't Richard's style to doss down on the covers fully-clothed for the night so he quickly summoned the strength to regain a standing position in order to undress and shower before turning in.

But out of the corner of his eye, he spotted the mini bar. Although he was not one to turn to alcohol on anything of a regular basis, the sight of a dozen or so bottles and cans of whatever he could wish for was just too tempting to pass on. He pulled out a single measure of a very appealing 25-year-old whisky, added a little ginger ale and two small ice cubes and had little trouble in convincing himself that, as well as helping him drop off to sleep, he deserved every last millilitre.

Having downed the beverage almost in one go, he carefully removed his suit jacket, loosened and took off his tie then systematically attended to unfastening his cufflinks. He'd gone to considerable trouble to present himself to the guests in a manner he felt befitted his status. But as he fiddled with his right cuff something felt wrong. In a mild panic he lifted the sleeve and found his smart watch had disappeared. He was immediately transformed to full panic mode. How could this be? The strap was fashioned from Kevlar – one of the strongest manmade materials available and secured by means of a lockable, stainless-steel clasp. The strap was of the continuous type in that it passed beneath the watch's body in one piece to preclude the need for sprung fixings. Then he noticed a tiny nick in the skin at the base of his hand just below the first metacarpal. He touched it and felt a slight soreness but no more than that. What could have caused this? There were no sharp edges on the watch. And it would have been impossible for the item to have come undone under its own volition. He knew for certainty that it was secured in place during the final demonstration only minutes before the end of the event.

Any signs of tiredness that may have been present prior to the discovery of the missing watch disappeared in an instant. Richard was as wide awake and as concerned about the loss as one could possibly imagine.

Without wasting time, he called the conference hall's security office number and was pleased when it answered almost immediately.

'King William V Conference Centre Security Office, Jim speaking – how can I help you?'

'Oh hi, Jim, this is Richard Stewart – I took part in tonight's presentation.'

'Yes, sir, I know who you are.'

'Oh, okay. Look, I'm sorry to trouble you but, on entering my hotel suite, I have discovered that my smart watch is missing. It was on my wrist at ten-thirty when the event began to draw to a close so I wonder if you might be good enough to carry out a check around the vicinity of the stage and, maybe, out towards the point at which I would have met with my taxi driver.'

'I'm sorry to hear that, sir, but, of course, I will walk those areas myself immediately and call you back in a couple of minutes.'

'That is kind of you, Jim. Thank you.'

While he waited for his cell phone to ring, Richard paced the floor of his suite in anticipation of the security manager's return call. But each minute he waited seemed to take an hour to pass. Then, true to his word, his instrument beeped before ten-minutes had elapsed.

'Hello Mr. Stewart. Unfortunately, I've found nothing. I've walked over the areas you mentioned several times and I am satisfied that the watch isn't there. Did you, perhaps, visit the washroom before leaving?'

'No, I simply left the stage, chatted to a number of people by the left-hand steps then made my way on to the taxi pickup point.'

'Well, I'm really sorry to hear that, sir, but I'll tell you what I'll do for you. I'll talk to each of my three stage technicians and ask them to carry out a more thorough search. Do you mind if I call you back in about half-an-hour with the result?'

'No, of course not, Jim. That will be most helpful of you. Thank you.'

Richard returned to his pacing routine feeling a little more anxious than he had the previous time but he had no option other than to exercise patience until the phone sounded again. He started to count his paces in a desperate attempt to divert his mind from the possibility that the watch would not be retrieved: one . . . two . . . three . . . four. Then something suddenly brought him up sharp. He was sure Jim mentioned three stage technicians. He was a mathematician and registering numbers, any numbers, unimportant numbers, just came naturally to him. When he walked along a pavement he'd automatically count the number of paving stones he trod. When he travelled on a train he'd count the number of bridges he passed beneath. When he listened to music he'd even count the number of bars. He didn't consciously count them rather than engage a sort of built-in, mental abacus that operated independently of his cognizance. It was just the way he was wired. To Richard, the world comprised of nothing that couldn't be counted. Its population, its surface area, the number of known animal species, the years since the Big Bang. In theory, even the grains of sand could be calculated though in practice only an estimation would be of any interest.

So, he had no doubt at all that Jim had suggested there were three technicians. But he also had no doubt that he'd counted four when he was standing around chatting at the end of the presentation. No doubt at all. He could even offer a brief description of the four individuals were he to be asked. He continued pacing with this in his mind until the phone rang for a second time. Without thinking, he hastily stabbed at the ANSWER button eager to learn the result of Jim's more detailed investigation.

'Richard here, Jim – how did it go?'

'Hello Mr. Stewart. I'm afraid we've had no luck. We've combed the whole area as best we can and have come up with nothing. I've even checked with the reception desk to see if it may have been handed in but still nothing. And the centre's principal, who's still on site, also knows nothing of it. I really am sorry but I don't believe there's anything else I can do.'

'Well, thank you, Jim, I'm sorry to have caused you and your staff any trouble. I will examine alternative avenues myself in the morning. But, before you go, would you mind if I asked you a question?'

'Fire away, Mr. Stewart, I am at your service.'

'Thank you, Jim. You mentioned your three stage technicians during our conversation but I feel certain I counted four when I was standing around chatting just after the event finished. Are you sure there wasn't a fourth staff member in the team?'

'As sure as the day is long, sir. I only have three registered on my books and all of them clocked in tonight with the prospect of it being such a full house.'

'Well, that's a mystery to me, Jim. Would you mind if I enquire further into their descriptions – I know I only saw them briefly but I feel I could account for each employee were you to roughly describe them.'

'That's no trouble, sir. No trouble at all. Right, there's Rodney – he's in his mid-thirties, short and a bit on the podgy side and an out-and-out cockney. Then there's Steve who you couldn't miss – forty-odd, slim as a rake with long, blond hair tied back in a ponytail. And lastly, Abraham, the loveliest, most friendly guy you'll ever wish to meet. He's a Jamaican – comes from Port Antonio. You couldn't fail to remember him.'

These descriptions all made perfect sense to Richard. He could clearly visualize each character's depiction and was sure he would be able to pick them out in a police identity parade should that be necessary.

'But there was a tall, well-built man in, let me think, probably his late twenties who stopped to talk to me. He was wearing the same uniform as the others and was carrying a large, coiled-up mains cable, I believe – wasn't English – middle-eastern, maybe – spoke with a deep voice. Does that sound like someone you might know, Jim?'

'That's a new one on me, sir. Certainly, no one I've ever taken on. Mind you, the locker room has several bits and pieces of uniform lying around – I suppose anyone could have borrowed some. We don't spend too much time worrying about security for that room as there really isn't anything of any value left in it.'

'Jim, you've been most helpful, thank you. And I really shouldn't keep you from your work any longer – you've a home and a bed to go to.'

'That's okay, Mr. Stewart. I'm sorry not to have been more helpful. You have a good night's sleep yourself, sir.'

'That's kind of you – you sleep tight as well, Jim. Goodnight to you.'

Richard flopped down on the bed in an unconscious symbolic gesture of hopelessness.

This was a problem, he thought. A big problem. If the smart watch were to find its way into the wrong hands security could be very much at risk. On the other hand, were it to have been simply swept up and shovelled into a trash bin before being taken off to a landfill site there would be nothing to worry about. But the fact that it really couldn't have just fallen off his wrist was of real concern. And, if he was to be honest with himself, it was looking far more likely that the watch was removed from his wrist by a professional thief wielding a sharp instrument. A sharp instrument that had, accidentally, nicked his skin in the process. There seemed no getting away from the thought that the fourth stage technician with the vigorous handshake was the most likely culprit.

Richard's mind was in something of a whirl. Although the watch had been deactivated with him having meticulously attended to all of the strict logging off procedures, the fact remained that the BG1 software resided intact on the device. And, as a highly trained, neurotechnological engineer, he was aware that nothing is one-hundred-percent foolproof. His only hope was that the watch was on its way to landfill and that the incident regarding the fourth stagehand had some other, yet unknown, plausible explanation.

Either way, he needed to alert the authorities and reckoned a call to Peter Williams would be the most sensible move at this time.

This was not part of the plan. Definitely not. Concluding the evening with the loss of the watch and the need to disturb Peter Williams at such an unsociable hour had cancelled out all of the positives the event had thus far provided.

'Peter, I'm so sorry to disturb you at this hour but I've something rather important to report.'

'Oh, hi Richard. Say nothing of it – I'm here to help. What is it?'

Richard gave a detailed account of what had happened over the course of the past hour-and-a-half and asked what Peter thought might be the best course of action.

'Mmm, this is difficult, Richard, very difficult. It clearly looks as though we have a phoney stagehand at play here and, from what you say of your conversation with Jim, security measures, where the locker room is concerned, were far too lax. Hopefully, the individual concerned was merely wanting to relieve you of your wristwatch and will simply dispose of it in the nearest garbage bin once he finds it impossible to activate.

'But we have to be realistic and consider, also, the

possibility of him being a professional with an agenda that might involve some kind of intellectual property sabotage. And, in which case, whether he's working alone or as part of a larger network.

'So, first things first. I will contact the head of security for the whole South Bank complex and request copies of the digital video cameras' footage that will have filmed the movements of every individual entering and leaving the hall tonight. I will then have one of my teams scrutinize the images in an attempt to obtain a still image of the, now infamous, fourth stagehand. But, Richard, with the best will in the world, this isn't going to happen until the morning so I suggest you get your head down and grab yourself a decent night's sleep after what has been a pretty hectic few hours.

'And try not to worry too much – the likelihood is that the guy was no more than a common thief who'll be known to us on the system. I'm sure we'll have an officer knocking on his door within a matter of hours.

'I'll put the call through to security now and will, hopefully, have an image on my desk first thing in the morning.'

'Peter, you have the perfect bedside manner – thank you. You've put my mind at rest and I will take your advice and get myself some quality shut-eye. Goodnight, Peter – sleep well.'

'You too, Richard.'

Chapter 24

Richard woke to a bright autumn morning with the sun's rays casting a swathe of partially diffused light through the windows' stylish venetian blinds. For some innate reason, he enjoyed the light reflected by the inwardly-upturned slats which seemed to offer a cooler, fresher, radiance to the room. But, once he'd opened his eyes fully, thoughts of the previous evening's events came flooding back to him. The elation following the extraordinarily successful presentation and the devastating disappointment at losing the smart watch became all too real again.

A dark, threatening cloud had descended over his room to offer a welcome he'd really rather reject.

But was he worrying unduly? It was true that the instrument could be wending its way to the landfill site, never to be seen again. And it was equally true that it could be in the hands of a network of individuals hell-bent on hacking into the software. The actual hardware value of the watch was negligible as Richard had secured a supply chain that could deliver at a highly competitive price in almost any quantities with no lead-in time to speak of. The subsequent uploading of the BG1 software would take place at IntuTech's headquarters in no time at all with an unlimited number of watches wirelessly linked to receive data simultaneously.

No, the potential problem was that, with someone possessive of the mind of a digital genius, Richard had no way of guaranteeing that the system's random mix of symmetrical and asymmetrical encryption algorithms couldn't be hacked. The odds were absurdly high in favour of the software being secure but Richard felt uncomfortable with any level of doubt above zero-percent.

Though for the moment he could do nothing. Peter Williams had the predicament firmly in hand and who could ask for a more reliable and resourceful individual to take charge of a case like this? No, he was in the safest hands imaginable and should put the matter to the back of his mind and get on with his day.

It was not yet seven-thirty and his solar express wasn't due to leave Paddington until 10.15 am so there was time to relax, wander down to the restaurant for breakfast, call a cab and check in with Jennie and Kate before commencing his return passage.

'Come on mate, there's nothing to worry about. You're being unduly pessimistic. The guy was no more than a common thief getting his kicks out of the whole masquerade business. Be honest with yourself, did he really look as though he had the intelligence to know what could be gained from a watch that looked like any other? He's probably using it to check the time.'

At 09.15 am he stepped into his black London taxi and was heartily greeted by his cabbie for the short trip.

'Morning guv'nor, I'm Charlie, where would you like me to take you?'

'Good morning, Charlie. I'm Richard and Paddington Station would be just perfect.'

'Your wish is my command, guv. And what makes you want to leave this beautiful city on a lovely morning like this, if you don't mind me asking?'

'Oh, nothing more interesting than business, Charlie. I was attending a conference last night that finished too late for me to return to my home on the southwest-coast.'

'Well, that's all right then. I don't s'pose it was that affair down on the South Bank that all the radio stations are on about this morning. Don't know if you heard about it but, Gordon Bennett, the things these scientists are getting up to these days. I mean, blimey, with the Bill having stuff like that, we'd all better keep our noses clean, I say.'

Richard was aware that bad news travelled fast – everyone knew that. But this was anything but bad news. Wow, he'd certainly made his mark on the capital.

Charlie bade Richard farewell as he brought his cab to a standstill by the entrance to the station's main concourse and made his way up to the coffee shop opposite platform twelve. With a cup of freshly-ground Hawaii Kona in a recyclable, synthetic cup, he sat down for the few minutes he had to spare and thought he'd call Jennie to see how things were looking in Falcombe.

'Hi Richard – how did it go? I've had your conference on my mind all night.'

'Oh, largely excellent, Jennie. Really excellent, except for a small hitch at the end of the evening. But no need to go into that now. I know it's still early but is there anything happening at base yet?'

'Well, nothing other than fifty-seven, no, it's now sixty-two, emails on the order purchasing account. I imagine they're a result of the presentation.'

'Oh, wow. I hadn't expected that. Maybe you could leave what you're doing, open them and draw up a summary for me to look at when I arrive back – which should be around lunchtime.'

'Yes, of course, Richard, leave that to me.'

'Okay, Jennie, good to catch up – I'll see you in a couple of hours, or so.'

Things were moving apace and Richard imagined each email was likely to include an attachment with a requisition order for the BG1 system. Sixty-two possible orders. Wow, jackpot time! The revenue from this volume of sales alone in no more than twelve hours could, if he wished, fund his retirement. But BG1 was not about no longer needing to work, it was about contributing to society. Making the UK a safer place. A more desirable place in which to live. Richard realised all too clearly that there was more to a career, a vocation even, than simply bagging a pay cheque at the end of each month.

But Jennie's good news was marred by his thoughts constantly harking back to the ominous fourth stagehand. Who was he and how was he able to act so quickly when the product barely had sufficient time to make itself known? If only he'd exercised more caution and taken the watch's security more seriously. It really was so remiss of him to have treated the instrument like any other timepiece. "Gordon Bennett", as Charlie would have exclaimed, what he was wearing on his wrist held the key to his future.

Haaziq Suleiman's parents had come to England as refugees in the early part of the twenty-first century. His father, a journalist from Damascus, needed desperately, to escape the Bashar al-Assad, Syrian regime following fallacious reports that he'd planned to condemn the leader's human rights record.

At that time, the attraction of resettling, by whatever means, in the UK, the land of peace, prosperity and opportunity, was nothing less than a dream. And Haaziq's father was a resourceful man who'd stop at nothing to achieve a secure home for his family. He found a route by a means of which he vowed never to breathe a word and his resolve remained steadfast throughout his days no matter how challenging they proved to be.

But settling in England had its problems too. Haaziq was a highly-gifted child who fell, all too easily, into the wrong company in his adoptive east London home. By the age of twelve, he had become a master petty thief pilfering and selling on any number of items of sufficient value to help put food on the table for his struggling family. A short visit to a local supermarket would yield enough women's purses, men's wallets or valuable items of supermarket stock to supplement his father's measly income as he moved from one menial job to another. It was all too easy for his parents to turn a blind eye to the rewards of Haaziq's daily excursions.

By the age of eighteen, his daily trading was easily earning him a lifestyle that was the envy of his friends and acquaintances. He drove an expensive German car and clothed himself in the finest Italian fashions. While class A drugs figured largely in his choice of commodities, whatever he turned his hand to never failed to pay dividends. And most importantly, no one, but no one, could ever manage to pin anything on him. Haaziq was simply untouchable.

But things had changed for Haaziq. The level he was now operating at brought him new clients. Wealthier clients. And he began to learn the ground rules: the higher the level the more remote the network. No longer was he aware of who he was working for. No longer did he know where his earnings were coming from. He was given commissions to fulfil. Commissions that could involve travel. Long distance travel, even. But he still saw no one. Talked to no one. Received his instructions in the most bizarre of ways. Notes scribbled on newspapers left in waste bins. Coded messages forming parts of travel departure boards at airports. Even cryptic communications hidden in social media ads. His orders could be anywhere but he never failed to locate them. One hidden message on a motorway matrix board would lead him to another on a discarded food wrapper. But he could never let his guard down for one second or it would be considerably more than the next assignment he would stand to lose.

Haaziq had brought himself up the hard way, the tough way. He'd learnt every trick in the book to maintain his survival and nobody but nobody knew the ways of the espionage world better than he did.

All in all, Haaziq's attention to detail guaranteed him that no trace of his activities, or his identity, found their way onto law enforcement agency records. Fingerprints, video images, DNA mapping, retinal scans – you name it, the police knew nothing about it.

So, with fifty-percent of his latest commission complete, all he needed to do was follow the next hidden instruction and his assignment would be fulfilled. The system worked so well because all, bar none, of the players were top-level professionals in their own fields. And not only that – the fact that they succeeded in operating undercover while undertaking duties demanded of them by their respective employers, deemed them superior to those simply carrying out everyday tasks in an honest fashion. Haaziq and his fellow networkers were the top dogs in their fields. Were their responsibilities to have been legitimate they'd have achieved PhDs or similar levels of qualification in their respective disciplines. But that's not the way of the world.

Within twenty-four hours of the close of the IntuTech presentation, Richard's smart watch was locked away in a high-security vault nearly two-thousand miles away without a landfill site in view.

Daniel Levin was a childhood genius. A child prodigy. At the age of twelve he was tested to have an IQ of one-hundred-and-sixty-two - two points higher than that of Albert Einstein. Born into a family of peasant farmers, nobody knew quite what to do with him. But news of his intellect travelled and by the time he was fourteen a small governmental delegation arrived at his cottage, in the small village where he'd grown up, to persuade his parents that it would be in his best interests to move to special accommodation in the capital where he would be trained for a career in the National Security Service. They felt they had no choice in the matter. But their patriotism served to value their son's fortuity and they duly bade him farewell in the hope that they would, one day, hear his name mentioned in high circles.

Daniel worked diligently as a trainee neurotechnologist at the State Academy of Sciences and received a salary he had no reason to believe wasn't commensurate with his position. By the time he was twenty-five, he became one of the youngest ever winners of the Samsonian Platinum Medal, the highest accolade awarded by the academy. But, by virtue of his extraordinary gifts, his future firmly resided in the control of his employer. Daniel would never be granted the option to travel the globe to achieve his rightful place as a world-leading scientist.

His superiors had chosen wisely. Not only was Daniel a top notch operator, he bore all the personality characteristics of an unambitious young man happy to deliver the products of his genius without demanding anything much by way of materialistic rewards in return. He was never likely to rattle his cage - they knew their business well.

But since the age of fourteen, he'd not known any different so life in the ten-storied, state-owned apartment where he was accommodated appeared to suit him perfectly. Daniel was quiet and retiring by nature and introverted to the point that socialising didn't feature on his radar. But his rooms were sufficiently spacious for him not to feel he was being taken advantage of and he was never expected to contribute to their maintenance other than by attending to regular housekeeping routines. In fact, the furnishings provided for him were more than adequate for his needs and the housing authorities had even stocked his bookshelves with volumes of literature ideally suited to his intellectual, recreational requirements: Shakespeare, Dostoevsky, Kafka, Steinbeck, they were all there. And when he fancied relaxing by listening to music, he had a wide selection of recordings by composers able to satisfy his every mood: Bach, Rachmaninoff, Mozart, Wagner. They had thought of everything.

Two days after the fourth stagehand incident in London, Daniel was approached by his immediate academy professor as he sat down at his desk first thing one morning. He was told to leave everything he was currently working on and attend to a task that was of the utmost importance. The directive had apparently come from the government itself and Daniel's progress would be closely monitored from the highest administrative level.

The professor placed a smart watch of regular appearance in front of Daniel and informed him that the software contained within the instrument was to be thoroughly hacked. And once hacked, the binary code should be formatted in such a way that it would be compatible with the operating systems currently running on the world's three major cell phone platforms. The professor then handed Daniel examples of the latest models of each of the phones.

With no hint of any kind of a facial expression, he held the three objects one at a time in front of him and appeared to regard the exercise as wholly unexceptional. All in a Daniel Levin's day's work.

He was told that the administration was granting him a generous period during which he was expected to complete the assignment. He had exactly two weeks. Furthermore, he was told that, due to the high priority that was attached to the undertaking, he would be working throughout extended hours and sleeping on the office couch rather than returning to his apartment at the end of each day. Food and drink would be brought to him at prescribed times and he should contact his immediate superior without leaving his office should he want for anything before the two weeks were up.

Daniel thanked the professor for selecting him amongst the many technologists working at the academy and promised to get to work straightaway.

Kim Hyori had graduated with a BSc (Hons) degree in computer sciences from one of South Korea's leading universities. She had grown to love her native country and, upon passing out, she chose to take up a post lecturing in the respective faculty at the university in which she had spent the past four years of her education. As an independent young woman, life in the capital city suited Kim Hyori perfectly. Her position at the university rewarded her handsomely and enabled her to lead a lifestyle very similar to that with which she might have enjoyed in the world of commerce.

South Korean fashions had been heavily influenced by the West in recent times and the culture, in general, had a positive cosmopolitan feel to it. The strong network of friends and family members she had left behind in the small village of Jeonpo Dong where she had grown up, not far from the southern city of Busan, kept in constant touch with her and she always imagined she'd settle back there at some future date. But, for now, life was good and the busy circle of friends and acquaintances she had built up in the short time she'd lived in the city, more than fulfilled her social needs.

Life for Kim Hyori was close to idyllic. Her pay grade at the university was commensurate with the final grades she'd been awarded upon graduation, her apartment had been furnished and equipped with the latest styles and technological devices and her future career prospects couldn't have looked healthier.

However, while she was taking a regular class at the campus

one morning, she was interrupted by a university official who entered the room and suggested she should go straight to the principal's office where some important information was awaiting her. The official was happy to take over tuition in the classroom until the end of the lesson.

Kim Hyori was intrigued to learn what it was that should so urgently concern her and immediately made her way to the university's administration block.

'Good morning Kim Hyori.' said the principal. 'May I introduce you to Garry Chaplin? He has come here especially to meet with you and to offer you a position in the city where you will hold the post of sub-technical under-manager to the development manager at Kangjeon Communications. I will now leave you to discuss the matter by yourselves.'

'Kim Hyori, I am honoured to meet you.' began the visitor. 'As you well know, Kangjeon is the leading organisation responsible for the manufacture and marketing of the world's most highly successful mobile telephones. The fulfilment of your position will not be subject to the usual application processes as it is considered that the qualifications and experience you hold are more than adequate for you to discharge the duties that will be required of you.

'Unfortunately you will not have a choice as to whether the position is to your liking and you will be starting your employment with Kangjeon next Monday morning. All necessary travel and accommodation arrangements will be made and paid for by your new employer and you will be required to comply with its strict contract of employment. I have a copy here on the desk for you to sign. Please use this pen.

'And please take note that you are not to mention this

meeting or your association with me to anyone if you value the lives of your family members in Jeonpo Dong. Is that understood?'

Out of the blue, she found herself in a situation that one could only imagine taking place in a movie. This couldn't be the real world, surely, she thought. But there was no evidence of a prank of any kind and this Chaplin guy was nothing but serious. Calmly threatening.

Kim Hyori was staggered. Lost for words. This gentleman was clearly not of South Korean ethnicity but appeared, instead, to be associated with some foreign culture where the breaching of human rights was not just an issue but a way of life. Where was he from and how did he gain entry into her place of work? She'd known nothing like this since working in the capital and had taken the human rights horror stories she'd heard about in various parts of the world with a pinch of salt. However, it was very clear that she had no option other than to conform with the directive and prepare to start a new life at a moment's notice. Kim Hyori duly signed the contract and was told a copy would be emailed to her within the hour.

Chapter 25

Kim Hyori climbed into the taxi that awaited her outside her apartment block at 08.30 am the following Monday morning and settled into her seat in readiness for the drive to her new place of work. She had thoroughly read the contract, several times over, during the course of the week since signing it in Garry Chaplin's presence. It was certainly no ordinary contract of employment. In fact, it wasn't a contract of employment at all, rather a set of instructions she was duty bound to obey if she wished to avoid consequences she'd prefer not to think about. In short, she was now working as an agent of some kind. An agent working for another government. An agent engaged on a mission to infiltrate the cell phone manufacturing giants operation to carry out the demands of a superior of whom she knew nothing. At the present time, she was unaware of the nature of the demands but was told she would receive the relevant information as and when it was deemed necessary.

This was a turn in her life she'd had no way of being prepared for. She had no allies. No means of contacting the authorities without the organisation under which she was being controlled being aware. Everything about her added up to her being a perfect catch.

All she knew, for the time being, was that a car would be waiting for her outside her home – the car in which she was now travelling. The driver of the vehicle had been furnished with a full description of her and was instructed to deliver her to the Seoul headquarters of Kangjeon Communications.

During the course of her deployment, she was to behave in a manner fitting for a senior executive and to take special care to socialise with colleagues in the same way one would expect a normal employee to do. She had been assigned living accommodation in Seoul's Gangnam district where she would enjoy exclusive use of a luxury penthouse apartment fully equipped to facilitate entertaining friends and acquaintances at her leisure. The lease on her present, rented accommodation would be terminated by others with all personal belongings transferred to her new home before she took up residence that day.

A detailed description of her assumed identity was listed out in an easily memorized fashion within the wording of her contract and she was instructed to recite the list to herself once every half-hour to avoid being found out.

A bank account was opened for her, in a fake surname, and her "employer" would be depositing funds representing a salary on the first day of every month. At no time would she be allowed to make contact with her family and friends who were, largely, situated in and around the south-eastern city of Busan, some 340 km away.

The drive proved uneventful but it enabled Kim Hyori to relax and mentally prepare for her new life. She had been promised that the assignment would be likely to last no longer than twelve months but, depending on certain possible events, her deployment could be terminated in half that time. An agent would be in constant touch with her and meetings would be arranged at regular intervals to closely monitor the success of the mission. The identity of the agent would remain confidential at all times.

To all intents and purposes, her new place of "employment" appeared as a perfectly normal career step and it was difficult for her to recognise any discomfit associated with the subterfuge she'd clearly got herself caught up in.

On arrival at Kangjeon, she was ushered up to a small office on the fourteenth floor and introduced to a stern looking man - possibly in his mid-fifties - wearing a dark business suit. He asked her, quite politely, to sit down on one of two chairs arranged to face each other by the window before positioning himself opposite her and looking her straight in the eye. Kim Hyori imagined he was another agent.

'Kim Hyori, welcome to Kangjeon Communications. I will be your contact, probably, for the duration of your mission here. If you have read your contract thoroughly, you will know that you will not be employed by Kangjeon but by a foreign government. This is an arrangement that will work much better for you.

'You will start work this morning after you have reported to the head of the Instrument Marketing and Formatting Division who controls the final preparation of the company's ubiquitous range of kCell mobile telephones. She will provide you with full details of everything you will need to know and I will be in touch with you, at least, on a daily basis to ensure you will be able to discharge your duties in the desired fashion.

'You are to assume that nobody at Kangjeon will know who you are working for and, throughout your term of office with the organisation, you will behave in a manner commensurate with that of an authentic employee. If you should fail to act in a convincing way at any time, I will be made aware of the fact and you will be removed from your duties without further notice. Please take my words seriously, Kim Hyori - there is no room for negotiation here, I'm afraid.'

Her new life could have come straight out of an Ian Fleming novel.

'Now, your job description. You will be engaged as a senior employee working in the department where the telephones are finally configured in readiness for export to their country of destination. As you can imagine, Kangjeon telephones are exported to virtually every sovereign state in the world.

'Just prior to the point at which the phones are sent for automated packing, a final check is carried out to see that all relevant software and accompanying application icons have been uploaded thereby rendering the instrument ready to be put into service. This process is, understandably, carried out by automatons under the control of the senior computer technicians. Kangjeon employs one technician for each country of destination and all other employees concerned with other aspects of production are accountable to these senior technicians. You will be one of the senior technicians and your responsibility will be for one sovereign state and one sovereign state only: the United Kingdom.

'And while you will be initially trained by a safe employee

to understand, precisely, the specification of the phones destined for the UK, you will receive further instructions concerning the surreptitious uploading of one additional piece of software. You do not need to know the nature of this software but you will be required to ensure that no application icon will be programmed to appear on the device's screen at the time of shipping. At a predetermined date, long after it has been commissioned by its end user in the UK, an appropriate icon will appear on the screen and the software will be available for use. Full instructions on its use will be included with the application.'

It wasn't easy for Kim Hyori to imagine what it was she was actually delivering to the UK customers. The phones were patently in good order and able to function exactly as one would expect. What could it possibly be that she was helping to ship to an unwitting clientele? No matter how long she dwelled on the question she was convinced she had no means of acquiring a logical answer.

'You will be responsible for seeing that the process takes place under your control at your designated computer terminal which will have been suitably primed before you take up your position. A simple piece of control software will be available to you for checking, each hour, that the phones being sent to final packing will meet with this specification. If you ever feel part of this system has been compromised in any way, you will simply apply a keystroke on your keyboard which will render the whole process null and void. It will leave no trace of the operation able to be detected by anybody at Kangjeon. If this should occur, we will be aware of the action you will have taken immediately.

'Furthermore, you will have partial control over updating

processes that Kangjeon programme for existing kCells currently in use in the UK. When these updates are due to be implemented, you are to ensure that the same software being applied to the new phones is duly included in the process. Once again, this software will be primed with a future activation date unknown to both you and the end user.

'Finally, when we decide that your purpose has been served here, you will be removed from your position and taken to a new apartment where, once again, your personal property will have been transferred. Our agents will see to this.

'That is all I need to tell you for now, Kim Hyori, but you are welcome to question any of the points raised during our regular communications. However, you will not know when my next contact with you will take place so be ready at all times to receive either a message or a voice call from me.

'Is everything clear?'

'Yes, sir, I think I understand everything fully but I will run over your instructions in my head and question you on anything I am unclear about when you next make contract.'

'I'm pleased to hear it, Kim Hyori. A colleague is waiting outside the door now and he will escort you to your new office. When you finish this afternoon, he will be waiting for you outside the main reception and you will be driven to the luxurious living quarters we have organised for you as part of your package. But, before you go, are you sure you don't have any immediate queries?'

'Thank you but, no. You have made everything very clear, sir.'

She felt defenceless, unable to contemplate an escape plan. Intellectually, these people were so far ahead of her she clearly had no choice but to play ball. To go along with their demands in the hope that she would eventually be released from their grip and allowed to return to the society she so desperately yearned for.

Kim Hyori was duly taken to her office where she was to await further instructions from her immediate superior before starting work.

'Rick, how are things going, my friend?'

The voice on the other end of the phone was that of Richard's one-time superior, Lukas Hoffman.

'Things are absolutely fine, Luke - it's so good to hear from you. How is life treating you?'

'Oh, my life has been unbelievably hectic since the launch of OT3. I could really be doing with some of your input if I'm to be totally honest. But, no worries, I'll manage one way or another. I called for nothing special really – just sitting here mulling things over in my head. How do you fancy meeting up some time to catch up on where we're both at?'

'Sounds good to me, Luke. When were you thinking?'

'Well, I won't be terribly far from you on Wednesday, how about lunch at the Harbour Café – say 12.30 pm?'

'Suits me fine – I'll see you there.'

'Lukas and Richard, welcome - I haven't seen you around here for some time – been wondering what'd happened to you.' said Freddie as soon as he spotted the two familiar customers.

'We're hard at work, Freddie – not like you just wandering around from table to table in between gazing out over the harbour.' Lukas jibed.

'He's kidding, Freddie, I'm sure you put in every bit as good a shift as the two of us put together.' added Richard.'

'Well, I don't know about that but it's good of you to mention it, Richard. Anyway, what can I get you, gentlemen?'

They placed their orders and, as the affable waiter walked away, they turned towards one another eager to learn how their respective projects were going.

If the truth be known, the two guys were missing each other's company, comradeship. They'd worked so closely together sharing the same aims and expectations that their individual pursuits, though lucrative and technologically satisfying, lacked a certain degree of brotherly support.

'So, tell me, Rick, what's the current state of play with that brainchild of yours? I've heard, through the grapevine, that things are moving along at apace.'

'They certainly are, Luke – don't really have time for anything else these days. You probably know that I reprogrammed the software from scratch to enable it to operate without the need for an implant and, frankly, I've not looked back since the day I was granted approval to market the system to the UK law enforcement establishments. How about you?'

'Likewise, since that evening in Brussels when I successfully demonstrated that I had a unique solution for the world's visually impaired, it's been absolutely manic.'

'That's marvellous, Luke, I'm so pleased for you.'

'Look, mate, I must come clean with you – I bumped into Beth the other day and we chatted for a while – seems things aren't going too well between the two of you. I have to say she didn't look her old self. I hope you don't mind me mentioning it – anything I can do?'

'Oh Luke, that's good of you but, no, of course not. It's for us to sort out – nothing anyone else can really do. But thanks a bunch for enquiring.'

'Well, you know where I am if you need me.'

'Yeah, thanks for that. Crazy really, but mine and Beth's situation is the other side of the coin that is my madly successful venture into the world of criminal investigation. Who would have thought it just a few years' ago when I graduated at Birmingham? We think we're in control of our destiny but, wow, someone certainly had a hand in mine. Luke, if you don't mind me saying so, like you, I am prosperous beyond my wildest dreams. And all in just a few short months after launching my product. But the reverse side of the coin has done a very good job of keeping my feet on the ground. I still haven't approached Beth on what I know of her and that Tremonti bastard but I'm going to have to get round to it sooner or later because I'm just not the guy she married anymore. Okay, I'm still friendly towards her and I still love her company. Do I love her, though? Mmm, that's a difficult question.'

Richard knew deep down in his heart that he had never stopped loving Beth. Not for one second. She was the light of his life without any question. But, somehow, to admit to a close buddy that this was the case seemed to suggest a weakness of character.

'But, Luke, the problem is so much bigger than Beth's and my marriage. I don't have a clue whether she's still seeing this guy and, if I'm absolutely honest, I'm inclined to think maybe she isn't. God, I've tried to catch her out so many times, without the use of BG1, but I haven't had so much as a sniff of anything untoward going on. I'm sorry, Luke, BG1 is the relabelled working title for the project – Brain Game version

1.0, in longhand.

'The way I see it is I have absolutely no problem, ethically, with the police nailing a criminal in a fraction of the time it would have taken with the old polygraph method. No, fair cop is what I say. But, and I know it's only a but, the philosophical implications of the ethos behind the invention have revealed something very real and very flawed about human relations.

'Look, there are no plans to release the system to the general public - we know that – and there is no need to worry about something that isn't likely to happen. But the fact remains that all good, decent, loving, responsible relationships that exist between any two people – Jesus - between any number of trusting people, just aren't what we've always believed them to be. You remember the tests we trialled when we were still working together? Well, there wasn't one that didn't reveal a sinister, negative side to the subject. And it didn't matter who it was or what the relationship was, the revelations were consistently enlightening in a depressing way.'

For Richard, this was the real nub of the outcome of BG1's functioning – a wholly unexpected result. And ironically, the philosophy it had revealed was, at the present time, unlikely to apply to its usage under the control of the criminal investigation agencies. Where it potentially posed real psychological problems – in otherwise stable human relationships – it was unlikely ever to be granted operational approval. Maybe a blessing, he thought.

'And since we parted company, I've carried out any number of experiments of my own with every single one resulting in the same outcome. Luke, whether we like it or not, we are all living in some kind of ghastly dystopian society without knowing it. Okay, we all know we have enemies and we all know that our friendly next-door neighbour might be secretly slagging us off for planting too high a hedge between our properties but, how many of us are prepared to accept that the same negative reservations exist between every one of us? Husband and wife, sister and brother, uncle and aunt, worker and employer, teacher and student, shopkeeper and customer . . . the list is endless.'

'Rick, I can't argue with that. I've seen the results as well as you have. Maybe it's because I don't have a close partner that it hasn't hit me quite as hard but, I have to say, wonderful though the creation is, it does paint an awfully dismal picture of the society we have all come to love. To rely on. To trust. God, you've not exactly lifted my spirits, mate.'

In Lukas' position, the psychological implications weren't anything like as significant as they appeared to Richard. For one, his OT3 product had no apparent side effects lurking beneath the surface and, two, his general lifestyle precluded the dependence Richard's was understandably required to sustain in his marriage to Beth.

'I'm so sorry, Luke. I didn't have any intention of depressing you but there just isn't any other way to look at it. Even if I was to pull the plug on the project, recall every device I've despatched to date and destroy the hard drives that hold the software, the fact would remain that no aspects of our society operate in the reliable, trustworthy way we've all grown to believe they did.

'The one redeeming factor is that only a relatively small number of people have realised how widespread the phenomenon is. Everyone knows that a lie has to be employed at some point in any relationship but the extent to which negative information is customarily withheld by even those closest to us is really quite alarming. So much so that, were BG1 to get into the wrong hands, I dread to think what would come of the world as we know it. This is more than a mere can of worms we've unleashed – it's a whole bloody sea container of snakes!'

Lukas and Richard sat there for a while not quite knowing what to say. Had they invented a miracle or had they invented a monster?

'Freddie, we need something to perk us up a bit.' called out Lukas. 'How about two double espressos to wash down our lunch?'

'Coming right up, sir.'

Chapter 26

Kim Hyori settled into her position at Kangjeon easily and comfortably as if she had negotiated the post herself through the normal channels. It was impossible for her to know who was a legitimate employee and who wasn't but she appreciated this was not her concern. At times she would almost forget the circumstances surrounding her "employment" status such was the meticulousness of the way the operation was being handled by her foreign superiors. She made friends with whom she would enjoy lunchtime breaks and even embarked, at one time, on a casual romance with one of the company's senior managers safe in the knowledge that she would receive a signal of some kind were matters to be deemed inappropriate. They had thought of everything and she found herself perfectly suited to the appointment that had been chosen for her.

She would often deliberate over the situation while alone in her apartment in the evenings wondering how widespread such arrangements were. How would one ever know? The world of undercover work almost dominated movie themes but why shouldn't its prevalence be reflected in real life? After all, most major nations were in constant conflict with each other in one way or another. For all she knew her position might be more commonplace than most people would realise. It certainly didn't appear to cause her any particular uneasiness.

Her own mobile phone was a kCell of the latest specification that had been specially formatted to ensure that its precise location could not be identified were any technologically-inclined members of her family or friends minded to attempt to seek out her daily whereabouts.

The development and manufacturing of the kCell brand at the Seoul plant was massive. The premises resembled a small town and the operation ran like clockwork with over seventy-percent of tasks being controlled by automatons. The hardware production and quality-control measures achieved were of such high standards that little appeared to be left to the responsibility of human beings. In fact, in some areas of the plant there were employees who would work day in and day out without ever coming across another person. Kim Hyori imagined that, one day, the whole operation could run without human intervention.

After she had been at Kangjeon for a little over six months, she received a message from her agent to notify het that her employment would be terminating soon and that she would receive good notice of what she needed to do when the time came for her to be transferred to alternative living accommodation. She estimated that, in the time she had been undertaking the role in the marketing and formatting division, something in the order of five million kCell telephones would have been despatched to distributors in the British Isles. This accounted for around five percent of the total number of service subscriptions in the four countries making up the union – significant but still a relatively small sum.

But when this number was augmented by the amount of updates being downloaded to existing UK kCell contracts, the figure was likely to be in the region of five times that amount. And, as she thought about it more, she realised there was every reason to believe she had counterparts working in precisely the same fashion at similar plants in Japan and Sweden for the other two major cell phone manufacturers. Why would the foreign government currently controlling her not have infiltrated those organisations as well? She was beginning to understand the way they worked but had absolutely no idea what the nature of the highly classified software was that she was heavily involved in. Though it wasn't her business to know – her remit was to see that the UK was suitably served whether or not it chose to be.

Kim Hyori began to talk herself into believing the whole setup was really nothing to worry about. She conjectured that it may all revolve around an advanced means of promoting exports. The UK kCell users might quite easily be the target of a sophisticated advertising programme designed to infiltrate their subconscious minds to subliminally persuade them make certain purchases. This seemed totally feasible to her and fitted in perfectly with the relaxed manner in which she was being required to carry out her duties.

She continued to work diligently knowing that at any time she would be receiving advice regarding her next move. Her agent would contact her regularly though at irregular times during the day or evening. But, as her life was relatively uncomplicated, she was inclined to welcome the contact. Her immediate superior at the office would generally schedule her working hours which could vary from day shifts to evening shifts depending on hardware production levels. And on this particular day, she was advised that she would not be needed at all the following day. This suited Kim Hyori ideally as she'd several things to clear up at her existing apartment and a bit of leisure time was always welcome.

At the allotted shutting-down time for the day, she packed her bag, locked her workstation drawers and headed for home in the usual manner: short walk to the bus terminus, twenty-odd-minute ride to the residential development and a two-minute stroll to her block – no more than half-an-hour all in.

As she offered her fob up to the tall, glass, main entrance doors to the ground floor reception of her apartment block, she was met by a suited gentleman who greeted her using her name. This didn't trouble her in the least because she was forever aware of the possibility of being visited by one of the agents at any time.

'Good evening to you, sir. I am sorry, I didn't catch your name.'

'My name isn't important, Kim Hyori, but please don't let that bother you.' he replied with a smile on his face. 'I am here to update you on your position with our organisation. May I come up to your suite so that we can talk in private?'

Her reassessment of the precariousness of her circumstances had the effect of her lowering her guard when it came to chance meetings such as this.

'I see no reason why not. Here, a lift car is just approaching level one.'

'Excellent - thank you.'

The anonymous foreign agent picked up his heavy bag and walked with Kim Hyori to the lift. When they arrived at the entrance door to her apartment, she stared momentarily at the iris recognition pad and the door duly swung open to admit its two guests. They duly removed their outdoor shoes and placed them tidily in a rack positioned adjacent to the door.

'Please make yourself comfortable over there.' Kim Hyori said as she pointed to her two matching sofas arranged adjacent to each other. 'I won't be a minute.'

The agent sat himself down before placing his bag on the floor beside him.

'There, I just needed to change out of my work clothes and hang my coat in the wardrobe. What can I do for you, sir?'

'I've come to advise you that you are booked on Korean Air flight number KE203 which will be leaving Seoul Incheon International Airport at 09.45 am tomorrow morning bound for Gimhae from where you will be able to travel the short distance to your family home. Your employment at Kangjeon has been terminated following the letter of termination that was delivered to their HR department thirty-days' ago.'

Kim Hyori's mind was thrown into a state of confusion. Everything she had begun to believe about the likely innocuous nature of her position with Kangjeon had now been put into question.

'But I don't understand, I thought . . .'

'Please don't interrupt me – everything will become clear in due course. Now, I have with me here, the belongings you left in your workstation and I would like you to see that everything is packed and ready for you to travel by 07.00 am in the morning. An agent will meet you in level one reception at that time to escort you to the airport in time for your journey to commence. Do you have any questions?'

Kim Hyori fell back into her usual subservient mode in response to the intimidation rather than for any purposeful objective.

'Oh, er, well, no, of course not. It's just that it has taken me by surprise. But I will see that I am ready for your agent in the morning – thank you for arranging these things.'

'That is my job, Kim Hyori. Now, I must tell you that you are quite correct in speculating about your counterparts in other countries around the world – Japan and Sweden in particular. You are a perceptive lady. Yes, when we have a mission to attend to, we attend to it properly. However, I would like to thank you for your diligence and conscientiousness over the past six months in discharging your duties at Kangjeon Communications in such a professional and efficient manner. It is always encouraging to witness employees carrying out important assignments without entertaining anything more than the most insignificant of negative thoughts towards their employer. I wish to thank you for this.'

'But how do you know these things . . . ?'

'Please, Kim Hyori, no interruptions. That is all I have to say to you now. If you have any questions for me before tomorrow morning, you will be able to express them when I next contact you.'

The agent promptly rose from the sofa and made his way to the door before bidding her a final farewell.'

Once the door closed behind him, Kim Hyori sat back on her sofa in contemplation of what the agent had just said to her. Not the instructions regarding her employment termination or the travel arrangements, but the parts concerning her thoughts on her counterparts. And her general lack of negative thoughts she'd had regarding her employer. What could he have meant by this? He could well have surmised that she was a faithful, appreciative employee imagining it unlikely for her to harbour unvoiced complaints about the manner in which she was treated. But the thoughts she'd had relating to the possibility that other personnel had been deployed to work in the same capacity for the other major cell phone manufacturers was plainly bizarre. It wasn't even as if she'd confided in her work colleagues about the subject. No, she'd only run over the prospect in her own head. Very strange, she thought.

Anyway, there was little she could do about it and felt it best to put to the matter to the back of her mind for further consideration at a later time. For now, she needed to prepare for her flight to Gimhae that awaited her the following day.

While her mind was in a general state of uncertainty she could at least gain a degree of solace in the knowledge that she would soon be reuniting with her family. A little time out from work in the comfort of her loved ones would hopefully enable her to reinstate some kind of order to her life.

In the event, Kim Hyori never arrived at her expected destination but, instead, found herself standing in the new arrivals concourse at Tennant Creek Airport in the Northern Territory of Australia. She remembered nothing of the flight but had awoken just minutes before her plane had begun its descent. Once in the main terminal building, she made her way to the luggage carousel and waited for her holdall to appear but, after half-an-hour when the conveyor began to circle in the absence of any further items of luggage, she resigned herself to realising that hers had not been stowed in the plane's hold. She had with her just a personal bag that she'd placed in the overhead locker but, on opening it, found her cell phone was missing along with her wallet, bankers' cards, identity documents, address book and several South Korean banknotes. She had no possessions and no access to cash. She had nothing. Where was she to sleep the night? How was she to make contact with her family and friends?

Kim Hyori found her way to the help desk where she explained her predicament and asked for advice on what she would best be advised to do. The officer manning the desk requested that she fill out a form to provide information on her precise position and the means by which she had arrived in Tennant Creek. She did so and handed it back to him. The officer picked up his telephone, dialled a number and proceeded to relate her circumstances to whoever was at the other end of the line. After five-minutes he replaced the receiver onto its base, looked at her and asked how she had really reached the airport. She repeated her previous words and, once again, quoted the flight number only to be told that he had checked and no one answering to her name and description had been booked on that particular flight.

She pinched herself several times hoping she might snap out of a nasty nightmare but, alas, to no avail. Kim Hyori had well and truly entered some kind of dystopian environment and couldn't begin to understand why *she* had been singled out for such treatment.

She walked away thoroughly dejected and realised what had happened to her. She had heard stories of other individuals' similar fates but never imagined something of this nature happening to her. With no resources and nowhere to live, she made her way to the police station where she found the duty officer decidedly unsympathetic.

'I've heard it all before my darling, and there's little I can do to help you. But, if it's of any use, we have a vacant cell that you are welcome to occupy for the next couple of nights if you wish.'

Kim Hyori's resourceful and resilient nature helped her muster the resolve to climb out of the metaphorical abyss she had, through no fault of her own, stumbled into.

But a police cell in the back of beyond appeared eminently preferrable to anything else she could possibly contemplate at that moment.

'Yes please, sir. I would like to take you up on your offer.'

Kim Hyori began the long, uphill trek back to civilisation by accepting part-time jobs here and there in whichever establishments found her energies of use: cafés, fuel station forecourts, supermarket stock rooms, automobile garages, construction sites etc., and she eventually worked her way back to some kind of normality. She'd sleep in railway stations' waiting rooms at first before graduating to homeless people's hostels and, finally, cheap backstreet lodgings. It was not in her repertoire to give up.

After a number of months she was fortunate enough to find a steady position with a small family-run computer repair business where she spent her days replacing various components that had failed in customers' aging machines - customers who were unable, financially, to replace their hardware with updated models. And before long she acquired sufficient cash to move on to the next town which would, hopefully, count as the first step on a planned journey back to Seoul. She spent her days dreaming of taking up a position at the university where she'd once enjoyed a credible level of employment.

Her long trek back was eased somewhat by her having been gifted, as a going away present, a second-hand laptop computer by the kind people at the repair shop and she cherished the machine as if it were one of the latest technological design. The modest little computer afforded her a window to the world via its, albeit often unreliable, connection to the internet and, perilous though it may prove to be, she was determined to expose the villainous behaviour of the foreign dictators who had connived to simply dispose of her once they judged she was of no further use.

But she had a resolve, a purpose, and, though she was a lone voice, she was possessed of a determination that knew no bounds. One way or another, Kim Hyori would rise to the surface and regain her rightful place in society.

It was now a good six months since her arrival at Tennant Creek and her resolve knew no boundaries. One night while sitting in her digs she decided to begin a blog for the purpose of openly revealing her plight and bringing the practice to the notice of other vulnerable young graduates. But for reasons of security, she felt it might be wise to adopt an alias rather than advertise her own name. For this purpose, she elected to be known to her followers as Stephanie Brown to avoid any immediate suspicion of her true identity. And she planned to pose a question relating to the dubious system she believed they had devised that, somehow, enabled them to read the minds of others once the site had attracted sufficient support. She was convinced this was the only way they could possibly have known what was in her mind when she considered the matter of possible counterparts existing in alternative cell phone plants while she was employed in Seoul.

She would spend much of her spare time developing controversial ideas to post to her rapidly-growing blog followers. Kim Hyori was not the kind of person to give up.

Richard, Jennie and Kate were working round the clock to keep all of their technological balls in the air and things were progressing at a rapid rate where the subject of BG1 sales and customer support services were concerned. Production of the necessary hardware, principally the smart watches, had been outsourced to specialist manufacturing plants in the far east from where they would be shipped directly to the IntuTech building for storage, software downloading and eventual despatching. Two further members of staff had been taken on: one to handle deliveries, management of the storage facility and the packaging up and mailing of all items of hardware and the other, a technically-qualified computer programmer able to deal with customer support issues. Extra security measures had, quite sensibly, been put in place, following the fourth stagehand incident many months' ago. These offered a level of protection way beyond that which was arguably necessary but Richard was taking no chances. There was to be no repeat performance of the fourth stagehand incident in any shape or form.

His mind rarely returned to the subject of the missing smart watch which, after so much time, led him to believe the instrument was most likely to have found its way to a landfill site as originally suspected. But, of course, it may, alternatively, be in the hands of an individual ignorant of just how much was at stake within the device's small, stainless steel casing.

Without the ability to access the heavily encrypted BG1 software, the watch would be perfectly able to serve as a timepiece, a heartbeat monitor, a step-counter or any other popular facilities demanded of such devices these days – all quite innocuous functions that could be found on any cheap, similar item available from most internet sites trading budget-priced goods. All his worrying late that night following the presentation was, he gladly accepted, completely misdirected. But there was a positive to the whole affair in that it prompted him to put some serious security procedures in place commensurate with the value of the products and intellectual property that were at stake.

He was now operating in the big league. The biggest league of them all and the idea of making savings when it came to security just made no sense. And it wasn't as if IntuTech was short on capital. Whatever needed to be done got done - signed off – no questions asked.

With BG1 having become so successful in the restricted marketplace that was the country's law enforcement agencies, life for him began to settle down to a canter rather than the gallop he had become accustomed to. In short, he was rapidly finding himself with time on his hands and little in the way of fences to jump. And, although he genuinely felt it was time he deserved after a non-stop period of high activity, he started to feel he needed something else to occupy the capacity he'd always had for new ventures. Ventures that demanded a creative, active mind. So, to this end, he decided to scan a number of internet sites in an attempt to glean snippets of information on current trends and lifestyle modes, that he felt he might find inspiring and, possibly, worthy of consideration as the basis for possible further technological developments.

He wasn't surprised that he stumbled upon a variety of off-beat ideas and quirky inventions that he doubted would ever see the light of day but, as he was trawling through one particular site, he hit upon an interesting blog account edited by a certain young lady going under the name of Stephanie Brown.

Chapter 27

On the face of it, Stephanie Brown appeared to be a highly interesting individual. Her blog had been running just a couple of months but, in that time, she had collected many thousands of followers. The subject matter tended to concentrate on human rights issues around the world but principally on those concerning a number of current foreign administrations for whom she had extraordinarily little respect.

Her short journey through life, so far, was briefly documented although she avoided including specifics with regard to her education, her employment, her country of origin and her present place of residence. Stephanie Brown was a lady to be reckoned with. Everything she seemed to stand for rang a bell in Richard's heart as if both of their brains had been hardwired by the same physiological designer. He immediately bookmarked her URL.

Richard trawled through Stephanie's pages from the

beginning of her posts and learned much, in principle, of her struggles to maintain her dignity through extremely difficult times and how she avoided sinking into the depths of despair when finding herself in the direst of situations through absolutely no fault of her own. Her quest was to highlight the dangers many innocent people had confronted as a result of foreign government policies of the kind she'd fallen foul of. It was the policies of administrations that showed a total disregard for the lives of otherwise hardworking, successful, highly-gifted individuals whose talents and skills had been customarily exploited for the purpose of political gain that she most wished to bring to people's attention. But she was careful to avoid exposing any personal details that could provide a traceable identity to those responsible for her own struggles.

Stephanie's personal story was one that she was clearly determined to keep under wraps. But it was a story that had opened her eyes to the most alarming accounts of young lives simply wasted and discarded by government agents and their henchmen whose only goals were power, greed and control.

Though she was unlucky in the extreme to fall into the hands of these despicable people she certainly wasn't on her own.

Examples of exploitation on industrial scales were cited where unassuming, highly-educated young people were used by the authorities to infiltrate commerce and influential world marketplaces for the sole purpose of achieving political advantage over honest, conscientious and diligent regimes.

But the particular blog that caught Richard's eye was one detailing a report that outlined a certain administration's involvement in a highly technological development that, and Stephanie wasn't very clear on the issue, apparently concerned an invasive neurological practice which intruded the human mind. She chose not to go into specific details and certainly didn't quote actual instances where the procedure had been used, but several respondents qualified her claims by citing instances where they had also personally experienced the same process.

While Richard found the blogger's reports on this specific issue extremely worrying, he couldn't help but wonder whether the incidents could have any connection with BG1. He felt it highly unlikely that the technology he had conceived and developed could have, simultaneously, conflicted with a totally independent body's virtually identical product. Without prior publication or advertisement of either the processes involved or the ideologies pursued, he had great difficulty in accepting that the two, apparently parallel technologies, were nothing more than coincidental.

Among Richard's university studies, mathematics and, in particular, the subject of probability had figured significantly. He was no fool when it came to the matter of random processes and what was contained within these reports were, without any question, way outside reasonable limits.

BG1 was his idea, his visualization, his creation and there was only one possible explanation as to how two identical technological developments, thousands of miles apart, could have manifested themselves at the same point in time. And that was by way of the fourth stagehand incident on the night of the presentation. Richard's smart watch never went anywhere near a landfill site but, instead, found its way into the duplicitous, ignominious organisation of some unidentified foreign government.

But how was he to take on what could, for all he knew,

prove to be one of the world's most powerful nations? How could he, Richard Stewart, begin to enter into a dispute through the auspices of the International Court of Justice with a formidable sovereign nation? The prospect was unthinkable. Was it possible, he wondered, to lead a genuinely honest and successful life without finding oneself involved in deception of one kind or another? One could follow as diligent a route as possible with integrity and veracity at the forefront of its principles but no account for the nefarious interventions of others could ever be ruled out.

His BG1 invention was an ethically-sound device providing it was restricted to use within a controlled environment. The law enforcement agencies were that controlled environment and its function as a worthy successor to the polygraph was unquestionably right and decent. If the proper application of BG1 led to the rightful conviction of a criminal responsible for an act against the very society upon which he, or she, depended, then there was no ethical question to answer. And the regulation authority's decision to grant consent for such use endorsed that view. But, like any item capable of inflicting damage or injury when put to inappropriate or nefarious use, such as a regular kitchen knife being used to sustain injury to a person, it is incumbent upon society to take tough action against the perpetrators to ensure that its use is restricted to applications only for the common good.

But so far, Stephanie Brown's vague reference to a system that Richard suspected was likely to have emanated from his own, diligent hard work could, he considered, be thousands of miles away on the other side of the planet. And, for the time being, he doubted anything would be gained if he were to spend undue time concerning himself with the issue. Were it to manifest itself in a way that impinged upon its current, ethical usage, then action would need to be taken but, for the time being, he had no reason to think anything untoward would necessarily ensue.

However, he continued to follow Stephanie's blog which seemed to gain followers from around the world on an exponential basis. And he imagined, as well as promoting the good cause that was the exposing of reprehensible human rights activities by certain sovereign states, she was managing to carve out a profitable career for herself in the process.

As the weeks passed, IntuTech's fortunes grew commensurately with the mounting reputation it was enjoying amongst the UK's police forces and Richard decided to put his mind to the development of an updated, version-two variant – BG2. Although he recognized BG1 to be the miracle product it was without one single competitor on the horizon, it stood to reason that even *it* could be improved.

After the South Bank incident, he had, periodically, felt uneasy about the ever-present possibility of an BG1-primed smart watch finding its way into the wrong hands. He was aware that its use was heavily regulated in the most controlled of environments but it would only take one slip-up by a serving officer or an act of dishonesty by a duplicitous employee for its security to be breached. He mulled over the possibilities and settled on maintaining the existing method of the smart watch being the control centre, the interface, for want of a better term, between the subject's and the examiner's nervous systems but he felt he could improve security by writing an algorithm that would render the smart watch inactive were it not first registered, neurologically, with the examiner's brain pattern "fingerprint". The registration process would need to be tailored individually for each person permitted to use the device and this would require more strenuous procedures at the time of deployment. But the advantages far outweighed the minimal, additional work needed in that the misplacement or misappropriation of the smart watch would prove to be of no consequence where the security of the software was concerned. He felt he was on to something and doubted the technological upgrading procedures would prove problematic providing he was able to set aside three, or four weeks to undertake the exercise.

In his leisure time, Richard would keep an eye on Stephanie Brown's blog page more as a matter of interest than for the distinct purpose of monitoring a foreign government's possible involvement with BG1. And he was encouraged to see that a small, but significant, body of dissidents within some of the key nations with poor human rights records seemed to be gaining ground and achieving a degree of exposure in various capacities: student publications, anti-government political movements, religious authorities etc. Keeping abreast of the site's developments took little in the way of time each day and he tacitly commended Stephanie, whoever she was, for the role she played in monitoring the subject on such a regular basis.

But, on logging on one morning as he stopped to grab a coffee in between working on the algorithm, a response to Stephanie from a UK follower caused him some alarm when it suggested that use of the BG1 system might possibly have been detected in Great Britain. Apparently, a schoolteacher in the Bristol area had reported an incident whereby a student was suspected of completing an examination paper in which he demonstrated a degree of knowledge to which the tutor believed it was impossible for him to have had access. The blog went on to suggest that the incident had come to the notice of the local media in Bristol who had interviewed both the teacher and the student.

Richard duly logged off the blog site and searched in his browser for the media report. The item came up immediately and he found the journalist had carried out a detailed investigation after questioning both the teacher and the student. What had, apparently, happened was that the class were set a mock examination having spent the previous school year studying the relevant syllabus in their English Language lessons. The teacher, a certain Sara Henshaw, had unintentionally omitted to cover a small aspect of the syllabus during term time due to her not having been sent the relevant details by the examining board.

No organisation was beyond making an error and the examining boards were certainly no exception. No matter how diligent Ms. Henshaw was in discharging her English Language duties to the current exam level students something or other was always able to slip through the net.

She was present at her desk in the examination room while an invigilator had also reported for duty and she passed the time by reading through the paper that had been handed out to the students. The particular question for which she had been unable to prepare them for appeared at the end of the paper and required the class to complete a lengthy passage involving a fictitious family's journey through an imaginary landscape while on an expedition in a northern European country. The question included the names of the various family members but, for no particular reason, excluded mention of one key individual and his place of work. These details appeared only in the original tutorial pages – the pages with which the examining board had failed to furnish Miss Henshaw. The papers she had in her possession on the day, included copies of the tutorial pages which she was now able to read and familiarize herself with.

But when a somewhat troublesome student named Harry Whittington handed in his completed work at the end of the one-and-a-half-hour examination period, he had included the name of the missing character – the character Sara Henshaw spent several minutes contemplating and deliberating over while the students did their best to complete the paper.

While Whittington could certainly be disruptive, he wasn't by any means the dumbest in the class. But he was the shifty one. Had the examination answers been available at a price on the internet it would've been Harry who'd found a way to download them. But in this case there had been no leaks whatsoever. The wayward student had discovered a means which had left everybody speechless.

While most examinees had made the best of a bad job using only the information featured on the actual examination paper, Harry, who had, unusually, positioned himself closest to the teacher's desk during the exam, provided a comprehensive answer which included the name and occupational details of the missing individual. Henshaw claimed that there was absolutely no way he could have had access to the information and called for an investigation into the possibility of his having gained access to the board's highly guarded documentation. No other educational establishment in the south west of the country had used the same examining board's syllabus.

On questioning, Whittington pleaded innocent to having,

surreptitiously, gained access to the board's records but refused to elaborate on how he managed to complete the question without compromise. The investigation was subsequently terminated and declared a mystery. But when, a week later, the very same Harry Whittington was suspected of having stolen an expensive bicycle from one of the city centre's main parking lots after having been seen loitering around the bike park at the time the owner had ridden in, parked his machine and set the combination lock, serious questions began to be asked.

Harry was approached by the city police department and questioned at the station for a good hour but to no avail. This bothered Harry not a jot as he was almost on first name terms with most of the regular station officers. Two officers subsequently paid his parents a visit to take a look around their property in search of the missing machine, but nothing in the way of evidence was found so the case was duly closed. Harry was a slippery character. No one had actually seen who had removed the cycle from the bike park so it was decided that no more valuable police time should be devoted to the incident. Two days later, a short item mentioning the two, slightly strange Harry Whittington events appeared almost as a footnote on a national internet media news site.

Richard found the whole episode fascinating but paid little attention to the similarity that Stephanie Brown and her followers might have found bizarrely coincidental.

But a week later, he stumbled upon a report from a regional newspaper that had made it onto a national media news site where the general theme was uncannily similar to that of the Bristol event. It concerned a married couple, in their mid-thirties, who had suddenly filed for divorce as a result of the husband's infidelity whilst away on a business trip. The relationship apparently broke down after the wife, an IT analyst, accused the husband of having slept with a prostitute in a German hotel he had been booked into by his financial services company employer. The wife had remained in the UK for the duration of his trip and had communicated with him by cell phone on two or three occasions. His European visit lasted just two days and he travelled alone. His contact in Germany was the CEO of a medium-sized manufacturing company and they met on only one occasion at a hotel adjacent to the host's premises. The hotel the husband stayed at was several miles away on the periphery of the city. Nobody from the host company accompanied the husband to the overnight hotel at any time during the visit. It was the kind of business trip that took place many thousands of times a week with those possessive of questionable moral compasses finding it easy to add the cost of some extra marital fun onto their expenses account with very little chance of being found out.

However, shortly after his return to his north of England home, he was confronted by his wife who asked him to explain the presence of a leggy blonde in his hotel bed with him. And when he suggested he'd been involved in nothing of the sort, she demanded to know why, in that case, there was a bright red bra and matching panties thrown on the white rug at the end of the hotel bed.

The husband immediately flushed and stumbled for words in an attempt to extricate himself from his predicament. But there were no words to be found because he had, in fact, just returned home from a business trip to Germany where he'd slept in his hotel room with a leggy blonde who'd tossed her bright red underwear, randomly, onto a white, fluffy rug situated at the end of the double bed they were occupying.

There was nothing inaccurate at all about the wife's accusations but how on earth could she have been privy to what he'd got up to seven-hundred miles away while she had been continuing in her usual routine at home?

When the wife provided even more intimate details of how he and his leggy blonde friend had entertained themselves, there was clearly no way back. Within twelve hours of him confidently turning the key in the lock of his front door, his wife was instructing her solicitor to commence divorce proceedings.

The unfortunate husband hadn't a clue how his hitherto loyal and faithful spouse had caught him out but there was no doubt at all about the veracity of her accusations.

This time, a report appeared not only in local news bulletins but in various prominent positions in most national press publications and online feeds.

So remarkable, in fact, was the dumbfounded husband's story that he was invited to appear on a late evening TV news programme in which the anchor grilled him on the details of the tale with a positive expression of disbelief on his face. It was a difficult tale to swallow.

Chapter 28

Colin Steadman's autonomous SUV was one month out of warranty when his problems started. It would transport him in a perfectly efficient manner for little over an hour before the troubles would begin. And were they troubles? Firstly, the navigation programme would have a habit of randomly selecting a route that bore no relevance to the journey he'd be halfway through then, the electronic stability control would fail and send an audible warning message to the audio system advising the driver to "bring the vehicle to a standstill at the soonest and safest opportunity." To say he was becoming infuriated at the dealer's inept attempts to resolve the issue would be an understatement.

Colin was not a young man. He could remember the days when a driver would enjoy total control over his vehicle and have no trouble overriding its satellite navigation system should he find himself at odds with its choice of route.

However, he had managed to deliver the vehicle back to the dealer for a third time requesting that they carry out a thorough investigation and fix it, once and for all - irrespective of cost. He was furious in the knowledge that, had the fault emerged just five weeks previously, the bill would have been covered by the manufacturer's warranty. However, be that as it may, he needed the vehicle for essential travelling connected with his job and had no option other than to confront the issue head on.

The dealer duly made contact at the end of the day advising him that the fault had, at last, been found and a replacement module was now fitted. The problem lay with some embedded software that couldn't, for some reason, be simply overwritten. The only way, apparently, was for the item to be replaced. And it wasn't cheap. But, the car had been fully road tested and the engineer who had undertaken the work was convinced there would be no further problems.

With the car's recent unreliable history, he was understandably suspicious with regard to the efficacy of the story behind the repair. He'd heard it all before. However, this time, with the fitting of a considerably costly, replacement unit he felt there just might be some dependable light at the end of the tunnel.

Colin promptly made his way over to the dealership to collect the vehicle, walked through to service reception and immediately asked the manager if he would be able to speak directly to the engineer himself.

'Of course, Mr. Steadman, I will call through to him now.'

While he was waiting he glanced at the bill in front of him and swallowed a couple of times before organizing a bank transfer on his new kCell mobile phone. The sum he had paid represented a significant proportion of the total cost of the vehicle he'd shelled out for just over twelve months previously.

Within a couple of minutes, a cheerful-looking, scruffy-overalled, middle-aged man appeared whilst, seemingly, being in the process of rubbing cleansing gel of some kind into his hands.

'Good afternoon, Mr. Steadman, my name is Ian - I won't shake hands if you don't mind.'

'No, I'd prefer you didn't, Ian.' Colin returned with a smile on his face. 'I thought, maybe, you wouldn't mind running through the details of the work you've carried out just to put me in the picture.'

On the face of it the fitter certainly looked like a decent guy. Not the type that didn't know his job and not the type to pull the wool over your eyes. But, of course, you could never be sure.

'That's no problem, sir. Once I'd located the fault, the solution was rather simple. One of the main control mechanisms was clearly malfunctioning and, to be absolutely safe, I decided to fit a replacement module to ensure it didn't trouble you again. I'm afraid there was no other way.'

'So, the solution was to unplug the faulty module and install a replacement.'

'Yes, sir, as simple as that. But it was the actual replacement cost of the item rather than the labour time involved that resulted in such a big bill. My time was mostly taken up with the initial diagnosis.'

'Well, why is the original module still fitted to the car, Ian?'

'I beg your pardon – I've just told you that the module was replaced with a new one.'

'I'm aware of what you told me, Ian, but, as I said, I'd like to know why the original is still in place.'

Ian became noticeably flushed and attempted to find an argument that might hold water but, in the process, failed miserably.

'Very well, but I must advise you that, first thing in the morning, I will be driving the vehicle directly to the UK importer to ask them to examine the item and report on its status. I believe the component will bear a coded date stamp revealing details of its original installation.'

Colin Steadman did exactly as he had promised the following day and had no trouble persuading the parts manager at the importer's premises to find someone to carry out the necessary examination. While this was being done, he relaxed in their stylish customer waiting area where drinks and snacks were available, free of charge, from a smart vending area at one side of the room.

As he sat there he had no doubt whatsoever that the engineer would be reporting shortly to say the module had not been replaced.

But he didn't have to dwell on this for too long as the appointed engineer soon appeared through a pair of double, stainless steel and glass doors to announce that the control module fitted to the vehicle was, indeed, the one installed during the original manufacturing process and that an email would be sent immediately confirming this point.

Colin was not surprised and duly thanked the man for his prompt and efficient service.

Rather than reapproach the dealership, Colin contacted his solicitor requesting that she should immediately institute proceedings against the fraudulent company and, within two months, he received the full cost of the repair back together with a significant sum in compensation. The dealer was duly fined and, quite appropriately, stripped of his franchise by the vehicle manufacturer's importer. When the court proceedings were picked up by several news agency reporters, the episode went on to generate substantial coverage in both online and printed news publications.

But one particular reviewer felt the case warranted further investigation. Investigation into the means by which Colin Steadman had known, so decisively, that the stated work had not been carried out. So far, there had been no explanation concerning this wholly significant aspect of the story. The journalist's thoughts on the matter made interesting reading in the periodical he contributed to and, following a whole page article on the subject - which included references to the previous, related incidents in Bristol and the north of England - he prompted a level of interest amongst his readership that manifested itself in a host of letters addressed to the publication's "Readers' Rants" column appearing in the subsequent week's issue.

One respondent suggested that "The ability to accurately comprehend, with absolute certainty, that which would seem to be beyond the scope of one's reasonable powers of perception is becoming something of a trend in specific parts of the country."

The variety of explanations reflected the wide range of mindsets prevalent within the UK population with each proposal making some kind of sense to its sponsor.

Another wrote in claiming to be comforted by increasing evidence that God was choosing to intervene in some areas of our culture where the rooting out of sinners' actions was something that could only lead to a better society in the long term.

Others believed that heightened powers of telepathy within certain members of society were becoming rightly enhanced and felt this could only be a good thing for the furtherance of truth and integrity amongst our people.

An awareness of the phenomenon was certainly spreading but the cause of its rapidly increasing occurrence remained a mystery for most rational thinkers. And this aspect of the event lent credence to the appetite held by both the media and its followers.

One strange aspect of the cases reported so far was the reluctance on the part of the perceptive parties to elaborate on their intuitive capabilities. None, to date, cared to be engaged on the subject as if they were adhering to some kind of confidentially agreement. They simply refused to be pressed when questioned. And this led to a growing interest amongst those following the publicity to become even more intrigued.

As time passed, more and more incidents were reported with a significant proportion involving infidelities amongst married couples and those in long-term, established relationships. And the instances started to escalate in an exponential manner as if people were jumping on the band wagon. But to most commentators, this view seemed non-sensical. How, they thought, could one acquire the ability to comprehend an accurate understanding of a situation in the total absence of evidence?

TV producers began to set aside time to feature programmes dedicated to examining the phenomenon in the presence of all kinds of studio guests. Some would take the matter seriously by inviting university professors whose specialist subjects were based around the sphere of neurological research whilst others would feature metaphysicians, clairvoyants, psychics and anyone who might profess to have an interesting perspective on the subject. But the one common thread that seemed to run through every discussion, every argument and every debate was the universal failure to come up with anything approaching a sustainable answer. No one, it appeared, knew anything of the mechanisms underlying the science behind the phenomenon.

'Hi, is that Richard?'

'Yes, Richard Stewart here. Who am I speaking to?'

'Richard, it's Peter here – Peter Williams – New Scotland Yard.'

'Oh Peter, how are you – good to hear from you.'

'I'm absolutely fine. Is it a good time?'

'Sure, it's always a good time to hear from you. Is there something particular you called for or did you just fancy a chat?'

'Well, yes, I suppose there is something. Look, we are so enthralled with the BG1 device that we really can't begin to comprehend how we ever managed to operate without it. It is an absolute godsend in that investigations are taking a fraction of the time they used to and guilty pleas almost seem to be the order of the day. Everyone is getting through so much work in so short a time that all but none of our investigating officers have yet to come down from the cloud they've been occupying since we first registered with IntuTech. So, a big thank you, Richard – you have revolutionized our working lives forever.'

Richard felt there was a "but" or a "however" on its way.

'Well, that's really good to know, Peter and thank you for expressing your appreciation so clearly. It is far more usual, unfortunately, to hear only the bad news in today's society – people seem either to take good news for granted or not to find interest in it all.'

'I'm aware of that but this system is really so exceptional that it would be impossible to ever put it to the back of one's mind. However, that wasn't, actually, the purpose of my call. What I wanted to run past you was the growing incidence of certain members of our society demonstrating, what would appear to be, an ability to emulate the techniques we are enjoying in our use of BG1 – have you seen the publicity it has been getting in the national media?'

'Peter, I *am* aware of what is going on and, frankly, I'm totally flummoxed. Without more information on the individuals involved and the execution of a proper controlled scientific examination, I really don't know what to say on the issue. What are your thoughts?'

'Well, very similar to yours. I've watched experts debate the subject on various broadcasting forums but nothing of any substance ever seems to come out of them. It was just a thought of mine to contact you to enquire of your opinion. And I half expected this to be your response, Richard. But never mind – look, do promise me you'll get in touch when you're next in this neck of the woods.'

Richard fleetingly imagined Peter wondering whether he was doubting his integrity with regard to his maintaining strict adherence to the criminal investigation limitations having been imposed on BG1's usage. Was he thinking that Richard might have breached the terms of their contract? Trust was everything to Richard. He felt uncomfortable.

'Without any doubt, Peter, you will be my first port of call. You take care and I'm sure we'll catch up soon.'

'Likewise, Richard – good chatting as always. Bye for now.'

'Cheers, Peter,'

Peter Williams walked over to the panoramic window in his Westminster office where he spent much of his thinking time. '*Come on, Peter, you're a highly experienced investigating police officer for goodness sake – if you can't solve this conundrum, who can?* He questioned himself. By nature, his mind wasn't happy when presented with a mystery that nobody appeared to be able to fathom out. To date, there had been something in the region of sixty-odd reports concerning people who seemed to possess psychic powers and this wasn't right. These things just didn't happen without a reason and he was determined to get to the bottom of it. *Could it just be possible that Richard Stewart is breaching the terms of his contract? No, I cannot believe this – Richard comes across as one of the most reliable individuals one could ever wish to meet.*

He picked up his phone and called his colleague, DI David O'Connor.

'David, it's Peter here, Peter Williams. How are things?'

'All good with me, Peter. What's up?'

'How aware are you of this mystery thing that's currently getting media time – you know, where people seem to be acquiring psychic powers?'

'Very, Peter. I'm totally confused by the whole business. Why do you ask?'

'Well, something's going on and, when there's no obvious reason for it and nobody's prepared to offer an explanation, it usually follows that the root of the situation is highly questionable.'

'Yep, I agree with that.'

'Well, if things with you aren't too hectic at present, I wonder whether you might put a little investigating team together to see what might turn up.'

'Not too hectic? You're kidding me – I've never had so much time on my hands what with this mind-reading device we took on all those months' ago. No, it's not a problem – I'll be interested to dig around.'

'Excellent. I can't be too involved myself but, if you're able to clear it with your immediate superior – tell him, by the way, that it came from me – I'll be extremely interested in what you might be able to uncover.'

'I'll check out my availability immediately, Peter, and will keep you posted on what transpires.'

'Thanks very much, David – speak soon.'

The two officers terminated the call and Peter already felt relieved that some progress might turn something up shortly. Within a half-hour, David O'Conner pinged him a message confirming that his supervising officer had no objection to him devoting whatever time he felt was necessary and he would begin to the carry out some enquiries.

David was a natural problem solver. If presented with a riddle, he'd lock his mind onto it for however long it took to solve. This aspect of his character could at times become irritating to those around him but that was the way his mind was wired. He'd never be any different. The Met loved him.

He began by searching the internet to compile a list of individuals reportedly connected to relevant incidents and, by the time he'd exhausted his study, he had a catalogue of names totalling sixty-seven individuals. The next item on his agenda was to set about obtaining contact details by some means or another. This was going to prove an arduous task and one that would best be tackled by a team of staff investigators whose job was to address assignments of this kind. In the event, he delegated the task to two young trainees on a lower floor who were more than eager to gain this type of experience.

'Well, thanks guys, if you could start by contacting the media organisations involved in publicizing the issue you might find you'll have something to go on. Telephone numbers, email addresses, residential locations, workplaces etc. – you name it. I'll leave you to get on then.'

Chapter 29

The software that Kim Hyori had unwittingly charged every new kCell phone with during her time in Seoul was ninety-nine-point-nine percent certain to be impregnable to penetration by hackers. Daniel Levin had seen to it that any attempt by anyone, whomsoever, to permeate the algorithms he had written, would automatically render the individual device's system inoperative. The modifications he had carried out simply caused the programme to self-destruct at the first sign of interference. And not only that, operational usage of the software was regulated to function only within the global positioning system confines of the UK. A similar, temporary, malfunction feature had been included in the encoding to preclude its ability to function in any other latitudes though, as soon as the instrument was returned to its global-friendly sphere of operation, the programming was immediately re-enabled making the software fully operational once again. Daniel was one serious computer wizard.

What was more, the point at which the BG1 application was programmed to become active on the end-users instrument coincided with the downloading of a full set of operating instructions ensuring the consumer had no difficulty in manipulating the settings to gain full use of its facilities. This very same software was also used for downloading to already-commissioned kCells by way of scheduled updates. In this way, the BG1 resource was guaranteed to achieve a presence in every existing, functioning kCell in the UK.

Furthermore, Kim Hyori's anonymous counterparts, who had been planted in similar divisions within the world's other two major cell phone manufacturers' premises, had effectively carried out carbon-copy exercises. The exercise had been carried out with military style precision. But this *was* military warfare - modern military warfare – spectacularly advanced when compared to the old-fashioned boots on the ground methodology. And infinitely more economical.

In doing so, the foreign government, whoever they were, had ensured that virtually every British cell phone owner would, at a particular, pre-meditated time, enjoy access to the IntuTech system. And with human nature being what it is, the unassuming inheritor of the technology was invariably inclined not to advertise its presence in order to maximise its effectiveness when in use. But, of course, in the fullness of time, the system would enjoy almost total ubiquity within the limitations of the United Kingdom's geographical locations rendering any effort to conceal its existence totally futile.

Whilst the BG1 applications on all new kCells shipped to the UK would become active within a prescribed number of weeks subsequent to their commissioning, update downloads on existing phones which, by definition, were far more numerous, would take place in a staggered fashion to avoid market overloading. It was considered that a graduated exposure of the system to the British public would prove more effective than a single-event flooding of the market.

Jason James, known to his friends as Jay-Jay, lived and worked in London. He resided in the north of the city and worked in the West End. Jason was a sixth-generation Afro-Caribbean – just about as far from his ethnic roots as an English Jamaican could be. Jay-Jay was an Englishman, through and through. His great-great-grandparents were among the first West Indian immigrants to arrive on HMT Empire Windrush in June 1948 and went on to settle in north London. His descendants were hard working people rarely without jobs - employed mostly on the capital's public transport systems and in its NHS hospitals, Jason's family contributed proudly and diligently to the British economy.

However, life was a struggle and there were often times when the rent was late and the table was short on food. But the James family were never deterred and continued to battle on in the face of whatever adversity they confronted. They were a tough bunch.

But each generation has its own take on how it sees it should fit in with the continual changes in society. And, of course, do its best to climb its way up the social ladder in the process.

So, Jason was determined to change certain parts of where the James's family was currently heading. Though he left school at the earliest legal age with only a handful of low-grade exam results to his name, he was confident he could turn things around and come out on top by the time he was thirty. He tried an assortment of jobs in and around London and was currently working as a night porter for a large, upmarket hotel on one of the capital's grandest of streets. But this wasn't offering him the kind of potential he needed to reach his three-decade goal. Though his wages were modest, he supplemented his income by deejay-ing at weekends when he wasn't scheduled to work. And, in doing so, managed to maintain a favourable lifestyle and meet the demands of his small, council flat rent.

Jay-Jay was no egotistical materialist yearning for the flashy pad with its swimming pool and attendant high end autonomous SUVs paraded behind electric gates. No, Jason wanted security for himself and his family but if he ever managed to hit the jackpot then so much the better.

And he would save, enthusiastically, to kit himself out with the kind of gear he considered suited his cool, part-time deejay image. Though shoes were his big thing and he loved them. All of them: sneakers, chukkas, loafers, Chelseas, Oxfords. But they had to be designer – had to have a designer label. And there was one West End shop that had them all, Chaussures de Mecs. It was of only a modest size as shops go but it was situated in the right property in the right street in the right part of town and Jay-Jay would scrimp and save to buy his deejay-ing footwear only from this retailer.

On his way to his night porter job on one particular evening, he made a detour for the sole pleasure of checking out the window display in Chaussures to tease himself into wanting another pair of their irresistible items of footwear. It wasn't too far out of his way and he knew that the lit-up displays in the night light would make the exhibits appear even more alluring. He approached the store from the lower end of the pedestrianised street so that the angled arcade shopfront would enhance his view and stand to seduce him even more. But what caught his eye before any of the store's products came into view was a smart, A3-sized notice on the left-hand door inviting applications for the post of a new shop under-manager. Wow, he thought, spending all day, every day amongst the stuff of his dreams would be the job of a lifetime. He stood staring at the wording as if in disbelief while he, simultaneously, memorized the email address via which he decided he would later submit a bid.

The following afternoon, when he woke from his morning's sleep, Jay-Jay carefully drafted an email, addressed it to the manager of the store, read it over and over several times then, finally, clicked the SEND icon. He sat back in his chair, stretched his limbs and mused over how cool it would be to replace his current, unsociable job with a daytime post at the Chaussures de Mecs outlet. He read through his communication several times over - viewing it as a kind of lottery ticket offering him the chance to elevate his humdrum job into a dream career.

And, within a matter of hours, he was thrilled to see a reply pop up in his inbox. Nervous to read the message in case there was a negative aspect to the response, he deliberated before clicking on OPEN, grabbed himself a black coffee from the kitchen and sat down to take in what the shop manager had to say.

Hi Jason, Thank you for your application for the post of under-manager. I will be delighted to see you to chat things over when it is convenient for you. Please contact me again to let me know when that might be. I'm available most times between 09.00 am and 06.00 pm weekdays. Saturdays are a little difficult, I'm afraid.

With best regards, Alexandre Moulin.

The message brought a big, wide smile to Jason's face and he set about punching out a reply immediately suggesting he'd call in at twelve noon the following day. And between clicking on SEND and a seeing a second response appear in his inbox, no more than five- or six-minutes had elapsed. The manager must have been staring at the screen of his computer as Jason was typing.

Hi Jason, Thank you for your prompt reply. Twelve noon tomorrow suits me fine. I will look forward to seeing you. With best regards, Alexandre.

"Alexandre!" Noting the absence of the manager's surname made Jason feel they were on first-name terms already.

He programmed an alarm to wake him at nine-thirty the following morning to give him adequate time to shower and sort out his trendiest outfit for the interview and by eleven-thirty he was relaxing drinking an Americano in a coffee shop just around the corner to Chaussures de Mecs. There was no way he was going to be late for this appointment.

Jay-Jay was out to impress. He looked the part, he'd rehearsed a number of responses to questions he imagined would be put to him and he intended to present himself to Alexandre in such a way that declining his application would make no sense to Chaussures de Mecs.

As he stepped inside the store he was immediately approached by a young saleslady asking him how she could be of help.

'Oh hi, I've come to see Mr. Moulin.'

'You must be Jason, then – here for the under-manager interview.'

'Yes, that's me – my apologies, I'm a few minutes early.'

'That's no problem, Jason, I will let Alexandre know you're here.'

Within what seemed like a lifetime to Jay-Jay, a tall, slim, decidedly French-looking gentleman appeared from the rear of the shop and beckoned Jason to follow him into an office. He did so while looking Jason straight in the eye with a welcoming, friendly smile and a casual glance down at his footwear.

The interview went exceptionally well in Jason's mind and he felt he and his would-be boss had got on famously. Alexandre was extremely impressed with his enthusiasm for the store's products, enthralled to learn that he had been a customer for at least two years and that he chose to wear his favourite Chaussures' Italian-made loafers for the meeting.

As the interview neared its end, Alexandre looked him in the eye.

'I have to tell you, Jason, that I have seen two other candidates who applied for this position and have decided not to consider any further applications. And, without wishing to build your hopes up unnecessarily, I am inclined to feel that you may well be the front runner. But the decision is not mine. I will be sending my reports to the owner of the store for him to make his choice. However, I should be able to get back to you with an answer in a day or two.'

'That sounds good to me, Mr. Moulin – thank you for seeing me.'

'You are very welcome, Jason – I hope I can look forward to meeting you again in the near future. Goodbye for now.'

Jason walked confidently out of the shop with his head aloft but as soon as he turned the corner into the main shopping thoroughfare, he leapt into the air giving out an audible 'YES' to the bemusement of the street's busy shoppers. And there was a positive spring in his step for the remainder of his journey home.

The following day he heard nothing, which didn't surprise him, but on the morning of the next day he saw a message in his inbox from Alexandre.

Hi Jason, I am sorry to inform you that the owner of Chaussures de Mecs has decided to offer the under-manager position to one of the other two applicants. I hope this does not disappoint you too much and wish you every success in your quest to secure a suitable position elsewhere. With very best regards, Alexandre Moulin.

Jason was gutted. He'd secretly been banking on being offered the post ever since he left the premises two days earlier and, frankly, couldn't imagine what had caused the owner to go against Alexandre's judgement. However, over the years he'd become hardened to certain discriminatory responses from some sections of the public to the point where he immediately became suspicious whenever something surfaced that appeared to possibly have an ethnic connotation.

So, not satisfied with the brief, albeit polite, message, he felt a visit to the store in the hope that a short chat with the manager might help ease his mind and offer him something positive by way of an explanation. Something that might help with future job applications.

He approached the shop late that same afternoon and saw Alexandre standing just inside talking to the saleslady he'd spoken to earlier in the week. On spotting Jason, Alexandre immediately waved him in and shuffled him through into the rear office.

'Sit down Jason, I presume you're here to ask me what went wrong.'

'Well, yes, Mr. Moulin, I must say I was a little surprised at not being awarded the position.'

'Yes, it surprised me too, Jason, but, as I said before, the decision was the preserve of the owner with whom I have little in the way of sway. Look, I have his email in front of me – would you like me to read it to you?'

Alexandre was sitting opposite Jason and had his laptop open.

'Well, yes please – it might help me when I apply for other posts.'

'Of course. '*Dear Alexandre, Thank you for sending me your reports on the three interviewees – it was most helpful. However, I have chosen to go with the second applicant on the list and I would like you to contact him to arrange another meeting during which we can discuss various details of the appointment.*' Alexandre paused momentarily before continuing with, '*Yours kindly, Mike Richardson.*'

'You see, it was his decision and his alone as to who would be offered the job, Jason.'

Alexandre had absolutely no idea that his position was highly compromised. He was doing his best but that wasn't nearly good enough when it came to a one-to-one confrontation with a BG1-equipped adversary.

'I understand that, Mr. Moulin, but why did you not read out the paragraph that stated: '*I have mentioned to you before, Alexandre, that I am not interested in employing staff of Caribbean origin. They have the wrong image, are unreliable and likely to get in late after having been stopped and searched on their way to work.*' Why did you choose for me not to know the owner's real reason for him declining my application?'

Alexandre flushed immediately and began to play for time.

'What do you mean, Jason?'

'You know precisely what I mean, Alexandre. And my solicitor, the Office of Fair Trading and ACAS will also know when I alert them to what has taken place here as soon as I leave this establishment.'

Alexandre looked shocked. He could understand exactly what Jason was objecting to but didn't have a clue as to how he was familiar with the contents of Mike Richardson's communication.

Then, without warning, Jason jumped up, leant over Alexandre's desk and photo-clicked the screen of the laptop with his kCell phone without giving his host a split second to react. He then turned and ran out of the premises before anyone had a chance to stop him.

Jason duly presented his evidence to the respective bodies who went on to bring a successful, perfectly justifiable racial discrimination case against the embarrassed employer ordering him to pay a substantial sum by way of a fine into the court office within seven days of the verdict. And Jason was awarded a sum several times that amount in compensation for the possible damage that may have been caused to his character.

But, although an innocent party throughout the whole incident, Alexandre was truly perplexed as to how young Jason James had managed to magic the information contained in the ultimate paragraph of Mike Richardson's email to bring about a case that went on to rightly justify the decision of the court.

Within three months of the court's ruling, the fine imposed on Mike Richardson's West End enterprise had a seriously damaging effect on his financial position and rendered him unable meet an increase in rent when an impending review became due. The landlord duly agreed to allow him to invoke a get-out clause in the lease and Chaussures de Mecs' exposure in London's trendy fashion quarters came to an abrupt end.

Chapter 30

David O'Connor's investigating team felt they were chasing an invisible target that was travelling at twice the speed of light. To say they were striving to produce a list of known individuals, savvy to the phenomenon, that was gaining more ground on them rather than the other way round was understating the case. No sooner did they obtain contact details for a significant number of the reported sixty-odd individuals known to have been in possession of magical powers of perception than the number of recognized cases escalated by factors out of all proportion with their ability to log the results. Put simply, it was an impossible task. The team may have well invented their statistics as nobody could ever have carried out a purposeful audit.

Within three days of being tasked to produce the list, the number had reached two-hundred-and-thirty-six. By 09.00 am the next morning it was over two thousand and by lunchtime that same day, news agencies were reporting having logged incoming calls close to half-a-million by persons purporting to have been duped by the system. Something was sweeping through the country and no one had the faintest clue what was going on.

So effective was the multiplying effect of the escalation of incidents that, within a matter of days, figures were being quoted in the tens of millions. The use of the cell phone app, which had been freely downloaded by the foreign government, had quickly reached epidemic proportions.

Kim Hyori and her anonymous cohorts had unwittingly taken control of the vast majority of the UK population's psyche which were now working their way, randomly, through all manner of relationships and destroying them one by one.

And the government was running out of representatives to undertake the job of persuading the public to keep calm while other media channels, previously unconcerned with topical news material, threw everything into live reports, interviews, warnings, helplines, you name it. Nothing anywhere or anyhow was being addressed except the subject of individuals either possessive of magical, mind-reading powers or dumbfounded by what everybody and his brother was mysteriously able to reveal about them. There were no more secrets. No one was able to hide one iota of information about themselves. No one had anything to conceal because everything was out in the open. Laid out on the table for all to see. If you didn't tell the truth it didn't matter – everyone knew what you were really thinking.

But, of course, what David O'Connor's team did manage to discover after interviewing just a few dozen respondents to their enquiries was that the activity was connected to mobile telephones. Mobile phones whose original function to provide a service by which two parties were able to communicate verbally with each other was so insignificant by comparison to their present ability to delve into the minds of their fellow human beings. The world was changing before its people's very eyes. But the UK was changing in a vastly different way.

No one had yet begun to establish a link to a nation responsible for the cell phone infiltration but several sovereign states found their way onto a list of likely culprits. And it wasn't clear why the UK should have been selected as the guinea pig although most intelligent researchers would have put money on it being the land of its invention with the idea that the UK deserved a taste of its own medicine.

A wave of bewilderment was sweeping across the country like a swarm of jet-propelled locusts. Nobody had time to consider how they should respond were the phenomenon to visit their neighbourhood. Before they had a chance to devise a means of countering its effects, they'd find themselves succumbing to its ravaging tactics of destroying every nuance of trust they'd previously had in their fellow folk. Folk who'd, in turn, lost every last vestige of hope in they themselves. The bootlegged version of BG1 took no prisoners, pulled no punches. It careened its way, indiscriminately, through a society that had spent centuries honing a system that allowed it, simultaneously, to survive successfully as a highly intellectual social species while retaining its ability to preserve every aspect of its capacity to behave like any other undeveloped class of animal whose existence depended, incontrovertibly, on unadulterated, ruthless principles. The UK's social system was being torn apart, limb by limb, by a foreign administrative animal hellbent on slaughtering its victim with a product of its own invention.

And the savage blow the British public were having to suffer was not selective in choosing its prey. While one may have, unjustifiably maybe, predicted that secondhand car dealers, carpet salesmen and real estate agents would, maybe, find themselves at the top of the list of vulnerable victims, no such bias appeared to exist. Instead, every sector of society found itself a casualty of the digital virus and failed to register as anything approaching a reputable entity.

There certainly were oodles of examples in areas where one would previously have judged its adherents to have figured towards the top of the caring and compassionate league table. And, contrastingly, there were others involved within whose trust the most unassuming and forgiving members of the community would avoid subscribing to at all lengths.

Retailers scored relatively highly as did the religious and educational bodies. But probably more numerous than any other sector was that concerning personal relationships. With the significant prevalence of sexual self-expansionism within partners in established relationships, revelations brought about through the operation of the now readily-available, mind-reading phone app, simply exposed unsuspecting partners to the realities of their otherwise honorably-perceived unions. Making love to your wife while concentrating your mind on the film star of your dreams now became a self-incriminating option. Nothing was sacred in this new, foreign-driven culture.

The process, in many ways, became a great leveller. No longer could one apply a meaningful label to any section of society as a means of distinguishing it ethically, honestly or decently from any other sector. When a league table of those claiming adherence to any of the above values could, in theory, be accurately compiled, it looked very much as though no one group could rightfully make claim to be occupying the moral high ground.

And the country had been taken by surprise. Caught with its pants down. Facilities that were traditionally available to cope with society's trials and tribulations were functioning on overload so much so that the legal profession, for example, was so bogged down with under-represented cases that virtually no disputes were standing any chance of being resolved. Partners in law firms up and down the country were unable to address their clients' needs for no reason other than their inability to address their own failed domestic situations.

The filing of cases in the law courts came to a halt when their internet registration processes crashed and elderly people's care homes were inundated with aging offspring demanding that their ailing parents be released following totally inappropriate thoughts on behalf of small numbers of the care staff.

No sections of society were exempt from the breakdown of the fabric which, for centuries, had served to bond its people in a semi-delusionary state of trust. A trust that was rarely questioned or simply discarded by a process of denial.

Theories were being bandied around by the thinking elite and university debates were being dedicated to the subject but no signs of a philosophy able to stem the flow of what was being termed, the new age of realisation, could be adopted by a society unable to properly grasp the enormity of a change it was being forced to undergo.

Neurological scientists were doing their best to explain to a bemused public that the problem lay with the brain's lack of ability to operate totally under the control of its consciousness

– it simply hadn't evolved that way. It had no need to evolve that way because it had always enjoyed the facility of being able to secrete thoughts it considered inappropriate or, in modern, social parlance, tactless if allowed to be revealed to an accomplice. And the secrecy aspect served also as a means of defence when used strategically to disarm an opponent.

The human mind had not developed in a way that would allow thoughts to be dependent upon one's ability to control what his, or her consciousness chose to consider. It simply didn't work that way. An individual's thought process was, in fact, the dominant partner to its thinkers need to think. Thoughts enjoyed an independence that enabled them to enter their subject's mind in order to influence its decision-making process. No human being had a natural ability to filter out unwanted thoughts but, instead, had to develop mind-training procedures that allowed them to focus on selected, invited concepts at the exclusion of those that would, otherwise, enter the mind on a random, involuntary basis.

This was not an easy discipline. Maybe those versed in the ancient, often far eastern, self-awareness arts would have a head start on the rest of society but even then the idea of eliminating random thought processes *before* they entered one's consciousness was a tall order indeed. After all, they only needed to present themselves for a millisecond for the BG1 transcriber to pick up the thread.

But there was a purpose to the randomness of the thoughts entering the untrained mind and that was, amongst other functions, to automatically alert the mind to imminent dangers that might have taken too long to recall manually. In this way, the subconscious mind was able to perform important functions, when required, without needing to interrupt the day-to-day activities when not required. It was a system that had stood the test of time but was dependent on the mind maintaining its ability to filter out thoughts as and when it considered them inappropriate.

The UK's long history of highly-sophisticated, intellectually-developed people became a broken system that no longer worked in any useful way. The levels of trust that had been instrumental in enabling society to develop a platform upon which its people could communicate and operate with confidence had been destroyed at its very roots. Democracy was no longer an option. It was only societies where authoritarian rule was allowed to prevail where an ignorance of the rules being imposed, elsewhere, by the new age of realisation enabled its people to live unencumbered by the knowledge that things were not what they appeared to be. The social order was about to change big time. The foreign administration responsible for this onslaught, it seemed, had successfully brought down the fabric of the UK's society without so much as firing a gun, flying over its airspace or disabling its cyber networks. It had simply infiltrated its mobile telephones. History finds its own way of entering into conflict with its political adversaries and the sands are shifting constantly. As a general rule, those administrations identifying themselves as falling behind in the endless quest for social and economic advancement develop a compulsion to arrest their neighbour's progress as a means of redressing the balance. Everybody wants to be top dog.

Lukas Hoffman had made his billions in the relatively short time he'd created and marketed his enormously successful OT3 retinal bypass system for those with sight impairment issues but, realising there was no future for him in his adoptive country, he elected to return to Germany and turn his efforts to helping its people fend off the inevitable threat of a similar attack on *its* democracy.

Peter Williams continued in his career at New Scotland Yard where crime had been on the decline since the BG1 system had gone viral. Every criminal seemed to recognise the fact that they were no longer capable of concealing the truth once they were brought in for questioning. The situation certainly didn't convert them to altruistic, responsibly-minded citizens but it made them rethink the relevance of their illicit tendencies which no longer served them well.

BG1 had quite miraculously transformed life in the UK in almost one fell swoop. Although the process caused massive disruption throughout all walks of life, the New Reality, as many referred to it, promised to produce a more honest society devoid of deception, deceit and defamation. In some ways the foreign administration had dealt the UK a trump card. But there was work to do to ensure matters unfolded in the correct order.

David O'Connor gratefully accepted the offer of a reduction in his working hours and agreed to a three-day working week with the advent of just a trickle of scheduled criminal investigation procedures to attend to most weeks. He'd always enjoyed a round of golf whenever he had time on his hands and he could now enjoy a game without being concerned as to whether his partner was cheating. Balls were no longer thrown down in the rough or kicked from under a tree. And no player dreamt of thinking about claiming a five when he had actually taken six shots to make a hole.

Mark Broderick took early retirement while the money was there to take. He'd enjoyed a career in the Met for several decades and, being the political animal he was, decided to spend his time working towards developing a new set of game rules for a society that needed serious remedial work if it was ever going to figure again as a force on the world stage. He appreciated that such a remedy could be some years off but society was dependent on the brightest minds available to devise a new set of rules, a new social system that would allow its members to integrate in a way that worked with total transparency. The old idea of trusting your partner, your work colleague, your teacher, your religious leader even, was not an option if society were to move forward in any sort of effective manner.

Life had become quite different indeed. Nobody needed to be concerned with whether they were being treated fairly. The real estate agent had no option but to disclose the fact that an industrial development was due to be built adjacent to the property you were viewing. The charity worker was compelled to divulge the proportion of your contribution that was heading for the administrators' investment account and the police officer had no way of hiding the real reason why he picked you out specifically for a stop and search exercise. Everybody was exposed to the truth whether they liked it or not.

Kim Hyori eventually found her way back to Seoul though

with the protection of her Stephanie Brown alias and a successfully encrypted blog site with several million followers. Her dream was to infiltrate every possible corner of every possible country with human rights issues and bring about change in the shape of a more honest and responsible approach to all aspects of human communication.

Richard Stewart had also made his billions with BG1 which was now ubiquitous amongst the UK's fifty-odd police forces so, frankly, he never needed to work again. But that alone didn't make life as ideal as it would have been were the original revelations concerning Beth and Ricky Tremonti never to have come to light. Or, better still, never to have occurred in the first place. But that was life. Life before BG1. Life before Stephanie Brown. And there was precious little he could do about it.

Richard had become a bit of an amateur philosopher as he steered his way through the twists and turns that figured on his road trip from student to celebrity and he believed the completed journey would never have been possible without the odd toll charge along the way. And there were indeed several of them - some costing considerably more than a few quid. But that was the cost of success and there was little argument over how much he had achieved. Richard had become a national treasure and that was never going to be an easy ride.

What was clearly needed was a new perspective. A new way of functioning within one's community. A way that no longer depended on ideals that simply weren't workable. In this New Reality its members needed to take on board the fact that previous illusions of commitment between two people, between any number of people, had to be consigned to the waste bin of outmoded philosophical beliefs. Trust in a partner's, or a group of colleagues' loyalty to oneself patently didn't apply. There never was a one-hundred-percent level of devotion to one's fellow human beings. Sure, there may have been fifty-percent and, in some instances – close romantic partnerships, for example – there may have been ninety-percent but there was never a level of commitment that was equal to that which one accorded to one's allegiance to oneself. Perhaps the commitment one had for one's offspring achieved the highest echelon of dedication. But that tended to apply only as long as their dependence existed. Once the nest was vacated, commitments were inclined to take flight simultaneously with those of its one-time inhabitants. And this duly led to the previous incumbents, once again, being left to their own devices. Nostalgia and guilt often took the place of earlier states of true faithfulness but, without a practical function in the particular pattern of behaviour, whatever remained, post flight, represented no more than a form of philanthropic idealism.

Richard Stewart, by way of BG1, had brought about more of a much-needed social revolution than the disaster the perpetrators had expected and within time there appeared to be no reason why the UK shouldn't become a shining light amongst the multitude of nations that would be racing with each other to catch up.

Beth had become used to the change in hers and Richard's lifestyle and now, in the wake of the foreign administration's intervention in virtually everybody's cell phone facilities, she had come to realise what it was in her husband's mind that had proved to be a game changer. But Beth was a student of psychology and was well versed in the workings of the human psyche. The idea of them separating to pursue relationships elsewhere made no sense to her. In this new age of technological enlightenment, one romantic liaison was no different to any other with regard to the matter of trust. No one, ever again, would lay faith in their partner when it could so easily be demonstrated to have been misplaced. A new, practical, basis for meaningful relationships was urgently needed and Beth wanted to be at the forefront of this essential, radical new movement. She felt the time would never be more appropriate to have a sober word with her loved one.

'Richard, I've been thinking. Thinking about you and me. Thinking of the times we enjoyed prior to this monumental societal change that's been foisted upon us. How would you feel about our having a serious chat? A chat about how we plan to face the future. Together.'

'Oh God, I can't think of anything we deserve more than to sort out this whole, ghastly mess, Beth. Yes, let's do it now. Here in the TV room okay?'

'No, I thought it might be better elsewhere – where we won't be distracted by the things we see around us all the time. How about the Harbour Café?'

'Sounds perfect.'

'Hi Beth, hi Richard, what can I get you on this beautiful afternoon?' Freddie greeted two of his regulars in his usual friendly manner.

'Just a pot of Earl Grey for two, if you wouldn't mind

Freddie, thank you.'

'Certainly - I'll be back in five minutes.'

'Richard, as you can imagine, we've been discussing this mind-reading business to death at uni and I don't feel we have to adopt quite such a dystopian view of our joint futures in this topsy-turvy society of ours. Somewhere along the way, civilization seemed to lose its way. It became, kind of, arrogant where the subject of how we should veer from God's - or whoever your preferred creator or evolutionary overseer may be – original plan to produce a number of species not only able to sustain their own lives but to maintain an unremitting dedication to the matter of procreation. Once created, these species would go on to manage their own lives in accordance with the original plan – the master blueprint, if you like. But the business of forever changing the ground rules somehow appealed to our species and it soon resulted in an attitude whereby the members felt more suited to re-writing the rule book than to adhering to the previous idea of following the original, highly-successful plan. The plan, we mustn't forget, that unequivocally facilitated our survival over countless millennia. To get to the point, I see no way of going forward other than to take the best bits of the creator's, or the evolutionary overseer's, original plan and put them together with the best bits of the human beings' re-written rule book.'

This was heavy stuff. The stuff of uni debating societies. The stuff of true, do-good revolutionaries. Richard needed to concentrate his mind on Beth's wise words.

'So, in a nutshell, we should retain the ideas relating to taking responsibility to look after ourselves and we'll continue to include the need to procreate on the agenda to ensure our presence on this planet doesn't terminate anytime soon. But we'll reinstate the concepts taken for granted in many less-developed animal species where the need to view oneself with such great importance does not figure and, instead, harbour expectations that don't tumble to the ground at the slightest signs of necessary evolutionary or creational behaviour. That way we'll be setting the bar at an achievable height without ever risking the stability we should always have strived to maintain. What do you think?'

'That's taken a lot of thinking, I'm sure, Beth. But, on the face of it, it makes absolutely perfect sense and I see no reason why we shouldn't take it on board. Ah, Freddie, just in time for us to toast a plan Beth has proposed that will allow us to spend the rest of our lives together in a state of pure harmonious jubilation. Why not take a seat and join us?'

'Don't mind if I do, Richard. Let me grab a cup.'

'You're very welcome, Freddie,' added Beth. 'as long as you don't mind being present while I announce to Richard that we will soon be welcoming another Stewart into the fold.'

With a pleasantly stunned look on Richard's face, the three of them held their cups aloft and toasted the new master plan.

Printed in Great Britain
by Amazon

11771440R10200